The Editor Ara.

BEVERLY LYON CLARK is Professor of English at Wheaton College. She is the author of *Kiddie Lit: The Cultural Construction of Children's Literature in America*, *Regendering the School Story: Sassy Sissies and Tattling Tomboys*, *Lewis Carroll*, and *Talking about Writing: A Guide for Tutor and Teacher Conferences*. Her edited or coedited works include *The Oxford Encyclopedia of Children's Literature*, *Louisa May Alcott: The Contemporary Reviews*, and *Girls, Boys, Books, Toys: Gender in Children's Literature and Culture*.

W. W. NORTON & COMPANY, INC.
Also Publishes

Mark Twain

THE ADVENTURES OF TOM SAWYER

AUTHORITATIVE TEXT
BACKGROUNDS AND CONTEXTS
CRITICISM

Edited by

BEVERLY LYON CLARK
WHEATON COLLEGE

W • W • **NORTON & COMPANY** • *New York* • *London*

W. W. Norton & Company has been independent since its founding in 1923, when William Warder Norton and Mary D. Herter Norton first published lectures delivered at the People's Institute, the adult education division of New York City's Cooper Union. The Nortons soon expanded their program beyond the Institute, publishing books by celebrated academics from America and abroad. By mid-century, the two major pillars of Norton's publishing program—trade books and college texts—were firmly established. In the 1950s, the Norton family transferred control of the company to its employees, and today—with a staff of four hundred and a comparable number of trade, college, and professional titles published each year—W. W. Norton & Company stands as the largest and oldest publishing house owned wholly by its employees.

The text of this book is composed in Fairfield Medium
with the display set in Bernhard Modern.
Composition by Binghamton Valley Composition.
Book design by Antonina Krass.
Manufacturing by the Courier Companies—Westford Division.
Production manager: Benjamin Reynolds.

Library of Congress Cataloging-in-Publication Data

Twain, Mark, 1835–1910.
The adventures of Tom Sawyer : authoritative text, backgrounds and contexts,
criticism / Mark Twain ; edited by Beverly Lyon Clark.
p. cm.—(Norton critical edition)
Includes bibliographical references.

ISBN-13: 978-0-393-92603-3 (pbk.)
ISBN-10: 0-393-92603-6 (pbk.)

1. Twain, Mark, 1835–1910. Adventures of Tom Sawyer.   2. Sawyer, Tom
(Fictitious character)—Fiction.   3. Adventure stories, American—History and
criticism.   4. Runaway children—Fiction.   5. Boys—Fiction.   6. Mississippi
River Valley—Fiction.   7. Missouri—Fiction.   I. Clark, Beverly Lyon.   II. Title.

PS1306.A1 2006b
813'.4—dc22
2006047302

W. W. Norton & Company, Inc., 500 Fifth Avenue,
New York, N.Y. 10110-0017
www.wwnorton.com

W. W. Norton & Company Ltd., Castle House,
75/76 Wells Street, London W1T 3QT

1 2 3 4 5 6 7 8 9 0

Contents

Criticism

Preface

Is *The Adventures of Tom Sawyer* a book for children? Or is it for adults? During much of the twentieth century it was generally relegated to children's literature, in contrast with its sequel, *Adventures of Huckleberry Finn*, which was considered suitable for adults: in 1950, for instance, T. S. Eliot called *Tom Sawyer* a "boys' book," whereas *Huckleberry Finn*, even if enjoyed by boys, "does not fall into the category of juvenile fiction." In the nineteenth century, though, when children's literature was less clearly differentiated from that for adults, both novels straddled the two readerships. Mark Twain himself vacillated about his audience, as is reflected in his exchange of letters with William Dean Howells, reprinted in this edition. And the initial critics rarely mentioned one book without the other; there were no sharp differentiations between the two. Now, in the twenty-first century, as the Harry Potter phenomenon once more erodes the boundaries between child and adult reading publics, and as children's literature is finding a place within the academy, *Tom Sawyer* is yet again repositioning itself.

A favorite of figures ranging from Pat Boone to George McGovern, from Ralph Ellison to Paul Newman, the book has been popular with a general audience ever since it was published in 1876. In the first half of the twentieth century *Tom Sawyer* was Twain's best-selling book—indeed, according to Frank Luther Mott in *Golden Multitudes*, one of the twenty-one top sellers in the United States. In the second half of the century, it was second, among Twain's works, only to *Huckleberry Finn*. *Books in Print* indexes 317 versions as currently available for *Tom Sawyer*, 382 for *Huckleberry Finn*.

In *Tom Sawyer* Twain consciously reacts against earlier didactic literature for children, a literature he satirized in "The Story of the Bad Little Boy" and "The Story of the Good Little Boy." At the same time the book celebrates a different kind of literature read by children, tales of pirates and Robin Hood, on the one hand, and stories in the emerging realistic genre of the "boy book," on the other—as Alan Gribben has noted. Indeed, like other boy books, it is partly autobiographical, as selections from Twain's *Chapters from My Autobiography*, reprinted in this edition, suggest.

The Adventures of Tom Sawyer is also one of Twain's most carefully structured novels, a fact that critics such as Walter Blair and Hamlin Hill pointed out in the mid twentieth century. More recently such critics as Judith Fetterley and Glenn Hendler have grappled with tonal inconsistencies and instabilities, with the nature of the relationship between Tom and the adult community, and with the construction of masculinity. One of the few scholars to explore the racial dynamics of the book is Carter Revard.

Finally, too little attention has thus far been accorded to the visual aspects of the book, a neglect remedied in this edition by Susan Gannon and also by the inclusion of a copy of the anatomy text page that Becky Thatcher presumably tore. Compared to other nineteenth-century works whose audience included children, *Tom Sawyer* is unusually direct in approaching sexuality: no other book allows a good girl so much interest in the human body (even if, in keeping with advice from Howells, Twain toned down the sexual implications of the scene). Yet it turns out that Becky did not learn a great deal from the picture: the figure was anatomically incorrect.

Other materials included in this edition provide nineteenth-century backgrounds on matters ranging from school curricula and discipline to boy culture, and from painkillers to graverobbing.

Let me conclude by acknowledging my gratitude to Carol Bemis, ever patient with my editorial questions, and Martha Mitchell, ever resourceful in finding interlibrary loan sources. I am grateful to Roger Clark and Alan Gribben for helpfully responding to drafts; to Sue Gannon, Glenn Hendler, and Robert Hirst for advice; and to Zephorene Stickney of the Madeleine Clark Wallace Library, Wheaton College, and Gladys I. Dratch of the Monroe C. Gutman Library, Harvard University, for archival assistance. Mark Baumer, Liz Brais, Anne Canada, Lindsay Codwise, Erica Hartnett, Tessa Manolopoulos, Stefanie Rosenblum, Jennifer Schuman, Amanda Seward, and Laura Tschop provided valuable assistance in deciding what to annotate.

The Text of
THE ADVENTURES OF
TOM SAWYER

THE ADVENTURES

OF

TOM SAWYER

BY

MARK TWAIN.

———————

THE AMERICAN PUBLISHING COMPANY,

HARTFORD, CONN.: CHICAGO, ILL.: CINCINNATI, OHIO.

A. ROMAN & CO., SAN FRANCISCO, CAL.

1876.

To

MY WIFE

This Book

is

Affectionately Dedicated.

PREFACE.

Most of the adventures recorded in this book really occurred; one or two were experiences of my own, the rest those of boys who were schoolmates of mine. Huck Finn is drawn from life; Tom Sawyer also, but not from an individual—he is a combination of the characteristics of three boys whom I knew, and therefore belongs to the composite order of architecture. ·

The odd superstitions touched upon were all prevalent among children and slaves in the West at the period of this story—that is to say, thirty or forty years ago.

Although my book is intended mainly for the entertainment of boys and girls, I hope it will not be shunned by men and women on that account, for part of my plan has been to try to pleasantly remind adults of what they once were themselves, and of how they felt and thought and talked, and what queer enterprises they sometimes engaged in.

THE AUTHOR.

HARTFORD, 1876.

CONTENTS.

CHAPTER XXVI.

CHAPTER XXVII.

CHAPTER XXVIII.

CHAPTER XXIX.

CHAPTER XXX.

CHAPTER XXXI.

CHAPTER XXXII.

CHAPTER XXXIII.

CHAPTER XXXIV.

CHAPTER XXXV.

Chapter I.

"Tom!"

No answer.

"Tom!"

No answer.

"What's gone with that boy, I wonder? You TOM!"

No answer.

The old lady pulled her spectacles down and looked over them, about the room; then she put them up and looked out under them. She seldom or never looked *through* them for so small a thing as a boy; they were her state pair, the pride of her heart, and were built for "style," not service;—she could have seen through a pair of stove lids just as well. She looked perplexed for a moment, and then said, not fiercely, but still loud enough for the furniture to hear:

"Well, I lay if I get hold of you I'll—"

She did not finish, for by this time she was bending down and punching under the bed with the broom, and so she needed breath to punctuate the punches with. She resurrected nothing but the cat.

"I never did see the beat of[1] that boy!"

She went to the open door and stood in it and looked out among the tomato vines and "jimpson" weeds[2] that constituted the garden. No Tom. So she lifted up her voice at an angle calculated for distance, and shouted:

"Y-o-u-u *Tom!*"

There was a slight noise behind her and she turned just in time to seize a small boy by the slack of his roundabout[3] and arrest his flight.

"There! I might 'a' thought of that closet. What you been doing in there?"

"Nothing."

"Nothing!" Look at your hands. And look at your mouth. What *is* that truck?"[4]

"*I* don't know, aunt."

"Well *I* know. It's jam—that's what it is. Forty times I've said if you didn't let that jam alone I'd skin you. Hand me that switch."

The switch hovered in the air—the peril was desperate—

"My! Look behind you, aunt!"

The old lady whirled around, and snatched her skirts out of danger. The lad fled, on the instant, scrambled up the high board fence, and disappeared over it.

1. Anything to top.
2. Poisonous weeds of the nightshade family.
3. Short jacket.
4. Rubbish.

11

His aunt Polly stood surprised a moment, and then broke into a gentle laugh.

"Hang the boy, can't I never learn anything? Ain't he played me tricks enough like that for me to be looking out for him by this time? But old fools is the biggest fools there is. Can't learn an old dog new tricks, as the saying is. But my goodness, he never plays them alike, two days, and how is a body to know what's coming? He 'pears to know just how long he can torment me before I get my dander up,[5] and he knows if he can make out to put me off for a minute or make me laugh, it's all down again and I can't hit him a lick. I ain't doing my duty by that boy, and that's the Lord's truth, goodness knows. Spare the rod and spile the child, as the Good Book says.[6] I'm a laying up sin and suffering for us both, *I* know. He's full of the Old Scratch,[7] but laws-a-me! he's my own dead sister's boy, poor thing, and I ain't got the heart to lash him, somehow. Every time I let him off my conscience does hurt me so, and every time I hit him my old heart most breaks. Well-a-well, man that is born of woman is of few days and full of trouble, as the Scripture says,[8] and I reckon it's so. He'll play hookey this evening,[9] and I'll just be obleeged to make him work, tomorrow, to punish him. It's mighty hard to make him work Saturdays, when all the boys is having holiday, but he hates work more than he hates anything else, and I've *got* to do some of my duty by him, or I'll be the ruination of the child."

Tom did play hookey, and he had a very good time. He got back home barely in season to help Jim, the small colored boy, saw next day's wood and split the kindlings before supper—at least he was there in time to tell his adventures to Jim while Jim did three-fourths of the work. Tom's younger brother (or rather, half-brother) Sid, was already through with his part of the work (picking up chips,) for he was a quiet boy and had no adventurous, troublesome ways.

While Tom was eating his supper, and stealing sugar as opportunity offered, aunt Polly asked him questions that were full of guile, and very deep—for she wanted to trap him into damaging revealments. Like many other simple-hearted souls, it was her pet vanity to believe she was endowed with a talent for dark and mysterious diplomacy and she loved to contemplate her most transparent devices as marvels of low cunning. Said she:

"Tom, it was middling warm in school, warn't it?"

"Yes'm."

"Powerful warm, warn't it?"

"Yes'm."

5. Become angry.
6. Proverbs 13.24: "He that spareth his rod hateth his son."
7. The devil.
8. Job 14.1: "Man that is born of a woman is of few days, and full of trouble."
9. "South-western for 'afternoon' " [Twain's note]. "Play hookey": skip school.

"Didn't you want to go in a-swimming, Tom?"

A bit of a scare shot through Tom—a touch of uncomfortable suspicion. He searched Aunt Polly's face, but it told him nothing. So he said:

"No'm—well, not very much."

The old lady reached out her hand and felt Tom's shirt, and said:

"But you ain't too warm now, though." And it flattered her to reflect that she had discovered that the shirt was dry without anybody knowing that that was what she had in her mind. But in spite of her, Tom knew where the wind lay, now. So he forestalled what might be the next move:

"Some of us pumped on our heads—mine's damp yet. See?"

Aunt Polly was vexed to think she had overlooked that bit of circumstantial evidence, and missed a trick. Then she had a new inspiration:

"Tom, you didn't have to undo your shirt collar where I sewed it, to pump on your head, did you? Unbutton your jacket!"

The trouble vanished out of Tom's face. He opened his jacket. His shirt collar was securely sewed.

"Bother! Well, go 'long with you. I'd made sure you'd played hookey and been a-swimming. But I forgive ye, Tom. I reckon you're a kind of singed cat, as the saying is—better'n you look. *This* time."

She was half sorry her sagacity had miscarried, and half glad that Tom had stumbled into obedient conduct for once.

But Sidney said:

"Well, now, if I didn't think you sewed his collar with white thread, but it's black."

"Why, I did sew it with white! Tom!"

But Tom did not wait for the rest. As he went out at the door he said:

"Siddy, I'll lick[1] you for that."

In a safe place Tom examined two large needles which were thrust into the lappels of his jacket, and had thread bound about them— one needle carried white thread and the other black. He said:

"She'd never noticed, if it hadn't been for Sid. Consound it! sometimes she sews it with white, and sometimes she sews it with black. I wish to geeminy she'd stick to one or t'other—*I* can't keep the run of 'em. But I bet you I'll lam[2] Sid for that. I'll learn him!"

He was not the Model Boy of the village. He knew the model boy very well though—and loathed him.

Within two minutes, or even less, he had forgotten all his troubles. Not because his troubles were one whit less heavy and bitter to him than a man's are to a man, but because a new and powerful interest bore them down and drove them out of his mind for the time—just

1. Beat.
2. Beat.

as men's misfortunes are forgotten in the excitement of new enterprises. This new interest was a valued novelty in whistling, which he
had just acquired from a negro, and he was suffering to practice it
undisturbed. It consisted in a peculiar bird-like turn, a sort of liquid
warble, produced by touching the tongue to the roof of the mouth
at short intervals in the midst of the music—the reader probably
remembers how to do it, if he has ever been a boy. Diligence and
attention soon gave him the knack of it, and he strode down the
street with his mouth full of harmony and his soul full of gratitude.
He felt much as an astronomer feels who has discovered a new
planet—no doubt, as far as strong, deep, unalloyed pleasure is concerned, the advantage was with the boy, not the astronomer.

The summer evenings were long. It was not dark, yet. Presently
Tom checked his whistle. A stranger was before him—a boy a shade
larger than himself. A new-comer of any age or either sex was an
impressive curiosity in the poor little shabby village of St. Petersburg.
This boy was well dressed, too—well dressed on a week-day. This
was simply astounding. His cap was a dainty thing, his close-
buttoned blue cloth roundabout was new and natty, and so were his
pantaloons. He had shoes on—and it was only Friday. He even wore
a necktie, a bright bit of ribbon. He had a citified air about him that
ate into Tom's vitals. The more Tom stared at the splendid marvel,
the higher he turned up his nose at his finery and the shabbier and
shabbier his own outfit seemed to him to grow. Neither boy spoke.
If one moved, the other moved—but only sidewise, in a circle; they
kept face to face and eye to eye all the time. Finally Tom said:

"I can lick you!"

"I'd like to see you try it."

"Well, I can do it."

"No you can't, either."

"Yes I can."

"No you can't."

"I can."

"You can't."

"Can!"

"Can't!"

An uncomfortable pause. Then Tom said:

"What's your name?"

" 'Tisn't any of your business, maybe."

"Well I 'low I'll *make* it my business."

"Well why don't you?"

"If you say much I will."

"Much—much—*much*. There now."

"Oh, you think you're mighty smart, *don't* you? I could lick you
with one hand tied behind me, if I wanted to."

"Well why don't you *do* it? You *say* you can do it."

"Well I *will*, if you fool with me."

"Oh yes—I've seen whole families in the same fix."

"Smarty! You think you're *some*, now, *don't* you? Oh what a hat!"

"You can lump that hat if you don't like it. I dare you to knock it off—and anybody that'll take a dare will suck eggs."

"You're a liar!"

"You're another."

"You're a fighting liar and dasn't take it up."

"Aw—take a walk!"

"Say—if you give me much more of your sass I'll take and bounce a rock off'n your head."

"Oh, of *course* you will."

"Well I *will*."

"Well why don't you *do* it then? What do you keep *saying* you will, for? Why don't you *do* it? It's because you're afraid."

"I *ain't* afraid."

"You are."

"I ain't."

"You are."

Another pause, and more eyeing and sidling around each other. Presently they were shoulder to shoulder. Tom said:

"Get away from here!"

"Get away yourself!"

"I won't."

"*I* won't either."

So they stood, each with a foot placed at an angle as a brace, and both shoving with might and main, and glowering at each other with hate. But neither could get an advantage. After struggling till both were hot and flushed, each relaxed his strain with watchful caution, and Tom said:

"You're a coward and a pup. I'll tell my big brother on you, and he can thrash you with his little finger, and I'll make him do it, too."

"What do I care for your big brother? I've got a brother that's bigger than he is—and what's more, he can throw him over that fence, too." [Both brothers were imaginary.]

"That's a lie."

"*Your* saying so don't make it so."

Tom drew a line in the dust with his big toe, and said:

"I dare you to step over that, and I'll lick you till you can't stand up. Anybody that'll take a dare will steal sheep."

The new boy stepped over promptly, and said:

"Now you said you'd do it, now let's see you do it."

"Don't you crowd me, now; you better look out."

"Well you *said* you'd do it—why don't you do it?"

"By jingo! for two cents I *will* do it."

The new boy took two broad coppers[3] out of his pocket and held them out with derision. Tom struck them to the ground. In an instant both boys were rolling and tumbling in the dirt, gripped together like cats; and for the space of a minute they tugged and tore at each other's hair and clothes, punched and scratched each other's noses, and covered themselves with dust and glory. Presently the confusion took form, and through the fog of battle Tom appeared, seated astride the new boy and pounding him with his fists.

"Holler 'nuff!" said he.

The boy only struggled to free himself. He was crying,—mainly from rage.

"Holler 'nuff!"—and the pounding went on.

At last the stranger got out a smothered " 'Nuff!" and Tom let him up and said:

"Now that'll learn you. Better look out who you're fooling with, next time."

The new boy went off brushing the dust from his clothes, sobbing, snuffling, and occasionally looking back and shaking his head and threatening what he would do to Tom the "next time he caught him out." To which Tom responded with jeers, and started off in high feather; and as soon as his back was turned the new boy snatched up a stone, threw it and hit him between the shoulders and then turned tail and ran like an antelope. Tom chased the traitor home, and thus found out where he lived. He then held a position at the gate for some time, daring the enemy to come outside, but the enemy only made faces at him through the window and declined. At last the enemy's mother appeared, and called Tom a bad, vicious, vulgar child, and ordered him away. So he went away; but he said he " 'lowed" to "lay"[4] for that boy.

He got home pretty late, that night, and when he climbed cautiously in at the window, he uncovered an ambuscade, in the person of his aunt; and when she saw the state his clothes were in her resolution to turn his Saturday holiday into captivity at hard labor became adamantine[5] in its firmness.

Chapter II.

SATURDAY morning was come, and all the summer world was bright and fresh, and brimming with life. There was a song in every heart;

3. Pennies.
4. Declared he'd lie in wait.
5. Unyielding, hard like a diamond. "Ambuscade": ambush.

and if the heart was young the music issued at the lips. There was cheer in every face and a spring in every step. The locust trees were in bloom and the fragrance of the blossoms filled the air. Cardiff Hill, beyond the village and above it, was green with vegetation, and it lay just far enough away to seem a Delectable Land,[6] dreamy, reposeful and inviting.

Tom appeared on the sidewalk with a bucket of whitewash and a long-handled brush. He surveyed the fence, and all gladness left him and a deep melancholy settled down upon his spirit. Thirty yards of board fence nine feet high. Life to him seemed hollow, and existence but a burden. Sighing, he dipped his brush and passed it along the topmost plank; repeated the operation; did it again; compared the insignificant whitewashed streak with the far-reaching continent of unwhitewashed fence, and sat down on a tree-box discouraged. Jim came skipping out at the gate with a tin pail, and singing "Buffalo Gals."[7] Bringing water from the town pump had always been hateful work in Tom's eyes, before, but now it did not strike him so. He remembered that there was company at the pump. White, mulatto, and negro boys and girls were always there waiting their turns, resting, trading playthings, quarreling, fighting, skylarking.[8] And he remembered that although the pump was only a hundred and fifty yards off, Jim never got back with a bucket of water under an hour—and even then somebody generally had to go after him. Tom said:

"Say, Jim, I'll fetch the water if you'll whitewash some."

Jim shook his head and said:

"Can't, Mars[9] Tom. Ole missis, she tole me I got to go an' git dis water an' not stop foolin' roun' wid anybody. She say she spec' Mars Tom gwyne to ax me to whitewash, an' so she tole me go 'long an' 'tend to my own business—she 'lowed *she'd* 'tend to de white-washin'."

"Oh, never you mind what she said, Jim. That's the way she always talks. Gimme the bucket—I won't be gone only a minute. *She* won't ever know."

"Oh, I dasn't, Mars Tom. Ole missis she'd take an' tar de head off'n me. 'Deed she would."

"*She!* She never licks anybody—whacks 'em over the head with her thimble—and who cares for that, I'd like to know. She talks awful, but talk don't hurt—anyways it don't if she don't cry. Jim, I'll give you a marvel. I'll give you a white alley!"[1]

6. In John Bunyan's *Pilgrim's Progress* (1678), Christian, the hero, views and eventually reaches the delightful Delectable Mountains on his way to heaven.
7. Minstrel song first published in 1844.
8. Frolicking, playing actively.
9. Master (dialect).
1. Alleys and marvels are marbles.

Jim began to waver.

"White alley, Jim! And it's a bully taw."[2]

"My! Dat's a mighty gay marvel, *I* tell you! But Mars Tom I's powerful 'fraid ole missis—"

"And besides, if you will I'll show you my sore toe."

Jim was only human—this attraction was too much for him. He put down his pail, took the white alley, and bent over the toe with absorbing interest while the bandage was being unwound. In another moment he was flying down the street with his pail and a tingling rear, Tom was whitewashing with vigor, and Aunt Polly was retiring from the field with a slipper in her hand and triumph in her eye.

But Tom's energy did not last. He began to think of the fun he had planned for this day, and his sorrows multiplied. Soon the free boys would come tripping along on all sorts of delicious expeditions, and they would make a world of fun of him for having to work—the very thought of it burnt him like fire. He got out his worldly wealth and examined it—bits of toys, marbles, and trash; enough to buy an exchange of *work*, maybe, but not half enough to buy so much as half an hour of pure freedom. So he returned his straightened means to his pocket, and gave up the idea of trying to buy the boys. At this dark and hopeless moment an inspiration burst upon him! Nothing less than a great, magnificent inspiration!

He took up his brush and went tranquilly to work. Ben Rogers hove in sight presently—the very boy, of all boys, whose ridicule he had been dreading. Ben's gait was the hop-skip-and-jump—proof enough that his heart was light and his anticipations high. He was eating an apple, and giving a long, melodious whoop, at intervals, followed by a deep-toned ding-dong-dong, ding-dong-dong, for he was personating a steamboat. As he drew near, he slackened speed, took the middle of the street, leaned far over to starboard and rounded to ponderously and with laborious pomp and circumstance—for he was personating the "Big Missouri," and considered himself to be drawing nine feet of water.[3] He was boat and captain and engine-bells combined, so he had to imagine himself standing on his own hurricane deck[4] giving the orders and executing them:

"Stop her, sir! Ting-a-ling-ling!" The headway ran almost out and he drew up slowly toward the side-walk.

"Ship up to back! Ting-a-ling-ling!" His arms straightened and stiffened down his sides.

"Set her back on the stabboard! Ting-a-ling-ling! Chow! ch-chow-wow! Chow!" His right hand, meantime, describing stately circles,— for it was representing a forty-foot wheel.

2. A type of marble used to shoot at other marbles. "Bully": excellent, jolly.
3. Nine feet of the boat was submerged in the water. "Starboard": right.
4. Upper deck.

"Let her go back on the labboard![5] Ting-a-ling-ling! Chow-ch-chow-chow!" The left hand began to describe circles.

"Stop the stabboard! Ting-a-ling-ling! Stop the labbord! Come ahead on the stabboard! Stop her! Let your outside turn over slow! Ting-a-ling-ling! Chow-ow-ow! Get out that head-line![6] *Lively* now! Come—out with your spring-line—what're you about there! Take a turn round that stump with the bight[7] of it! Stand by that stage, now—let her go! Done with the engines, sir! Ting-a-ling-ling! *Sh't! s'sh't! sh't!*" (trying the gauge-cocks.)

Tom went on whitewashing—paid no attention to the steamboat. Ben stared a moment and then said:

"Hi-*yi! You're* up a stump,[8] ain't you!"

No answer. Tom surveyed his last touch with the eye of an artist; then he gave his brush another gentle sweep and surveyed the result, as before. Ben ranged up alongside of him. Tom's mouth watered for the apple, but he stuck to his work. Ben said:

"Hello, old chap, you got to work, hey?"

Tom wheeled suddenly and said:

"Why it's you, Ben! I warn't noticing."

"Say—*I'm* going in a swimming, *I* am. Don't you wish you could? But of course you'd druther *work*—wouldn't you? 'Course you would!"

Tom contemplated the boy a bit, and said:

"What do you call work?"

"Why ain't *that* work?"

Tom resumed his whitewashing, and answered carelessly:

"Well, maybe it is, and maybe it ain't. All I know, is, it suits Tom Sawyer."

"Oh come, now, you don't mean to let on that you *like* it?"

The brush continued to move.

"Like it? Well I don't see why I oughtn't to like it. Does a boy get a chance to whitewash a fence every day?"

That put the thing in a new light. Ben stopped nibbling his apple. Tom swept his brush daintily back and forth—stepped back to note the effect—added a touch here and there—criticised the effect again—Ben watching every move and getting more and more interested, more and more absorbed. Presently he said:

"Say, Tom, let *me* whitewash a little."

Tom considered; was about to consent; but he altered his mind:

"No—no—I reckon it wouldn't hardly do, Ben. You see, Aunt Polly's awful particular about this fence—right here on the street,

---

5. I.e., larboard, left.
6. On a boat, ropes are called lines.
7. Loop.
8. Stumped, in trouble.

you know—but if it was the back fence I wouldn't mind and *she* wouldn't. Yes, she's awful particular about this fence; it's got to be done very careful; I reckon there ain't one boy in a thousand, maybe two thousand, that can do it the way it's got to be done.

"No—is that so? Oh come, now—lemme just try. Only just a little—I'd let *you*, if you was me, Tom."

"Ben, I'd like to, honest injun;[9] but aunt Polly—well Jim wanted to do it, but she wouldn't let him; Sid wanted to do it, and she wouldn't let Sid. Now don't you see how I'm fixed? If you was to tackle this fence and anything was to happen to it—"

"Oh, shucks, I'll be just as careful. Now lemme try. Say—I'll give you the core of my apple."

"Well, here—. No, Ben, now don't. I'm afeard—"

"I'll give you *all* of it!"

Tom gave up the brush with reluctance in his face but alacrity in his heart. And while the late steamer "Big Missouri" worked and sweated in the sun, the retired artist sat on a barrel in the shade close by, dangled his legs, munched his apple, and planned the slaughter of more innocents.[1] There was no lack of material; boys happened along every little while; they came to jeer, but remained to whitewash. By the time Ben was fagged out, Tom had traded the next chance to Billy Fisher for a kite, in good repair; and when *he* played out, Johnny Miller bought in for a dead rat and a string to swing it with—and so on, and so on, hour after hour. And when the middle of the afternoon came, from being a poor poverty-stricken boy in the morning, Tom was literally rolling in wealth. He had, beside the things before mentioned, twelve marbles, part of a jews-harp,[2] a piece of blue bottle-glass to look through, a spool cannon, a key that wouldn't unlock anything, a fragment of chalk, a glass stopper of a decanter, a tin soldier, a couple of tadpoles, six firecrackers, a kitten with only one eye, a brass door-knob, a dog collar—but no dog—the handle of a knife, four pieces of orange peel, and a dilapidated old window-sash.

He had had a nice, good, idle time all the while—plenty of company—and the fence had three coats of whitewash on it! If he hadn't run out of whitewash, he would have bankrupted every boy in the village.

Tom said to himself that it was not such a hollow world, after all. He had discovered a great law of human action, without knowing it—namely, that in order to make a man or a boy covet a thing, it is

---

9. Indian (derogatory).
1. Alarmed by reports of the birth of a future king (namely, Jesus), Herod ordered the killing of all Jewish boys "from two years old and under" (Matthew 2.16), an action later called the slaughter of the innocents.
2. Small musical instrument with a frame and a steel tongue for twanging.

only necessary to make the thing difficult to attain. If he had been a great and wise philosopher, like the writer of this book, he would now have comprehended that Work consists of whatever a body is *obliged* to do and that Play consists of whatever a body is not obliged to do. And this would help him to understand why constructing artificial flowers or performing on a treadmill is work, while rolling tenpins or climbing Mont Blanc is only amusement. There are wealthy gentlemen in England who drive four-horse passenger-coaches twenty or thirty miles on a daily line, in the summer, because the privilege costs them considerable money; but if they were offered wages for the service, that would turn it into work and then they would resign.

The boy mused a while over the substantial change which had taken place in his worldly circumstances, and then wended[3] toward head-quarters to report.

Chapter III.

TOM presented himself before aunt Polly, who was sitting by an open window in a pleasant rearward apartment which was bed-room, breakfast-room, dining room, and library combined. The balmy summer air, the restful quiet, the odor of the flowers, and the drowsing murmur of the bees had had their effect, and she was nodding over her knitting—for she had no company but the cat, and it was asleep in her lap. Her spectacles were propped up on her gray head for safety. She had thought that of course Tom had deserted long ago, and she wondered to see him place himself in her power again in this intrepid way. He said:

"Mayn't I go and play now, aunt?"

"What, a'ready? How much have you done?"

"It's all done, aunt."

"Tom, don't lie to me—I can't bear it."

"I ain't, aunt; it *is* all done."

Aunt Polly placed small trust in such evidence. She went out to see for herself; and she would have been content to find twenty per cent of Tom's statement true. When she found the entire fence whitewashed, and not only whitewashed but elaborately coated and recoated, and even a streak added to the ground, her astonishment was almost unspeakable. She said:

"Well, I never! There's no getting around it, you *can* work when you're a mind to, Tom." And then she diluted the compliment by adding, "But it's powerful seldom you're a mind to, I'm bound to say.

3. Went.

Well, go 'long and play; but mind you get back some time in a week, or I'll tan[4] you."

She was so overcome by the splendor of his achievement that she took him into the closet and selected a choice apple and delivered it to him, along with an improving lecture upon the added value and flavor a treat took to itself when it came without sin through virtuous effort. And while she closed with a happy Scriptural flourish, he "hooked"[5] a doughnut.

Then he skipped out, and saw Sid just starting up the outside stairway that led to the back rooms on the second floor. Clods[6] were handy and the air was full of them in a twinkling. They raged around Sid like a hail-storm; and before aunt Polly could collect her surprised faculties and sally to the rescue, six or seven clods had taken personal effect, and Tom was over the fence and gone. There was a gate, but as a general thing he was too crowded for time to make use of it. His soul was at peace, now that he had settled with Sid for calling attention to his black thread and getting him into trouble.

Tom skirted the block, and came around into a muddy alley that led by the back of his aunt's cow-stable. He presently got safely beyond the reach of capture and punishment, and hasted toward the public square of the village, where two "military" companies of boys had met for conflict, according to previous appointment. Tom was General of one of these armies, Joe Harper (a bosom friend,) General of the other. These two great commanders did not condescend to fight in person—that being better suited to the still smaller fry—but sat together on an eminence and conducted the field operations by orders delivered through aides-de-camp. Tom's army won a great victory, after a long and hard-fought battle. Then the dead were counted, prisoners exchanged, the terms of the next disagreement agreed upon and the day for the necessary battle appointed; after which the armies fell into line and marched away, and Tom turned homeward alone.

As he was passing by the house where Jeff Thatcher lived, he saw a new girl in the garden—a lovely little blue-eyed creature with yellow hair plaited into two long tails, white summer frock and embroidered pantalettes.[7] The fresh-crowned hero fell without firing a shot. A certain Amy Lawrence vanished out of his heart and left not even a memory of herself behind. He had thought he loved her to distraction, he had regarded his passion as adoration; and behold it was only a poor little evanescent partiality. He had been months winning her; she had confessed hardly a week ago; he had been the happiest

4. Whip.
5. Pilfered, stole.
6. Lumps of earth.
7. Ruffled undergarment extending below the skirt. "Plaited": braided. "Frock": dress.

and the proudest boy in the world only seven short days, and here, in one instant of time she had gone out of his heart like a casual stranger whose visit is done.

He worshiped this new angel with furtive[8] eye, till he saw that she had discovered him; then he pretended he did not know she was present, and began to "show off" in all sorts of absurd boyish ways in order to win her admiration. He kept up this grotesque foolishness for some time; but by and by, while he was in the midst of some dangerous gymnastic performances, he glanced aside and saw that the little girl was wending her way toward the house. Tom came up to the fence and leaned on it, grieving, and hoping she would tarry yet a while longer. She halted a moment on the steps and then moved toward the door. Tom heaved a great sigh as she put her foot on the threshold. But his face lit up, right away, for she tossed a pansy over the fence a moment before she disappeared.

The boy ran around and stopped within a foot or two of the flower, and then shaded his eyes with his hand and began to look down street as if he had discovered something of interest going on in that direction. Presently he picked up a straw and began trying to balance it on his nose, with his head tilted far back; and as he moved from side to side, in his efforts, he edged nearer and nearer toward the pansy; finally his bare foot rested upon it, his pliant toes closed upon it and he hopped away with the treasure, and disappeared around the corner. But only for a minute—only while he could button the flower inside his jacket, next his heart—or next his stomach, possibly, for he was not much posted in anatomy, and not hypercritical, anyway.

He returned, now, and hung about the fence till nightfall, "showing off," as before; but the girl never exhibited herself again, though Tom comforted himself a little with the hope that she had been near some window, meantime, and been aware of his attentions. Finally he went home reluctantly, with his poor head full of visions.

All through supper his spirits were so high that his aunt wondered "what had got into the child." He took a good scolding about clodding Sid, and did not seem to mind it in the least. He tried to steal sugar under his aunt's very nose, and got his knuckles rapped for it. He said:

"Aunt, you don't whack Sid when he takes it."

"Well, Sid don't torment a body the way you do. You'd be always into that sugar if I warn't watching you."

Presently she stepped into the kitchen, and Sid, happy in his immunity, reached for the sugar-bowl—a sort of glorying over Tom which was well-nigh unbearable. But Sid's fingers slipped and the bowl dropped and broke. Tom was in ecstasies. In such ecstasies

8. Secret, sly.

that he even controlled his tongue and was silent. He said to himself that he would not speak a word, even when his aunt came in, but would sit perfectly still till she asked who did the mischief; and then he would tell and there would be nothing so good in the world as to see that pet model "catch it." He was so brim-full of exultation that he could hardly hold himself when the old lady came back and stood above the wreck discharging lightnings of wrath from over her spectacles. He said to himself, "Now it's coming!" And the next instant he was sprawling on the floor! The potent palm was uplifted to strike again when Tom cried out:

"Hold on, now, what 're you belting *me*, for?—Sid broke it!"

Aunt Polly paused, perplexed, and Tom looked for healing pity. But when she got her tongue again, she only said:

"Umf! Well, you didn't get a lick amiss, I reckon. You been into some other owdacious mischief when I wasn't around, like enough."

Then her conscience reproached her, and she yearned to say something kind and loving; but she judged that this would be construed into a confession that she had been in the wrong, and discipline forbade that. So she kept silence, and went about her affairs with a troubled heart. Tom sulked in a corner and exalted his woes. He knew that in her heart his aunt was on her knees to him, and he was morosely gratified by the consciousness of it. He would hang out no signals, he would take notice of none. He knew that a yearning glance fell upon him, now and then, through a film of tears, but he refused recognition of it. He pictured himself lying sick unto death and his aunt bending over him beseeching one little forgiving word, but he would turn his face to the wall, and die with that word unsaid. Ah, how would she feel then? And he pictured himself brought home from the river, dead, with his curls all wet, and his poor hands still forever, and his sore heart at rest. How she would throw herself upon him, and how her tears would fall like rain, and her lips pray God to give her back her boy and she would never, never abuse him any more! But he would lie there cold and white and make no sign—a poor little sufferer whose griefs were at an end. He so worked upon his feelings with the pathos[9] of these dreams that he had to keep swallowing, he was so like to choke; and his eyes swam in a blur of water, which overflowed when he winked, and ran down and trickled from the end of his nose. And such a luxury to him was this petting of his sorrows, that he could not bear to have any worldly cheeriness or any grating delight intrude upon it; it was too sacred for such contact; and so, presently, when his cousin Mary danced in, all alive with the joy of seeing home again after an age-long visit of one week to the country, he got up and moved in clouds and darkness

9. Quality arousing pity.

out at one door as she brought song and sunshine in at the other.

He wandered far from the accustomed haunts of boys, and sought desolate places that were in harmony with his spirit. A log raft in the river invited him, and he seated himself on its outer edge and contemplated the dreary vastness of the stream, wishing, the while, that he could only be drowned, all at once and unconsciously, without undergoing the uncomfortable routine devised by nature. Then he thought of his flower. He got it out, rumpled and wilted, and it mightily increased his dismal felicity. He wondered if *she* would pity him if she knew? Would she cry, and wish that she had a right to put her arms around his neck and comfort him? Or would she turn coldly away like all the hollow world? This picture brought such an agony of pleasurable suffering that he worked it over and over again in his mind and set it up in new and varied lights till he wore it threadbare. At last he rose up sighing, and departed in the darkness.

About half past nine or ten o'clock, he came along the deserted street to where the Adored Unknown lived; he paused a moment; no sound fell upon his listening ear; a candle was casting a dull glow upon the curtain of a second-story window. Was the sacred presence there? He climbed the fence, threaded his stealthy way through the plants, till he stood under that window; he looked up at it long, and with emotion; then he laid him down on the ground under it, disposing himself upon his back, with his hands clasped upon his breast and holding his poor wilted flower. And thus he would die—out in the cold world, with no shelter over his homeless head, no friendly hand to wipe the death-damps from his brow, no loving face to bend pityingly over him when the great agony came. And thus *she* would see him when she looked out upon the glad morning—and oh! would she drop one little tear upon his poor lifeless form, would she heave one little sigh to see a bright young life so rudely blighted, so untimely cut down?

The window went up, a maid-servant's discordant voice profaned the holy calm, and a deluge of water drenched the prone martyr's remains!

The strangling hero sprang up with a relieving snort. There was a whiz as of a missile in the air, mingled with the murmur of a curse, a sound as of shivering glass followed, and a small vague form went over the fence and shot away in the gloom.

Not long after, as Tom, all undressed for bed, was surveying his drenched garments by the light of a tallow dip,[1] Sid woke up; but if he had any dim idea of making any "references to allusions," he thought better of it and held his peace—for there was danger in Tom's eye.

1. Dipped candle made with animal fat.

Tom turned in without the added vexation[2] of prayers, and Sid made mental note of the omission.

Chapter IV.

THE sun rose upon a tranquil world, and beamed down upon the peaceful village like a benediction. Breakfast over, aunt Polly had family worship; it began with a prayer built from the ground up of solid courses of Scriptural quotations, welded together with a thin mortar of originality; and from the summit of this she delivered a grim chapter of the Mosaic Law, as from Sinai.[3]

Then Tom girded up his loins,[4] so to speak, and went to work to "get his verses." Sid had learned his lesson days before. Tom bent all his energies to the memorizing of five verses, and he chose part of the Sermon on the Mount, because he could find no verses that were shorter. At the end of half an hour Tom had a vague general idea of his lesson, but no more, for his mind was traversing the whole field of human thought, and his hands were busy with distracting recreations. Mary took his book to hear him recite, and he tried to find his way through the fog:

"Blessed are the—a—a—"

"Poor—"

"Yes—poor; blessed are the poor—a—a—"

"In spirit—"

"In spirit; blessed are the poor in spirit, for they—they—"

"*Theirs*—"

"For *theirs*. Blessed are the poor in spirit, for *theirs*—is the kingdom of heaven. Blessed are they that mourn, for they—they—"

"Sh—"

"For they—a—"

"S, H, A—"

"For they S, H—Oh I don't know what it is!"

"*Shall!*"

"Oh, *shall!* for they shall—for they shall—a—a—shall mourn—a—a—blessed are they that shall—they that—a—they that shall mourn, for they shall—a—shall *what?* Why don't you tell me, Mary?—what do you want to be so mean, for?"

"Oh, Tom, you poor thick-headed thing, I'm not teasing you. I wouldn't do that. You must go and learn it again. Don't you be dis-

---

2. Irritation, bother.
3. One or more of the Ten Commandments, which Moses received on Mount Sinai.
4. Readied for action. Jeremiah 1.17: "Thou therefore gird up thy loins, and arise, and speak unto them all that I command thee."

couraged, Tom, you'll manage it—and if you do, I'll give you something ever so nice. There, now, that's a good boy."

"All right! What is it, Mary, tell me what it is."

"Never you mind, Tom. You know if I say it's nice, it *is* nice."

"You bet you that's so, Mary. All right, I'll tackle it again."

And he did "tackle it again"—and under the double pressure of curiosity and prospective gain, he did it with such spirit that he accomplished a shining success. Mary gave him a bran-new "Barlow" knife[5] worth twelve and a half cents; and the convulsion of delight that swept his system shook him to his foundations. True, the knife would not cut anything, but it was a "sure-enough" Barlow, and there was inconceivable grandeur in that—though where the western boys ever got the idea that such a weapon could possibly be counterfeited to its injury, is an imposing mystery and will always remain so, perhaps. Tom contrived to scarify the cupboard with it, and was arranging to begin on the bureau, when he was called off to dress for Sunday-School.

Mary gave him a tin basin of water and a piece of soap, and he went outside the door and set the basin on a little bench there; then he dipped the soap in the water and laid it down; turned up his sleeves; poured out the water on the ground, gently, and then entered the kitchen and began to wipe his face diligently on the towel behind the door. But Mary removed the towel and said:

"Now ain't you ashamed, Tom. You mustn't be so bad. Water won't hurt you."

Tom was a trifle disconcerted. The basin was refilled, and this time he stood over it a little while, gathering resolution; took in a big breath and began. When he entered the kitchen presently, with both eyes shut, and groping for the towel with his hands, an honorable testimony of suds and water was dripping from his face. But when he emerged from the towel, he was not yet satisfactory, for the clean territory stopped short at his chin and his jaws, like a mask; below and beyond this line there was a dark expanse of unirrigated soil that spread downward in front and backward around his neck. Mary took him in hand, and when she was done with him he was a man and a brother, without distinction of color,[6] and his saturated hair was neatly brushed, and its short curls wrought into a dainty and symmetrical general effect. [He privately smoothed out the curls, with labor and difficulty, and plastered his hair close down to his head; for he held curls to be effeminate, and his own filled his life with bitterness.] Then Mary got out a suit of his clothing that had been used only on Sundays during two years—they were simply called his

5. Single-bladed pocketknife.
6. Phrases frequently invoked by abolitionists: e.g., am I not a man and a brother?

"other clothes"—and so by that we know the size of his wardrobe. The girl "put him to rights" after he had dressed himself; she buttoned his neat roundabout up to his chin, turned his vast shirt collar down over his shoulders, brushed him off and crowned him with his speckled straw hat. He now looked exceedingly improved and uncomfortable. And he was fully as uncomfortable as he looked; for there was a restraint about whole clothes and cleanliness that galled him. He hoped that Mary would forget his shoes, but the hope was blighted; she coated them thoroughly with tallow, as was the custom, and brought them out. He lost his temper and said he was always being made to do everything he didn't want to do. But Mary said, persuasively:

"Please, Tom—that's a good boy."

So he got into the shoes, snarling. Mary was soon ready, and the three children set out for Sunday-school—a place that Tom hated with his whole heart; but Sid and Mary were fond of it.

Sabbath-school hours were from nine to half past ten; and then church service. Two of the children always remained for the sermon, voluntarily; and the other always remained, too—for stronger reasons. The church's high-backed, uncushioned pews would seat about three hundred persons; the edifice was but a small, plain affair, with a sort of pine board tree-box on top of it for a steeple. At the door Tom dropped back a step and accosted a Sunday-dressed comrade:

"Say, Billy, got a yaller ticket?"

"Yes."

"What'll you take for her?"

"What'll you give?"

"Piece of lickrish and a fish-hook."

"Less see 'em."

Tom exhibited. They were satisfactory, and the property changed hands. Then Tom traded a couple of white alleys for three red tickets, and some small trifle or other for a couple of blue ones. He waylaid other boys as they came, and went on buying tickets of various colors ten or fifteen minutes longer. He entered the church, now, with a swarm of clean and noisy boys and girls, proceeded to his seat and started a quarrel with the first boy that came handy. The teacher, a grave, elderly man, interfered; then turned his back a moment and Tom pulled a boy's hair in the next bench, and was absorbed in his book when the boy turned around; stuck a pin in another boy, presently, in order to hear him say "Ouch!" and got a new reprimand from his teacher. Tom's whole class were of a pattern—restless, noisy and troublesome. When they came to recite their lessons, not one of them knew his verses perfectly, but had to be prompted all along. However, they worried through, and each got his reward—in small blue tickets, each with a passage of Scripture on it; each blue ticket was pay for two verses of the recitation. Ten blue tickets equaled a red one, and could be exchanged for it; ten red tickets equaled a yellow one: for ten yellow tickets the Superintendent gave a very plainly bound Bible, (worth forty cents in those easy times,) to the pupil. How many of my readers would have the industry and the application to memorize two thousand verses, even for a Doré Bible? And yet Mary had acquired two Bibles in this way—it was the patient work of two years; and a boy of German parentage had won four or five. He once recited three thousand verses without stopping; but the strain upon his mental faculties was too great, and he was little better than an idiot from that day forth—a grievous misfortune for the school, for on great occasions, before company, the Superintendent (as Tom expressed it) had always made this boy come out and "spread himself." Only the older pupils managed to keep their tickets and stick to their tedious work long enough to get a Bible, and so the delivery of one of these prizes was a rare and noteworthy circumstance; the successful pupil was so great and conspicuous for that day that on the spot every scholar's breast was fired with a fresh ambition that often lasted a couple of weeks. It is possible that Tom's mental stomach had never really hungered for one of those prizes, but unquestionably his entire being had for many a day longed for the glory and the eclat[7] that came with it.

In due course the Superintendent stood up in front of the pulpit, with a closed hymn book in his hand and his forefinger inserted between its leaves, and commanded attention. When a Sunday-school Superintendent makes his customary little speech, a hymn-book in the hand is as necessary as is the inevitable sheet of music in the hand of a singer who stands forward on the platform and sings a solo at a concert—though why, is a mystery: for neither the hymn-book nor the sheet of music is ever referred to by the sufferer. This Superintendent was a slim creature of thirty-five, with a sandy goatee and short sandy hair; he wore a stiff standing-collar whose upper edge almost reached his ears and whose sharp points curved forward abreast the corners of his mouth—a fence that compelled a straight lookout ahead, and a turning of the whole body when a side view was required; his chin was propped on a spreading cravat[8] which was as broad and as long as a bank note, and had fringed ends; his boot toes were turned sharply up, in the fashion of the day, like sleigh-runners—an effect patiently and laboriously produced by the young men by sitting with their toes pressed against a wall for hours together. Mr. Walters was very earnest of mien, and very sincere and honest at heart; and he held sacred things and places in such reverence, and so separated them from worldly matters, that uncon-

7. Brilliant success.
8. Necktie.

sciously to himself his Sunday-school voice had acquired a peculiar intonation which was wholly absent on week-days. He began after this fashion:

"Now children, I want you all to sit up just as straight and pretty as you can and give me all your attention for a minute or two. There—that is it. That is the way good little boys and girls should do. I see one little girl who is looking out of the window—I am afraid she thinks I am out there somewhere—perhaps up in one of the trees making a speech to the little birds. [Applausive titter.[9]] I want to tell you how good it makes me feel to see so many bright, clean little faces assembled in a place like this, learning to do right and be good."

And so forth and so on. It is not necessary to set down the rest of the oration.[1] It was of a pattern which does not vary, and so it is familiar to us all.

The latter third of the speech was marred by the resumption of fights and other recreations among certain of the bad boys, and by fidgetings and whisperings that extended far and wide, washing even to the bases of isolated and incorruptible rocks like Sid and Mary. But now every sound ceased suddenly, with the subsidence of Mr. Walters's voice, and the conclusion of the speech was received with a burst of silent gratitude.

A good part of the whispering had been occasioned by an event which was more or less rare—the entrance of visitors; lawyer Thatcher, accompanied by a very feeble and aged man; a fine, portly, middle-aged gentleman with iron-gray hair; and a dignified lady who was doubtless the latter's wife. The lady was leading a child. Tom had been restless and full of chafings and repinings; conscience-smitten, too—he could not meet Amy Lawrence's eye, he could not brook her loving gaze. But when he saw this small new-comer his soul was all ablaze with bliss in a moment. The next moment he was "showing off" with all his might—cuffing boys, pulling hair, making faces—in a word, using every art that seemed likely to fascinate a girl and win her applause. His exaltation had but one alloy—the memory of his humiliation in this angel's garden—and that record in sand was fast washing out, under the waves of happiness that were sweeping over it now.

The visitors were given the highest seat of honor, and as soon as Mr. Walters's speech was finished, he introduced them to the school. The middle-aged man turned out to be a prodigious personage—no less a one than the county judge—altogether the most august[2] creation these children had ever looked upon—and they wondered what kind of material he was made of—and they half wanted to hear him

9. Restrained laughter.
1. Formal speech.
2. Awe-inspiring.

roar, and were half afraid he might, too. He was from Constantinople, twelve miles away—so he had traveled, and seen the world—these very eyes had looked upon the county court house—which was said to have a tin roof. The awe which these reflections inspired was attested by the impressive silence and the ranks of staring eyes. This was the great Judge Thatcher, brother of their own lawyer. Jeff Thatcher immediately went forward, to be familiar with the great man and be envied by the school. It would have been music to his soul to hear the whisperings:

"Look at him, Jim! He's a going up there. Say—look! he's a-going to shake hands with him—he *is* a shaking hands with him! By jings, don't you wish you was Jeff?"

Mr. Walters fell to "showing off," with all sorts of official bustlings and activities, giving orders, delivering judgments, discharging directions here, there, everywhere that he could find a target. The librarian "showed off"—running hither and thither with his arms full of books and making a deal of the splutter and fuss that insect authority delights in. The young lady teachers "showed off"—bending sweetly over pupils that were lately being boxed, lifting pretty warning fingers at bad little boys and patting good ones lovingly. The young gentlemen teachers "showed off" with small scoldings and other little displays of authority and fine attention to discipline—and most of the teachers, of both sexes, found business up at the library, by the pulpit; and it was business that frequently had to be done over again two or three times, (with much seeming vexation.) The little girls "showed off" in various ways, and the little boys "showed off" with such diligence that the air was thick with paper wads and the murmur of scufflings. And above it all the great man sat and beamed a majestic judicial smile upon all the house, and warmed himself in the sun of his own grandeur—for he was "showing off," too.

There was only one thing wanting, to make Mr. Walters's ecstasy complete, and that was, a chance to deliver a Bible-prize and exhibit a prodigy. Several pupils had a few yellow tickets, but none had enough—he had been around among the star pupils inquiring. He would have given worlds, now, to have that German lad back again with a sound mind.

And now at this moment, when hope was dead, Tom Sawyer came forward with nine yellow tickets, nine red tickets, and ten blue ones, and demanded a Bible. This was a thunderbolt out of a clear sky. Walters was not expecting an application from this source for the next ten years. But there was no getting around it—here were the certified checks, and they were good for their face. Tom was therefore elevated to a place with the Judge and the other elect, and the great news was announced from head-quarters. It was the most stunning surprise of the decade; and so profound was the sensation that it lifted the new hero up to the judicial one's altitude, and the school had two marvels to gaze upon in place of one. The boys were all eaten up with envy—but those that suffered the bitterest pangs were those who perceived too late that they themselves had contributed to this hated splendor by trading tickets to Tom for the wealth he had amassed in selling whitewashing privileges. These despised themselves, as being the dupes of a wily fraud, a guileful snake in the grass.

The prize was delivered to Tom with as much effusion as the Superintendent could pump up under the circumstances; but it lacked somewhat of the true gush, for the poor fellow's instinct taught him that there was a mystery here that could not well bear the light, perhaps; it was simply preposterous that *this* boy had warehoused two thousand sheaves of Scriptural wisdom on his premises—a dozen would strain his capacity, without a doubt.

Amy Lawrence was proud and glad, and she tried to make Tom see it in her face—but he wouldn't look. She wondered; then she was just a grain troubled; next a dim suspicion came and went—came again; she watched; a furtive glance told her worlds—and then her heart broke, and she was jealous, and angry, and the tears came and she hated everybody: Tom most of all, (she thought.)

Tom was introduced to the Judge; but his tongue was tied, his breath would hardly come, his heart quaked—partly because of the awful greatness of the man, but mainly because he was *her* parent. He would have liked to fall down and worship him, if it were in the dark. The Judge put his hand on Tom's head and called him a fine little man, and asked him what his name was. The boy stammered, gasped, and got it out:

"Tom."

"Oh, no, not Tom—it is—"

"Thomas."

"Ah, that's it. I thought there was more to it, maybe. That's very well. But you've another one I daresay, and you'll tell it to me, won't you?"

"Tell the gentleman your other name, Thomas," said Walters, "and say *sir.*—You mustn't forget your manners."

"Thomas Sawyer—sir."

"That's it! That's a good boy. Fine boy. Fine, manly little fellow. Two thousand verses is a great many—very, very great many. And you never can be sorry for the trouble you took to learn them; for knowledge is worth more than anything there is in the world; it's what makes great men and good men; you'll be a great man and a good man yourself, some day, Thomas, and then you'll look back and say, It's all owing to the precious Sunday-school privileges of my boyhood—it's all owing to my dear teachers that taught me to learn—it's all owing to the good Superintendent, who encouraged me, and watched over me, and gave me a beautiful Bible—a splendid elegant Bible, to keep and have it all for my own, always—it's all owing to right bringing up! That is what you will say, Thomas—and you wouldn't take any money for those two thousand verses then— no indeed you wouldn't. And now you wouldn't mind telling me and this lady some of the things you've learned—no, I know you wouldn't—for we are proud of little boys that learn. Now no doubt you know the names of all the twelve disciples. Won't you tell us the names of the first two that were appointed?"

Tom was tugging at a button and looking sheepish. He blushed, now, and his eyes fell. Mr. Walters's heart sank within him. He said to himself, It is not possible that the boy can answer the simplest question—why *did* the Judge ask him? Yet he felt obliged to speak up and say:

"Answer the gentleman, Thomas—don't be afraid."

Tom still hung fire.

"Now I know you'll tell *me*" said the lady. "The names of the first two disciples were—"

"DAVID AND GOLIAH!"[3]

Let us draw the curtain of charity over the rest of the scene.

Chapter V.

ABOUT half past ten the cracked bell of the small church began to ring, and presently the people began to gather for the morning sermon. The Sunday school children distributed themselves about the house and occupied pews with their parents, so as to be under supervision. Aunt Polly came, and Tom and Sid and Mary sat with her— Tom being placed next the aisle, in order that he might be as far away from the open window and the seductive outside summer scenes as possible. The crowd filed up the aisles: the aged and needy postmaster, who had seen better days; the mayor and his wife—for they had a mayor there, among other unnecessaries; the justice of the peace; the widow Douglas, fair, smart and forty, a generous, good-hearted soul and well-to-do, her hill mansion the only palace in the town, and the most hospitable and much the most lavish in the matter of festivities that St. Petersburg could boast; the bent and venerable Major and Mrs. Ward; lawyer Riverson, the new notable from a distance; next the belle of the village, followed by a troop of lawn-clad[4] and ribbon-decked young heart-breakers; then all the

3. Not disciples. In the Old Testament the young hero David brought down the giant Goliath using only a slingshot.
4. Dressed in a kind of fine linen or cotton cloth.

young clerks in town in a body—for they had stood in the vestibule sucking their cane-heads, a circling wall of oiled and simpering admirers, till the last girl had run their gauntlet; and last of all came the Model Boy, Willie Mufferson, taking as heedful care of his mother as if she were cut glass. He always brought his mother to church, and was the pride of all the matrons. The boys all hated him, he was so good. And besides, he had been "thrown up to them" so much. His white handkerchief was hanging out of his pocket behind, as usual on Sundays—accidentally. Tom had no handkerchief, and he looked upon boys who had, as snobs.

The congregation being fully assembled, now, the bell rang once more, to warn laggards and stragglers, and then a solemn hush fell upon the church which was only broken by the tittering and whispering of the choir in the gallery. The choir always tittered and whispered all through service. There was once a church choir that was not ill-bred, but I have forgotten where it was, now. It was a great many years ago, and I can scarcely remember anything about it, but I think it was in some foreign country.

The minister gave out the hymn, and read it through with a relish, in a peculiar style which was much admired in that part of the country. His voice began on a medium key and climbed steadily up till it reached a certain point, where it bore with strong emphasis upon the topmost word and then plunged down as if from a spring-board:

Shall I be car-ri-ed toe the skies, on flow'ry *beds*

of ease,

Whilst others fight to win the prize, and sail thro' *blood-*

-y seas?

He was regarded as a wonderful reader. At church "sociables" he was always called upon to read poetry; and when he was through, the ladies would lift up their hands and let them fall helplessly in their laps, and "wall" their eyes, and shake their heads, as much as to say, "Words cannot express it; it is too beautiful, *too* beautiful for this mortal earth."

After the hymn had been sung, the Rev. Mr. Sprague turned himself into a bulletin board and read off "notices" of meetings and societies and things till it seemed that the list would stretch out to the crack of doom—a queer custom which is still kept up in America, even in cities, away here in this age of abundant newspapers. Often, the less there is to justify a traditional custom, the harder it is to get rid of it.

And now the minister prayed. A good, generous prayer, it was, and went into details: it pleaded for the church, and the little children of the church; for the other churches of the village; for the village itself; for the county; for the State; for the State officers; for the United States; for the churches of the United States; for Congress; for the President; for the officers of the Government; for poor sailors, tossed by stormy seas; for the oppressed millions groaning under the heel of European monarchies and Oriental despotisms; for such as have the light and the good tidings, and yet have not eyes to see nor ears to hear withal; for the heathen in the far islands of the sea; and closed with a supplication that the words he was about to speak might find grace and favor, and be as seed sown in fertile ground, yielding in time a grateful harvest of good. Amen.

There was a rustling of dresses, and the standing congregation sat down. The boy whose history this book relates, did not enjoy the prayer, he only endured it—if he even did that much. He was restive,[5] all through it; he kept tally of the details of the prayer, unconsciously—for he was not listening, but he knew the ground of old, and the clergyman's regular route over it—and when a little trifle of new matter was interlarded, his ear detected it and his whole nature resented it; he considered additions unfair, and scoundrelly. In the midst of the prayer a fly had lit on the back of the pew in front of him and tortured his spirit by calmly rubbing its hands together; embracing its head with its arms, and polishing it so vigorously that it seemed to almost part company with the body, and the slender thread of a neck was exposed to view; scraping its wings with its hind legs and smoothing them to its body as if they had been coat tails; going through its whole toilet as tranquilly as if it knew it was perfectly safe. As indeed it was; for as sorely as Tom's hands itched to grab for it they did not dare—he believed his soul would be instantly destroyed if he did such a thing while the prayer was going on. But with the closing sentence his hand began to curve and steal forward; and the instant the "Amen" was out the fly was a prisoner of war. His aunt detected the act and made him let it go.

The minister gave out his text and droned along monotonously through an argument that was so prosy that many a head by and by began to nod—and yet it was an argument that dealt in limitless fire and brimstone and thinned the predestined elect[6] down to a company so small as to be hardly worth the saving. Tom counted the pages of the sermon; after church he always knew how many pages there had been, but he seldom knew anything else about the discourse. However, this time he was really interested for a little while. The minister made a grand and moving picture of the assembling

5. Restless.
6. Those destined for heaven.

together of the world's hosts at the millennium when the lion and the lamb should lie down together and a little child should lead them.[7] But the pathos, the lesson, the moral of the great spectacle were lost upon the boy; he only thought of the conspicuousness of the principal character before the on-looking nations; his face lit with the thought, and he said to himself that he wished he could be that child, if it was a tame lion.

Now he lapsed into suffering again, as the dry argument was resumed. Presently he bethought him of a treasure he had and got it out. It was a large black beetle with formidable jaws—a "pinch-bug," he called it. It was in a percussion-cap box. The first thing the beetle did was to take him by the finger. A natural fillip[8] followed, the beetle went floundering into the aisle and lit on its back, and the hurt finger went into the boy's mouth. The beetle lay there working its helpless legs, unable to turn over. Tom eyed it, and longed for it; but it was safe out of his reach. Other people uninterested in the sermon, found relief in the beetle, and they eyed it too. Presently a vagrant[9] poodle dog came idling along, sad at heart, lazy with the summer softness and the quiet, weary of captivity, sighing for change. He spied the beetle; the drooping tail lifted and wagged. He surveyed the prize; walked around it; smelt at it from a safe distance; walked around it again; grew bolder, and took a closer smell; then lifted his lip and made a gingerly snatch at it, just missing it; made another, and another; began to enjoy the diversion; subsided to his stomach with the beetle between his paws, and continued his experiments; grew weary at last, and then indifferent and absent-minded. His head nodded, and little by little his chin descended and touched the enemy, who seized it. There was a sharp yelp, a flirt of the poodle's head, and the beetle fell a couple of yards away, and lit on its back once more. The neighboring spectators shook with a gentle inward joy, several faces went behind fans and handkerchiefs, and Tom was entirely happy. The dog looked foolish, and probably felt so; but there was resentment in his heart, too, and a craving for revenge. So he went to the beetle and began a wary attack on it again; jumping at it from every point of a circle, lighting with his fore paws within an inch of the creature, making even closer snatches at it with his teeth, and jerking his head till his ears flapped again. But he grew tired once more, after a while; tried to amuse himself with a fly but found no relief; followed an ant around, with his nose close to the floor, and quickly wearied of that; yawned, sighed, forgot the beetle entirely, and sat down on it! Then there was a wild yelp of agony and

7. At the second coming of Christ, "The wolf also shall dwell with the lamb, and the leopard shall lie down with the kid; and the calf and the young lion and the fatling together; and a little child shall lead them" (Isaiah 11.6).
8. Excitement.
9. Stray, wandering.

the poodle went sailing up the aisle; the yelps continued, and so did the dog; he crossed the house in front of the altar; he flew down the other aisle; he crossed before the doors; he clamored up the home-stretch; his anguish grew with his progress, till presently he was but a woolly comet moving in its orbit with the gleam and the speed of light. At last the frantic sufferer sheered from its course, and sprang into its master's lap; he flung it out of the window, and the voice of distress quickly thinned away and died in the distance.

By this time the whole church was red-faced and suffocating with suppressed laughter, and the sermon had come to a dead stand-still. The discourse was resumed presently, but it went lame and halting, all possibility of impressiveness being at an end; for even the gravest sentiments were constantly being received with a smothered burst of unholy mirth, under cover of some remote pew-back, as if the poor parson had said a rarely facetious[1] thing. It was a genuine relief to the whole congregation when the ordeal was over and the bene-diction pronounced.

Tom Sawyer went home quite cheerful, thinking to himself that there was some satisfaction about divine service when there was a bit of variety in it. He had but one marring thought; he was willing that the dog should play with his pinch-bug, but he did not think it was upright in him to carry it off.

Chapter VI.

MONDAY morning found Tom Sawyer miserable. Monday morning always found him so—because it began another week's slow suffer-ing in school. He generally began that day with wishing he had had no intervening holiday, it made the going into captivity and fetters again so much more odious.[2]

Tom lay thinking. Presently it occurred to him that he wished he was sick; then he could stay home from school. Here was a vague possibility. He canvassed his system. No ailment was found, and he investigated again. This time he thought he could detect colicky symptoms,[3] and he began to encourage them with considerable hope. But they soon grew feeble, and presently died wholly away. He reflected further. Suddenly he discovered something. One of his upper front teeth was loose. This was lucky; he was about to begin to groan, as a "starter," as he called it, when it occurred to him that if he came into court with that argument, his aunt would pull it out, and that would hurt. So he thought he would hold the tooth in

1. Flippant, humorous.
2. Hateful, offensive. "Fetters": chains.
3. Severe abdominal pain.

reserve for the present, and seek further. Nothing offered for some little time, and then he remembered hearing the doctor tell about a certain thing that laid up a patient for two or three weeks and threatened to make him lose a finger. So the boy eagerly drew his sore toe from under the sheet and held it up for inspection. But now he did not know the necessary symptoms. However, it seemed well worth while to chance it, so he fell to groaning with considerable spirit.

But Sid slept on unconscious.

Tom groaned louder, and fancied that he began to feel pain in the toe. No result from Sid.

Tom was panting with his exertions by this time. He took a rest and then swelled himself up and fetched a succession of admirable groans.

Sid snored on.

Tom was aggravated. He said, "Sid, Sid!" and shook him. This course worked well, and Tom began to groan again. Sid yawned, stretched, then brought himself up on his elbow with a snort, and began to stare at Tom. Tom went on groaning. Sid said:

"Tom! Say, Tom!" [No response.] "Here, Tom! *Tom!* What is the matter, Tom?" And he shook him and looked in his face anxiously.

Tom moaned out:

"O don't, Sid. Don't joggle me."

"Why what's the matter, Tom? I must call auntie."

"No—never mind. It'll be over by and by, maybe. Don't call anybody."

"But I must! *Don't* groan so, Tom, it's awful. How long you been this way?"

"Hours. Ouch! O don't stir so, Sid, you'll kill me."

"Tom, why didn't you wake me sooner? O, Tom, *don't!* It makes my flesh crawl to hear you. Tom, what *is* the matter?"

"I forgive you everything, Sid. [Groan.] Everything you've ever done to me. When I'm gone—"

"O, Tom, you ain't dying, are you? Don't, Tom—O, don't. Maybe—"

"I forgive everybody, Sid. [Groan.] Tell 'em so, Sid. And Sid, you give my window-sash and my cat with one eye to that new girl that's come to town, and tell her—"

But Sid had snatched his clothes and gone. Tom was suffering in reality, now, so handsomely was his imagination working, and so his groans had gathered quite a genuine tone.

Sid flew down stairs and said:

"O, aunt Polly, come! Tom's dying!"

"Dying!"

"Yes'm. Don't wait—come quick!"

"Rubbage! I don't believe it!"

But she fled up stairs, nevertheless, with Sid and Mary at her heels. And her face grew white, too, and her lip trembled. When she reached the bedside she gasped out:

"You Tom! Tom, what's the matter with you!"

"O, auntie, I'm—"

"What's the matter with you—what *is* the matter with you, child!"

"O, auntie, my sore toe's mortified!"[4]

The old lady sank down into a chair and laughed a little, then cried a little, then did both together. This restored her and she said:

"Tom, what a turn you did give me. Now you shut up that nonsense and climb out of this."

The groans ceased and the pain vanished from the toe. The boy felt a little foolish, and he said:

"Aunt Polly it *seemed* mortified, and it hurt so I never minded my tooth at all."

"Your tooth, indeed! What's the matter with your tooth?"

"One of them's loose, and it aches perfectly awful."

"There, there, now, don't begin that groaning again. Open your mouth. Well—your tooth *is* loose, but you're not going to die about that. Mary, get me a silk thread, and a chunk of fire out of the kitchen."

Tom said:

"O, please auntie, don't pull it out. It don't hurt any more. I wish I may never stir if it does. Please don't, auntie. *I* don't want to stay home from school."

"Oh, you don't, don't you? So all this row was because you thought you'd get to stay home from school and go a fishing? Tom, Tom, I love you so, and you seem to try every way you can to break my old heart with your outrageousness."

By this time the dental instruments were ready. The old lady made one end of the silk thread fast to Tom's tooth with a loop and tied the other to the bed-post. Then she seized the chunk of fire and suddenly thrust it almost into the boy's face. The tooth hung dangling by the bedpost, now.

But all trials bring their compensations. As Tom wended to school after breakfast, he was the envy of every boy he met because the gap in his upper row of teeth enabled him to expectorate[5] in a new and admirable way. He gathered quite a following of lads interested in the exhibition; and one that had cut his finger and had been a centre of fascination and homage up to this time, now found himself suddenly without an adherent, and shorn of his glory. His heart was heavy, and he said with a disdain which he did not feel, that it wasn't anything to spit like Tom Sawyer; but another boy said "Sour grapes!" and he wandered away a dismantled hero.

4. Infected to the point of becoming gangrenous.
5. Spit.

Shortly Tom came upon the juvenile pariah[6] of the village, Huckleberry Finn, son of the town drunkard. Huckleberry was cordially hated and dreaded by all the mothers of the town, because he was idle, and lawless, and vulgar and bad—and because all their children admired him so, and delighted in his forbidden society, and wished they dared to be like him. Tom was like the rest of the respectable boys, in that he envied Huckleberry his gaudy outcast condition, and was under strict orders not to play with him. So he played with him every time he got a chance. Huckleberry was always dressed in the cast-off clothes of full-grown men, and they were in perennial bloom and fluttering with rags. His hat was a vast ruin with a wide crescent lopped out of its brim; his coat, when he wore one, hung nearly to his heels and had the rearward buttons far down the back; but one suspender supported his trousers; the seat of the trousers bagged low and contained nothing; the fringed legs dragged in the dirt when not rolled up.

Huckleberry came and went, at his own free will. He slept on doorsteps in fine weather and in empty hogsheads[7] in wet; he did not have to go to school or to church, or call any being master or obey anybody; he could go fishing or swimming when and where he chose, and stay as long as it suited him; nobody forbade him to fight; he could sit up as late as he pleased; he was always the first boy that went barefoot in the spring and the last to resume leather in the fall; he never had to wash, nor put on clean clothes; he could swear wonderfully. In a word, everything that goes to make life precious, that boy had. So thought every harassed, hampered, respectable boy in St. Petersburg.

Tom hailed the romantic outcast:

"Hello, Huckleberry!"

"Hello yourself, and see how you like it."

"What's that you got?"

"Dead cat."

"Lemme see him, Huck. My, he's pretty stiff. Where'd you get him?"

"Bought him off'n a boy."

"What did you give?"

"I give a blue ticket and a bladder that I got at the slaughter house."

"Where'd you get the blue ticket?"

"Bought it off'n Ben Rogers two weeks ago for a hoop-stick."

"Say—what is dead cats good for, Huck?"

"Good for? Cure warts with."

"No! Is that so? I know something that's better."

"I bet you don't. What is it?"

6. Outcast.
7. Large barrel, at least twice as large as regular ones.

"Why, spunk-water."[8]

"Spunk-water! I wouldn't give a dern for spunk-water."

"You wouldn't, wouldn't you? D'you ever try it?"

"No, I hain't. But Bob Tanner did."

"Who told you so!"

"Why he told Jeff Thatcher, and Jeff told Johnny Baker, and Johnny told Jim Hollis, and Jim told Ben Rogers, and Ben told a nigger, and the nigger told me. There, now!"

"Well, what of it? They'll all lie. Leastways all but the nigger. I don't know *him*. But I never see a nigger that *wouldn't* lie. Shucks! Now you tell me how Bob Tanner done it, Huck."

"Why he took and dipped his hand in a rotten stump where the rain water was."

"In the day time?"

"Cert'nly."

"With his face to the stump?"

"Yes. Least I reckon so."

"Did he *say* anything?"

"I don't reckon he did. I don't know."

"Aha! Talk about trying to cure warts with spunk-water such a blame fool way as that! Why that ain't going to do any good. You got to go all by yourself, to the middle of the woods, where you know there's a spunk-water stump, and just as it's midnight you back up against the stump and jam your hand in and say:

> "Barley-corn, barley-corn, injun-meal shorts,
> Spunk-water, spunk-water, swaller these warts;"

and then walk away quick, eleven steps, with your eyes shut, and then turn around three times and walk home without speaking to anybody. Because if you speak the charm's busted."

"Well that sounds like a good way; but that ain't the way Bob Tanner done."

"No, sir, you can bet he didn't; becuz he's the wartiest boy in this town; and he wouldn't have a wart on him if he'd knowed how to work spunk-water. I've took off thousands of warts off of my hands that way Huck. I play with frogs so much that I've always got considerable many warts. Sometimes I take 'em off with a bean."

"Yes, bean's good. I've done that."

"Have you? What's your way?"

"You take and split the bean, and cut the wart so as to get some blood, and then you put the blood on one piece of the bean and take and dig a hole and bury it 'bout midnight at the cross-roads in the dark of the moon, and then you burn up the rest of the bean. You

8. Standing water in a tree stump.

see that piece that's got the blood on it will keep drawing and drawing, trying to fetch the other piece to it, and so that helps the blood
to draw the wart, and pretty soon off she comes."

"Yes, that's it Huck—that's it; though when you're burying it if you
say 'Down bean; off, wart; come no more to bother me!' it's better.
That's the way Joe Harper does, and he's ben nearly to Coonville and
most everywheres. But say—how do you cure 'em with dead cats?"

"Why you take your cat and go and get in the graveyard 'long about
midnight when somebody that was wicked has been buried; and
when it's midnight a devil will come, or maybe two or three, but you
can't see 'em, you can only hear something like the wind, or maybe
hear 'em talk; and when they're taking that feller away, you heave
your cat after 'em and say 'Devil follow corpse, cat follow devil, warts
follow cat, I'm done with ye!' That'll fetch *any* wart."

"Sounds right. D'you ever try it, Huck?"

"No, but old Mother Hopkins told me."

"Well I reckon it's so, then. Becuz they say she's a witch."

"*Say!* Why, Tom, I *know* she is. She witched pap. Pap says so his
own self. He come along one day, and he see she was a witching
him, so he took up a rock, and if she hadn't dodged he'd a got her.
Well that very night he rolled off'n a shed wher' he was a layin' drunk,
and broke his arm."

"Why that's awful. How did he know she was a witching him."

"Lord, pap can tell, easy. Pap says when they keep looking at you
right stiddy, they're a witching you. Specially if they mumble. Becuz
when they mumble they're a saying the Lord's Prayer back'ards."

"Say, Hucky, when you going to try the cat?"

"To-night. I reckon they'll come after old Hoss Williams to-night."

"But they buried him Saturday. Didn't they get him Saturday
night?"

"Why how you talk! How could their charms work till midnight?—
and *then* it's Sunday. Devils don't slosh around much of a Sunday,
I don't reckon."

"I never thought of that. That's so. Lemme go with you?"

"Of course—if you ain't afeard."

"Afeard! 'Tain't likely. Will you meow?"

"Yes—and you meow back, if you get a chance. Last time, you kep'
me a meowing around till old Hays went to throwing rocks at me
and says 'Dern that cat!' and so I hove a brick through his window—
but don't you tell."

"I won't. I couldn't meow that night, becuz auntie was watching
me, but I'll meow this time. Say—what's that?"

"Nothing but a tick."

"Where'd you get him?"

"Out in the woods."

"What'll you take for him?"

"I don't know. I don't want to sell him."

"All right. It's a mighty small tick, anyway."

"O, anybody can run a tick down that don't belong to them. I'm satisfied with it. It's a good enough tick for me."

"Sho, there's ticks a plenty. I could have a thousand of 'em if I wanted to."

"Well why don't you? Becuz you know mighty well you can't. This is a pretty early tick, I reckon. It's the first one I've seen this year."

"Say Huck—I'll give you my tooth for him."

"Less see it."

Tom got out a bit of paper and carefully unrolled it. Huckleberry viewed it wistfully. The temptation was very strong. At last he said:

"Is it genuwyne?"

Tom lifted his lip and showed the vacancy.

"Well, all right," said Huckleberry, "it's a trade."

Tom enclosed the tick in the percussion-cap box that had lately been the pinch-bug's prison, and the boys separated, each feeling wealthier than before.

When Tom reached the little isolated frame school-house, he strode in briskly, with the manner of one who had come with all honest speed. He hung his hat on a peg and flung himself into his seat with business-like alacrity. The master, throned on high in his great splint-bottom arm-chair, was dozing, lulled by the drowsy hum of study. The interruption roused him.

"Thomas Sawyer!"

Tom knew that when his name was pronounced in full, it meant trouble.

"Sir!"

"Come up here. Now sir, why are you late again, as usual?"

Tom was about to take refuge in a lie, when he saw two long tails of yellow hair hanging down a back that he recognized by the electric sympathy of love; and by that form[9] was *the only vacant place* on the girl's side of the school-house. He instantly said:

"I STOPPED TO TALK WITH HUCKLEBERRY FINN!"

The master's pulse stood still, and he stared helplessly. The buzz of study ceased. The pupils wondered if this fool-hardy boy had lost his mind. The master said:

"You—you did what?"

"Stopped to talk with Huckleberry Finn."

There was no mistaking the words.

9. Long bench.

"Thomas Sawyer, this is the most astounding confession I have ever listened to. No mere ferule[1] will answer for this offence. Take off your jacket."

The master's arm performed until it was tired and the stock of switches notably diminished. Then the order followed:

"Now sir, go and sit with the *girls!* And let this be a warning to you."

The titter that rippled around the room appeared to abash the boy, but in reality that result was caused rather more by his worshipful awe of his unknown idol and the dread pleasure that lay in his high good fortune. He sat down upon the end of the pine bench and the girl hitched herself away from him with a toss of her head. Nudges and winks and whispers traversed the room, but Tom sat still, with his arms upon the long, low desk before him, and seemed to study his book.

By and by attention ceased from him, and the accustomed school murmur rose upon the dull air once more. Presently the boy began to steal furtive glances at the girl. She observed it, "made a mouth" at him and gave him the back of her head for the space of a minute. When she cautiously faced around again, a peach lay before her. She thrust it away. Tom gently put it back. She thrust it away, again, but with less animosity. Tom patiently returned it to its place. Then she let it remain. Tom scrawled on his slate, "Please take it—I got more." The girl glanced at the words, but made no sign. Now the boy began to draw something on the slate, hiding his work with his left hand. For a time the girl refused to notice; but her human curiosity presently began to manifest itself by hardly perceptible signs. The boy worked on, apparently unconscious. The girl made a sort of noncommittal attempt to see, but the boy did not betray that he was aware of it. At last she gave in and hesitatingly whispered:

"Let me see it."

Tom partly uncovered a dismal caricature of a house with two gable ends to it and a cork-screw of smoke issuing from the chimney. Then the girl's interest began to fasten itself upon the work and she forgot everything else. When it was finished, she gazed a moment, then whispered:

"It's nice—make a man."

The artist erected a man in the front yard, that resembled a derrick.[2] He could have stepped over the house; but the girl was not hypercritical; she was satisfied with the monster, and whispered:

"It's a beautiful man—now make me coming along."

Tom drew an hour-glass with a full moon and straw limbs to it and armed the spreading fingers with a portentous fan. The girl said:

1. Ruler; reference to striking a student's hand with a ruler as a punishment.
2. Mast-like apparatus, used for lifting.

"It's ever so nice—I wish I could draw."

"It's easy," whispered Tom, "I'll learn you."

"O, will you? When?"

"At noon. Do you go home to dinner?"

"I'll stay if you will."

"Good,—that's a whack.[3] What's your name?"

"Becky Thatcher. What's yours? Oh, I know. It's Thomas Sawyer."

"That's the name they lick me by. I'm Tom when I'm good. You call me Tom, will you?"

"Yes."

Now Tom began to scrawl something on the slate, hiding the words from the girl. But she was not backward this time. She begged to see. Tom said:

"Oh it ain't anything."

"Yes it is."

"No it ain't. You don't want to see."

"Yes I do, indeed I do. Please let me."

"You'll tell."

"No I won't—deed and deed and double deed I won't."

"You won't tell anybody at all?—Ever, as long as you live?"

"No I won't ever tell *any*body. Now let me."

"Oh, *you* don't want to see!"

"Now that you treat me so, I *will* see." And she put her small hand upon his and a little scuffle ensued, Tom pretending to resist in earnest but letting his hand slip by degrees till these words were revealed: *"I love you."*

"O, you bad thing!" And she hit his hand a smart rap, but reddened and looked pleased, nevertheless.

Just at this juncture the boy felt a slow, fateful grip closing on his ear, and a steady, lifting impulse. In that vise he was borne across the house and deposited in his own seat, under a peppering fire of giggles from the whole school. Then the master stood over him during a few awful moments, and finally moved away to his throne without saying a word. But although Tom's ear tingled, his heart was jubilant.

As the school quieted down Tom made an honest effort to study, but the turmoil within him was too great. In turn he took his place in the reading class and made a botch of it; then in the geography class and turned lakes into mountains, mountains into rivers, and rivers into continents, till chaos was come again; then in the spelling class, and got "turned down,"[4] by a succession of mere baby words till he brought up at the foot and yielded up the pewter medal which he had worn with ostentation for months.

3. Bargain.
4. Sent lower in the class.

Chapter VII.

THE harder Tom tried to fasten his mind on his book, the more his ideas wandered. So at last, with a sigh and a yawn, he gave it up. It seemed to him that the noon recess would never come. The air was utterly dead. There was not a breath stirring. It was the sleepiest of sleepy days. The drowsing murmur of the five and twenty studying scholars soothed the soul like the spell that is in the murmur of bees. Away off in the flaming sunshine, Cardiff Hill lifted its soft green sides through a shimmering veil of heat, tinted with the purple of distance; a few birds floated on lazy wing high in the air; no other living thing was visible but some cows, and they were asleep. Tom's heart ached to be free, or else to have something of interest to do to pass the dreary time. His hand wandered into his pocket and his face lit up with a glow of gratitude that was prayer, though he did not know it. Then furtively the percussion-cap box came out. He released the tick and put him on the long flat desk. The creature probably glowed with a gratitude that amounted to prayer, too, at this moment, but it was premature: for when he started thankfully to travel off, Tom turned him aside with a pin and made him take a new direction.

Tom's bosom friend sat next him, suffering just as Tom had been, and now he was deeply and gratefully interested in this entertainment in an instant. This bosom friend was Joe Harper. The two boys were sworn friends all the week, and embattled enemies on Saturdays. Joe took a pin out of his lappel and began to assist in exercising the prisoner. The sport grew in interest momently. Soon Tom said that they were interfering with each other, and neither getting the fullest benefit of the tick. So he put Joe's slate on the desk and drew a line down the middle of it from top to bottom.

"Now," said he, "as long as he is on your side you can stir him up and I'll let him alone; but if you let him get away and get on my side, you're to leave him alone as long as I can keep him from crossing over."

"All right—go ahead—start him up."

The tick escaped from Tom, presently, and crossed the equator. Joe harassed him a while, and then he got away and crossed back again. This change of base occurred often. While one boy was worrying the tick with absorbing interest, the other would look on with interest as strong, the two heads bowed together over the slate, and the two souls dead to all things else. At last luck seemed to settle and abide with Joe. The tick tried this, that, and the other course, and got as excited and as anxious as the boys themselves, but time and again just as he would have victory in his very grasp, so to speak, and Tom's fingers would be twitching to begin, Joe's pin would deftly head him off and keep possession. At last Tom could stand it no longer. The temptation was too strong. So he reached out and lent a hand with his pin. Joe was angry in a moment. Said he:

"Tom, you let him alone."

"I only just want to stir him up a little, Joe."

"No, sir, it ain't fair; you just let him alone."

"Blame it, I ain't going to stir him much."

"Let him alone, I tell you!"

"I won't!"

"You shall—he's on my side of the line."

"Look here, Joe Harper, whose is that tick?"

"*I* don't care whose tick he is—he's on my side of the line, and you shan't touch him."

"Well I'll just bet I will, though. He's my tick and I'll do what I blame please with him, or die!"

A tremendous whack came down on Tom's shoulders, and its duplicate on Joe's; and for the space of two minutes the dust continued to fly from the two jackets and the whole school to enjoy it. The boys had been too absorbed to notice the hush that had stolen upon the school a while before when the master came tip-toeing down the room and stood over them. He had contemplated a good part of the performance before he contributed his bit of variety to it.

When school broke up at noon, Tom flew to Becky Thatcher, and whispered in her ear:

"Put on your bonnet and let on you're going home; and when you get to the corner, give the rest of 'em the slip, and turn down through the lane and come back. I'll go the other way and come it over 'em the same way."

So the one went off with one group of scholars, and the other with another. In a little while the two met at the bottom of the lane, and when they reached the school they had it all to themselves. Then they sat together, with a slate before them, and Tom gave Becky the pencil and held her hand in his, guiding it, and so created another surprising house. When the interest in art began to wane, the two fell to talking. Tom was swimming in bliss. He said:

"Do you love rats?"

"No! I hate them!"

"Well, I do too—*live* ones. But I mean dead ones, to swing round your head with a string."

"No, I don't care for rats much, anyway. What *I* like is chewing-gum."

"O, I should say so! I wish I had some now."

"Do you? I've got some. I'll let you chew it awhile, but you must give it back to me."

That was agreeable, so they chewed it turn about, and dangled their legs against the bench in excess of contentment.

"Was you ever at a circus?" said Tom.

"Yes, and my pa's going to take me again some time, if I'm good."

"I been to the circus three or four times—lots of times. Church ain't shucks to a circus. There's things going on at a circus all the time. I'm going to be a clown in a circus when I grow up."

"O, are you! That will be nice. They're so lovely, all spotted up."

"Yes, that's so. And they get slathers of money—most a dollar a day, Ben Rogers says. Say, Becky, was you ever engaged?"

"What's that?"

"Why, engaged to be married."

"No."

"Would you like to?"

"I reckon so. I don't know. What is it like?"

"Like? Why it ain't like anything. You only just tell a boy you won't ever have any body but him, ever ever *ever*, and then you kiss and that's all. Anybody can do it."

"Kiss? What do you kiss for?"

"Why that, you know, is to—well, they always do that."

"Everybody?"

"Why yes, everybody that's in love with each other. Do you remember what I wrote on the slate?"

"Ye—yes."

"What was it?"

"I shan't tell you."

"Shall I tell *you*?"

"Ye—Yes—but some other time."

"No, now."

"No, not now—to-morrow."

"O, no, *now*. Please Becky—I'll whisper it, I'll whisper it ever so easy."

Becky hesitating, Tom took silence for consent, and passed his arm about her waist and whispered the tale ever so softly, with his mouth close to her ear. And then he added:

"Now you whisper it to me—just the same."

She resisted, for a while, and then said:

"You turn your face away so you can't see, and then I will. But you mustn't ever tell anybody—*will* you, Tom? Now you won't, *will* you?"

"No, indeed indeed I won't. Now Becky."

He turned his face away. She bent timidly around till her breath stirred his curls and whispered, "I—love—you!"

Then she sprang away and ran around and around the desks and benches, with Tom after her, and took refuge in a corner at last, with her little white apron to her face. Tom clasped her about her neck and pleaded:

"Now Becky, it's all done—all over but the kiss. Don't you be afraid of that—it ain't anything at all. Please, Becky."—And he tugged at the apron and the hands.

By and by she gave up, and let her hands drop; her face, all glowing with the struggle, came up and submitted. Tom kissed the red lips and said:

"Now it's all done, Becky. And always after this, you know, you ain't ever to love anybody but me, and you ain't ever to marry anybody but me, never never and forever. Will you?"

"No, I'll never love anybody but you, Tom, and I'll never marry anybody but you—and you ain't to ever marry anybody but me, either."

"Certainly. Of course. That's *part* of it. And always coming to school or when we're going home, you're to walk with me, when there ain't anybody looking—and you choose me and I choose you at parties, because that's the way you do when you're engaged."

"It's so nice. I never heard of it before."

"Oh it's ever so gay! Why me and Amy Lawrence—"

The big eyes told Tom his blunder and he stopped, confused.

"O, Tom! Then I ain't the first you've ever been engaged to!"

The child began to cry. Tom said:

"O don't cry, Becky, I don't care for her any more."

"Yes you do, Tom—you know you do."

Tom tried to put his arm about her neck, but she pushed him away and turned her face to the wall, and went on crying. Tom tried again, with soothing words in his mouth, and was repulsed again. Then his pride was up, and he strode away and went outside. He stood about, restless and uneasy, for a while, glancing at the door, every now and then, hoping she would repent and come to find him. But she did not. Then he began to feel badly and fear that he was in the wrong. It was a hard struggle with him to make new advances, now, but he nerved himself to it and entered. She was still standing back there in the corner, sobbing, with her face to the wall. Tom's heart smote him. He went to her and stood a moment, not knowing exactly how to proceed. Then he said hesitatingly:

"Becky, I—I don't care for anybody but you."

No reply—but sobs.

"Becky,"—pleadingly. "Becky, won't you say something?"

More sobs.

Tom got out his chiefest jewel, a brass knob from the top of an andiron,[5] and passed it around her so that she could see it, and said:

---

5. Metal support for holding wood in a fireplace.

"Please, Becky, won't you take it?"

She struck it to the floor. Then Tom marched out of the house and over the hills and far away,[6] to return to school no more that day. Presently Becky began to suspect. She ran to the door; he was not in sight; she flew around to the play-yard; he was not there. Then she called:

"Tom! Come back Tom!"

She listened intently, but there was no answer. She had no companions but silence and loneliness. So she sat down to cry again and upbraid herself; and by this time the scholars began to gather again, and she had to hide her griefs and still her broken heart and take up the cross of a long, dreary, aching afternoon, with none among the strangers about her to exchange sorrows with.

Chapter VIII.

Tom dodged hither and thither through lanes until he was well out of the track of returning scholars, and then fell into a moody jog. He crossed a small "branch" two or three times, because of a prevailing juvenile superstition that to cross water baffled pursuit. Half an hour later he was disappearing behind the Douglas mansion on the summit of Cardiff Hill, and the school-house was hardly distinguishable away off in the valley behind him. He entered a dense wood, picked his pathless way to the centre of it, and sat down on a mossy spot under a spreading oak. There was not even a zephyr[7] stirring; the dead noonday heat had even stilled the songs of the birds; nature lay in a trance that was broken by no sound but the occasional far-off hammering of a woodpecker, and this seemed to render the pervading silence and sense of loneliness the more profound. The boy's soul was steeped in melancholy; his feelings were in happy accord with his surroundings. He sat long with his elbows on his knees and his chin in his hands, meditating. It seemed to him that life was but a trouble, at best, and he more than half envied Jimmy Hodges, so lately released; it must be very peaceful, he thought, to lie and slumber and dream forever and ever, with the wind whispering through the trees and caressing the grass and the flowers over the grave, and nothing to bother and grieve about, ever any more. If he only had a clean Sunday-school record he could be willing to go, and be done with it all. Now as to this girl. What had he done? Nothing. He had meant the best in the world, and been treated like a dog—like a very

6. Much-repeated phrase from a ballad in, e.g., Thomas D'Urfey's *Pills to Purge Melancholy* (1706).
7. Gentle west wind.

dog. She would be sorry some day—maybe when it was too late. Ah, if he could only die *temporarily!*

But the elastic heart of youth cannot be kept compressed into one constrained shape long at a time. Tom presently began to drift insensibly back into the concerns of this life again. What if he turned his back, now, and disappeared mysteriously? What if he went away—ever so far away, into unknown countries beyond the seas—and never came back any more! How would she feel then! The idea of being a clown recurred to him now, only to fill him with disgust. For frivolity, and jokes, and spotted tights were an offense, when they intruded themselves upon a spirit that was exalted into the vague august realm of the romantic. No, he would be a soldier, and return, after long years, all war-worn and illustrious. No—better still, he would join the Indians, and hunt buffaloes and go on the warpath in the mountain ranges and the trackless great plains of the Far West, and away in the future come back a great chief, bristling with feathers, hideous with paint, and prance into Sunday-school, some drowsy summer morning, with a blood-curdling war-whoop, and sear the eye-balls of all his companions with unappeasable envy. But no, there was something gaudier even than this. He would be a pirate! That was it! *Now* his future lay plain before him, and glowing with unimaginable splendor. How his name would fill the world, and make people shudder! How gloriously he would go plowing the dancing seas, in his long, low, black-hulled racer, the "Spirit of the Storm," with his grisly flag flying at the fore! And at the zenith[8] of his fame, how he would suddenly appear at the old village and stalk into church, all brown and weather-beaten, in his black velvet doublet and trunks, his great jack-boots, his crimson sash, his belt bristling with horse-pistols, his crime-rusted cutlass at his side, his slouch hat with waving plumes, his black flag unfurled, with the skull and cross-bones on it, and hear with swelling ecstasy the whisperings, "It's Tom Sawyer the Pirate!—the Black Avenger of the Spanish Main!"[9]

Yes, it was settled; his career was determined. He would run away from home and enter upon it. He would start the very next morning. Therefore he must now begin to get ready. He would collect his resources together. He went to a rotten log near at hand and began to dig under one end of it with his Barlow knife. He soon struck wood that sounded hollow. He put his hand there and uttered this incantation[1] impressively:

"What hasn't come here, *come!* What's here, *stay* here!"

8. Highest point.
9. Title of an 1847 adventure story by Ned Buntline (E. Z. C. Judson).
1. Words spoken to produce magic.

Then he scraped away the dirt, and exposed a pine shingle. He took it up and disclosed a shapely little treasure-house whose bottom and sides were of shingles. In it lay a marble. Tom's astonishment was boundless! He scratched his head with a perplexed air, and said:

"Well, that beats anything!"

Then he tossed the marble away pettishly, and stood cogitating.[2] The truth was, that a superstition of his had failed, here, which he and all his comrades had always looked upon as infallible. If you buried a marble with certain necessary incantations, and left it alone a fortnight,[3] and then opened the place with the incantation he had just used, you would find that all the marbles you had ever lost had gathered themselves together there, meantime, no matter how widely they had been separated. But now, this thing had actually and unquestionably failed. Tom's whole structure of faith was shaken to its foundations. He had many a time heard of this thing succeeding, but never of its failing before. It did not occur to him that he had tried it several times before, himself, but could never find the hiding places afterwards. He puzzled over the matter some time, and finally decided that some witch had interfered and broken the charm. He thought he would satisfy himself on that point; so he searched around till he found a small sandy spot with a little funnel-shaped depression in it. He laid himself down and put his mouth close to this depression and called:

"Doodle-bug, doodle-bug, tell me what I want to know! Doodle-bug, doodle-bug tell me what I want to know!"

The sand began to work, and presently a small black bug appeared for a second and then darted under again in a fright.

"He dasn't tell! So it *was* a witch that done it. I just knowed it."

He well knew the futility of trying to contend against witches, so he gave up, discouraged. But it occurred to him that he might as well have the marble he had just thrown away, and therefore he went and made a patient search for it. But he could not find it. Now he went back to his treasure-house and carefully placed himself just as he had been standing when he tossed the marble away; then he took another marble from his pocket and tossed it in the same way, saying:

"Brother go find your brother!"

He watched where it stopped, and went there and looked. But it must have fallen short or gone too far; so he tried twice more. The last repetition was successful. The two marbles lay within a foot of each other.

Just here the blast of a toy tin trumpet came faintly down the green aisles of the forest. Tom flung off his jacket and trousers, turned a

2. Thinking.
3. Two weeks.

suspender into a belt, raked away some brush behind the rotten log, disclosing a rude bow and arrow, a lath[4] sword and a tin trumpet, and in a moment had seized these things and bounded away, bare-legged, with fluttering shirt. He presently halted under a great elm, blew an answering blast, and then began to tip-toe and look warily out, this way and that. He said cautiously—to an imaginary company:

"Hold, my merry men! Keep hid till I blow."

Now appeared Joe Harper, as airily clad and elaborately armed as Tom. Tom called:

"Hold! Who comes here into Sherwood Forest without my pass?"

"Guy of Guisborne wants no man's pass. Who are thou that—that—"

"Dares to hold such language," said Tom, prompting—for they talked "by the book," from memory.

"Who art thou that dares to hold such language?"

"I, indeed! I am Robin Hood, as thy caitiff carcase soon shall know."

"Then art thou indeed that famous outlaw? Right gladly will I dispute with thee the passes of the merry wood. Have at thee!"

They took their lath swords, dumped their other traps on the ground, struck a fencing attitude, foot to foot, and began a grave, careful combat, "two up and two down." Presently Tom said:

"Now if you've got the hang, go it lively!"

So they "went it lively," panting and perspiring with the work. By and by Tom shouted:

"Fall! fall! Why don't you fall?"

"I shan't! Why don't you fall yourself? You're getting the worst of it."

"Why that ain't anything. *I* can't fall; that ain't the way it is in the book. The book says 'Then with one back-handed stroke he slew poor Guy of Guisborne.' You're to turn around and let me hit you in the back."

There was no getting around the authorities, so Joe turned, received the whack, and fell.

"Now," said Joe—getting up, "You got to let me kill *you*. That's fair."

"Why I can't do that, it ain't in the book."

"Well it's blamed mean,—that's all."

"Well, say, Joe—you can be Friar Tuck or Much the miller's son and lam me with a quarter-staff; or I'll be the Sheriff of Nottingham and you be Robin Hood a little while and kill me."

This was satisfactory, and so these adventures were carried out.

4. Thin strip of wood.

Then Tom became Robin Hood again, and was allowed by the treacherous nun to bleed his strength away through his neglected wound. And at last Joe, representing a whole tribe of weeping outlaws, dragged him sadly forth, gave his bow into his feeble hands, and Tom said, "Where this arrow falls, there bury poor Robin Hood under the greenwood tree." Then he shot the arrow and fell back and would have died but he lit on a nettle and sprang up too gaily for a corpse.

The boys dressed themselves, hid their accoutrements, and went off grieving that there were no outlaws any more, and wondering what modern civilization could claim to have done to compensate for their loss. They said they would rather be outlaws a year in Sherwood Forest than President of the United States forever.

Chapter IX.

AT half past nine, that night, Tom and Sid were sent to bed, as usual. They said their prayers, and Sid was soon asleep. Tom lay awake and waited, in restless impatience. When it seemed to him that it must be nearly daylight, he heard the clock strike ten! This was despair. He would have tossed and fidgeted, as his nerves demanded, but he was afraid he might wake Sid. So he lay still, and stared up into the dark. Everything was dismally still. By and by, out of the stillness, little, scarcely perceptible noises began to emphasize themselves. The ticking of the clock began to bring itself into notice. Old beams began to crack mysteriously. The stairs creaked faintly. Evidently spirits were abroad. A measured, muffled snore issued from Aunt Polly's chamber. And now the tiresome chirping of a cricket that no human ingenuity could locate, began. Next the ghastly ticking of a death-watch[5] in the wall at the bed's head made Tom shudder—it meant that somebody's days were numbered. Then the howl of a far-off dog rose on the night air, and was answered by a fainter howl from a remoter distance. Tom was in an agony. At last he was satisfied that time had ceased and eternity begun; he began to doze, in spite of himself; the clock chimed eleven but he did not hear it. And then there came mingling with his half-formed dreams, a most melancholy caterwauling.[6] The raising of a neighboring window disturbed him. A cry of "S'cat! you devil!" and the crash of an empty bottle against the back of his aunt's woodshed brought him wide

---

5. Wood beetle, whose tapping is thought to announce death.
6. Screeching, like a cat. "Melancholy": excessively gloomy.

awake, and a single minute later he was dressed and out of the window and creeping along the roof of the "ell"[7] on all fours. He "meow'd" with caution once or twice, as he went; then jumped to the roof of the woodshed and thence to the ground. Huckleberry Finn was there, with his dead cat. The boys moved off and disappeared in the gloom. At the end of half an hour they were wading through the tall grass of the graveyard.

It was a graveyard of the old-fashioned western kind. It was on a hill, about a mile and a half from the village. It had a crazy board fence around it, which leaned inward in places, and outward the rest of the time, but stood upright nowhere. Grass and weeds grew rank over the whole cemetery. All the old graves were sunken in. There was not a tombstone on the place; round-topped, worm-eaten boards staggered over the graves, leaning for support and finding none. "Sacred to the Memory of" So-and-so had been painted on them once, but it could no longer have been read, on the most of them, now, even if there had been light.

A faint wind moaned through the trees, and Tom feared it might be the spirits of the dead complaining at being disturbed. The boys talked little, and only under their breath, for the time and the place and the pervading solemnity and silence oppressed their spirits. They found the sharp new heap they were seeking, and ensconced themselves within the protection of three great elms that grew in a bunch within a few feet of the grave.

Then they waited in silence for what seemed a long time. The hooting of a distant owl was all the sound that troubled the dead stillness. Tom's reflections grew oppressive. He must force some talk. So he said in a whisper:

"Hucky, do you believe the dead people like it for us to be here?"

Huckleberry whispered:

"I wisht I knowed. It's awful solemn like, *ain't* it?"

"I bet it is."

There was a considerable pause, while the boys canvassed this matter inwardly. Then Tom whispered:

"Say, Hucky—do you reckon Hoss Williams hears us talking?"

"O' course he does. Least his sperrit does."

Tom, after a pause:

"I wish I'd said *Mister* Williams. But I never meant any harm. Everybody calls him Hoss."

"A body can't be too partic'lar how they talk 'bout these-yer dead people, Tom."

---

7. Addition to a building.

This was a damper, and conversation died again. Presently Tom seized his comrade's arm and said:

"Sh!"

"What is it, Tom?" And the two clung together with beating hearts.

"Sh! There 'tis again! Didn't you hear it?"

"I—"

"There! Now you hear it."

"Lord, Tom they're coming! They're coming, sure. What'll we do?"

"I dono. Think they'll see us?"

"O, Tom, they can see in the dark, same as cats. I wisht I hadn't come."

"O, don't be afeard. *I* don't believe they'll bother us. We ain't doing any harm. If we keep perfectly still, maybe they won't notice us at all."

"I'll try to, Tom, but Lord I'm all of a shiver."

"Listen!"

The boys bent their heads together and scarcely breathed. A muffled sound of voices floated up from the far end of the graveyard.

"Look! See there!" whispered Tom. "What is it?"

"It's devil-fire. O, Tom, this is awful."

Some vague figures approached through the gloom, swinging an old-fashioned tin lantern that freckled the ground with innumerable little spangles of light. Presently Huckleberry whispered with a shudder:

"It's the devils sure enough. Three of 'em! Lordy, Tom, we're goners! Can you pray?"

"I'll try, but don't you be afeard. They ain't going to hurt us. Now I lay me down to sleep, I—"

"Sh!"

"What is it, Huck?"

"They're *humans*! One of 'em is, anyway. One of 'em's old Muff Potter's voice."

"No—'tain't so, is it?"

"I bet I know it. Don't you stir nor budge. *He* ain't sharp enough to notice us. Drunk, same as usual, likely—blamed old rip!"

"All right, I'll keep still. Now they're stuck. Can't find it. Here they come again. Now they're hot. Cold again. Hot again. Red hot! They're p'inted right, this time. Say Huck, I know another o' them voices; it's Injun Joe."

"That's so—that murderin' half-breed![8] I'd druther they was devils, a dern sight. What kin they be up to?"

---

8. Offspring of a white and an Indian. Considered by some 19th-century whites to be morally inferior to full-blooded Native Americans.

The whispers died wholly out, now, for the three men had reached the grave and stood within a few feet of the boys' hiding place.

"Here it is," said the third voice; and the owner of it held the lantern up and revealed the face of young Dr. Robinson.

Potter and Injun Joe were carrying a handbarrow with a rope and a couple of shovels on it. They cast down their load and began to open the grave. The doctor put the lantern at the head of the grave and came and sat down with his back against one of the elm trees. He was so close the boys could have touched him.

"Hurry, men!" he said in a low voice; "the moon might come out at any moment."

They growled a response and went on digging. For some time there was no noise but the grating sound of the spades discharging their freight of mould and gravel. It was very monotonous. Finally a spade struck upon the coffin with a dull woody accent, and within another minute or two the men had hoisted it out on the ground. They pried off the lid with their shovels, got out the body and dumped it rudely on the ground. The moon drifted from behind the clouds and exposed the pallid face. The barrow was got ready and the corpse placed on it, covered with a blanket, and bound to its place with the rope. Potter took out a large spring-knife and cut off the dangling end of the rope and then said:

"Now the cussed thing's ready, Sawbones,[9] and you'll just out with another five, or here she stays."

"That's the talk!" said Injun Joe.

"Look here, what does this mean?" said the doctor. "You required your pay in advance, and I've paid you."

"Yes, and you done more than that," said Injun Joe, approaching the doctor, who was now standing. "Five year ago you drove me away from your father's kitchen one night, when I come to ask for something to eat, and you said I warn't there for any good; and when I swore I'd get even with you if it took a hundred years, your father had me jailed for a vagrant. Did you think I'd forget? The Injun blood ain't in me for nothing. And now I've *got* you, and you got to *settle*, you know!"

He was threatening the doctor, with his fist in his face, by this time. The doctor struck out suddenly and stretched the ruffian on the ground. Potter dropped his knife, and exclaimed:

"Here, now, don't you hit my pard!" And the next moment he had grappled with the doctor and the two were struggling with might and main, trampling the grass and tearing the ground with their heels.

9. Doctor, especially a surgeon (slang).

Injun Joe sprang to his feet, his eyes flaming with passion, snatched up Potter's knife, and went creeping, catlike and stooping, round and round about the combatants, seeking an opportunity. All at once the doctor flung himself free, seized the heavy head board of Williams's grave and felled Potter to the earth with it—and in the same instant the half-breed saw his chance and drove the knife to the hilt in the young man's breast. He reeled and fell partly upon Potter, flooding him with his blood, and in the same moment the clouds blotted out the dreadful spectacle and the two frightened boys went speeding away in the dark.

Presently, when the moon emerged again, Injun Joe was standing over the two forms, contemplating them. The doctor murmured inarticulately, gave a long gasp or two and was still. The half-breed muttered:

"*That* score is settled—damn you."

Then he robbed the body. After which he put the fatal knife in Potter's open right hand, and sat down on the dismantled coffin. Three—four—five minutes passed, and then Potter began to stir and moan. His hand closed upon the knife; he raised it, glanced at it, and let it fall, with a shudder. Then he sat up, pushing the body from him, and gazed at it, and then around him, confusedly. His eyes met Joe's.

"Lord, how is this, Joe?" he said.

"It's a dirty business," said Joe, without moving. "What did you do it for?"

"I! I never done it!"

"Look here! That kind of talk won't wash."

Potter trembled and grew white.

"I thought I'd got sober. I'd no business to drink to-night. But it's in my head yet—worse'n when we started here. I'm all in a muddle; can't recollect anything of it hardly. Tell me, Joe—*honest*, now, old feller—did I do it? Joe, I never meant to—'pon my soul and honor I never meant to, Joe. Tell me how it was Joe. O, it's awful—and him so young and promising."

"Why you two was scuffling, and he fetched you one with the head-board and you fell flat; and then up you come, all reeling and staggering, like, and snatched the knife and jammed it into him, just as he fetched you another awful clip—and here you've laid, dead as a wedge till now."

"O, I didn't know what I was a doing. I wish I may die this minute if I did. It was all on accounts of the whisky; and the excitement, I reckon. I never used a weapon in my life before, Joe. I've fought, but never with weepons. They'll all say that. Joe, don't tell! Say you won't tell, Joe—that's a good feller. I always liked you Joe, and stood up for you, too. Don't you remember? You *won't* tell, *will* you Joe?" And the poor creature dropped on his knees before the stolid[1] murderer, and clasped his appealing hands.

"No, you've always been fair and square with me, Muff Potter, and I won't go back on you.—There, now, that's as fair as a man can say."

"O, Joe, you're an angel. I'll bless you for this the longest day I live." And Potter began to cry.

"Come, now, that's enough of that. This ain't any time for blubbering. You be off yonder way and I'll go this. Move, now, and don't leave any tracks behind you."

Potter started on a trot that quickly increased to a run. The half-breed stood looking after him. He muttered:

"If he's as much stunned with the lick and fuddled with the rum as he had the look of being, he won't think of the knife till he's gone so far he'll be afraid to come back after it to such a place by himself—chicken-heart!"

Two or three minutes later the murdered man, the blanketed corpse, the lidless coffin and the open grave were under no inspection but the moon's. The stillness was complete again, too.

Chapter X.

THE two boys flew on and on, toward the village, speechless with horror. They glanced backward over their shoulders from time to time, apprehensively, as if they feared they might be followed. Every stump that started up in their path seemed a man and an enemy, and made them catch their breath; and as they sped by some outlying cottages that lay near the village, the barking of the aroused watch-dogs seemed to give wings to their feet.

"If we can only get to the old tannery, before we break down!" whispered Tom, in short catches between breaths, "I can't stand it much longer."

Huckleberry's hard pantings were his only reply, and the boys fixed their eyes on the goal of their hopes and bent to their work to win it. They gained steadily on it, and at last, breast to breast they burst through the open door and fell grateful and exhausted in the sheltering shadows beyond. By and by their pulses slowed down, and Tom whispered:

"Huckleberry, what do you reckon 'll come of this?"

"If Dr. Robinson dies, I reckon hanging 'll come of it."

"Do you though?"

"Why I *know* it, Tom."

1. Impassive, showing little feeling.

Tom thought a while, then he said:

"Who'll tell? We?"

"What are you talking about? S'pose something happened and Injun Joe *didn't* hang? Why he'd kill us some time or other, just as dead sure as we're a laying here."

"That's just what I was thinking to myself, Huck."

"If anybody tells, let Muff Potter do it, if he's fool enough. He's generally drunk enough."

Tom said nothing—went on thinking. Presently he whispered:

"Huck, Muff Potter don't *know* it. How can he tell?"

"What's the reason he don't know it?"

"Because he'd just got that whack when Injun Joe done it. D' you reckon he could see anything? D' you reckon he knowed anything?"

"By hokey, that's so Tom!"

"And besides, look-a-here—maybe that whack done for *him*!"

"No, 'tain't likely Tom. He had liquor in him; I could see that; and besides, he always has. Well when pap's full, you might take and belt him over the head with a church and you couldn't phase him. He says so, his own self. So it's the same with Muff Potter, of course. But if a man was dead sober, I reckon maybe that whack might fetch him; I dono."

After another reflective silence, Tom said:

"Hucky, you sure you can keep mum?"[2]

"Tom, we *got* to keep mum. *You* know that. That Injun devil wouldn't make any more of drownding us than a couple of cats, if we was to squeak 'bout this and they didn't hang him. Now look-a-here, Tom, less take and swear to one another—that's what we got to do—swear to keep mum."

"I'm agreed. It's the best thing. Would you just hold hands and swear that we—"

"O, no, that wouldn't do for this. That's good enough for little rubbishy common things—specially with gals, cuz *they* go back on you anyway, and blab if they get in a huff—but there orter be writing 'bout a big thing like this. And blood."

Tom's whole being applauded this idea. It was deep, and dark, and awful; the hour, the circumstances, the surroundings, were in keeping with it. He picked up a clean pine shingle that lay in the moonlight, took a little fragment of "red keel"[3] out of his pocket, got the moon on his work, and painfully scrawled these lines, emphasizing each slow down-stroke by clamping his tongue between his teeth, and letting up the pressure on the up-strokes:

2. Silent.
3. Chalk.

"Huck Finn and
Tom Sawyer swears
they will keep mum
about this and they
wish they may drop
down dead in their
tracks if they ever
tell and Rot."

Huckleberry was filled with admiration of Tom's facility in writing, and the sublimity of his language. He at once took a pin from his lappel and was going to prick his flesh, but Tom said:

"Hold on! Don't do that. A pin's brass. It might have verdigrease[4] on it."

"What's verdigrease?"

"It's p'ison. That's what it is. You just swaller some of it once—you'll see."

So Tom unwound the thread from one of his needles, and each boy pricked the ball of his thumb and squeezed out a drop of blood. In time, after many squeezes, Tom managed to sign his initials, using the ball of his little finger for a pen. Then he showed Huckleberry how to make an H and an F, and the oath was complete. They buried the shingle close to the wall, with some dismal ceremonies and incantations, and the fetters that bound their tongues were considered to be locked and the key thrown away.

A figure crept stealthily through a break in the other end of the ruined building, now, but they did not notice it.

4. I.e., verdigris, the greenish substance that forms on copper or brass when exposed to the air.

"Tom," whispered Huckleberry, "does this keep us from *ever* telling—*always*?"

"Of course it does. It don't make any difference *what* happens, we got to keep mum. We'd drop down dead—don't *you* know that?"

"Yes, I reckon that's so."

They continued to whisper for some little time. Presently a dog set up a long, lugubrious[5] howl just outside—within ten feet of them. The boys clasped each other suddenly, in an agony of fright.

"Which of us does he mean?" gasped Huckleberry.

"I dono—peep through the crack. Quick!"

"No, *you*, Tom!"

"I can't—I can't *do* it, Huck!"

"Please, Tom. There 'tis again!"

"O, lordy, I'm thankful!" whispered Tom. "I know his voice. It's Bull Harbison."[6]

"O, that's good—I tell you, Tom, I was most scared to death; I'd a bet anything it was a *stray* dog."

The dog howled again. The boys' hearts sank once more.

"O, my! that ain't no Bull Harbison!" whispered Huckleberry. "*Do*, Tom!"

Tom, quaking with fear, yielded, and put his eye to the crack. His whisper was hardly audible when he said:

"O, Huck, IT'S A STRAY DOG!"

"Quick, Tom, quick! Who does he mean?"

"Huck, he must mean us both—we're right together."

"O, Tom, I reckon we're goners. I reckon there ain't no mistake 'bout where *I'll* go to. I been so wicked."

"Dad fetch it! This comes of playing hookey and doing everything a feller's told *not* to do. I might a been good, like Sid, if I'd a tried—but no, I wouldn't, of course. But if ever I get off this time, I lay I'll just *waller*[7] in Sunday-schools!" And Tom began to snuffle a little.

"*You* bad!" and Huckleberry began to snuffle too. "Consound it, Tom Sawyer, you're just old pie, 'longside o' what *I* am. O, *lordy*, lordy, lordy, I wisht I only had half your chance."

Tom choked off and whispered:

"Look, Hucky, look! He's got his *back* to us!"

Hucky looked, with joy in his heart.

"Well he has, by jingoes! Did he before?"

"Yes, he did. But I, like a fool, never thought. O, this is bully, you know. *Now* who can he mean?"

5. Very mournful.
6. "If Mr. Harbison had owned a slave named Bull, Tom would have spoken of him as 'Harbison's Bull,' but a son or a dog of that name was 'Bull Harbison' " [Twain's note].
7. Wallow (dialect).

The howling stopped. Tom pricked up his ears.

"Sh! What's that?" he whispered.

"Sounds like—like hogs grunting. No—it's somebody snoring, Tom."

"That *is* it? Where 'bouts is it, Huck?"

"I bleeve it's down at t'other end. Sounds so, anyway. Pap used to sleep there, sometimes, 'long with the hogs, but laws bless you, he just lifts things when *he* snores. Besides, I reckon he ain't ever coming back to this town any more."

The spirit of adventure rose in the boys' souls once more.

"Hucky, do you das't to go if I lead?"

"I don't like to, much. Tom, s'pose it's Injun Joe!"

Tom quailed. But presently the temptation rose up strong again and the boys agreed to try, with the understanding that they would take to their heels if the snoring stopped. So they went tip-toeing stealthily down, the one behind the other. When they had got to within five steps of the snorer, Tom stepped on a stick, and it broke with a sharp snap. The man moaned, writhed a little, and his face came into the moonlight. It was Muff Potter. The boys' hearts had stood still, and their bodies too, when the man moved, but their fears passed away now. They tip-toed out, through the broken weatherboarding, and stopped at a little distance to exchange a parting word. That long, lugubrious howl rose on the night air again! They turned and saw the strange dog standing within a few feet of where Potter was lying, and *facing* Potter, with his nose pointing heavenward.

"O, geeminy it's *him*!" exclaimed both boys, in a breath.

"Say, Tom—they say a stray dog come howling around Johnny Miller's house, 'bout midnight, as much as two weeks ago; and a whipporwill come in and lit on the bannisters and sung, the very same evening; and there ain't anybody dead there yet."

"Well I know that. And suppose there ain't. Didn't Gracie Miller fall in the kitchen fire and burn herself terrible the very next Saturday?"

"Yes, but she ain't *dead*. And what's more, she's getting better, too."

"All right, you wait and see. She's a goner, just as dead sure as Muff Potter's a goner. That's what the niggers say, and they know all about these kind of things, Huck."

Then they separated, cogitating. When Tom crept in at his bedroom window, the night was almost spent. He undressed with excessive caution, and fell asleep congratulating himself that nobody knew of his escapade. He was not aware that the gently-snoring Sid was awake, and had been so for an hour.

When Tom awoke, Sid was dressed and gone. There was a late look in the light, a late sense in the atmosphere. He was startled.

Why had he not been called—persecuted till he was up, as usual? The thought filled him with bodings.[8] Within five minutes he was dressed and down stairs, feeling sore and drowsy. The family were still at table, but they had finished breakfast. There was no voice of rebuke; but there were averted eyes; there was a silence and an air of solemnity that struck a chill to the culprit's heart. He sat down and tried to seem gay, but it was up-hill work; it roused no smile, no response, and he lapsed into silence and let his heart sink down to the depths.

After breakfast his aunt took him aside, and Tom almost brightened in the hope that he was going to be flogged; but it was not so. His aunt wept over him and asked him how he could go and break her old heart so; and finally told him to go on, and ruin himself and bring her gray hairs with sorrow to the grave, for it was no use for her to try any more. This was worse than a thousand whippings, and Tom's heart was sorer now than his body. He cried, he pleaded for forgiveness, promised reform over and over again and then received his dismissal feeling that he had won but an imperfect forgiveness and established but a feeble confidence.

He left the presence too miserable to even feel vengeful toward Sid; and so the latter's prompt retreat through the back gate was unnecessary. He moped to school gloomy and sad, and took his flogging, along with Joe Harper, for playing hookey the day before, with the air of one whose heart was busy with heavier woes and wholly dead to trifles. Then he betook himself to his seat, rested his elbows on his desk and his jaws in his hands and stared at the wall with the stony stare of suffering that has reached the limit and can no further go. His elbow was pressing against some hard substance. After a long time he slowly and sadly changed his position, and took up this object with a sigh. It was in a paper. He unrolled it. A long, lingering, colossal sigh followed, and his heart broke. It was his brass andiron knob!

This final feather broke the camel's back.

Chapter XI.

CLOSE upon the hour of noon the whole village was suddenly electrified with the ghastly news. No need of the as yet undreamed-of telegraph; the tale flew from man to man, from group to group, from house to house with little less than telegraphic speed. Of course the schoolmaster gave holiday for that afternoon; the town would have thought strangely of him if he had not.

A gory knife had been found close to the murdered man, and it

8. Forebodings.

had been recognized by somebody as belonging to Muff Potter—so the story ran. And it was said that a belated citizen had come upon Potter washing himself in the "branch" about one or two o'clock in the morning, and that Potter had at once sneaked off—suspicious circumstances, especially the washing, which was not a habit with Potter. It was also said that the town had been ransacked for this "murderer" (the public are not slow in the matter of sifting evidence and arriving at a verdict,) but that he could not be found. Horsemen had departed down all the roads in every direction, and the Sheriff "was confident" that he would be captured before night.

All the town was drifting toward the graveyard. Tom's heart-break vanished and he joined the procession, not because he would not a thousand times rather go anywhere else, but because an awful, unaccountable fascination drew him on. Arrived at the dreadful place, he wormed his small body through the crowd and saw the dismal spectacle. It seemed to him an age since he was there before. Somebody pinched his arm. He turned, and his eyes met Huckleberry's. Then both looked elsewhere at once, and wondered if anybody had noticed anything in their mutual glance. But everybody was talking, and intent upon the grisly spectacle before them.

"Poor fellow!" "Poor young fellow!" "This ought to be a lesson to grave-robbers!" "Muff Potter'll hang for this if they catch him!" This was the drift of remark; and the minister said, "It was a judgment; His hand is here."

Now Tom shivered from head to heel; for his eye fell upon the stolid face of Injun Joe. At this moment the crowd began to sway and struggle, and voices shouted, "It's him! it's him! he's coming himself!"

"Who? Who?" from twenty voices.

"Muff Potter!"

"Hallo, he's stopped!—Look out, he's turning! Don't let him get away!"

People in the branches of the trees over Tom's head, said he wasn't trying to get away—he only looked doubtful and perplexed.

"Infernal impudence!" said a bystander; "wanted to come and take a quiet look at his work, I reckon—didn't expect any company."

The crowd fell apart, now, and the Sheriff came through, ostentatiously leading Potter by the arm. The poor fellow's face was haggard, and his eyes showed the fear that was upon him. When he stood before the murdered man, he shook as with a palsy, and he put his face in his hands and burst into tears.

"I didn't do it, friends," he sobbed; " 'pon my word and honor I never done it."

"Who's accused you?" shouted a voice.

This shot seemed to carry home. Potter lifted his face and looked around him with a pathetic hopelessness in his eyes. He saw Injun Joe, and exclaimed:

"O, Injun Joe, you promised me you'd never—"

"Is that your knife?"—and it was thrust before him by the Sheriff.

Potter would have fallen if they had not caught him and eased him to the ground. Then he said:

"Something *told* me 't if I didn't come back and get—" He shuddered; then waved his nerveless hand with a vanquished gesture and said, "Tell 'em, Joe, tell 'em—it ain't any use any more."

Then Huckleberry and Tom stood dumb and staring, and heard the stony-hearted liar reel off his serene statement, they expecting every moment that the clear sky would deliver God's lightnings upon his head, and wondering to see how long the stroke was delayed. And when he had finished and still stood alive and whole, their wavering impulse to break their oath and save the poor betrayed prisoner's life faded and vanished away, for plainly this miscreant had sold himself to Satan and it would be fatal to meddle with the property of such a power as that.

"Why didn't you leave? What did you want to come here for?" somebody said.

"I couldn't help it—I couldn't help it," Potter moaned. "I wanted to run away, but I couldn't seem to come anywhere but here." And he fell to sobbing again.

Injun Joe repeated his statement, just as calmly, a few minutes afterward on the inquest, under oath; and the boys, seeing that the lightnings were still withheld, were confirmed in their belief that Joe had sold himself to the devil. He was now become, to them, the most balefully[9] interesting object they had ever looked upon, and they could not take their fascinated eyes from his face. They inwardly resolved to watch him, nights, when opportunity should offer, in the hope of getting a glimpse of his dread master.

Injun Joe helped to raise the body of the murdered man and put it in a wagon for removal; and it was whispered through the shuddering crowd that the wound bled a little![1] The boys thought that this happy circumstance would turn suspicion in the right direction; but they were disappointed, for more than one villager remarked:

"It was within three feet of Muff Potter when it done it."

Tom's fearful secret and gnawing conscience disturbed his sleep for as much as a week after this; and at breakfast one morning Sid said:

"Tom, you pitch around and talk in your sleep so much that you keep me awake about half the time."

---

9. Menacingly, evilly.
1. Some believe that the wound of a murdered person bleeds when the murderer passes near.

Tom blanched[2] and dropped his eyes.

"It's a bad sign," said Aunt Polly, gravely. "What you got on your mind, Tom?"

"Nothing. Nothing 't I know of." But the boy's hand shook so that he spilled his coffee.

"And you do talk such stuff," Sid said. "Last night you said 'it's blood, it's blood, that's what it is!' You said that over and over. And you said 'Don't torment me so—I'll tell.' Tell *what*? What is it you'll tell?"

Everything was swimming before Tom. There is no telling what might have happened, now, but luckily the concern passed out of Aunt Polly's face and she came to Tom's relief without knowing it. She said:

"Sho! It's that dreadful murder. I dream about it most every night myself. Sometimes I dream it's me that done it."

Mary said she had been affected much the same way. Sid seemed satisfied. Tom got out of the presence as quickly as he plausibly could, and after that he complained of toothache for a week and tied up his jaws every night. He never knew that Sid lay nightly watching, and frequently slipped the bandage free and then leaned on his elbow listening a good while at a time, and afterward slipped the bandage back to its place again. Tom's distress of mind wore off gradually and the toothache grew irksome and was discarded. If Sid really managed to make anything out of Tom's disjointed mutterings, he kept it to himself.

It seemed to Tom that his schoolmates never would get done holding inquests on dead cats, and thus keeping his trouble present to his mind. Sid noticed that Tom never was coroner[3] at one of these inquiries, though it had been his habit to take the lead in all new enterprises; he noticed, too, that Tom never acted as a witness,— and that was strange; and Sid did not overlook the fact that Tom even showed a marked aversion to these inquests, and always avoided them when he could. Sid marveled, but said nothing. However, even inquests went out of vogue at last, and ceased to torture Tom's conscience.

Every day or two, during this time of sorrow, Tom watched his opportunity and went to the little grated jail-window and smuggled such small comforts through to the "murderer" as he could get hold of. The jail was a trifling little brick den that stood in a marsh at the edge of the village, and no guards were afforded for it; indeed it was seldom occupied. These offerings greatly helped to ease Tom's conscience.

2. Turned pale.
3. Official who investigates whether a death is natural, sometimes conducting an inquest to determine whether there should be a trial.

The villagers had a strong desire to tar-and-feather Injun Joe and ride him on a rail,[4] for body-snatching, but so formidable was his character that nobody could be found who was willing to take the lead in the matter, so it was dropped. He had been careful to begin both of his inquest-statements with the fight, without confessing the grave-robbery that preceded it; therefore it was deemed wisest not to try the case in the courts at present.

Chapter XII.

ONE of the reasons why Tom's mind had drifted away from its secret troubles was, that it had found a new and weighty matter to interest itself about. Becky Thatcher had stopped coming to school. Tom had struggled with his pride a few days, and tried to "whistle her down the wind,"[5] but failed. He began to find himself hanging around her father's house, nights, and feeling very miserable. She was ill. What if she should die! There was distraction in the thought. He no longer took an interest in war, nor even in piracy. The charm of life was gone; there was nothing but dreariness left. He put his hoop away, and his bat; there was no joy in them any more. His aunt was concerned. She began to try all manner of remedies on him. She was one of those people who are infatuated with patent medicines and all new-fangled methods of producing health or mending it. She was an inveterate experimenter in these things. When something fresh in this line came out she was in a fever, right away, to try it; not on herself, for she was never ailing, but on anybody else that came handy. She was a subscriber for all the "Health" periodicals and phrenological[6] frauds; and the solemn ignorance they were inflated with was breath to her nostrils. All the "rot" they contained about ventilation, and how to go to bed, and how to get up, and what to eat, and what to drink, and how much exercise to take, and what frame of mind to keep one's self in, and what sort of clothing to wear, was all gospel to her, and she never observed that her health-journals of the current month customarily upset everything they had recommended the month before. She was as simple-hearted and honest as the day was long, and so she was an easy victim. She gathered together her quack periodicals and her quack medicines, and thus armed with death, went about on her pale horse, metaphorically

---

4. Punishments. Tarring and feathering entailed covering the person first with tar then with feathers. Riding on a rail involved getting the person to straddle or hang from a rail while men paraded him around the town.
5. Dismiss her.
6. Determining a person's characteristics on the basis of the shape of the skull.

speaking, with "hell following after."[7] But she never suspected that she was not an angel of healing and the balm of Gilead[8] in disguise, to the suffering neighbors.

The water treatment was new, now, and Tom's low condition was a windfall to her. She had him out at daylight every morning, stood him up in the woodshed and drowned him with a deluge of cold water; then she scrubbed him down with a towel like a file, and so brought him to; then she rolled him up in a wet sheet and put him away under blankets till she sweated his soul clean and "the yellow stains of it came through his pores"—as Tom said.

Yet notwithstanding all this, the boy grew more and more melancholy and pale and dejected. She added hot baths, sitz baths, shower baths and plunges. The boy remained as dismal as a hearse. She began to assist the water with a slim oatmeal diet and blister plasters. She calculated his capacity as she would a jug's, and filled him up every day with quack cure-alls.

Tom had become indifferent to persecution, by this time. This phase filled the old lady's heart with consternation. This indifference must be broken up at any cost. Now she heard of Pain-Killer for the first time. She ordered a lot at once. She tasted it and was filled with gratitude. It was simply fire in a liquid form. She dropped the water treatment and everything else, and pinned her faith to Pain-Killer. She gave Tom a tea-spoonful and watched with the deepest anxiety for the result. Her troubles were instantly at rest, her soul at peace again; for the "indifference" was broken up. The boy could not have shown a wilder, heartier interest, if she had built a fire under him.

Tom felt that it was time to wake up; this sort of life might be romantic enough, in his blighted condition, but it was getting to have too little sentiment and too much distracting variety about it. So he thought over various plans for relief, and finally hit upon that of professing to be fond of Pain-Killer. He asked for it so often that he became a nuisance, and his aunt ended by telling him to help himself and quit bothering her. If it had been Sid, she would have had no misgivings to alloy her delight; but since it was Tom, she watched the bottle clandestinely. She found that the medicine did really diminish, but it did not occur to her that the boy was mending the health of a crack in the sitting-room floor with it.

One day Tom was in the act of dosing the crack when his aunt's yellow cat came along, purring, eyeing the tea-spoon avariciously, and begging for a taste. Tom said:

7. After Revelation 6.8: "And I looked, and behold a pale horse: and his name that sat on him was Death, and Hell followed with him." "Quack": medically false.
8. Soothing ointment from a land east of the Jordan River. "Go up into Gilead and take balm, O virgin, the daughter of Egypt: in vain shalt thou use many medicines; for thou shalt not be cured" (Jeremiah 46.11).

"Don't ask for it unless you want it, Peter."

But Peter signified that he did want it.

"You better make sure."

Peter was sure.

"Now you've asked for it, and I'll give it to you, because there ain't anything mean about *me*; but if you find you don't like it, you mustn't blame anybody but your own self."

Peter was agreeable. So Tom pried his mouth open and poured down the Pain-Killer. Peter sprang a couple of yards into the air, and then delivered a war-whoop and set off round and round the room, banging against furniture, upsetting flower pots and making general havoc. Next he rose on his hind feet and pranced around, in a frenzy of enjoyment, with his head over his shoulder and his voice proclaiming his unappeasable happiness. Then he went tearing around the house again spreading chaos and destruction in his path. Aunt Polly entered in time to see him throw a few double summersets, deliver a final mighty hurrah, and sail through the open window, carrying the rest of the flower-pots with him. The old lady stood petrified with astonishment, peering over her glasses; Tom lay on the floor expiring with laughter.

"Tom, what on earth ails that cat?"

"*I* don't know, aunt," gasped the boy.

"Why I never see anything like it. What *did* make him act so?"

"Deed I don't know aunt Polly; cats always act so when they're having a good time."

"They do, do they?" There was something in the tone that made Tom apprehensive.

"Yes'm. That is, I believe they do."

"You *do*?"

"Yes'm."

The old lady was bending down, Tom watching, with interest emphasized by anxiety. Too late he divined her "drift." The handle of the tell-tale tea-spoon was visible under the bed-valance.[9] Aunt Polly took it, held it up. Tom winced, and dropped his eyes. Aunt Polly raised him by the usual handle—his ear—and cracked his head soundly with her thimble.

"Now, sir, what did you want to treat that poor dumb beast so, for?"

"I done it out of pity for him—because he hadn't any aunt."

"Hadn't any aunt!—you numscull. What has that got to do with it?"

"Heaps. Because if he'd a had one she'd a burnt him out herself!

_____

9. Curtain around the base of a bed.

She'd a roasted his bowels out of him 'thout any more feeling than if he was a human!"

Aunt Polly felt a sudden pang of remorse. This was putting the thing in a new light; what was cruelty to a cat *might* be cruelty to a boy, too. She began to soften; she felt sorry. Her eyes watered a little, and she put her hand on Tom's head and said gently:

"I was meaning for the best, Tom. And Tom, it *did* do you good."

Tom looked up in her face with just a perceptible twinkle peeping through his gravity:

"I know you was meaning for the best, aunty, and so was I with Peter. It done *him* good, too. I never see him get around so since—"

"O, go 'long with you, Tom, before you aggravate me again. And you try and see if you can't be a good boy, for once, and you needn't take any more medicine."

Tom reached school ahead of time. It was noticed that this strange thing had been occurring every day latterly. And now, as usual of late, he hung about the gate of the school yard instead of playing with his comrades. He was sick, he said; and he looked it. He tried to seem to be looking everywhere but whither he really was looking— down the road. Presently Jeff Thatcher hove in sight, and Tom's face lighted; he gazed a moment, and then turned sorrowfully away. When Jeff arrived, Tom accosted him, and "led up" warily to opportunities for remark about Becky, but the giddy lad never could see the bait. Tom watched and watched, hoping whenever a frisking frock came in sight, and hating the owner of it as soon as he saw she was not the right one. At last frocks ceased to appear, and he dropped hopelessly into the dumps; he entered the empty school house and sat down to suffer. Then one more frock passed in at the gate, and Tom's heart gave a great bound. The next instant he was out, and "going on" like an Indian; yelling, laughing, chasing boys, jumping over the fence at risk of life and limb, throwing hand-springs, standing on his head—doing all the heroic things he could conceive of, and keeping a furtive eye out, all the while, to see if Becky Thatcher was noticing. But she seemed to be unconscious of it all; she never looked. Could it be possible that she was not aware that he was there? He carried his exploits to her immediate vicinity; came war-whooping around, snatched a boy's cap, hurled it to the roof of the school-house, broke through a group of boys, tumbling them in every direction, and fell sprawling, himself, under Becky's nose, almost upsetting her—and she turned, with her nose in the air, and he heard her say. "Mf! some people think they're mighty smart— always showing off!"

Tom's cheeks burned. He gathered himself up and sneaked off, crushed and crestfallen.

Chapter XIII.

Tom's mind was made up, now. He was gloomy and desperate. He was a forsaken, friendless boy, he said; nobody loved him; when they found out what they had driven him to, perhaps they would be sorry; he had tried to do right and get along, but they would not let him; since nothing would do them but to be rid of him, let it be so; and let them blame *him* for the consequences—why shouldn't they? what right had the friendless to complain? Yes, they had forced him to it at last: he would lead a life of crime. There was no choice.

By this time he was far down Meadow Lane, and the bell for school to "take up" tinkled faintly upon his ear. He sobbed, now, to think he should never, never hear that old familiar sound any more—it was very hard, but it was forced on him; since he was driven out into the cold world, he must submit—but he forgave them. Then the sobs came thick and fast.

Just at this point he met his soul's sworn comrade, Joe Harper—hard-eyed, and with evidently a great and dismal purpose in his heart. Plainly here were "two souls with but a single thought."[1] Tom, wiping his eyes with his sleeve, began to blubber out something about a resolution to escape from hard usage and lack of sympathy at home by roaming abroad into the great world never to return; and ended by hoping that Joe would not forget him.

But it transpired that this was a request which Joe had just been going to make of Tom, and had come to hunt him up for that purpose. His mother had whipped him for drinking some cream which he had never tasted and knew nothing about; it was plain that she was tired of him and wished him to go; if she felt that way, there was nothing for him to do but succumb; he hoped she would be happy, and never regret having driven her poor boy out into the unfeeling world to suffer and die.

As the two boys walked sorrowing along, they made a new compact to stand by each other and be brothers and never separate till death relieved them of their troubles. Then they began to lay their plans. Joe was for being a hermit, and living on crusts in a remote cave, and dying, some time, of cold, and want, and grief; but after listening to Tom, he conceded that there were some conspicuous advantages about a life of crime, and so he consented to be a pirate.

Three miles below St. Petersburg, at a point where the Mississippi river was a trifle over a mile wide, there was a long, narrow, wooded island, with a shallow bar at the head of it, and this offered well as a rendezvous. It was not inhabited; it lay far over toward the further shore, abreast a dense and almost wholly unpeopled forest. So Jack-

1. Phrase from *Ingomar the Barbarian* (1842) by von Münch-Bellinghausen.

son's Island was chosen. Who were to be the subjects of their piracies, was a matter that did not occur to them. Then they hunted up
Huckleberry Finn, and he joined them promptly, for all careers were
one to him; he was indifferent. They presently separated to meet at
a lonely spot on the river bank two miles above the village at the
favorite hour—which was midnight. There was a small log raft there
which they meant to capture. Each would bring hooks and lines, and
such provision as he could steal in the most dark and mysterious
way—as became outlaws. And before the afternoon was done, they
had all managed to enjoy the sweet glory of spreading the fact that
pretty soon the town would "hear something." All who got this vague
hint were cautioned to "be mum and wait."

About midnight Tom arrived with a boiled ham and a few trifles,
and stopped in a dense undergrowth on a small bluff overlooking the
meeting-place. It was starlight, and very still. The mighty river lay
like an ocean at rest. Tom listened a moment, but no sound disturbed
the quiet. Then he gave a low, distinct whistle. It was answered from
under the bluff. Tom whistled twice more; these signals were
answered in the same way. Then a guarded voice said:

"Who goes there?"

"Tom Sawyer, the Black Avenger of the Spanish Main. Name your
names."

"Huck Finn the Red-Handed, and Joe Harper the Terror of the
Seas." Tom had furnished these titles, from his favorite literature.

" 'Tis well. Give the countersign."[2]

Two hoarse whispers delivered the same awful word simultaneously to the brooding night:

"BLOOD!"

Then Tom tumbled his ham over the bluff and let himself down
after it, tearing both skin and clothes to some extent in the effort.
There was an easy, comfortable path along the shore under the bluff,
but it lacked the advantages of difficulty and danger so valued by a
pirate.

The Terror of the Seas had brought a side of bacon, and had about
worn himself out with getting it there. Finn the Red-Handed had
stolen a skillet, and a quantity of half cured leaf tobacco, and had
also brought a few corn-cobs to make pipes with. But none of the
pirates smoked or "chewed" but himself. The Black Avenger of the
Spanish Main said it would never do to start without some fire. That
was a wise thought; matches were hardly known there in that day.
They saw a fire smouldering upon a great raft a hundred yards above,
and they went stealthily thither and helped themselves to a chunk.
They made an imposing adventure of it, saying, "Hist!" every now

2. Password.

and then and suddenly halting with finger on lip; moving with hands on imaginary dagger-hilts; and giving orders in dismal whispers that if "the foe" stirred to "let him have it to the hilt," because "dead men tell no tales." They knew well enough that the raftsmen were all down at the village laying in stores or having a spree, but still that was no excuse for their conducting this thing in an unpiratical way.

They shoved off, presently, Tom in command, Huck at the after oar and Joe at the forward. Tom stood amidships, gloomy-browed, and with folded arms, and gave his orders in a low, stern whisper:

"Luff,[3] and bring her to the wind!"

"Aye-aye, sir!"

"Steady, steady-y-y-y!"

"Steady it is, sir!"

"Let her go off a point!"

"Point it is, sir!"

As the boys steadily and monotonously drove the raft toward midstream it was no doubt understood that these orders were given only for "style," and were not intended to mean anything in particular.

"What sail's she carrying?"

"Courses, tops'ls, and flying-jib,[4] sir."

"Send the r'yals up! Lay out aloft, there, half a dozen of ye,—foretopmaststuns'l! Lively, now!"

"Aye-aye, sir!"

"Shake out that maintogalans'l! Sheets and braces![5] *Now*, my hearties!"

"Aye-aye, sir!"

"Hellum-a-lee—hard a port! Stand by to meet her when she comes! Port, port! *Now*, men! With a will! Stead-y-y-y!"

"Steady it is, sir!"

The raft drew beyond the middle of the river; the boys pointed her head right, and then lay on their oars. The river was not high, so there was not more than a two- or three-mile current. Hardly a word was said during the next three-quarters of an hour. Now the raft was passing before the distant town. Two or three glimmering lights showed where it lay, peacefully sleeping, beyond the vague vast sweep of star-gemmed water, unconscious of the tremendous event that was happening. The Black Avenger stood, still with folded arms, "looking his last" upon the scene of his former joys and his later sufferings, and wishing "she" could see him now, abroad on the wild sea, facing peril and death with dauntless heart, going to his doom with a grim smile on his lips. It was but a small strain on his imag-

3. Sail close to or into the wind.
4. Among the thirty or more sails used on three-masted ships are the relatively small flying jibs and royals. Other sails are the fore and main courses, the foretopmast studding sail (stun's'l), the main topgallant sail, and various topsails.
5. Sheets and braces are ropes.

ination to remove Jackson's Island beyond eye-shot of the village, and so he "looked his last" with a broken and satisfied heart. The other pirates were looking their last, too; and they all looked so long that they came near letting the current drift them out of the range of the island. But they discovered the danger in time, and made shift to avert it. About two o'clock in the morning the raft grounded on the bar two hundred yards above the head of the island, and they waded back and forth until they had landed their freight. Part of the little raft's belongings consisted of an old sail, and this they spread over a nook in the bushes for a tent to shelter their provisions; but they themselves would sleep in the open air in good weather, as became outlaws.

They built a fire against the side of a great log twenty or thirty steps within the sombre depths of the forest, and then cooked some bacon in the frying-pan for supper, and used up half of the corn "pone" stock they had brought. It seemed glorious sport to be feasting in that wild free way in the virgin forest of an unexplored and uninhabited island, far from the haunts of men, and they said they never would return to civilization. The climbing fire lit up their faces and threw its ruddy glare upon the pillared tree trunks of their forest temple, and upon the varnished foliage and festooning vines.

When the last crisp slice of bacon was gone, and the last allowance of corn pone devoured, the boys stretched themselves out on the grass, filled with contentment. They could have found a cooler place, but they would not deny themselves such a romantic feature as the roasting camp-fire.

"*Ain't* it gay?" said Joe.

"It's *nuts!*" said Tom. "What would the boys say if they could see us?"

"Say? Well they'd just die to be here—hey Hucky!"

"I reckon so," said Huckleberry; "anyways *I'm* suited. I don't want nothing better'n this. I don't ever get enough to eat, gen'ally—and here they can't come and pick at a feller and bullyrag[6] him so."

"It's just the life for me," said Tom. "You don't have to get up, mornings, and you don't have to go to school, and wash, and all that blame foolishness. You see a pirate don't have to do *anything*, Joe, when he's ashore, but a hermit *he* has to be praying considerable, and then he don't have any fun, anyway, all by himself that way."

"O yes, that's so," said Joe, "but I hadn't thought much about it, you know. I'd a good deal ruther be a pirate, now that I've tried it."

"You see," said Tom, "people don't go much on hermits, now-a-days, like they used to in old times, but a pirate's always respected. And a hermit's got to sleep on the hardest place he can find, and put

6. Bully, intimidate.

sack-cloth[7] and ashes on his head, and stand out in the rain, and—"

"What does he put sack-cloth and ashes on his head for?" inquired Huck.

"*I* dono. But they've *got* to do it. Hermits always do. You'd have to do that if you was a hermit."

"Dern'd if I would," said Huck.

"Well what would you do?"

"I dono. But I wouldn't do that."

"Why Huck you'd *have* to. How'd you get around it?"

"Why I just wouldn't stand it. I'd run away."

"Run away! Well you *would* be a nice old slouch of a hermit. You'd be a disgrace."

The Red-Handed made no response, being better employed. He had finished gouging out a cob, and now he fitted a weed stem to it, loaded it with tobacco, and was pressing a coal to the charge and blowing a cloud of fragrant smoke—he was in the full bloom of luxurious contentment. The other pirates envied him this majestic vice, and secretly resolved to acquire it shortly. Presently Huck said:

"What does pirates have to do?"

Tom said:

"Oh they have just a bully time—take ships, and burn them, and get the money and bury it in awful places in their island where there's ghosts and things to watch it, and kill everybody in the ships—make 'em walk a plank."

"And they carry the women to the island," said Joe; "they don't kill the women."

"No," assented Tom, "they don't kill the women—they're too noble. And the women's always beautiful, too."

"And don't they wear the bulliest clothes! Oh, no! All gold and silver and di'monds," said Joe, with enthusiasm.

"Who?" said Huck.

"Why the pirates."

Huck scanned his own clothing forlornly.

"I reckon I ain't dressed fitten for a pirate," said he, with a regretful pathos in his voice; "but I ain't got none but these."

But the other boys told him the fine clothes would come fast enough, after they should have begun their adventures. They made him understand that his poor rags would do to begin with, though it was customary for wealthy pirates to start with a proper wardrobe.

Gradually their talk died out and drowsiness began to steal upon the eyelids of the little waifs. The pipe dropped from the fingers of the Red-Handed, and he slept the sleep of the conscience-free and the weary. The Terror of the Seas and the Black Avenger of the

7. Coarse cloth, sometimes worn by one seeking to be absolved of sin. Not usually worn on the head.

Spanish Main had more difficulty in getting to sleep. They said their prayers inwardly, and lying down, since there was nobody there with authority to make them kneel and recite aloud; in truth they had a mind not to say them at all, but they were afraid to proceed to such lengths as that, lest they might call down a sudden and special thunderbolt from Heaven. Then at once they reached and hovered upon the imminent verge of sleep—but an intruder came, now, that would not "down." It was conscience. They began to feel a vague fear that they had been doing wrong to run away; and next they thought of the stolen meat, and then the real torture came. They tried to argue it away by reminding conscience that they had purloined sweetmeats and apples scores of times; but conscience was not to be appeased by such thin plausibilities; it seemed to them, in the end, that there was no getting around the stubborn fact that taking sweetmeats was only "hooking," while taking bacon and hams and such valuables was plain simple *stealing*—and there was a command against that in the Bible. So they inwardly resolved that so long as they remained in the business, their piracies should not again be sullied with the crime of stealing. Then conscience granted a truce, and these curiously inconsistent pirates fell peacefully to sleep.

Chapter XIV.

WHEN Tom awoke in the morning, he wondered where he was. He sat up and rubbed his eyes and looked around. Then he comprehended. It was the cool gray dawn, and there was a delicious sense of repose and peace in the deep pervading calm and silence of the woods. Not a leaf stirred; not a sound obtruded upon great Nature's meditation. Beaded dew-drops stood upon the leaves and grasses. A white layer of ashes covered the fire, and a thin blue breath of smoke rose straight into the air. Joe and Huck still slept.

Now, far away in the woods a bird called; another answered; presently the hammering of a woodpecker was heard. Gradually the cool dim gray of the morning whitened, and as gradually sounds multiplied and life manifested itself. The marvel of Nature shaking off sleep and going to work unfolded itself to the musing boy. A little green worm came crawling over a dewy leaf, lifting two-thirds of his body into the air from time to time and "sniffing around," then proceeding again—for he was measuring, Tom said; and when the worm approached him, of its own accord, he sat as still as a stone, with his hopes rising and falling, by turns, as the creature still came toward him or seemed inclined to go elsewhere; and when at last it considered a painful moment with its curved body in the air and then came decisively down upon Tom's leg and began a journey over him, his whole heart was glad—for that meant that he was going to have a new suit of clothes—without the shadow of a doubt a gaudy piratical uniform. Now a procession of ants appeared, from nowhere in particular, and went about their labors; one struggled manfully by with a dead spider five times as big as itself in its arms, and lugged it straight up a tree-trunk. A brown spotted lady-bug climbed the dizzy height of a grass-blade, and Tom bent down close to it and said, "Lady-bug, lady-bug, fly away home, your house is on fire, your children's alone," and she took wing and went off to see about it—which did not surprise the boy, for he knew of old that this insect was credulous about conflagrations[8] and he had practiced upon its simplicity more than once. A tumble-bug came next, heaving sturdily at its ball, and Tom touched the creature, to see it shut its legs against its body and pretend to be dead. The birds were fairly rioting, by this time. A cat-bird, the northern mocker, lit in a tree over Tom's head, and trilled out her imitations of her neighbors in a rapture of enjoyment; then a shrill jay swept down, a flash of blue flame, and stopped on a twig almost within the boy's reach, cocked his head to one side and eyed the strangers with a consuming curiosity; a gray squirrel and a big fellow of the "fox" kind came skurrying along, sitting up at intervals to inspect and chatter at the boys, for the wild things had probably never seen a human being before and scarcely knew whether to be afraid or not. All Nature was wide awake and stirring, now; long lances of sunlight pierced down through the dense foliage far and near, and a few butterflies came fluttering upon the scene.

Tom stirred up the other pirates and they all clattered away with a shout, and in a minute or two were stripped and chasing after and tumbling over each other in the shallow limpid water of the white sand-bar. They felt no longing for the little village sleeping in the distance beyond the majestic waste of water. A vagrant current or a slight rise in the river had carried off their raft, but this only gratified them, since its going was something like burning the bridge between them and civilization.

They came back to camp wonderfully refreshed, glad-hearted, and ravenous; and they soon had the camp-fire blazing up again. Huck found a spring of clear cold water close by, and the boys made cups of broad oak or hickory leaves, and felt that water, sweetened with such a wild-wood charm as that, would be a good enough substitute for coffee. While Joe was slicing bacon for breakfast, Tom and Huck asked him to hold on a minute; they stepped to a promising nook in the river bank and threw in their lines; almost immediately they had reward. Joe had not had time to get impatient before they were back

8. Willing to believe anything about fires.

again with some handsome bass; a couple of sun-perch and a small catfish—provision enough for quite a family. They fried the fish with the bacon and were astonished; for no fish had ever seemed so delicious before. They did not know that the quicker a fresh water fish is on the fire after he is caught the better he is; and they reflected little upon what a sauce open air sleeping, open air exercise, bathing, and a large ingredient of hunger makes, too.

They lay around in the shade, after breakfast, while Huck had a smoke, and then went off through the woods on an exploring expedition. They tramped gaily along, over decaying logs, through tangled underbrush, among solemn monarchs of the forest, hung from their crowns to the ground with a drooping regalia of grape-vines. Now and then they came upon snug nooks carpeted with grass and jeweled with flowers.

They found plenty of things to be delighted with but nothing to be astonished at. They discovered that the island was about three miles long and a quarter of a mile wide, and that the shore it lay closest to was only separated from it by a narrow channel hardly two hundred yards wide. They took a swim about every hour, so it was close upon the middle of the afternoon when they got back to camp. They were too hungry to stop to fish, but they fared sumptuously upon cold ham, and then threw themselves down in the shade to talk. But the talk soon began to drag, and then died. The stillness, the solemnity that brooded in the woods, and the sense of loneliness, began to tell upon the spirits of the boys. They fell to thinking. A sort of undefined longing crept upon them. This took dim shape, presently—it was budding home-sickness. Even Finn the Red-Handed was dreaming of his door-steps and empty hogsheads. But they were all ashamed of their weakness, and none was brave enough to speak his thought.

For some time, now, the boys had been dully conscious of a peculiar sound in the distance, just as one sometimes is of the ticking of a clock which he takes no distinct note of. But now this mysterious sound became more pronounced, and forced a recognition. The boys started, glanced at each other, and then each assumed a listening attitude. There was a long silence, profound and unbroken; then a deep, sullen boom came floating down out of the distance.

"What is it!" exclaimed Joe, under his breath.

"I wonder," said Tom in a whisper.

" 'Tain't thunder," said Huckleberry, in an awed tone, "becuz thunder—"

"Hark!" said Tom. "Listen—don't talk."

They waited a time that seemed an age, and then the same muffled boom troubled the solemn hush.

"Let's go and see."

They sprang to their feet and hurried to the shore toward the town. They parted the bushes on the bank and peered out over the water. The little steam ferry boat was about a mile below the village, drifting with the current. Her broad deck seemed crowded with people. There were a great many skiffs[9] rowing about or floating with the stream in the neighborhood of the ferry-boat, but the boys could not determine what the men in them were doing. Presently a great jet of white smoke burst from the ferry-boat's side, and as it expanded and rose in a lazy cloud, that same dull throb of sound was borne to the listeners again.

"I know now!" exclaimed Tom; "somebody's drownded!"

"That's it!" said Huck; "they done that last summer, when Bill Turner got drownded; they shoot a cannon over the water, and that makes him come up to the top. Yes, and they take loaves of bread and put quicksilver[1] in 'em and set 'em afloat, and wherever there's anybody that's drownded, they'll float right there and stop."

"Yes, I've heard about that," said Joe. "I wonder what makes the bread do that."

"Oh it ain't the bread, so much," said Tom; "I reckon it's mostly what they *say* over it before they start it out."

"But they don't say anything over it," said Huck. "I've seen 'em, and they don't."

"Well that's funny," said Tom. "But maybe they say it to themselves. Of *course* they do. Anybody might know that."

The other boys agreed that there was reason in what Tom said, because an ignorant lump of bread, uninstructed by an incantation, could not be expected to act very intelligently when sent upon an errand of such gravity.

"By jings I wish I was over there, now," said Joe.

"I do too," said Huck. "I'd give heaps to know who it is."

The boys still listened and watched. Presently a revealing thought flashed through Tom's mind, and he exclaimed:

"Boys, I know who's drownded—it's us!"

They felt like heroes in an instant. Here was a gorgeous triumph; they were missed; they were mourned; hearts were breaking on their account; tears were being shed; accusing memories of unkindnesses to these poor lost lads were rising up, and unavailing regrets and remorse were being indulged; and best of all, the departed were the talk of the whole town, and the envy of all the boys, as far as this dazzling notoriety was concerned. This was fine. It was worth while to be a pirate, after all.

As twilight drew on, the ferry boat went back to her accustomed business and the skiffs disappeared. The pirates returned to camp.

9. Small boats.
1. Mercury.

They were jubilant with vanity over their new grandeur and the illustrious trouble they were making. They caught fish, cooked supper and ate it, and then fell to guessing at what the village was thinking and saying about them; and the pictures they drew of the public distress on their account were gratifying to look upon—from their point of view. But when the shadows of night closed them in, they gradually ceased to talk, and sat gazing into the fire, with their minds evidently wandering elsewhere. The excitement was gone, now, and Tom and Joe could not keep back thoughts of certain persons at home who were not enjoying this fine frolic as much as they were. Misgivings came; they grew troubled and unhappy; a sigh or two escaped, unawares. By and by Joe timidly ventured upon a round-about "feeler" as to how the others might look upon a return to civilization—not right now, but—

Tom withered him with derision! Huck, being uncommitted, as yet, joined in with Tom, and the waverer quickly "explained," and was glad to get out of the scrape with as little taint of chicken-hearted home-sickness clinging to his garments as he could. Mutiny[2] was effectually laid to rest for the moment.

As the night deepened, Huck began to nod, and presently to snore. Joe followed next. Tom lay upon his elbow motionless, for some time, watching the two intently. At last he got up cautiously, on his knees, and went searching among the grass and the flickering reflections flung by the camp-fire. He picked up and inspected several large semi-cylinders of the thin white bark of a sycamore, and finally chose two which seemed to suit him. Then he knelt by the fire and painfully wrote something upon each of these with his "red keel;" one he rolled up and put in his jacket pocket, and the other he put in Joe's hat and removed it to a little distance from the owner. And he also put into the hat certain school-boy treasures of almost inestimable value—among them a lump of chalk, an India rubber ball, three fish-hooks, and one of that kind of marbles known as a "sure 'nough crystal." Then he tip-toed his way cautiously among the trees till he felt that he was out of hearing, and straightway broke into a keen run in the direction of the sand-bar.

Chapter XV.

A FEW minutes later Tom was in the shoal[3] water of the bar, wading toward the Illinois shore. Before the depth reached his middle he was half-way over; the current would permit no more wading, now,

2. Rebellion against authority, especially among sailors and soldiers.
3. Shallow.

so he struck out confidently to swim the remaining hundred yards. He swam quartering[4] up stream, but still was swept downward rather faster than he had expected. However, he reached the shore finally, and drifted along till he found a low place and drew himself out. He put his hand on his jacket pocket, found his piece of bark safe, and then struck through the woods, following the shore, with streaming garments. Shortly before ten o'clock he came out into an open place opposite the village, and saw the ferry boat lying in the shadow of the trees and the high bank. Everything was quiet under the blinking stars. He crept down the bank, watching with all his eyes, slipped into the water, swam three or four strokes and climbed into the skiff that did "yawl" duty at the boat's stern.[5] He laid himself down under the thwarts[6] and waited, panting.

Presently the cracked bell tapped and a voice gave the order to "cast off." A minute or two later the skiff's head was standing high up, against the boat's swell, and the voyage was begun. Tom felt happy in his success, for he knew it was the boat's last trip for the night. At the end of a long twelve or fifteen minutes the wheels stopped, and Tom slipped overboard and swam ashore in the dusk, landing fifty yards down stream, out of danger of possible stragglers.

He flew along unfrequented alleys, and shortly found himself at his aunt's back fence. He climbed over, approached the "ell" and looked in at the sitting-room window, for a light was burning there. There sat Aunt Polly, Sid, Mary, and Joe Harper's mother, grouped together, talking. They were by the bed, and the bed was between them and the door. Tom went to the door and began to softly lift the latch; then he pressed gently and the door yielded a crack; he continued pushing cautiously, and quaking every time it creaked, till he judged he might squeeze through on his knees; and so he put his head through and began, warily.

"What makes the candle blow so?" said Aunt Polly. Tom hurried up. "Why that door's open, I believe. Why of course it is. No end of strange things now. Go 'long and shut it, Sid."

Tom disappeared under the bed just in time. He lay and "breathed" himself for a time, and then crept to where he could almost touch his aunt's foot.

"But as I was saying," said aunt Polly, "he warn't *bad*, so to say— only misch*ee*vous. Only just giddy, and harum-scarum,[7] you know. He warn't any more responsible than a colt. *He* never meant any harm, and he was the best-hearted boy that ever was"—and she began to cry.

---

4. Moving from one side to another while advancing.
5. Rear of a boat. "Yawl": small boat aboard a larger one.
6. Seats extending across a boat.
7. Reckless.

"It was just so with my Joe—always full of his devilment, and up to every kind of mischief, but he was just as unselfish and kind as he could be—and laws bless me, to think I went and whipped him for taking that cream, never once recollecting that I throwed it out myself because it was sour, and I never to see him again in this world, never, never, never, poor abused boy!" And Mrs. Harper sobbed as if her heart would break.

"I hope Tom's better off where he is," said Sid, "but if he'd been better in some ways—"

"Sid!" Tom felt the glare of the old lady's eye, though he could not see it. "Not a word against my Tom, now that he's gone! God'll take care of him—never you trouble yourself, sir! Oh, Mrs. Harper, I don't know how to give him up, I don't know how to give him up! He was such a comfort to me, although he tormented my old heart out of me, 'most."

"The Lord giveth and the Lord hath taken away.—Blessed be the name of the Lord![8] But it's so hard—Oh, it's so hard! Only last Saturday my Joe busted a fire-cracker right under my nose and I knocked him sprawling. Little did I know then, how soon—O, if it was to do over again I'd hug him and bless him for it."

"Yes, yes, yes, I know just how you feel, Mrs. Harper, I know just exactly how you feel. No longer ago than yesterday noon, my Tom took and filled the cat full of Pain-Killer, and I did think the cretur would tear the house down. And God forgive me, I cracked Tom's head with my thimble, poor boy, poor dead boy. But he's out of all his troubles now. And the last words I ever heard him say was to reproach—"

But this memory was too much for the old lady, and she broke entirely down. Tom was snuffling, now, himself—and more in pity of himself than anybody else. He could hear Mary crying, and putting in a kindly word for him from time to time. He began to have a nobler opinion of himself than ever before. Still he was sufficiently touched by his aunt's grief to long to rush out from under the bed and overwhelm her with joy—and the theatrical gorgeousness of the thing appealed strongly to his nature, too, but he resisted and lay still.

He went on listening, and gathered, by odds and ends that it was conjectured at first that the boys had got drowned while taking a swim; then the small raft had been missed; next, certain boys said the missing lads had promised that the village should "hear something" soon; the wise-heads had "put this and that together" and decided that the lads had gone off on that raft and would turn up at the next town below, presently; but toward noon the raft had been found, lodged against the Missouri shore some five or six miles below

8. Job 1.21: "The Lord gave, and the Lord hath taken away; blessed be the name of the Lord."

the village,—and then hope perished; they must be drowned, else hunger would have driven them home by nightfall if not sooner. It was believed that the search for the bodies had been a fruitless effort merely because the drowning must have occurred in mid-channel, since the boys, being good swimmers, would otherwise have escaped to shore. This was Wednesday night. If the bodies continued missing until Sunday, all hope would be given over, and the funerals would be preached on that morning. Tom shuddered.

Mrs. Harper gave a sobbing good-night and turned to go. Then with a mutual impulse the two bereaved women flung themselves into each other's arms and had a good, consoling cry, and then parted. Aunt Polly was tender far beyond her wont, in her good-night to Sid and Mary. Sid snuffled a bit and Mary went off crying with all her heart.

Aunt Polly knelt down and prayed for Tom so touchingly, so appealingly, and with such measureless love in her words and her old trembling voice, that he was weltering in tears again, long before she was through.

He had to keep still long after she went to bed, for she kept making broken-hearted ejaculations[9] from time to time, tossing unrestfully, and turning over. But at last she was still, only moaning a little in her sleep. Now the boy stole out, rose gradually by the bedside, shaded the candle-light with his hand, and stood regarding her. His heart was full of pity for her. He took out his sycamore scroll and placed it by the candle. But something occurred to him, and he lingered, considering. His face lighted with a happy solution of his thought; he put the bark hastily in his pocket. Then he bent over and kissed the faded lips, and straightway made his stealthy exit, latching the door behind him.

He threaded his way back to the ferry landing, found nobody at large there, and walked boldly on board the boat, for he knew she was tenantless except that there was a watchman, who always turned in and slept like a graven image.[1] He untied the skiff at the stern, slipped into it, and was soon rowing cautiously up stream. When he had pulled a mile above the village, he started quartering across and bent himself stoutly to his work. He hit the landing on the other side neatly, for this was a familiar bit of work to him. He was moved to capture the skiff, arguing that it might be considered a ship and therefore legitimate prey for a pirate, but he knew a thorough search would be made for it and that might end in revelations. So he stepped ashore and entered the wood.

He sat down and took a long rest, torturing himself meantime to

9. Exclamations.
1. Carved idol. One of the Ten Commandments reads "Thou shalt not make unto thee any graven image" (Exodus 20.4).

keep awake, and then started wearily down the home-stretch. The night was far spent. It was broad daylight before he found himself fairly abreast the island bar. He rested again until the sun was well up and gilding the great river with its splendor, and then he plunged into the stream. A little later he paused, dripping, upon the threshold of the camp, and heard Joe say:

"No, Tom's true-blue, Huck, and he'll come back. He won't desert. He knows that would be a disgrace to a pirate, and Tom's too proud for that sort of thing. He's up to something or other. Now I wonder what?"

"Well, the things is ours, anyway, ain't they?"

"Pretty near, but not yet, Huck. The writing says they are if he ain't back here to breakfast."

"Which he is!" exclaimed Tom, with fine dramatic effect, stepping grandly into camp.

A sumptuous breakfast of bacon and fish was shortly provided, and as the boys set to work upon it, Tom recounted (and adorned) his adventures. They were a vain and boastful company of heroes when the tale was done. Then Tom hid himself away in a shady nook to sleep till noon, and the other pirates got ready to fish and explore.

Chapter XVI.

AFTER dinner all the gang turned out to hunt for turtle eggs on the bar. They went about poking sticks into the sand, and when they found a soft place they went down on their knees and dug with their hands. Sometimes they would take fifty or sixty eggs out of one hole. They were perfectly round white things a trifle smaller than an English walnut. They had a famous fried-egg feast that night, and another on Friday morning.

After breakfast they went whooping and prancing out on the bar, and chased each other round and round, shedding clothes as they went, until they were naked, and then continued the frolic far away up the shoal water of the bar, against the stiff current, which latter tripped their legs from under them from time to time and greatly increased the fun. And now and then they stooped in a group and splashed water in each other's faces with their palms, gradually approaching each other, with averted faces to avoid the strangling sprays and finally gripping and struggling till the best man ducked his neighbor, and then they all went under in a tangle of white legs and arms and came up blowing, sputtering, laughing and gasping for breath at one and the same time.

When they were well exhausted, they would run out and sprawl on the dry, hot sand, and lie there and cover themselves up with it, and by and by break for the water again and go through the original performance once more. Finally it occurred to them that their naked skin represented flesh-colored "tights" very fairly; so they drew a ring in the sand and had a circus—with three clowns in it, for none would yield this proudest post to his neighbor.

Next they got their marbles and played "knucks" and "ring-taw" and "keeps"[2] till that amusement grew stale. Then Joe and Huck had another swim, but Tom would not venture, because he found that in kicking off his trousers he had kicked his string of rattlesnake rattles off his ankle, and he wondered how he had escaped cramp so long without the protection of this mysterious charm. He did not venture again until he had found it, and by that time the other boys were tired and ready to rest. They gradually wandered apart, dropped into the "dumps," and fell to gazing longingly across the wide river to where the village lay drowsing in the sun. Tom found himself writing "BECKY" in the sand with his big toe; he scratched it out, and was angry with himself for his weakness. But he wrote it again, nevertheless; he could not help it. He erased it once more and then took himself out of temptation by driving the other boys together and joining them.

But Joe's spirits had gone down almost beyond resurrection. He was so homesick that he could hardly endure the misery of it. The tears lay very near the surface. Huck was melancholy, too. Tom was down-hearted, but tried hard not to show it. He had a secret which he was not ready to tell, yet, but if this mutinous depression was not broken up soon, he would have to bring it out. He said, with a great show of cheerfulness:

"I bet there's been pirates on this island before, boys. We'll explore it again. They've hid treasures here somewhere. How'd you feel to light on a rotten chest full of gold and silver—hey?"

But it roused only a faint enthusiasm, which faded out, with no reply. Tom tried one or two other seductions; but they failed, too. It was discouraging work. Joe sat poking up the sand with a stick and looking very gloomy. Finally he said:

"O, boys, let's give it up. I want to go home. It's so lonesome."

"Oh, no, Joe, you'll feel better by and by," said Tom. "Just think of the fishing that's here."

"I don't care for fishing. I want to go home."

"But Joe, there ain't such another swimming place anywhere."

"Swimming's no good. I don't seem to care for it, somehow, when there ain't anybody to say I shan't go in. I mean to go home."

"O, shucks! Baby! You want to see your mother, I reckon."

2. Marble games that entail, respectively, shooting at a marble held between the opponent's knuckles, shooting at marbles in a circle, and playing for keeps.

"Yes, I *do* want to see my mother—and you would too, if you had one. I ain't any more baby than you are." And Joe snuffled a little.

"Well, we'll let the cry-baby go home to his mother, *won't* we Huck? Poor thing—does it want to see its mother? And so it shall. *You* like it here, *don't* you Huck? We'll stay, won't we?"

Huck said "Y-e-s"—without any heart in it.

"I'll never speak to you again as long as I live," said Joe, rising. "There now!" And he moved moodily away and began to dress himself.

"Who cares!" said Tom. "Nobody wants you to. Go 'long home and get laughed at. O, you're a nice pirate. Huck and me ain't cry-babies. We'll stay, won't we Huck? Let him go if he wants to. I reckon we can get along without him, per'aps."

But Tom was uneasy, nevertheless, and was alarmed to see Joe go sullenly on with his dressing. And then it was discomforting to see Huck eyeing Joe's preparations so wistfully, and keeping up such an ominous silence. Presently, without a parting word, Joe began to wade off toward the Illinois shore. Tom's heart began to sink. He glanced at Huck. Huck could not bear the look, and dropped his eyes. Then he said:

"I want to go, too, Tom. It was getting so lonesome anyway, and now it'll be worse. Let us go too, Tom."

"I won't! You can all go, if you want to. I mean to stay."

"Tom, I better go."

"Well go 'long—who's hendering you."

Huck began to pick up his scattered clothes. He said:

"Tom, I wisht you'd come too. Now you think it over. We'll wait for you when we get to shore."

"Well you'll wait a blame long time, that's all."

Huck started sorrowfully away, and Tom stood looking after him, with a strong desire tugging at his heart to yield his pride and go along too. He hoped the boys would stop, but they still waded slowly on. It suddenly dawned on Tom that it was become very lonely and still. He made one final struggle with his pride, and then darted after his comrades, yelling:

"Wait! Wait! I want to tell you something!"

They presently stopped and turned around. When he got to where they were, he began unfolding his secret, and they listened moodily till at last they saw the "point" he was driving at, and then they set up a war-whoop of applause and said it was "splendid!" and said if he had told them that at first, they wouldn't have started away. He made a plausible excuse; but his real reason had been the fear that not even the secret would keep them with him any very great length of time, and so he had meant to hold it in reserve as a last seduction.

The lads came gaily back and went at their sports again with a will, chattering all the time about Tom's stupendous plan and admiring the genius of it. After a dainty egg and fish dinner, Tom said he wanted to learn to smoke, now. Joe caught at the idea and said he would like to try, too. So Huck made pipes and filled them. These novices had never smoked anything before but cigars made of grapevine and they "bit" the tongue and were not considered manly, anyway.

Now they stretched themselves out on their elbows and began to puff, charily, and with slender confidence. The smoke had an unpleasant taste, and they gagged a little, but Tom said:

"Why it's just as easy! If I'd a knowed *this* was all, I'd a learnt long ago."

"So would I," said Joe. "It's just nothing."

"Why many a time I've looked at people smoking, and thought well I wish I could do that; but I never thought I could," said Tom.

"That's just the way with me, hain't it Huck? You've heard me talk just that away—haven't you Huck? I'll leave it to Huck if I haven't."

"Yes—heaps of times," said Huck.

"Well I have too," said Tom; "O, hundreds of times. Once down there by the slaughter-house. Don't you remember, Huck? Bob Tanner was there, and Johnny Miller, and Jeff Thatcher, when I said it. Don't you remember Huck, 'bout me saying that?"

"Yes, that's so," said Huck. "That was the day after I lost a white alley. No, 'twas the day before."

"There—I told you so," said Tom. "Huck recollects it."

"I bleeve I could smoke this pipe all day," said Joe. "*I* don't feel sick.'

"Neither do I," said Tom. "*I* could smoke it all day. But I bet you Jeff Thatcher couldn't."

"Jeff Thatcher! Why he'd keel over just with two draws. Just let him try it once. *He'd* see!"

"I bet he would. And Johnny Miller—I wish I could see Johnny Miller tackle it once."

"O, don't *I!*" said Joe. "Why I bet you Johnny Miller couldn't any more do this than nothing. Just one little snifter would fetch *him.*"

" 'Deed it would, Joe. Say—I wish the boys could see us now."

"So do I."

"Say,—boys, don't say anything about it, and some time when they're around, I'll come up to you and say 'Joe, got a pipe? I want a smoke.' And you'll say, kind of careless like, as if it warn't anything, you'll say, 'Yes, I got my *old* pipe, and another one, but my tobacker ain't very good.' And I'll say, 'Oh, that's all right, if it's *strong* enough.' And then you'll out with the pipes, and we'll light up just as ca'm, and then just see 'em look!"

"By jings that'll be gay, Tom! I wish it was *now!*"

"So do I! And when we tell 'em we learned when we was off pirating, won't they wish they'd been along?"

"O, I reckon not! I'll just *bet* they will!"

So the talk ran on. But presently it began to flag a trifle, and grow disjointed. The silences widened; the expectoration marvelously increased. Every pore inside the boys' cheeks became a spouting fountain; they could scarcely bail out the cellars under their tongues fast enough to prevent an inundation; little overflowings down their throats occurred in spite of all they could do, and sudden retchings followed every time. Both boys were looking very pale and miserable, now. Joe's pipe dropped from his nerveless fingers. Tom's followed. Both fountains were going furiously and both pumps bailing with might and main. Joe said feebly:

"I've lost my knife. I reckon I better go and find it."

Tom said, with quivering lip and halting utterance:

"I'll help you. You go over that way and I'll hunt around by the spring. No, you needn't come, Huck—we can find it."

So Huck sat down again, and waited an hour. Then he found it lonesome and went to find his comrades. They were wide apart in the woods, both very pale, both fast asleep. But something informed him that if they had had any trouble they had got rid of it.

They were not talkative at supper that night. They had a humble look; and when Huck prepared his pipe after the meal and was going to prepare theirs, they said no, they were not feeling very well— something they ate at dinner had disagreed with them.

About midnight Joe awoke, and called the boys. There was a brooding oppressiveness in the air that seemed to bode something. The boys huddled themselves together and sought the friendly companionship of the fire, though the dull dead heat of the breathless atmosphere was stifling. They sat still, intent and waiting. The solemn hush continued. Beyond the light of the fire everything was swallowed up in the blackness of darkness.[3] Presently there came a quivering glow that vaguely revealed the foliage for a moment and then vanished. By and by another came, a little stronger. Then another. Then a faint moan came sighing through the branches of the forest and the boys felt a fleeting breath upon their cheeks, and shuddered with the fancy that the Spirit of the Night had gone by. There was a pause. Now a weird flash turned night into day and showed every little grass-blade, separate and distinct, that grew about their feet. And it showed three white, startled faces, too. A deep peal of thunder went rolling and tumbling down the heavens and lost itself in sullen rumblings in the distance. A sweep of chilly air passed by, rustling all the leaves and snowing the flaky ashes broadcast

---

3. In Jude 1.13, godless men are compared to "wandering stars, to whom is reserved the blackness of darkness for ever."

about the fire. Another fierce glare lit up the forest and an instant crash followed that seemed to rend the tree-tops right over the boys' heads. They clung together in terror, in the thick gloom that followed. A few big rain-drops fell pattering upon the leaves.

"Quick! boys, go for the tent!" exclaimed Tom.

They sprang away, stumbling over roots and among vines in the dark, no two plunging in the same direction. A furious blast roared through the trees, making everything sing as it went. One blinding flash after another came, and peal on peal of deafening thunder. And now a drenching rain poured down and the rising hurricane drove it in sheets along the ground. The boys cried out to each other, but the roaring wind and the booming thunder-blasts drowned their voices utterly. However, one by one they straggled in at last and took shelter under the tent, cold, scared, and streaming with water; but to have company in misery seemed something to be grateful for. They could not talk, the old sail flapped so furiously, even if the other noises would have allowed them. The tempest rose higher and higher, and presently the sail tore loose from its fastenings and went winging away on the blast. The boys seized each others' hands and fled, with many tumblings and bruises, to the shelter of a great oak that stood upon the river bank. Now the battle was at its highest. Under the ceaseless conflagration of lightnings that flamed in the skies, everything below stood out in clean-cut and shadowless distinctness: the bending trees, the billowy river, white with foam, the driving spray of spume-flakes, the dim outlines of the high bluffs on the other side, glimpsed through the drifting cloud-rack and the slanting veil of rain. Every little while some giant tree yielded the fight and fell crashing through the younger growth; and the unflagging thunder-peals came now in ear-splitting explosive bursts, keen and sharp, and unspeakably appalling. The storm culminated in one matchless effort that seemed likely to tear the island to pieces, burn it up, drown it to the tree tops, blow it away, and deafen every creature in it, all at one and the same moment. It was a wild night for homeless young heads to be out in.

But at last the battle was done, and the forces retired with weaker and weaker threatenings and grumblings, and peace resumed her sway. The boys went back to camp, a good deal awed; but they found there was still something to be thankful for, because the great sycamore, the shelter of their beds, was a ruin, now, blasted by the lightnings, and they were not under it when the catastrophe happened.

Everything in camp was drenched, the camp-fire as well; for they were but heedless lads, like their generation, and had made no provision against rain. Here was matter for dismay, for they were soaked through and chilled. They were eloquent in their distress; but they presently discovered that the fire had eaten so far up under the great log it had been built against, (where it curved upward and separated itself from the ground,) that a hand-breadth or so of it had escaped wetting; so they patiently wrought until, with shreds and bark gathered from the under sides of sheltered logs, they coaxed the fire to burn again. Then they piled on great dead boughs till they had a roaring furnace and were glad-hearted once more. They dried their boiled ham and had a feast, and after that they sat by the fire and expanded and glorified their midnight adventure until morning, for there was not a dry spot to sleep on, anywhere around.

As the sun began to steal in upon the boys, drowsiness came over them and they went out on the sand-bar and lay down to sleep. They got scorched out, by and by, and drearily set about getting breakfast. After the meal they felt rusty, and stiff-jointed, and a little homesick once more. Tom saw the signs, and fell to cheering up the pirates as well as he could. But they cared nothing for marbles, or circus, or swimming, or anything. He reminded them of the imposing secret, and raised a ray of cheer. While it lasted, he got them interested in a new device. This was to knock off being pirates, for a while, and be Indians for a change. They were attracted by this idea; so it was not long before they were stripped, and striped from head to heel with black mud, like mud, like so many zebras,—all of them chiefs, of course—and then they went tearing through the woods to attack an English settlement.

By and by, they separated into three hostile tribes, and darted upon each other from ambush with dreadful war-whoops, and killed and scalped each other by thousands. It was a gory day. Consequently it was an extremely satisfactory one.

They assembled in camp toward supper time, hungry and happy; but now a difficulty arose—hostile Indians could not break the bread of hospitality together without first making peace, and this was a simple impossibility without smoking a pipe of peace. There was no other process that ever they had heard of. Two of the savages almost wished they had remained pirates. However, there was no other way; so with such show of cheerfulness as they could muster they called for the pipe and took their whiff as it passed, in due form.

And behold they were glad they had gone into savagery, for they had gained something; they found that they could now smoke a little without having to go and hunt for a lost knife; they did not get sick enough to be seriously uncomfortable. They were not likely to fool away this high promise for lack of effort. No, they practiced cautiously, after supper, with right fair success, and so they spent a jubilant evening. They were prouder and happier in their new acquirement than they would have been in the scalping and skinning of the Six Nations.[4] We will leave them to smoke and chatter and brag, since we have no further use for them at present.

Chapter XVII.

BUT there was no hilarity in the little town that same tranquil Saturday afternoon. The Harpers, and Aunt Polly's family, were being put into mourning, with great grief and many tears. An unusual quiet possessed the village, although it was ordinarily quiet enough, in all conscience. The villagers conducted their concerns with an absent air, and talked little; but they sighed often. The Saturday holiday seemed a burden to the children. They had no heart in their sports, and gradually gave them up.

In the afternoon Becky Thatcher found herself moping about the deserted school-house yard, and feeling very melancholy. But she found nothing there to comfort her. She soliloquised:

"Oh, if I only had his brass andiron-knob again! But I haven't got anything now to remember him by." And she choked back a little sob.

Presently she stopped, and said to herself:

"It was right here. O, if it was to do over again, I wouldn't say that—I wouldn't say it for the whole world. But he's gone now; I'll never never never see him any more."

This thought broke her down and she wandered away, with the tears rolling down her cheeks. Then quite a group of boys and girls,— playmates of Tom's and Joe's—came by, and stood looking over the paling fence and talking in reverent tones of how Tom did so-and-so, the last time they saw him, and how Joe said this and that small trifle (pregnant with awful prophecy, as they could easily see now!)— and each speaker pointed out the exact spot where the lost lads stood at the time, and then added something like "and I was a standing just so—just as I am now, and as if you was him—I was as close as that—and he smiled, just this way—and then something seemed to go all over me, like,—awful, you know—and I never thought what it meant, of course, but I can see now!"

Then there was a dispute about who saw the dead boys last in life, and many claimed that dismal distinction, and offered evidences, more or less tampered with by the witness; and when it was ultimately decided who *did* see the departed last, and exchanged the last words with them, the lucky parties took upon themselves a sort of sacred importance, and were gaped at and envied by all the rest. One

4. Iroquois Confederacy.

poor chap, who had no other grandeur to offer, said with tolerably manifest pride in the remembrance:

"Well, Tom Sawyer he licked me once."

But that bid for glory was a failure. Most of the boys could say that, and so that cheapened the distinction too much. The group loitered away, still recalling memories of the lost heroes, in awed voices.

When the Sunday-school hour was finished, the next morning, the bell began to toll, instead of ringing in the usual way. It was a very still Sabbath, and the mournful sound seemed in keeping with the musing hush that lay upon nature. The villagers began to gather, loitering a moment in the vestibule to converse in whispers about the sad event. But there was no whispering in the house; only the funereal rustling of dresses as the women gathered to their seats, disturbed the silence there. None could remember when the little church had been so full before. There was finally a waiting pause, an expectant dumbness, and then Aunt Polly entered, followed by Sid and Mary, and they by the Harper family, all in deep black, and the whole congregation, the old minister as well, rose reverently and stood, until the mourners were seated in the front pew. There was another communing silence, broken at intervals by muffled sobs, and then the minister spread his hands abroad and prayed. A moving hymn was sung, and the text followed: "I am the Resurrection and the Life."[5]

As the service proceeded, the clergyman drew such pictures of the graces, the winning ways and the rare promise of the lost lads, that every soul there, thinking he recognized these pictures, felt a pang in remembering that he had persistently blinded himself to them, always before, and had as persistently seen only faults and flaws in the poor boys. The minister related many a touching incident in the lives of the departed, too, which illustrated their sweet, generous natures, and the people could easily see, now, how noble and beautiful those episodes were, and remembered with grief that at the time they occurred they had seemed rank rascalities, well deserving of the cowhide.[6] The congregation became more and more moved, as the pathetic tale went on, till at last the whole company broke down and joined the weeping mourners in a chorus of anguished sobs, the preacher himself giving way to his feelings, and crying in the pulpit.

There was a rustle in the gallery, which nobody noticed; a moment later the church door creaked; the minister raised his streaming eyes above his handkerchief, and stood transfixed! First one and then

---

5. Text frequently used at funerals. It continues, "He that believeth in me, though he were dead, yet shall he live" (John 11.25).
6. Leather whip.

another pair of eyes followed the minister's, and then almost with one impulse the congregation rose and stared while the three dead boys came marching up the aisle, Tom in the lead, Joe next, and Huck, a ruin of drooping rags, sneaking sheepishly in the rear! They had been hid in the unused gallery listening to their own funeral sermon!

Aunt Polly, Mary and the Harpers threw themselves upon their restored ones, smothered them with kisses and poured out thanksgivings, while poor Huck stood abashed and uncomfortable, not knowing exactly what to do or where to hide from so many unwelcoming eyes. He wavered, and started to slink away, but Tom seized him and said:

"Aunt Polly, it ain't fair. Somebody's got to be glad to see Huck."

"And so they shall. I'm glad to see him, poor motherless thing!" And the loving attentions Aunt Polly lavished upon him were the one thing capable of making him more uncomfortable than he was before.

Suddenly the minister shouted at the top of his voice:

"Praise God from whom all blessings flow—SING!—and put your hearts in it!"

And they did. Old Hundred[7] swelled up with a triumphant burst, and while it shook the rafters Tom Sawyer the Pirate looked around upon the envying juveniles about him and confessed in his heart that this was the proudest moment of his life.

As the "sold"[8] congregation trooped out they said they would almost be willing to be made ridiculous again to hear Old Hundred sung like that once more.

Tom got more cuffs and kisses that day—according to Aunt Polly's varying moods—than he had earned before in a year; and he hardly knew which expressed the most gratefulness to God and affection for himself.

Chapter XVIII.

THAT was Tom's great secret—the scheme to return home with his brother pirates and attend their own funerals. They had paddled over to the Missouri shore on a log, at dusk on Saturday, landing five or six miles below the village; they had slept in the woods at the edge of town till nearly daylight, and had then crept through back lanes and alleys and finished their sleep in the gallery of the church among a chaos of invalided benches.

7. The music of the Doxology, which begins, "Praise God, from whom all blessings flow."
8. Deceived.

At breakfast, Monday morning, Aunt Polly and Mary were very loving to Tom, and very attentive to his wants. There was an unusual amount of talk. In the course of it Aunt Polly said:

"Well, I don't say it wasn't a fine joke, Tom, to keep everybody suffering 'most a week so you boys had a good time, but it is a pity you could be so hard-hearted as to let *me* suffer so. If you could come over on a log to go to your funeral, you could have come over and give me a hint some way that you warn't *dead,* but only run off."

"Yes, you could have done that, Tom," said Mary; "and I believe you would if you had thought of it."

"Would you Tom?" said Aunt Polly, her face lighting wistfully. "Say, now, would you, if you'd thought of it?"

"I—well I don't know. 'Twould a spoiled everything."

"Tom, I hoped you loved me that much," said Aunt Polly, with a grieved tone that discomforted the boy. "It would been something if you'd cared enough to *think* of it, even if you didn't *do* it."

"Now auntie, that ain't any harm," pleaded Mary; "it's only Tom's giddy way—he is always in such a rush that he never thinks of anything."

"More's the pity. Sid would have thought. And Sid would have come and *done* it, too. Tom, you'll look back, some day, when it's too late, and wish you'd cared a little more for me when it would have cost you so little."

"Now auntie, you know I do care for you," said Tom.

"I'd know it better if you acted more like it."

"I wish now I'd thought," said Tom, with a repentant tone; "but I dreamed about you, anyway. That's something, ain't it?"

"It ain't much—a cat does that much—but it's better than nothing. What did you dream?"

"Why Wednesday night I dreamt that you was sitting over there by the bed, and Sid was sitting by the wood-box, and Mary next to him."

"Well, so we did. So we always do. I'm glad your dreams could take even that much trouble about us."

"And I dreamt that Joe Harper's mother was here."

"Why, she *was* here! Did you dream any more?"

"O, lots. But it's so dim, now."

"Well, *try* to recollect—can't you?"

"Some how it seems to me that the wind—the wind blowed the—the—"

"Try harder, Tom! The wind did blow something. Come!"

Tom pressed his fingers on his forehead an anxious minute, and then said:

"I've got it now! I've got it now! It blowed the candle!"

"Mercy on us! Go on, Tom—go on!"

"And it seems to me that you said, 'Why I believe that that door—' "

"Go *on*, Tom!"

"Just let me study a moment—just a moment. Oh, yes—you said you believed the door was open."

"As I'm a sitting here, I did! Didn't I, Mary! Go on!"

"And then—and then—well I won't be certain, but it seems like as if you made Sid go and—and—"

"Well? Well? What did I make him do, Tom? What did I make him do?"

"You made him—you—O, you made him shut it."

"Well for the land's sake! I never heard the beat of that in all my days! Don't tell *me* there ain't anything in dreams, any more. Sereny Harper shall know of this before I'm an hour older. I'd like to see her get around *this* with her rubbage 'bout superstition. Go on, Tom!"

"Oh, it's all getting just as bright as day, now. Next you said I warn't *bad*, only mischeevous and harum-scarum, and not any more responsible than—than—I think it was a colt, or something."

"And so it was! Well, goodness gracious! Go on, Tom!"

"And then you began to cry."

"So I did. So I did. Not the first time, neither. And then—"

"Then Mrs. Harper she began to cry, and said Joe was just the same and she wished she hadn't whipped him for taking cream when she'd throwed it out her own self—"

"Tom! The sperrit was upon you! You was a prophecying—that's what you was doing! Land alive, go on, Tom!"

"Then Sid he said—he said—"

"I don't think I said anything," said Sid.

"Yes you did, Sid," said Mary.

"Shut your heads and let Tom go on! What did he say, Tom?"

"He said—I *think* he said he hoped I was better off where I was gone to, but if I'd been better sometimes—"

"*There*, d'you hear that! It was his very words!"

"And you shut him up sharp."

"I lay I did! There must a been an angel there. There *was* an angel there, somewheres!"

"And Mrs. Harper told about Joe scaring her with a fire-cracker, and you told about Peter and the Pain-Killer—"

"Just as true as I live!"

"And then there was a whole lot of talk 'bout dragging the river for us, and 'bout having the funeral Sunday, and then you and old Miss Harper hugged and cried, and she went."

"It happened just so! It happened just so, as sure as I'm a sitting in these very tracks. Tom you couldn't told it more like, if you'd a seen it! And *then* what? Go on, Tom?"

"Then I thought you prayed for me—and I could see you and hear every word you said. And you went to bed, and I was so sorry that I took and wrote on a piece of sycamore bark, '*We ain't dead—we are only off being pirates,*' and put it on the table by the candle; and then you looked so good, laying there asleep, that I thought I went and leaned over and kissed you on the lips."

"Did you, Tom, *did* you! I just forgive you everything for that!" And she seized the boy in a crushing embrace that made him feel like the guiltiest of villains.

"It was very kind, even though it was only a—dream," Sid soliloquised just audibly.

"Shut up, Sid! A body does just the same in a dream as he'd do if he was awake. Here's a big Milum apple[9] I've been saving for you Tom, if you was ever found again—now go 'long to school. I'm thankful to the good God and Father of us all I've got you back, that's long-suffering and merciful to them that believe on Him and keep His word, though goodness knows I'm unworthy of it, but if only the worthy ones got His blessings and had His hand to help them over the rough places, there's few enough would smile here or ever enter into His rest when the long night comes. Go 'long Sid, Mary, Tom— take yourselves off—you've hendered me long enough."

The children left for school, and the old lady to call on Mrs. Harper and vanquish her realism with Tom's marvelous dream. Sid had better judgment than to utter the thought that was in his mind as he left the house. It was this: "Pretty thin—as long a dream as that, without any mistakes in it!"

What a hero Tom was become, now! He did not go skipping and prancing, but moved with a dignified swagger as became a pirate who felt that the public eye was on him. And indeed it was; he tried not to seem to see the looks or hear the remarks as he passed along, but they were food and drink to him. Smaller boys than himself flocked at his heels, as proud to be seen with him, and tolerated by him, as if he had been the drummer at the head of a procession or the elephant leading a menagerie into town. Boys of his own size pretended not to know he had been away at all; but they were consuming with envy, nevertheless. They would have given anything to have that swarthy sun-tanned skin of his, and his glittering notoriety; and Tom would not have parted with either for a circus.

At school the children made so much of him and of Joe, and delivered such eloquent admiration from their eyes, that the two heroes

9. A kind of sweet apple.

were not long in becoming insufferably "stuck-up." They began to tell their adventures to hungry listeners—but they only began; it was not a thing likely to have an end, with imaginations like theirs to furnish material. And finally, when they got out their pipes and went serenely puffing around, the very summit of glory was reached.

Tom decided that he could be independent of Becky Thatcher now. Glory was sufficient. He would live for glory. Now that he was distinguished, maybe she would be wanting to "make up." Well, let her—she should see that he could be as indifferent as some other people. Presently she arrived. Tom pretended not to see her. He moved away and joined a group of boys and girls and began to talk. Soon he observed that she was tripping gayly back and forth with flushed face and dancing eyes, pretending to be busy chasing school-mates, and screaming with laughter when she made a capture; but he noticed that she always made her captures in his vicinity, and that she seemed to cast a conscious eye in his direction at such times, too. It gratified all the vicious vanity that was in him; and so, instead of winning him it only "set him up" the more and made him the more diligent to avoid betraying that he knew she was about. Presently she gave over skylarking, and moved irresolutely about, sighing once or twice and glancing furtively and wistfully toward Tom. Then she observed that now Tom was talking more particularly to Amy Lawrence than to any one else. She felt a sharp pang and grew disturbed and uneasy at once. She tried to go away, but her feet were treacherous, and carried her to the group instead. She said to a girl almost at Tom's elbow—with sham vivacity:

"Why Mary Austin! you bad girl, why didn't you come to Sunday-school?"

"I did come—didn't you see me?"

"Why no! Did you? Where did you sit?"

"I was in Miss Peters's class, where I always go. I saw *you.*"

"Did you? Why it's funny I didn't see you. I wanted to tell you about the pic-nic."

"O, that's jolly. Who's going to give it?"

"My ma's going to let me have one."

"O, goody; I hope she'll let *me* come."

"Well she will. The pic-nic's for me. She'll let anybody come that I want, and I want you."

"That's ever so nice. When is it going to be?"

"By and by. Maybe about vacation."

"O, won't it be fun! You going to have all the girls and boys?"

"Yes, every one that's friends to me—or wants to be;" and she glanced ever so furtively at Tom, but he talked right along to Amy Lawrence about the terrible storm on the island, and how the lightning tore the great sycamore tree "all to flinders" while he was "stand-ing within three feet of it."

"O, may I come?" said Gracie Miller.

"Yes."

"And me?" said Sally Rogers.

"Yes."

"And me, too?" said Susy Harper. "And Joe?"

"Yes."

And so on, with clapping of joyful hands till all the group had begged for invitations but Tom and Amy. Then Tom turned coolly away, still talking, and took Amy with him. Becky's lip trembled and the tears came to her eyes; she hid these signs with a forced gayety and went on chattering, but the life had gone out of the pic-nic, now, and out of everything else; she got away as soon as she could and hid herself and had what her sex call "a good cry." Then she sat moody, with wounded pride till the bell rang. She roused up, now, with a vindictive cast in her eye, and gave her plaited tails a shake and said she knew what *she*'d do.

At recess Tom continued his flirtation with Amy with jubilant self-satisfaction. And he kept drifting about to find Becky and lacerate her with the performance. At last he spied her, but there was a sud-den falling of his mercury. She was sitting cosily on a little bench behind the school-house looking at a picture book with Alfred Tem-ple—and so absorbed were they, and their heads so close together over the book that they did not seem to be conscious of anything in the world beside. Jealousy ran red hot through Tom's veins. He began to hate himself for throwing away the chance Becky had offered for a reconciliation. He called himself a fool, and all the hard names he could think of. He wanted to cry with vexation. Amy chatted happily along, as they walked, for her heart was singing, but Tom's tongue had lost its function. He did not hear what Amy was saying, and whenever she paused expectantly he could only stammer an awkward assent, which was as often misplaced as otherwise. He kept drifting to the rear of the school-house, again and again, to sear his eye-balls with the hateful spectacle there. He could not help it. And it mad-dened him to see, as he thought he saw, that Becky Thatcher never once suspected that he was even in the land of the living. But she did see, nevertheless; and she knew she was winning her fight, too, and was glad to see him suffer as she had suffered.

Amy's happy prattle became intolerable. Tom hinted at things he had to attend to; things that must be done; and time was fleeting. But in vain—the girl chirped on. Tom thought, "O hang her, ain't I ever going to get rid of her?" At last he *must* be attending to those things—and she said artlessly that she would be "around" when school let out. And he hastened away, hating her for it.

"Any other boy!" Tom thought, grating his teeth. "Any boy in the whole town but that Saint Louis smarty that thinks he dresses so fine and is aristocracy! O, all right, I licked you the first day you ever saw this town, mister, and I'll lick you again! You just wait till I catch you out! I'll just take and—"

And he went through the motions of thrashing an imaginary boy—pummeling the air, and kicking and gouging. "Oh, you do, do you? You holler 'nough, do you? Now, then, let that learn you!" And so the imaginary flogging was finished to his satisfaction.

Tom fled home at noon. His conscience could not endure any more of Amy's grateful happiness, and his jealousy could bear no more of the other distress. Becky resumed her picture-inspections with Alfred, but as the minutes dragged along and no Tom came to suffer, her triumph began to cloud and she lost interest; gravity and absent-mindedness followed, and then melancholy; two or three times she pricked up her ear at a footstep, but it was a false hope; no Tom came. At last she grew entirely miserable and wished she hadn't carried it so far. When poor Alfred, seeing that he was losing her, he did not know how, and kept exclaiming: "O here's a jolly one! look at this!" she lost patience at last, and said, "Oh, don't bother me! I don't care for them!" and burst into tears, and got up and walked away.

Alfred dropped alongside and was going to try to comfort her, but she said:

"Go away and leave me alone, can't you! I hate you!"

So the boy halted, wondering what he could have done—for she had said she would look at pictures all through the nooning—and she walked on, crying. Then Alfred went musing into the deserted school-house. He was humiliated and angry. He easily guessed his way to the truth—the girl had simply made a convenience of him to vent her spite upon Tom Sawyer. He was far from hating Tom the less when this thought occurred to him. He wished there was some way to get that boy into trouble without much risk to himself. Tom's spelling book fell under his eye. Here was his opportunity. He gratefully opened to the lesson for the afternoon and poured ink upon the page.

Becky, glancing in at a window behind him at the moment, saw the act, and moved on, without discovering herself. She started homeward, now, intending to find Tom and tell him; Tom would be thankful and their troubles would be healed. Before she was half way home, however, she had changed her mind. The thought of Tom's treatment of her when she was talking about her pic-nic came scorching back and filled her with shame. She resolved to let him get whipped on the damaged spelling-book's account, and to hate him forever, into the bargain.

Chapter XIX.

Tom arrived at home in a dreary mood, and the first thing his aunt said to him showed him that he had brought his sorrows to an unpromising market:

"Tom, I've a notion to skin you alive!"

"Auntie, what have I done?"

"Well, you've done enough. Here I go over to Sereny Harper, like an old softy, expecting I'm going to make her believe all that rubbage about that dream, when lo and behold you she'd found out from Joe that you was over here and heard all the talk we had that night. Tom I don't know what is to become of a boy that will act like that. It makes me feel so bad to think you could let me go to Sereny Harper and make such a fool of myself and never say a word."

This was a new aspect of the thing. His smartness of the morning had seemed to Tom a good joke before, and very ingenious. It merely looked mean and shabby now. He hung his head and could not think of anything to say for a moment. Then he said:

"Auntie, I wish I hadn't done it—but I didn't think."

"O, child you never think. You never think of anything but your own selfishness. You could think to come all the way over here from Jackson's Island in the night to laugh at our troubles, and you could think to fool me with a lie about a dream; but you couldn't ever think to pity us and save us from sorrow."

"Auntie, I know now it was mean, but I didn't mean to be mean. I didn't, honest. And besides I didn't come over here to laugh at you that night."

"What did you come for, then?"

"It was to tell you not to be uneasy about us, because we hadn't got drowned."

"Tom, Tom, I would be the thankfullest soul in this world if I could believe you ever had as good a thought as that, but you know you never did—and I know it, Tom."

"Indeed and 'deed I did, auntie—I wish I may never stir if I didn't."

"O, Tom, don't lie—don't do it. It only makes things a hundred times worse."

"It ain't a lie, auntie, it's the truth. I wanted to keep you from grieving—that was all that made me come."

"I'd give the whole world to believe that—it would cover up a power of sins Tom. I'd 'most be glad you'd run off and acted so bad. But it ain't reasonable; because, why didn't you tell me, child?"

"Why, you see, auntie, when you got to talking about the funeral, I just got all full of the idea of our coming and hiding in the church, and I couldn't somehow bear to spoil it. So I just put the bark back in my pocket and kept mum."

"What bark?"

"The bark I had wrote on to tell you we'd gone pirating. I wish, now, you'd waked up when I kissed you—I do, honest."

The hard lines in his aunt's face relaxed and a sudden tenderness dawned in her eyes.

"*Did* you kiss me, Tom?"

"Why yes I did."

"Are you sure you did, Tom?"

"Why yes I did, auntie—certain sure."

"What did you kiss me for, Tom?"

"Because I loved you so, and you laid there moaning and I was so sorry."

The words sounded like truth. The old lady could not hide a tremor in her voice when she said:

"Kiss me again, Tom!—and be off with you to school, now, and don't bother me any more."

The moment he was gone, she ran to a closet and got out the ruin of a jacket which Tom had gone pirating in. Then she stopped, with it in her hand, and said to herself:

"No, I don't dare. Poor boy, I reckon he's lied about it—but it's a blessed, blessed lie, there's such comfort come from it. I hope the Lord—I *know* the Lord will forgive him, because it was such good-heartedness in him to tell it. But I don't want to find out it's a lie. I won't look."

She put the jacket away, and stood by musing a minute. Twice she put out her hand to take the garment again, and twice she refrained. Once more she ventured, and this time she fortified herself with the thought: "It's a good lie—it's a good lie—I won't let it grieve me." So she sought the jacket pocket. A moment later she was reading Tom's piece of bark through flowing tears and saying: "I could forgive the boy, now, if he'd committed a million sins!"

Chapter XX.

THERE was something about Aunt Polly's manner, when she kissed Tom, that swept away his low spirits and made him light-hearted and happy again. He started to school and had the luck of coming upon Becky Thatcher at the head of Meadow Lane. His mood always determined his manner. Without a moment's hesitation he ran to her and said:

"I acted mighty mean to-day, Becky, and I'm so sorry. I won't ever, ever do that way again, as long as ever I live—please make up, won't you?"

The girl stopped and looked him scornfully in the face:

"I'll thank you to keep yourself *to* yourself, Mr. Thomas Sawyer. I'll never speak to you again."

She tossed her head and passed on. Tom was so stunned that he had not even presence of mind enough to say "Who cares, Miss Smarty?" until the right time to say it had gone by. So he said nothing. But he was in a fine rage, nevertheless. He moped into the school-yard wishing she were a boy, and imagining how he would trounce her if she were. He presently encountered her and delivered a stinging remark as he passed. She hurled one in return, and the angry breach was complete. It seemed to Becky, in her hot resentment, that she could hardly wait for school to "take in," she was so impatient to see Tom flogged for the injured spelling-book. If she had had any lingering notion of exposing Alfred Temple, Tom's offensive fling had driven it entirely away.

Poor girl, she did not know how fast she was nearing trouble herself. The master, Mr. Dobbins, had reached middle age with an unsatisfied ambition. The darling of his desires was, to be a doctor, but poverty had decreed that he should be nothing higher than a village schoolmaster. Every day he took a mysterious book out of his desk and absorbed himself in it at times when no classes were reciting. He kept that book under lock and key. There was not an urchin in school but was perishing to have a glimpse of it, but the chance never came. Every boy and girl had a theory about the nature of that book; but no two theories were alike, and there was no way of getting at the facts in the case. Now, as Becky was passing by the desk, which stood near the door, she noticed that the key was in the lock! It was a precious moment. She glanced around; found herself alone, and the next instant she had the book in her hands. The title-page—Professor somebody's "Anatomy"—carried no information to her mind; so she began to turn the leaves. She came at once upon a handsomely engraved and colored frontispiece—a human figure, stark naked. At that moment a shadow fell on the page and Tom Sawyer stepped in at the door, and caught a glimpse of the picture. Becky snatched at the book to close it, and had the hard luck to tear the pictured page half down the middle. She thrust the volume into the desk, turned the key, and burst out crying with shame and vexation.

"Tom Sawyer, you are just as mean as you can be, to sneak up on a person and look at what they're looking at."

"How could *I* know you was looking at anything?"

"You ought to be ashamed of yourself Tom Sawyer; you know you're going to tell on me, and O, what shall I do, what shall I do! I'll be whipped, and I never was whipped in school."

Then she stamped her little foot and said:

"*Be* so mean if you want to! *I* know something that's going to happen. You just wait and you'll see! Hateful, hateful, hateful!"— and she flung out of the house with a new explosion of crying.

Tom stood still, rather flustered by this onslaught. Presently he said to himself:

"What a curious kind of a fool a girl is. Never been licked in school! Shucks, what's a licking! That's just like a girl—they're so thin-skinned and chicken-hearted. Well, of course *I* ain't going to tell old Dobbins on this little fool, because there's other ways of getting even on her, that ain't so mean; but what of it? Old Dobbins will ask who it was tore his book. Nobody'll answer. Then he'll do just the way he always does—ask first one and then t'other, and when he comes to the right girl he'll know it, without any telling. Girls' faces always tell on them. They ain't got any backbone. She'll get licked. Well, it's a kind of a tight place for Becky Thatcher, because there ain't any way out of it." Tom conned[1] the thing a moment longer, and then added: "All right, though; she'd like to see me in just such a fix—let her sweat it out!"

Tom joined the mob of skylarking scholars outside. In a few moments the master arrived and school "took in." Tom did not feel a strong interest in his studies. Every time he stole a glance at the girls' side of the room Becky's face troubled him. Considering all things, he did not want to pity her, and yet it was all he could do to help it. He could get up no exultation that was really worthy the name. Presently the spelling-book discovery was made, and Tom's mind was entirely full of his own matters for a while after that. Becky roused up from her lethargy of distress and showed good interest in the proceedings. She did not expect that Tom could get out of his trouble by denying that he spilt the ink on the book himself; and she was right. The denial only seemed to make the thing worse for Tom. Becky supposed she would be glad of that, and she tried to believe she was glad of it, but she found she was not certain. When the worst came to the worst, she had an impulse to get up and tell on Alfred Temple, but she made an effort and forced herself to keep still—because, said she to herself, "he'll tell about me tearing the picture, sure. I wouldn't say a word, not to save his life!"

Tom took his whipping and went back to his seat not at all broken-hearted, for he thought it was possible that he had unknowingly upset the ink on the spelling-book himself, in some skylarking bout—

1. Studied.

he had denied it for form's sake and because it was custom, and had stuck to the denial from principle.

A whole hour drifted by, the master sat nodding in his throne, the air was drowsy with the hum of study. By and by, Mr. Dobbins straightened himself up, yawned, then unlocked his desk, and reached for his book, but seemed undecided whether to take it out or leave it. Most of the pupils glanced up languidly, but there were two among them that watched his movements with intent eyes. Mr. Dobbins fingered his book absently for a while, then took it out and settled himself in his chair to read! Tom shot a glance at Becky. He had seen a hunted and helpless rabbit look as she did, with a gun leveled at its head. Instantly he forgot his quarrel with her. Quick— something must be done!—done in a flash, too! But the very imminence of the emergency paralyzed his invention. Good!—he had an inspiration! He would run and snatch the book, spring through the door and fly! But his resolution shook for one little instant, and the chance was lost—the master opened the volume. If Tom only had the wasted opportunity back again! Too late; there was no help for Becky now, he said. The next moment the master faced the school. Every eye sunk under his gaze. There was that in it which smote even the innocent with fear. There was silence while one might count ten; the master was gathering his wrath. Then he spoke:

"Who tore this book?"

There was not a sound. One could have heard a pin drop. The stillness continued; the master searched face after face for signs of guilt.

"Benjamin Rogers, did you tear this book?"

A denial. Another pause.

"Joseph Harper, did you?"

Another denial. Tom's uneasiness grew more and more intense under the slow torture of these proceedings. The master scanned the ranks of boys—considered a while, then turned to the girls:

"Amy Lawrence?"

A shake of the head.

"Gracie Miller?"

The same sign.

"Susan Harper, did you do this?"

Another negative. The next girl was Becky Thatcher. Tom was trembling from head to foot with excitement and a sense of the hopelessness of the situation.

"Rebecca Thatcher," [Tom glanced at her face—it was white with terror,]—"did you tear—no, look me in the face"—[her hands rose in appeal]—"did you tear this book?"

A thought shot like lightning through Tom's brain. He sprang to his feet and shouted—

"*I* done it!"

The school stared in perplexity at this incredible folly. Tom stood a moment, to gather his dismembered faculties; and when he stepped forward to go to his punishment the surprise, the gratitude, the adoration that shone upon him out of poor Becky's eyes seemed pay enough for a hundred floggings. Inspired by the splendor of his own act, he took without an outcry the most merciless flaying that even Mr. Dobbins had ever administered; and also received with indifference the added cruelty of a command to remain two hours after school should be dismissed—for he knew who would wait for him outside till his captivity was done, and not count the tedious time as loss, either.

Tom went to bed that night planning vengeance against Alfred Temple; for with shame and repentance Becky had told him all, not forgetting her own treachery; but even the longing for vengeance had to give way, soon, to pleasanter musings, and he fell asleep at last, with Becky's latest words lingering dreamily in his ear—

"Tom, how *could* you be so noble!"

Chapter XXI.

VACATION was approaching. The schoolmaster, always severe, grew severer and more exacting than ever, for he wanted the school to make a good showing on "Examination" day. His rod and his ferule were seldom idle now—at least among the smaller pupils. Only the biggest boys, and young ladies of eighteen and twenty escaped lashing. Mr. Dobbins's lashings were very vigorous ones, too; for although he carried, under his wig, a perfectly bald and shiny head, he had only reached middle age and there was no sign of feebleness in his muscle. As the great day approached, all the tyranny that was in him came to the surface; he seemed to take a vindictive pleasure in punishing the least shortcomings. The consequence was, that the smaller boys spent their days in terror and suffering and their nights in plotting revenge. They threw away no opportunity to do the master a mischief. But he kept ahead all the time. The retribution that followed every vengeful success was so sweeping and majestic that the boys always retired from the field badly worsted. At last they conspired together and hit upon a plan that promised a dazzling victory. They swore-in the sign-painter's boy, told him the scheme, and asked his help. He had his own reasons for being delighted, for the master boarded in his father's family and had given the boy ample cause to hate him. The master's wife would go on a visit to the country in a few days, and there would be nothing to interfere with the plan; the master always prepared himself for great occasions by getting pretty well fuddled, and the sign-painter's boy said that when the dominie[2] had reached the proper condition on Examination Evening he would "manage the thing" while he napped in his chair; then he would have him awakened at the right time and hurried away to school.

In the fulness of time the interesting occasion arrived. At eight in the evening the schoolhouse was brilliantly lighted, and adorned with wreaths and festoons of foliage and flowers. The master sat throned in his great chair upon a raised platform, with his blackboard behind him. He was looking tolerably mellow. Three rows of benches on each side and six rows in front of him were occupied by the dignitaries of the town and by the parents of the pupils. To his left, back of the rows of citizens, was a spacious temporary platform upon which were seated the scholars who were to take part in the exercises of the evening; rows of small boys, washed and dressed to an intolerable state of discomfort; rows of gawky big boys; snow-banks of girls and young ladies clad in lawn and muslin and conspicuously conscious of their bare arms, their grandmothers' ancient trinkets, their bits of pink and blue ribbon and the flowers in their hair. All the rest of the house was filled with non-participating scholars.

The exercises began. A very little boy stood up and sheepishly recited, "You'd scarce expect one of my age to speak in public on the stage, etc"[3]—accompanying himself with the painfully exact and spasmodic gestures which a machine might have used—supposing the machine to be a trifle out of order. But he got through safely, though cruelly scared, and got a fine round of applause when he made his manufactured bow and retired.

A little shame-faced girl lisped "Mary had a little lamb, etc.," performed a compassion-inspiring curtsy, got her meed of applause, and sat down flushed and happy.

Tom Sawyer stepped forward with conceited confidence and soared into the unquenchable and indestructible "Give me liberty or give me death" speech,[4] with fine fury and frantic gesticulation, and broke down in the middle of it. A ghastly stage-fright seized him, his legs quaked under him and he was like to choke. True, he had the manifest sympathy of the house—but he had the house's silence, too, which was even worse than its sympathy. The master frowned, and this completed the disaster. Tom struggled a while and then retired, utterly defeated. There was a weak attempt at applause, but it died early.

---

2. Teacher. "Fuddled": confused or drunk.
3. Poem by David Everett (1769–1813).
4. By Patrick Henry to the Virginia House of Delegates in 1775, on the eve of the American Revolution.

"The Boy Stood on the Burning Deck" followed; also "The Assyrian Came Down," and other declamatory gems.[5] Then there were reading exercises, and a spelling fight. The meager Latin class recited with honor. The prime feature of the evening was in order, now—original "compositions" by the young ladies. Each in her turn stepped forward to the edge of the platform, cleared her throat, held up her manuscript (tied with dainty ribbon), and proceeded to read, with labored attention to "expression" and punctuation. The themes were the same that had been illuminated upon similar occasions by their mothers before them, their grandmothers, and doubtless all their ancestors in the female line clear back to the Crusades. "Friendship" was one; "Memories of Other Days;" "Religion in History;" "Dream Land;" "The Advantages of Culture;" "Forms of Political Government Compared and Contrasted;" "Melancholy;" "Filial Love;" "Heart Longings," etc., etc.

A prevalent feature in these compositions was a nursed and petted melancholy; another was a wasteful and opulent gush of "fine language;" another was a tendency to lug in by the ears particularly prized words and phrases until they were worn entirely out; and a peculiarity that conspicuously marked and marred them was the inveterate and intolerable sermon that wagged its crippled tail at the end of each and every one of them. No matter what the subject might be, a brain-racking effort was made to squirm it into some aspect or other that the moral and religious mind could contemplate with edification.[6] The glaring insincerity of these sermons was not sufficient to compass the banishment of the fashion from the schools, and it is not sufficient to-day; it never will be sufficient while the world stands, perhaps. There is no school in all our land where the young ladies do not feel obliged to close their compositions with a sermon; and you will find that the sermon of the most frivolous and least religious girl in the school is always the longest and the most relentlessly pious. But enough of this. Homely truth is unpalatable.

Let us return to the "Examination." The first composition that was read was one entitled "Is this, then, Life?" Perhaps the reader can endure an extract from it:

> "In the common walks of life, with what delightful emotions does the youthful mind look forward to some anticipated scene of festivity! Imagination is busy sketching rose-tinted pictures of joy. In fancy, the voluptuous votary of fashion sees herself amid the festive throng, 'the observed of all observers.'[7] Her

5. Poems by Felicia Hemans (1793–1835) and George Gordon Lord Byron (1788–1824), respectively.
6. Improvement.
7. Ophelia thus describes how all eyes are drawn to Hamlet (*Hamlet* 3.1.154). "Voluptuous votary": luxurious devotee.

graceful form, arrayed in snowy robes, is whirling through the mazes of the joyous dance; her eye is brightest, her step is lightest in the gay assembly.

"In such delicious fancies time quickly glides by, and the welcome hour arrives for her entrance into the elysian world, of which she has had such bright dreams. How fairy-like does every thing appear to her enchanted vision! each new scene is more charming than the last. But after a while she finds that beneath this goodly exterior, all is vanity: the flattery which once charmed her soul, now grates harshly upon her ear; the ballroom has lost its charms; and with wasted health and imbittered heart, she turns away with the conviction that earthly pleasures cannot satisfy the longings of the soul!"

And so forth and so on. There was a buzz of gratification from time to time during the reading, accompanied by whispered ejaculations of "How sweet!" "How eloquent!" "So true!" etc., and after the thing had closed with a peculiarly afflicting sermon the applause was enthusiastic.

Then arose a slim, melancholy girl, whose face had the "interesting" paleness that comes of pills and indigestion, and read a "poem." Two stanzas of it will do:

A MISSOURI MAIDEN'S FAREWELL TO ALABAMA.

ALABAMA, good-bye! I love thee well!
　　But yet for awhile do I leave thee now!
Sad, yes, sad thoughts of thee my heart doth swell,
　　And burning recollections throng my brow!
For I have wandered through thy flowery woods;
　　Have roamed and read near Tallapoosa's stream;
Have listened to Tallassee's[8] warring floods,
　　And wooed on Coosa's side Aurora's[9] beam.

Yet shame I not to bear an o'er-full heart,
　　Nor blush to turn behind my tearful eyes;
'Tis from no stranger land I now must part,
　　'Tis to no strangers left I yield these sighs.
Welcome and home were mine within this State,
　　Whose vales I leave—whose spires fade fast from me;
And cold must be mine eyes, and heart, and tête,
　　When, dear Alabama! they turn cold on thee!

There were very few there who knew what "*tête*"[1] meant, but the poem was very satisfactory, nevertheless.

8. An Alabama town on the Tallapoosa River.
9. Roman goddess of the dawn. Coosa is a river.
1. Head (French).

Next appeared a dark complexioned, black eyed, black haired young lady, who paused an impressive moment, assumed a tragic expression and began to read in a measured, solemn tone.

A VISION.

Dark and tempestuous was night. Around the throne on high not a single star quivered; but the deep intonations of the heavy thunder constantly vibrated upon the ear; whilst the terrific lightning revelled in angry mood through the cloudy chambers of heaven, seeming to scorn the power exerted over its terror by the illustrious Franklin! Even the boisterous winds unanimously came forth from their mystic homes, and blustered about as if to enhance by their aid the wildness of the scene.

At such a time, so dark, so dreary, for human sympathy my very spirit sighed; but instead thereof,

"My dearest friend, my counsellor, my comforter and guide—
My joy in grief, my second bliss in joy," came to my side.[2]

She moved like one of those bright beings pictured in the sunny walks of fancy's Eden by the romantic and young, a queen of beauty unadorned save by her own transcendent loveliness. So soft was her step, it failed to make even a sound, and but for the magical thrill imparted by her genial touch, as other unobtrusive beauties, she would have glided away unperceived—unsought. A strange sadness rested upon her features, like icy tears upon the robe of December, as she pointed to the contending elements without, and bade me contemplate the two beings presented.

This nightmare occupied some ten pages of manuscript and wound up with a sermon so destructive of all hope to non-Presbyterians that it took the first prize. This composition was considered to be the very finest effort of the evening. The mayor of the village, in delivering the prize to the author of it, made a warm speech in which he said that it was by far the most "eloquent" thing he had ever listened to, and that Daniel Webster[3] himself might well be proud of it.

It may be remarked, in passing, that the number of compositions in which the word "beauteous" was over-fondled, and human experience referred to as "life's page," was up to the usual average.

Now the master, mellow almost to the verge of geniality, put his chair aside, turned his back to the audience, and began to draw a map of America on the blackboard, to exercise the geography class

2. Based loosely on a passage in *The Course of Time* (1827) by Robert Pollok.
3. U.S. statesman (1782–1852), known for his eloquent—fluent and effective—speeches.

upon. But he made a sad business of it with his unsteady hand, and a smothered titter rippled over the house. He knew what the matter was, and set himself to right it. He sponged out lines and re-made them; but he only distorted them more than ever, and the tittering was more pronounced. He threw his entire attention upon his work, now, as if determined not to be put down by the mirth. He felt that all eyes were fastened upon him; he imagined he was succeeding, and yet the tittering continued; it even manifestly increased. And well it might. There was a garret above, pierced with a scuttle[4] over his head; down through this scuttle came a cat, suspended around the haunches by a string; she had a rag tied about her head and jaws to keep her from mewing; as she slowly descended she curved upward and clawed at the string, she swung downward and clawed at the intangible air. The tittering rose higher and higher—the cat was within six inches of the absorbed teacher's head—down, down, a little lower, and she grabbed his wig with her desperate claws, clung to it and was snatched up into the garret in an instant with her trophy still in her possession! And how the light did blaze abroad from the master's bald pate—for the sign-painter's boy had *gilded* it![5]

That broke up the meeting. The boys were avenged. Vacation had come.[6]

Chapter XXII.

TOM joined the new order of Cadets of Temperance,[7] being attracted by the showy character of their "regalia." He promised to abstain from smoking, chewing and profanity as long as he remained a member. Now he found out a new thing—namely, that to promise not to do a thing is the surest way in the world to make a body want to go and do that very thing. Tom soon found himself tormented with a desire to drink and swear; the desire grew to be so intense that nothing but the hope of a chance to display himself in his red sash kept him from withdrawing from the order. Fourth of July was coming; but he soon gave that up—gave it up before he had worn his shackles over forty-eight hours—and fixed his hopes upon old Judge Frazer, justice of the peace, who was apparently on his death-bed and would have a big public funeral, since he was so high an official. During

4. Opening with a lid.
5. Painted it gold.
6. "NOTE.—The pretended 'compositions' quoted in this chapter are taken without alteration from a volume entitled 'Prose and Poetry, by a Western Lady'—but they are exactly and precisely after the school-girl pattern and hence are much happier than any mere imitations could be" [Twain's note].
7. Organization of young people who promised, usually, not to drink liquor; Twain once belonged to such a society and pledged not to use tobacco.

three days Tom was deeply concerned about the Judge's condition and hungry for news of it. Sometimes his hopes ran high—so high that he would venture to get out his regalia and practice before the looking-glass. But the Judge had a most discouraging way of fluctuating. At last he was pronounced upon the mend—and then convalescent. Tom was disgusted; and felt a sense of injury, too. He handed in his resignation at once—and that night the Judge suffered a relapse and died. Tom resolved that he would never trust a man like that again. The funeral was a fine thing. The Cadets paraded in a style calculated to kill the late member with envy. Tom was a free boy again, however—there was something in that. He could drink and swear, now—but found to his surprise that he did not want to. The simple fact that he could, took the desire away, and the charm of it.

Tom presently wondered to find that his coveted vacation was beginning to hang a little heavily on his hands.

He attempted a diary—but nothing happened during three days, and so he abandoned it.

The first of all the negro minstrel shows[8] came to town, and made a sensation. Tom and Joe Harper got up a band of performers and were happy for two days.

Even the Glorious Fourth was in some sense a failure, for it rained hard, there was no procession in consequence, and the greatest man in the world (as Tom supposed) Mr. Benton,[9] an actual United States Senator, proved an overwhelming disappointment—for he was not twenty-five feet high, nor even anywhere in the neighborhood of it.

A circus came. The boys played circus for three days afterward in tents made of rag carpeting—admission, three pins for boys, two for girls—and then circusing was abandoned.

A phrenologist and a mesmerizer[1] came—and went again and left the village duller and drearier than ever.

There were some boys-and-girls' parties, but they were so few and so delightful that they only made the aching voids between ache the harder.

Becky Thatcher was gone to her Constantinople home to stay with her parents during vacation—so there was no bright side to life anywhere.

The dreadful secret of the murder was a chronic misery. It was a very cancer for permanency and pain.

Then came the measles.

During two long weeks Tom lay a prisoner, dead to the world and its happenings. He was very ill, he was interested in nothing. When

8. Entertainments in which whites performed in blackface.
9. Thomas Hart Benton (1782–1858), first U.S. senator from Missouri (1821–51).
1. Hypnotist.

he got upon his feet at last and moved feebly down town, a melancholy change had come over everything and every creature. There had been a "revival,"[2] and everybody had "got religion;" not only the adults, but even the boys and girls. Tom went about, hoping against hope for the sight of one blessed sinful face, but disappointment crossed him everywhere. He found Joe Harper studying a Testament, and turned sadly away from the depressing spectacle. He sought Ben Rogers, and found him visiting the poor with a basket of tracts. He hunted up Jim Hollis, who called his attention to the precious blessing of his late measles as a warning. Every boy he encountered added another ton to his depression; and when, in desperation, he flew for refuge at last to the bosom of Huckleberry Finn and was received with a scriptural quotation, his heart broke and he crept home and to bed realizing that he alone of all the town was lost, forever and forever.

And that night there came on a terrific storm, with driving rain, awful claps of thunder and blinding sheets of lightning. He covered his head with the bedclothes and waited in a horror of suspense for his doom; for he had not the shadow of a doubt that all this hubbub was about him. He believed he had taxed the forbearance of the powers above to the extremity of endurance and that this was the result. It might have seemed to him a waste of pomp and ammunition to kill a bug with a battery of artillery, but there seemed nothing incongruous about the getting up such an expensive thunderstorm as this to knock the turf from under an insect like himself.

By and by the tempest spent itself and died without accomplishing its object. The boy's first impulse was to be grateful, and reform. His second was to wait—for there might not be any more storms.

The next day the doctors were back; Tom had relapsed. The three weeks he spent on his back this time seemed an entire age. When he got abroad at last he was hardly grateful that he had been spared, remembering how lonely was his estate, how companionless and forlorn he was. He drifted listlessly down the street and found Jim Hollis acting as judge in a juvenile court that was trying a cat for murder, in the presence of her victim, a bird. He found Joe Harper and Huck Finn up an alley eating a stolen melon. Poor lads! they—like Tom— had suffered a relapse.

Chapter XXIII.

AT last the sleepy atmosphere was stirred—and vigorously: the murder trial came on in the court. It became the absorbing topic of

2. Religious meeting to reawaken faith.

village talk immediately. Tom could not get away from it. Every reference to the murder sent a shudder to his heart, for his troubled conscience and his fears almost persuaded him that these remarks were put forth in his hearing as "feelers;" he did not see how he could be suspected of knowing anything about the murder, but still he could not be comfortable in the midst of this gossip. It kept him in a cold shiver all the time. He took Huck to a lonely place to have a talk with him. It would be some relief to unseal his tongue for a little while; to divide his burden of distress with another sufferer. Moreover, he wanted to assure himself that Huck had remained discreet.

"Huck, have you ever told anybody about—that?"

" 'Bout what?"

"You know what."

"Oh—'course I haven't."

"Never a word?"

"Never a solitry word, so help me. What makes you ask?"

"Well, I was afeard."

"Why Tom Sawyer, we wouldn't be alive two days if that got found out. *You* know that."

Tom felt more comfortable. After a pause:

"Huck, they couldn't anybody get you to tell, could they?"

"Get me to tell? Why if I wanted that half-breed devil to drownd me they could get me to tell. They ain't no different way."

"Well, that's all right, then. I reckon we're safe as long as we keep mum. But let's swear again, anyway. It's more surer."

"I'm agreed."

So they swore again with dread solemnities.

"What is the talk around, Huck? I've heard a power of it."

"Talk? Well, it's just Muff Potter, Muff Potter, Muff Potter all the time. It keeps me in a sweat, constant, so's I want to hide som'ers."

"That's just the same way they go on round me. I reckon he's a goner. Don't you feel sorry for him, sometimes?"

"Most always—most always. He ain't no account; but then he hain't ever done anything to hurt anybody. Just fishes a little, to get money to get drunk on—and loafs around considerable; but lord we all do that—leastways most of us,—preachers and such like. But he's kind of good—he give me half a fish, once, when there warn't enough for two; and lots of times he's kind of stood by me when I was out of luck."

"Well, he's mended kites for me, Huck, and knitted hooks on to my line. I wish we could get him out of there."

"My! we couldn't get him out Tom. And besides, 'twouldn't do any good; they'd ketch him again."

"Yes—so they would. But I hate to hear 'em abuse him so like the dickens when he never done—that."

"I do too, Tom. Lord, I hear 'em say he's the bloodiest looking villain in this country, and they wonder he wasn't ever hung before."

"Yes, they talk like that, all the time. I've heard 'em say that if he was to get free they'd lynch him."

"And they'd do it, too."

The boys had a long talk, but it brought them little comfort. As the twilight drew on, they found themselves hanging about the neighborhood of the little isolated jail, perhaps with an undefined hope that something would happen that might clear away their difficulties. But nothing happened; there seemed to be no angels or fairies interested in this luckless captive.

The boys did as they had often done before—went to the cell grating and gave Potter some tobacco and matches. He was on the ground floor and there were no guards.

His gratitude for their gifts had always smote their consciences before—it cut deeper than ever, this time. They felt cowardly and treacherous to the last degree when Potter said:

"You've ben mighty good to me, boys—better'n anybody else in this town. And I don't forget it, I don't. Often I says to myself, says I, 'I used to mend all the boys' kites and things, and show 'em where the good fishin' places was, and befriend 'em what I could, and now they've all forgot old Muff when he's in trouble; but Tom don't, and Huck don't—*they* don't forget him,' says I, 'and I don't forget them.' Well, boys, I done an awful thing—drunk and crazy at the time— that's the only way I account for it—and now I got to swing for it, and it's right. Right, and *best,* too I reckon—hope so, anyway. Well, we won't talk about that. I don't want to make *you* feel bad; you've befriended me. But what I want to say, is, don't *you* ever get drunk— then you won't ever get here. Stand a little furder west—so—that's it; it's a prime comfort to see faces that's friendly when a body's in such a muck of trouble,—and there don't none come here but yourn. Good friendly faces—good friendly faces. Git up on one another's backs and let me touch 'em. That's it. Shake hands—yourn'll come through the bars, but mine's too big. Little hands, and weak—but they've helped Muff Potter a power, and they'd help him more if they could."

Tom went home miserable, and his dreams that night were full of horrors. The next day and the day after, he hung about the court room, drawn by an almost irresistible impulse to go in, but forcing himself to stay out. Huck was having the same experience. They studiously avoided each other. Each wandered away, from time to time, but the same dismal fascination always brought them back presently. Tom kept his ears open when idlers sauntered out of the court room, but invariably heard distressing news—the toils were closing more and more relentlessly around poor Potter. At the end of the second day the village talk was to the effect that Injun Joe's evidence stood firm and unshaken, and that there was not the slightest question as to what the jury's verdict would be.

Tom was out late, that night, and came to bed through the window. He was in a tremendous state of excitement. It was hours before he got to sleep. All the village flocked to the Court house the next morning, for this was to be the great day. Both sexes were about equally represented in the packed audience. After a long wait the jury filed in and took their places; shortly afterward, Potter, pale and haggard, timid and hopeless, was brought in, with chains upon him, and seated where all the curious eyes could stare at him; no less conspicuous was Injun Joe, stolid as ever. There was another pause, and then the judge arrived and the sheriff proclaimed the opening of the court. The usual whisperings among the lawyers and gathering together of papers followed. These details and accompanying delays worked up an atmosphere of preparation that was as impressive as it was fascinating.

Now a witness was called who testified that he found Muff Potter washing in the brook, at an early hour of the morning that the murder was discovered, and that he immediately sneaked away. After some further questioning, counsel for the prosecution said—

"Take the witness."

The prisoner raised his eyes for a moment, but dropped them again when his own counsel said—

"I have no questions to ask him."

The next witness proved the finding of the knife near the corpse. Counsel for the prosecution said:

"Take the witness."

"I have no questions to ask him," Potter's lawyer replied.

A third witness swore he had often seen the knife in Potter's possession.

"Take the witness."

Counsel for Potter declined to question him. The faces of the audience began to betray annoyance. Did this attorney mean to throw away his client's life without an effort?

Several witnesses deposed concerning Potter's guilty behavior when brought to the scene of the murder. They were allowed to leave the stand without being cross-questioned.

Every detail of the damaging circumstances that occurred in the graveyard upon that morning which all present remembered so well, was brought out by credible witnesses, but none of them were cross-examined by Potter's lawyer. The perplexity and dissatisfaction of the house expressed itself in murmurs and provoked a reproof from the bench. Counsel for the prosecution now said:

"By the oaths of citizens whose simple word is above suspicion, we have fastened this awful crime beyond all possibility of question, upon the unhappy prisoner at the bar. We rest our case here."

A groan escaped from poor Potter, and he put his face in his hands and rocked his body softly to and fro, while a painful silence reigned in the courtroom. Many men were moved, and many women's compassion testified itself in tears. Counsel for the defence rose and said:

"Your honor, in our remarks at the opening of this trial, we foreshadowed our purpose to prove that our client did this fearful deed while under the influence of a blind and irresponsible delirium produced by drink. We have changed our mind. We shall not offer that plea." [Then to the clerk]: "Call Thomas Sawyer!"

A puzzled amazement awoke in every face in the house, not even excepting Potter's. Every eye fastened itself with wondering interest upon Tom as he rose and took his place upon the stand. The boy looked wild enough, for he was badly scared. The oath was administered.

"Thomas Sawyer, where were you on the seventeenth of June, about the hour of midnight?"

Tom glanced at Injun Joe's iron face and his tongue failed him. The audience listened breathless, but the words refused to come. After a few moments, however, the boy got a little of his strength back, and managed to put enough of it into his voice to make part of the house hear:

"In the graveyard!"

"A little bit louder, please. Don't be afraid. You were—"

"In the graveyard."

A contemptuous smile flitted across Injun Joe's face.

"Were you anywhere near Horse Williams's grave?"

"Yes, sir."

"Speak up—just a trifle louder. How near were you?"

"Near as I am to you."

"Were you hidden, or not?"

"I was hid."

"Where?"

"Behind the elms that's on the edge of the grave."

Injun Joe gave a barely perceptible start.

"Any one with you?"

"Yes, sir. I went there with—"

"Wait—wait a moment. Never mind mentioning your companion's name. We will produce him at the proper time. Did you carry anything there with you?"

Tom hesitated and looked confused.

"Speak out my boy—don't be diffident. The truth is always respectable. What did you take there?"

"Only a—a—dead cat."

There was a ripple of mirth, which the court checked.

"We will produce the skeleton of that cat. Now my boy, tell us everything that occurred—tell it in your own way—don't skip anything, and don't be afraid."

Tom began—hesitatingly at first, but as he warmed to his subject his words flowed more and more easily; in a little while every sound ceased but his own voice; every eye fixed itself upon him; with parted lips and bated breath the audience hung upon his words, taking no note of time, rapt in the ghastly fascinations of the tale. The strain upon pent emotion reached its climax when the boy said—

"—and as the doctor fetched the board around and Muff Potter fell, Injun Joe jumped with the knife and—"

Crash! Quick as lightning the half-breed sprang for a window, tore his way through all opposers, and was gone!

Chapter XXIV.

TOM was a glittering hero once more—the pet of the old, the envy of the young. His name even went into immortal print, for the village paper magnified him. There were some that believed he would be President, yet, if he escaped hanging.

As usual, the fickle, unreasoning world took Muff Potter to its bosom and fondled him as lavishly as it had abused him before. But that sort of conduct is to the world's credit; therefore it is not well to find fault with it.

Tom's days were days of splendor and exultation to him, but his nights were seasons of horror. Injun Joe infested all his dreams, and always with doom in his eye. Hardly any temptation could persuade the boy to stir abroad after nightfall. Poor Huck was in the same state of wretchedness and terror, for Tom had told the whole story to the lawyer the night before the great day of the trial, and Huck was sore afraid that his share in the business might leak out, yet, notwithstanding Injun Joe's flight had saved him the suffering of testifying in court. The poor fellow had got the attorney to promise secrecy, but what of that? Since Tom's harrassed conscience had managed to drive him to the lawyer's house by night and wring a dread tale from lips that had been sealed with the dismalest and most formidable of oaths, Huck's confidence in the human race was well nigh obliterated. Daily Muff Potter's gratitude made Tom glad he had spoken; but nightly he wished he had sealed up his tongue.

Half the time Tom was afraid Injun Joe would never be captured; the other half he was afraid he would be. He felt sure he never could draw a safe breath again until that man was dead and he had seen the corpse.

Rewards had been offered, the country had been scoured, but no Injun Joe was found. One of those omniscient and awe-inspiring marvels, a detective, came up from St. Louis, moused around, shook his head, looked wise, and made that sort of astounding success which members of that craft usually achieve. That is to say he "found a clew." But you can't hang a "clew" for murder, and so after that detective had got through and gone home, Tom felt just as insecure as he was before.

The slow days drifted on, and each left behind it a slightly lightened weight of apprehension.

Chapter XXV.

THERE comes a time in every rightly constructed boy's life when he has a raging desire to go somewhere and dig for hidden treasure. This desire suddenly came upon Tom one day. He sallied out to find Joe Harper, but failed of success. Next he sought Ben Rogers; he had gone fishing. Presently he stumbled upon Huck Finn the Red-Handed. Huck would answer. Tom took him to a private place and opened the matter to him confidentially. Huck was willing. Huck was always willing to take a hand in any enterprise that offered entertainment and required no capital,[3] for he had a troublesome super-abundance of that sort of time which is *not* money.

"Where'll we dig?" said Huck.

"O, most anywhere."

"Why, is it hid all around?"

"No indeed it ain't. It's hid in mighty particular places, Huck— sometimes on islands, sometimes in rotten chests under the end of a limb of an old dead tree, just where the shadow falls at midnight; but mostly under the floor in ha'nted houses."

"Who hides it?"

"Why robbers, of course—who'd you reckon? Sunday-school sup'rintendents?"

"I don't know. If 'twas mine I wouldn't hide it; I'd spend it and have a good time."

"So would I. But robbers don't do that way. They always hide it and leave it there."

"Don't they come after it any more?"

3. Wealth used to produce more wealth.

"No, they think they will, but they generally forget the marks, or else they die. Anyway it lays there a long time and gets rusty; and by and by somebody finds an old yellow paper that tells how to find the marks—a paper that's got to be ciphered over about a week because it's mostly signs and hy'rogliphics."[4]

"Hyro—which?"

"Hy'rogliphics—pictures and things, you know, that don't seem to mean anything."

"Have you got one of them papers, Tom?"

"No."

"Well then, how you going to find the marks?"

"I don't want any marks. They always bury it under a ha'nted house or on an island, or under a dead tree that's got one limb sticking out. Well, we've tried Jackson's Island a little, and we can try it again some time; and there's the old ha'nted house up the Still-House branch, and there's lots of dead-limb trees—dead loads of 'em."

"Is it under all of them?"

"How you talk! No!"

"Then how you going to know which one to go for?"

"Go for all of 'em!"

"Why Tom, it'll take all summer."

"Well, what of that? Suppose you find a brass pot with a hundred dollars in it, all rusty and gay, or a rotten chest full of di'monds. How's that?"

Huck's eyes glowed.

"That's bully. Plenty bully enough for me. Just you gimme the hundred dollars and I don't want no di'monds."

"All right. But I bet you *I* ain't going to throw off on di'monds. Some of 'em's worth twenty dollars apiece—there ain't any, hardly, but's worth six bits[5] or a dollar."

"No! Is that so?"

"Cert'nly—anybody'll tell you so. Hain't you ever seen one, Huck?"

"Not as I remember."

"O, kings have slathers of them."

"Well, I don't know no kings, Tom."

"I reckon you don't. But if you was to go to Europe you'd see a raft of 'em hopping around."

"Do they hop?"

"Hop?—your granny! No!"

"Well what did you say they did, for?"

"Shucks, I only meant you'd *see* 'em—not hopping, of course— what do they want to hop for?—but I mean you'd just see 'em—

---

4. I.e., hieroglyphics; Egyptian picture writing, first deciphered, in modern times, in 1822. "Ciphered": worked out.
5. Seventy-five cents.

scattered around, you know, in a kind of a general way. Like that old hump-backed Richard."[6]

"Richard? What's his other name?"

"He didn't have any other name. Kings don't have any but a given name."

"No?"

"But they don't."

"Well, if they like it, Tom, all right; but I don't want to be a king and have only just a given name, like a nigger. But say—where you going to dig first?"

"Well, I don't know. S'pose we tackle that old dead-limb tree on the hill t'other side of Still-House branch?"

"I'm agreed."

So they got a crippled pick and a shovel, and set out on their three-mile tramp. They arrived hot and panting, and threw themselves down in the shade of a neighboring elm to rest and have a smoke.

"I like this," said Tom.

"So do I."

"Say, Huck, if we find a treasure here, what you going to do with your share?"

"Well I'll have pie and a glass of soda every day, and I'll go to every circus that comes along. I bet I'll have a gay time."

"Well ain't you going to save any of it?"

"Save it? What for?"

"Why so as to have something to live on, by and by."

"O, that ain't any use. Pap would come back to thish-yer town some day and get his claws on it if I didn't hurry up, and I tell you he'd clean it out pretty quick. What you going to do with yourn, Tom?"

"I'm going to buy a new drum, and a sure-'nough sword, and a red neck-tie and a bull pup, and get married."

"Married!"

"That's it."

"Tom, you—why you ain't in your right mind."

"Wait—you'll see."

"Well that's the foolishest thing you could do. Look at pap and my mother. Fight? Why they used to fight all the time. I remember, mighty well."

"That ain't anything. The girl I'm going to marry won't fight."

"Tom, I reckon they're all alike. They'll all comb[7] a body. Now you better think 'bout this a while. I tell you you better. What's the name of the gal?"

6. Richard III (1452–1485), king of England (1483–85), who presumably murdered two young nephews to gain the crown.
7. Search, rake.

"It ain't a gal at all—it's a girl."

"It's all the same, I reckon; some says gal, some says girl—both's right, like enough. Anyway, what's her name, Tom?"

"I'll tell you some time—not now."

"All right—that'll do. Only if you get married I'll be more lonesomer than ever."

"No you won't. You'll come and live with me. Now stir out of this and we'll go to digging."

They worked and sweated for half an hour. No result. They toiled another half hour. Still no result. Huck said:

"Do they always bury it as deep as this?"

"Sometimes—not always. Not generally. I reckon we haven't got the right place."

So they chose a new spot and began again. The labor dragged a little, but still they made progress. They pegged away in silence for some time. Finally Huck leaned on his shovel, swabbed the beaded drops from his brow with his sleeve, and said:

"Where you going to dig next, after we get this one?"

"I reckon maybe we'll tackle the old tree that's over yonder on Cardiff Hill back of the widow's."

"I reckon that'll be a good one. But won't the widow take it away from us Tom? It's on her land."

"*She* take it away! Maybe she'd like to try it once. Whoever finds one of these hid treasures, it belongs to him. It don't make any difference whose land it's on."

That was satisfactory. The work went on. By and by Huck said:—

"Blame it, we must be in the wrong place again. What do you think?"

"It *is* mighty curious Huck. I don't understand it. Sometimes witches interfere. I reckon maybe that's what's the trouble now."

"Shucks, witches ain't got no power in the daytime."

"Well, that's so. I didn't think of that. Oh, *I* know what the matter is! What a blamed lot of fools we are! You got to find out where the shadow of the limb falls at midnight, and that's where you dig!"

"Then consound it, we've fooled away all this work for nothing. Now hang it all, we got to come back in the night. It's an awful long way. Can you get out?"

"I bet I will. We've got to do it to night, too, because if some body sees these holes they'll know in a minute what's here and they'll go for it."

"Well, I'll come around and maow to-night."

"All right. Let's hide the tools in the bushes."

The boys were there that night, about the appointed time. They sat in the shadow waiting. It was a lonely place, and an hour made solemn by old traditions. Spirits whispered in the rustling leaves, ghosts lurked in the murky nooks, the deep baying of a hound floated up out of the distance, an owl answered with his sepulchral note. The boys were subdued by these solemnities, and talked little. By and by they judged that twelve had come; they marked where the shadow fell, and began to dig. Their hopes commenced to rise. Their interest grew stronger, and their industry kept pace with it. The hole deepened and still deepened, but every time their hearts jumped to hear the pick strike upon something, they only suffered a new disappointment. It was only a stone or a chunk. At last Tom said:—

"It ain't any use, Huck, we're wrong again."

"Well but we *can't* be wrong. We spotted the shadder to a dot."

"I know it, but then there's another thing."

"What's that?"

"Why we only guessed at the time. Like enough it was too late or too early."

Huck dropped his shovel.

"That's it," said he. "That's the very trouble. We got to give this one up. We can't ever tell the right time, and besides this kind of thing's too awful, here this time of night with witches and ghosts a-fluttering around so. I feel as if something's behind me all the time; and I'm afeard to turn around, becuz maybe there's others in front a-waiting for a chance. I been creeping all over, ever since I got here."

"Well, I've been pretty much so, too, Huck. They most always put in a dead man when they bury a treasure under a tree, to look out for it."

"Lordy!"

"Yes, they do. I've always heard that."

"Tom I don't like to fool around much where there's dead people. A body's bound to get into trouble with 'em, sure."

"I don't like to stir 'em up, either. S'pose this one here was to stick his skull out and say something!"

"Don't, Tom! It's awful."

"Well it just is. Huck, I don't feel comfortable a bit."

"Say, Tom, let's give this place up, and try somewheres else."

"All right, I reckon we better."

"What'll it be?"

Tom considered a while; and then said—

"The ha'nted house. That's it!"

"Blame it, I don't like ha'nted houses Tom. Why they're a dern sight worse'n dead people. Dead people might talk, maybe, but they don't come sliding around in a shroud, when you ain't noticing, and peep over your shoulder all of a sudden and grit their teeth, the way a ghost does. I couldn't stand such a thing as that, Tom—nobody could."

"Yes, but Huck, ghosts don't travel around only at night—they won't hender us from digging there in the day time."

"Well that's so. But you know mighty well people don't go about that ha'nted house in the day nor the night."

"Well, that's mostly because they don't like to go where a man's been murdered, anyway—but nothing's ever been seen around that house except in the night—just some blue lights slipping by the windows—no regular ghosts."

"Well where you see one of them blue lights flickering around, Tom, you can bet there's a ghost mighty close behind it. It stands to reason. Becuz *you* know that they don't anybody but ghosts use 'em."

"Yes, that's so. But anyway they don't come around in the daytime, so what's the use of our being afeared?"

"Well, all right. We'll tackle the ha'nted house if you say so—but I reckon it's taking chances."

They had started down the hill by this time. There in the middle of the moonlit valley below them stood the "ha'nted" house, utterly isolated, its fences gone long ago, rank weeds smothering the very doorstep, the chimney crumbled to ruin, the window-sashes vacant, a corner of the roof caved in. The boys gazed a while, half expecting to see a blue light flit past a window; then talking in a low tone, as befitted the time and the circumstances, they struck far off to the right, to give the haunted house a wide berth, and took their way homeward through the woods that adorned the rearward side of Cardiff Hill.

Chapter XXVI.

ABOUT noon the next day the boys arrived at the dead tree; they had come for their tools. Tom was impatient to go to the haunted house; Huck was measurably so, also—but suddenly said—

"Lookyhere, Tom, do you know what day it is?"

Tom mentally ran over the days of the week, and then quickly lifted his eyes with a startled look in them—

"My! I never once thought of it, Huck!"

"Well I didn't neither, but all at once it popped onto me that it was Friday."

"Blame it, a body can't be too careful, Huck. We might a got into an awful scrape, tackling such a thing on a Friday."

"*Might!* Better say we *would!* There's some lucky days, maybe, but Friday ain't."

"Any fool knows that. I don't reckon *you* was the first that found it out, Huck."

"Well, I never said I was, did I? And Friday ain't all, neither. I had a rotten bad dream last night—dreampt about rats."

"No! Sure sign of trouble. Did they fight?"

"No."

"Well that's good, Huck. When they don't fight it's only a sign that there's trouble around, you know. All we got to do is to look mighty sharp and keep out of it. We'll drop this thing for to-day, and play. Do you know Robin Hood, Huck?"

"No. Who's Robin Hood?"

"Why he was one of the greatest men that was ever in England— and the best. He was a robber."

"Cracky, I wisht I was. Who did he rob?"

"Only sheriffs and bishops and rich people and kings, and such like. But he never bothered the poor. He loved 'em. He always divided up with 'em—perfectly square."

"Well, he must 'a' been a brick."[8]

"I bet you he was, Huck. Oh, he was the noblest man that ever was. They ain't any such men now, I can tell you. He could lick any man in England, with one hand tied behind him; and he could take his yew[9] bow and plug a ten cent piece every time, a mile and a half."

"What's a *yew* bow?"

"*I* don't know. It's some kind of a bow, of course. And if he hit that dime only on the edge he would set down and cry—and curse. But we'll play Robin Hood—it's noble fun. I'll learn you."

"I'm agreed."

So they played Robin Hood all the afternoon, now and then casting a yearning eye down upon the haunted house and passing a remark about the morrow's prospects and possibilities there. As the sun began to sink into the west they took their way homeward athwart the long shadows of the trees and soon were buried from sight in the forests of Cardiff Hill.

On Saturday, shortly after noon, the boys were at the dead tree again. They had a smoke and a chat in the shade, and then dug a little in their last hole, not with great hope, but merely because Tom said there were so many cases where people had given up a treasure after getting down within six inches of it, and then somebody else had come along and turned it up with a single thrust of a shovel. The thing failed this time, however, so the boys shouldered their tools and went away feeling that they had not trifled with fortune but had fulfilled all the requirements that belong to the business of treasure-hunting.

When they reached the haunted house there was something so weird and grisly about the dead silence that reigned there under the baking sun, and something so depressing about the loneliness and desolation of the place, that they were afraid, for a moment, to ven-

8. Admirable person.
9. Slow-growing evergreen that produces a fine-grained wood well suited to bows.

ture in. Then they crept to the door and took a trembling peep. They saw a weed-grown, floorless room, unplastered, an ancient fireplace, vacant windows, a ruinous staircase; and here, there, and everywhere, hung ragged and abandoned cobwebs. They presently entered, softly, with quickened pulses, talking in whispers, ears alert to catch the slightest sound, and muscles tense and ready for instant retreat.

In a little while familiarity modified their fears and they gave the place a critical and interested examination, rather admiring their own boldness, and wondering at it, too. Next they wanted to look up stairs. This was something like cutting off retreat, but they got to daring each other, and of course there could be but one result—they threw their tools into a corner and made the ascent. Up there were the same signs of decay. In one corner they found a closet that promised mystery, but the promise was a fraud—there was nothing in it. Their courage was up, now, and well in hand. They were about to go down and begin work when—

"Sh!" said Tom.

"What is it?" whispered Huck, blanching with fright.

"Sh! . . . . . There! . . . . . Hear it?"

"Yes! . . . . . O, my! Let's run!"

"Keep still! Don't you budge! They're coming right toward the door."

The boys stretched themselves upon the floor with their eyes to knot holes in the planking, and lay waiting, in a misery of fear.

"They've stopped . . . . . . No—coming . . . . . . Here they are. Don't whisper another word, Huck. My goodness, I wish I was out of this!"

Two men entered. Each boy said to himself: "There's the old deef and dumb Spaniard that's been about town once or twice lately—never saw t'other man before."

"T'other" was a ragged, unkempt creature, with nothing very pleasant in his face. The Spaniard was wrapped in a *serape*; he had bushy white whiskers; long white hair flowed from under his sombrero, and he wore green goggles.[1] When they came in, "t'other" was talking in a low voice; they sat down on the ground, facing the door, with their backs to the wall, and the speaker continued his remarks. His manner became less guarded and his words more distinct as he proceeded:

"No," said he, "I've thought it all over, and I don't like it. It's dangerous."

"Dangerous!" grunted the "deaf and dumb" Spaniard,—to the vast surprise of the boys. "Milksop!"[2]

1. Glasses. "Serape": blanket-like outer garment, often worn in Latin America.
2. Sissy.

This voice made the boys gasp and quake. It was Injun Joe's! There was silence for some time. Then Joe said:

"What's any more dangerous than that job up yonder—but nothing's come of it."

"That's different. Away up the river so, and not another house about. 'Twon't ever be known that we tried, anyway, long as we didn't succeed."

"Well, what's more dangerous than coming here in the day time?—anybody would suspicion us that saw us."

"*I* know that. But there warn't any other place as handy after that fool of a job. I want to quit this shanty. I wanted to yesterday, only it warn't any use trying to stir out of here, with those infernal boys playing over there on the hill right in full view."

"Those infernal boys," quaked again under the inspiration of this remark, and thought how lucky it was that they had remembered it was Friday and concluded to wait a day. They wished in their hearts they had waited a year.

The two men got out some food and made a luncheon. After a long and thoughtful silence, Injun Joe said:

"Look here, lad—you go back up the river where you belong. Wait there till you hear from me. I'll take the chances on dropping into this town just once more, for a look. We'll do that 'dangerous' job after I've spied around a little and think things look well for it. Then for Texas! We'll leg it together!"

This was satisfactory. Both men presently fell to yawning, and Injun Joe said:

"I'm dead for sleep! It's your turn to watch."

He curled down in the weeds and soon began to snore. His comrade stirred him once or twice and he became quiet. Presently the watcher began to nod; his head drooped lower and lower; both men began to snore now.

The boys drew a long, grateful breath. Tom whispered—

"Now's our chance—come!"

Huck said:

"I can't—I'd die if they was to wake."

Tom urged—Huck held back. At last Tom rose slowly and softly, and started alone. But the first step he made wrung such a hideous creak from the crazy floor that he sank down almost dead with fright. He never made a second attempt. The boys lay there counting the dragging moments till it seemed to them that time must be done and eternity growing gray; and then they were grateful to note that at last the sun was setting.

Now one snore ceased. Injun Joe sat up, stared around—smiled grimly upon his comrade, whose head was drooping upon his knees—stirred him up with his foot and said—

"Here! *You're* a watchman, ain't you! All right, though—nothing's happened."

"My! Have I been asleep?"

"Oh, partly, partly. Nearly time for us to be moving, pard. What'll we do with what little swag[3] we've got left?"

"I don't know—leave it here as we've always done, I reckon. No use to take it away till we start south. Six hundred and fifty in silver's something to carry."

"Well—all right—it won't matter to come here once more."

"No—but I'd say come in the night as we used to do—it's better."

"Yes; but look here; it may be a good while before I get the right chance at that job; accidents might happen; 'tain't in such a very good place; we'll just regularly bury it—and bury it deep."

"Good idea," said the comrade, who walked across the room, knelt down, raised one of the rearward hearthstones and took out a bag that jingled pleasantly. He subtracted from it twenty or thirty dollars for himself and as much for Injun Joe and passed the bag to the latter, who was on his knees in the corner, now, digging with his bowie knife.[4]

The boys forgot all their fears, all their miseries in an instant. With gloating eyes they watched every movement. Luck!—the splendor of it was beyond all imagination! Six hundred dollars was money enough to make half a dozen boys rich! Here was treasure-hunting under the happiest auspices—there would not be any bothersome uncertainty as to where to dig. They nudged each other every moment—eloquent nudges and easily understood, for they simply meant "O, but ain't you glad *now* we're here!"

Joe's knife struck upon something.

"Hello!" said he.

"What is it?" said his comrade.

"Half-rotten plank—no it's a box, I believe. Here—bear a hand and we'll see what it's here for. Never mind, I've broke a hole."

He reached his hand in and drew it out—

"Man, it's money!"

The two men examined the handful of coins. They were gold. The boys above were as excited as themselves, and as delighted.

Joe's comrade said—

"We'll make quick work of this. There's an old rusty pick over amongst the weeds in the corner the other side of the fire-place—I saw it a minute ago."

He ran and brought the boys' pick and shovel. Injun Joe took the pick, looked it over critically, shook his head, muttered something to himself, and then began to use it. The box was soon unearthed.

3. Loot, plunder.
4. Hunting knife with a crosspiece between handle and blade.

It was not very large; it was iron bound and had been very strong before the slow years had injured it. The men contemplated the treasure a while in blissful silence.

"Pard, there's thousands of dollars here," said Injun Joe.

" 'Twas always said that Murrel's gang used around here one summer," the stranger observed.

"I know it," said Injun Joe; "and this looks like it, I should say."

"*Now* you won't need to do that job."

The half-breed frowned. Said he—

"You don't know me. Least you don't know all about that thing. 'Tain't robbery altogether—it's *revenge!*" and a wicked light flamed in his eyes. "I'll need your help in it. When it's finished—then Texas. Go home to your Nance and your kids, and stand by till you hear from me."

"Well—if you say so, what'll we do with this—bury it again?"

"Yes." [Ravishing delight overhead.] "*No!* by the great Sachem,[5] no!" [Profound distress overhead.] "I'd nearly forgot. That pick had fresh earth on it!" [The boys were sick with terror in a moment.] "What business has a pick and a shovel here? What business with fresh earth on them? Who brought them here—and where are they gone? Have you heard anybody?—seen anybody? What! bury it again and leave them to come and see the ground disturbed? Not exactly—not exactly. We'll take it to my den."

"Why of course! Might have thought of that before. You mean Number One?"

"No—Number Two—under the cross. The other place is bad—too common."

"All right. It's nearly dark enough to start."

Injun Joe got up and went about from window to window cautiously peeping out. Presently he said:

"Who could have brought those tools here? Do you reckon they can be up stairs?"

The boys' breath forsook them. Injun Joe put his hand on his knife, halted a moment, undecided, and then turned toward the stairway. The boys thought of the closet, but their strength was gone. The steps came creaking up the stairs—the intolerable distress of the situation woke the stricken resolution of the lads—they were about to spring for the closet, when there was a crash of rotten timbers and Injun Joe landed on the ground amid the debris of the ruined stairway. He gathered himself up cursing, and his comrade said:

"Now what's the use of all that? If it's anybody, and they're up there, let them *stay* there—who cares? If they want to jump down, now, and get into trouble, who objects? It will be dark in fifteen

---

5. North American Indian chief, especially Algonquian. Used here as a synonym for *Lord*.

minutes—and then let them follow us if they want to. I'm willing. In my opinion, whoever hove those things in here caught a sight of us and took us for ghosts or devils or something. I'll bet they're running yet."

Joe grumbled a while; then he agreed with his friend that what daylight was left ought to be economised in getting things ready for leaving. Shortly afterward they slipped out of the house in the deepening twilight, and moved toward the river with their precious box.

Tom and Huck rose up, weak but vastly relieved, and stared after them through the chinks between the logs of the house. Follow? Not they. They were content to reach ground again without broken necks, and take the townward track over the hill. They did not talk much. They were too much absorbed in hating themselves—hating the ill luck that made them take the spade and the pick there. But for that, Injun Joe never would have suspected. He would have hidden the silver with the gold to wait there till his "revenge" was satisfied, and then he would have had the misfortune to find that money turn up missing. Bitter, bitter luck that the tools were ever brought there!

They resolved to keep a lookout for that Spaniard when he should come to town spying out for chances to do his revengeful job, and follow him to "Number Two," wherever that might be. Then a ghastly thought occurred to Tom:

"Revenge? What if he means us, Huck!"

"O, don't!" said Huck, nearly fainting.

They talked it all over, and as they entered town they agreed to believe that he might possibly mean somebody else—at least that he might at least mean nobody but Tom, since only Tom had testified.

Very, very small comfort it was to Tom to be alone in danger! Company would be a palpable improvement, he thought.

Chapter XXVII.

THE adventure of the day mightily tormented Tom's dreams that night. Four times he had his hands on that rich treasure and four times it wasted to nothingness in his fingers as sleep forsook him and wakefulness brought back the hard reality of his misfortune. As he lay in the early morning recalling the incidents of his great adventure, he noticed that they seemed curiously subdued and far away—somewhat as if they had happened in another world, or in a time long gone by. Then it occurred to him that the great adventure itself must be a dream! There was one very strong argument in favor of this idea—namely, that the quantity of coin he had seen was too vast to be real. He had never seen as much as fifty dollars in one mass before, and he was like all boys of his age and station in life, in that he imagined that all references to "hundreds" and "thousands" were mere fanciful forms of speech, and that no such sums really existed in the world. He never had supposed for a moment that so large a sum as a hundred dollars was to be found in actual money in any one's possession. If his notions of hidden treasure had been analyzed, they would have been found to consist of a handful of real dimes and a bushel of vague, splendid, ungraspable dollars.

But the incidents of his adventure grew sensibly sharper and clearer under the attrition of thinking them over, and so he presently found himself leaning to the impression that the thing might not have been a dream, after all. This uncertainty must be swept away. He would snatch a hurried breakfast and go and find Huck.

Huck was sitting on the gunwale[6] of a flatboat, listlessly dangling his feet in the water and looking very melancholy. Tom concluded to let Huck lead up to the subject. If he did not do it, then the adventure would be proved to have been only a dream.

"Hello, Huck!"

"Hello, yourself."

[Silence, for a minute.]

"Tom, if we'd a left the blame tools at the dead tree, we'd 'a' got the money. O, ain't it awful!"

" 'Tain't a dream, then, 'tain't a dream! Somehow I most wish it was. Dog'd if I don't, Huck."

"What ain't a dream?"

"Oh, that thing yesterday. I been half thinking it was."

"Dream! If them stairs hadn't broke down you'd 'a' seen how much dream it was! I've had dreams enough all night—with that patch-eyed Spanish devil going for me all through 'em—rot him!"

"No, not rot him. *Find* him! Track the money!"

"Tom, we'll never find him. A feller don't have only one chance for such a pile—and that one's lost. I'd feel mighty shaky if I was to see him, anyway."

"Well, so'd I; but I'd like to see him, anyway—and track him out—to his Number Two."

"Number Two—yes, that's it. I ben thinking 'bout that. But I can't make nothing out of it. What do you reckon it is?"

"I dono. It's too deep. Say, Huck—maybe it's the number of a house!"

"Goody! . . . . . . No, Tom, that ain't it. If it is, it ain't in this one-horse town. They ain't no numbers here."

6. Edge at the side of a boat.

"Well, that's so. Lemme think a minute. Here—it's the number of a room—in a tavern, you know!"

"O, that's the trick! They ain't only two taverns. We can find out quick."

"You stay here, Huck, till I come."

Tom was off at once. He did not care to have Huck's company in public places. He was gone half an hour. He found that in the best tavern, No. 2 had long been occupied by a young lawyer, and was still so occupied. In the less ostentatious house No. 2 was a mystery. The tavern-keeper's young son said it was kept locked all the time, and he never saw anybody go into it or come out of it except at night; he did not know any particular reason for this state of things; had had some little curiosity, but it was rather feeble; had made the most of the mystery by entertaining himself with the idea that that room was "ha'nted;" had noticed that there was a light in there the night before.

"That's what I've found out, Huck. I reckon that's the very No. 2 we're after."

"I reckon it is, Tom. Now what you going to do?"

"Lemme think."

Tom thought a long time. Then he said:

"I'll tell you. The back door of that No. 2 is the door that comes out into that little close alley between the tavern and the old rattle-trap of a brick store. Now you get hold of all the door-keys you can find, and I'll nip all of Auntie's and the first dark night we'll go there and try 'em. And mind you keep a lookout for Injun Joe, because he said he was going to drop into town and spy around once more for a chance to get his revenge. If you see him, you just follow him; and if he don't go to that No. 2, that ain't the place."

"Lordy I don't want to foller him by myself!"

"Why it'll be night, sure. He mightn't ever see you—and if he did, maybe he'd never think anything."

"Well, if it's pretty dark I reckon I'll track him. I dono—I dono. I'll try."

"You bet I'll follow him, if it's dark, Huck. Why he might 'a' found out he couldn't get his revenge, and be going right after that money."

"It's so, Tom, it's so. I'll foller him; I will, by jingoes!"

"Now you're *talking!* Don't you ever weaken, Huck, and I won't."

Chapter XXVIII.

THAT night Tom and Huck were ready for their adventure. They hung about the neighborhood of the tavern until after nine, one watching the alley at a distance and the other the tavern door. Nobody entered the alley or left it; nobody resembling the Spaniard entered or left the tavern door. The night promised to be a fair one; so Tom went home with the understanding that if a considerable degree of darkness came on, Huck was to come and "maow," whereupon he would slip out and try the keys. But the night remained clear, and Huck closed his watch and retired to bed in an empty sugar hogshead about twelve.

Tuesday the boys had the same ill luck. Also Wednesday. But Thursday night promised better. Tom slipped out in good season with his aunt's old tin lantern, and a large towel to blindfold it with. He hid the lantern in Huck's sugar hogshead and the watch began. An hour before midnight the tavern closed up and its lights (the only ones thereabouts) were put out. No Spaniard had been seen. Nobody had entered or left the alley. Everything was auspicious. The blackness of darkness reigned, the perfect stillness was interrupted only by occasional mutterings of distant thunder.

Tom got his lantern, lit it in the hogshead, wrapped it closely in the towel, and the two adventurers crept in the gloom toward the tavern. Huck stood sentry and Tom felt his way into the alley. Then there was a season of waiting anxiety that weighed upon Huck's spirits like a mountain. He began to wish he could see a flash from the lantern—it would frighten him, but it would at least tell him that Tom was alive yet. It seemed hours since Tom had disappeared. Surely he must have fainted; maybe he was dead; maybe his heart had burst under terror and excitement. In his uneasiness Huck found himself drawing closer and closer to the alley; fearing all sorts of dreadful things, and momentarily expecting some catastrophe to happen that would take away his breath. There was not much to take away, for he seemed only able to inhale it by thimblefuls, and his heart would soon wear itself out, the way it was beating. Suddenly there was a flash of light and Tom came tearing by him:

"Run!" said he; "run, for your life!"

He needn't have repeated it; once was enough; Huck was making thirty or forty miles an hour before the repetition was uttered. The boys never stopped till they reached the shed of a deserted slaughter-house at the lower end of the village. Just as they got within its shelter the storm burst and the rain poured down. As soon as Tom got his breath he said:

"Huck, it was awful! I tried two of the keys, just as soft as I could; but they seemed to make such a power of racket that I couldn't hardly get my breath I was so scared. They wouldn't turn in the lock, either. Well, without noticing what I was doing, I took hold of the knob, and open comes the door! It warn't locked! I hopped in, and shook off the towel, and, *great Caesar's ghost!*"

"What!—what 'd you see, Tom!"

"Huck, I most stepped onto Injun Joe's hand!"

"No!"

"Yes! He was laying there, sound asleep on the floor, with his old patch on his eye and his arms spread out."

"Lordy, what did you do? Did he wake up?"

"No, never budged. Drunk, I reckon. I just grabbed that towel and started!"

"I'd never 'a' thought of the towel, I bet!"

"Well, *I* would. My aunt would make me mighty sick if I lost it."

"Say, Tom, did you see that box?"

"Huck I didn't wait to look around. I didn't see the box, I didn't see the cross. I didn't see anything but a bottle and a tin cup on the floor by Injun Joe; yes, and I saw two barrels and lots more bottles in the room. Don't you see, now, what's the matter with that ha'nted room?"

"How?"

"Why it's ha'nted with whisky! Maybe *all* the Temperance Taverns[7] have got a ha'nted room, hey Huck?"

"Well I reckon maybe that's so. Who'd 'a' thought such a thing? But say, Tom, now's a mighty good time to get that box, if Injun Joe's drunk."

"It is, that! You try it!"

Huck shuddered.

"Well, no—I reckon not."

"And *I* reckon not, Huck. Only one bottle alongside of Injun Joe ain't enough. If there'd been three, he'd be drunk enough and I'd do it."

There was a long pause for reflection, and then Tom said:

"Lookyhere, Huck, less not try that thing any more till we know Injun Joe's not in there. It's too scary. Now if we watch every night, we'll be dead sure to see him go out, some time or other, and then we'll snatch that box quicker'n lightning."

"Well, I'm agreed. I'll watch the whole night long, and I'll do it every night, too, if you'll do the other part of the job."

"All right, I will. All you got to do is to trot up Hooper street a block and maow—and if I'm asleep, you throw some gravel at the window and that'll fetch me."

"Agreed, and good as wheat!"

"Now Huck, the storm's over, and I'll go home. It'll begin to be daylight in a couple of hours. You go back and watch that long, will you?"

"I said I would, Tom, and I will. I'll ha'nt that tavern every night for a year! I'll sleep all day and I'll stand watch all night."

---

7. Taverns that presumably do not serve liquor.

"That's all right. Now where you going to sleep?"

"In Ben Rogers's hayloft. He lets me, and so does his pap's nigger man, Uncle Jake. I tote water for Uncle Jake whenever he wants me to, and any time I ask him he gives me a little something to eat if he can spare it. That's a mighty good nigger, Tom. He likes me, becuz I don't ever act as if I was above him. Sometimes I've set right down and eat *with* him. But you needn't tell that. A body's got to do things when he's awful hungry he wouldn't want to do as a steady thing."

"Well, if I don't want you in the day time, I'll let you sleep. I won't come bothering around. Any time you see something's up, in the night, just skip right around and maow."

Chapter XXIX.

THE first thing Tom heard on Friday morning was a glad piece of news—Judge Thatcher's family had come back to town the night before. Both Injun Joe and the treasure sunk into secondary importance for a moment, and Becky took the chief place in the boy's interest. He saw her and they had an exhausting good time playing "hi-spy" and "gully-keeper"[8] with a crowd of their schoolmates. The day was completed and crowned in a peculiarly satisfactory way: Becky teased her mother to appoint the next day for the long-promised and long-delayed pic-nic, and she consented. The child's delight was boundless; and Tom's not more moderate. The invitations were sent out before sunset, and straightway the young folks of the village were thrown into a fever of preparation and pleasurable anticipation. Tom's excitement enabled him to keep awake until a pretty late hour, and he had good hopes of hearing Huck's "maow," and of having his treasure to astonish Becky and the pic-nickers with, next day; but he was disappointed. No signal came that night.

Morning came, eventually, and by ten or eleven o'clock a giddy and rollicking company were gathered at Judge Thatcher's, and everything was ready for a start. It was not the custom for elderly people to mar pic-nics with their presence. The children were considered safe enough under the wings of a few young ladies of eighteen and a few young gentlemen of twenty-three or thereabouts. The old steam ferry boat was chartered for the occasion; presently the gay throng filed up the main street laden with provision baskets. Sid was sick and had to miss the fun; Mary remained at home to entertain him. The last thing Mrs. Thatcher said to Becky, was—

"You'll not get back till late. Perhaps you'd better stay all night with some of the girls that live near the ferry landing, child."

8. Games of tag.

"Then I'll stay with Susy Harper, mamma."

"Very well. And mind and behave yourself and don't be any trouble."

Presently, as they tripped along, Tom said to Becky:

"Say—I'll tell you what we'll do. 'Stead of going to Joe Harper's, we'll climb right up the hill and stop at Widow Douglas's. She'll have ice cream! She has it 'most every day—dead loads of it. And she'll be awful glad to have us."

"O, that will be fun!"

Then Becky reflected a moment and said:

"But what will mamma say?"

"How'll she ever know?"

The girl turned the idea over in her mind, and said reluctantly:

"I reckon it's wrong—but—"

"But shucks! Your mother won't know, and so what's the harm? All she wants is that you'll be safe; and I bet you she'd 'a' said go there if she'd 'a' thought of it. I know she would!"

The widow Douglas's splendid hospitality was a tempting bait. It and Tom's persuasions presently carried the day. So it was decided to say nothing to anybody about the night's programme. Presently it occurred to Tom that maybe Huck might come this very night and give the signal. The thought took a deal of the spirit out of his anticipations. Still he could not bear to give up the fun at Widow Douglas's. And why should he give it up, he reasoned—the signal did not come the night before, so why should it be any more likely to come to-night? The sure fun of the evening outweighed the uncertain treasure; and boy like, he determined to yield to the stronger inclination and not allow himself to think of the box of money another time that day.

Three miles below town the ferry boat stopped at the mouth of a woody hollow and tied up. The crowd swarmed ashore and soon the forest distances and craggy heights echoed far and near with shoutings and laughter. All the different ways of getting hot and tired were gone through with, and by and by the rovers straggled back to camp fortified with responsible appetites, and then the destruction of the good things began. After the feast there was a refreshing season of rest and chat in the shade of spreading oaks. By and by somebody shouted—

"Who's ready for the cave?"

Everybody was. Bundles of candles were produced, and straightway there was a general scamper up the hill. The mouth of the cave was high up the hillside—an opening shaped like a letter A. Its massive oaken door stood unbarred. Within was a small chamber, chilly as an ice-house, and walled by Nature with solid limestone that was dewy with a cold sweat. It was romantic and mysterious to stand here in the deep gloom and look out upon the green valley shining in the sun. But the impressiveness of the situation quickly wore off, and the romping began again. The moment a candle was lighted there was a general rush upon the owner of it; a struggle and a gallant defense followed, but the candle was soon knocked down or blown out, and then there was a glad clamor of laughter and a new chase. But all things have an end. By and by the procession went filing down the steep descent of the main avenue, the flickering rank of lights dimly revealing the lofty walls of rock almost to their point of junction sixty feet overhead. This main avenue was not more than eight or ten feet wide. Every few steps other lofty and still narrower crevices branched from it on either hand—for McDougal's cave was but a vast labyrinth of crooked aisles that ran into each other and out again and led nowhere. It was said that one might wander days and nights together through its intricate tangle of rifts and chasms, and never find the end of the cave; and that he might go down, and down, and still down, into the earth, and it was just the same—labyrinth underneath labyrinth, and no end to any of them. No man "knew" the cave. That was an impossible thing. Most of the young men knew a portion of it, and it was not customary to venture much beyond this known portion. Tom Sawyer knew as much of the cave as any one.

The procession moved along the main avenue some three quarters of a mile, and then groups and couples began to slip aside into branch avenues, fly along the dismal corridors, and take each other by surprise at points where the corridors joined again. Parties were able to elude each other for the space of half an hour without going beyond the "known" ground.

By and by, one group after another came straggling back to the mouth of the cave, panting, hilarious, smeared from head to foot with tallow drippings, daubed with clay, and entirely delighted with the success of the day. Then they were astonished to find that they had been taking no note of time and that night was about at hand. The clanging bell had been calling for half an hour. However, this sort of close to the day's adventures was romantic and therefore satisfactory. When the ferry-boat with her wild freight pushed into the stream, nobody cared sixpence[9] for the wasted time but the captain of the craft.

Huck was already upon his watch when the ferry-boat's lights went glinting past the wharf. He heard no noise on board, for the young people were as subdued and still as people usually are who are nearly tired to death. He wondered what boat it was, and why she did not stop at the wharf—and then he dropped her out of his mind and put

9. British coin worth six pennies.

his attention upon his business. The night was growing cloudy and dark. Ten o'clock came, and the noise of vehicles ceased, scattered lights began to wink out, all straggling foot passengers disappeared, the village betook itself to its slumbers and left the small watcher alone with the silence and the ghosts. Eleven o'clock came, and the tavern lights were put out; darkness everywhere, now. Huck waited what seemed a weary long time, but nothing happened. His faith was weakening. Was there any use? Was there really any use? Why not give it up and turn in?

A noise fell upon his ear. He was all attention in an instant. The alley door closed softly. He sprang to the corner of the brick store. The next moment two men brushed by him, and one seemed to have something under his arm. It must be that box! So they were going to remove the treasure. Why call Tom now? It would be absurd—the men would get away with the box and never be found again. No, he would stick to their wake and follow them; he would trust to the darkness for security from discovery. So communing with himself, Huck stepped out and glided along behind the men, cat-like, with bare feet, allowing them to keep just far enough ahead not to be invisible.

They moved up the river street three blocks, then turned to the left up a cross street. They went straight ahead, then, until they came to the path that led up Cardiff Hill; this they took. They passed by the old Welchman's house, half way up the hill, without hesitating, and still climbed upward. Good, thought Huck, they will bury it in the old quarry. But they never stopped at the quarry. They passed on, up the summit. They plunged into the narrow path between the tall sumach bushes, and were at once hidden in the gloom. Huck closed up and shortened his distance, now, for they would never be able to see him. He trotted along a while; then slackened his pace, fearing he was gaining too fast; moved on a piece, then stopped alto-gether; listened; no sound; none, save that he seemed to hear the beating of his own heart. The hooting of an owl came from over the hill—ominous sound! But no footsteps. Heavens, was everything lost! He was about to spring with winged feet, when a man cleared his throat not four feet from him! Huck's heart shot into his throat, but he swallowed it again; and then he stood there shaking as if a dozen agues[1] had taken charge of him at once, and so weak that he thought he must surely fall to the ground. He knew where he was. He knew he was within five steps of the stile[2] leading into widow Douglas's grounds. Very well, he thought, let them bury it there; it won't be hard to find.

Now there was a voice—a very low voice—Injun Joe's:

1. Fevers with chills.
2. Set of steps for going over a fence or wall.

"Damn her, maybe she's got company—there's lights, late as it is."

"I can't see any."

This was that stranger's voice—the stranger of the haunted house. A deadly chill went to Huck's heart—this, then, was the "revenge" job! His thought was, to fly. Then he remembered that the widow Douglas had been kind to him more than once, and maybe these men were going to murder her. He wished he dared venture to warn her; but he knew he didn't dare—they might come and catch him. He thought all this and more in the moment that lapsed between the stranger's remark and Injun Joe's next—which was—

"Because the bush is in your way. Now—this way—now you see, don't you?"

"Yes. Well there *is* company there, I reckon. Better give it up."

"Give it up, and I just leaving this country forever! Give it up and maybe never have another chance. I tell you again, as I've told you before, I don't care for her swag—you may have it. But her husband was rough on me—many times he was rough on me—and mainly he was the justice of the peace that jugged[3] me for a vagrant. And that ain't all. It ain't the millionth part of it! He had me *horsewhipped!*—horsewhipped in front of the jail, like a nigger!—with all the town looking on! HORSEWHIPPED!—do you understand? He took advantage of me and died. But I'll take it out of *her*."

"Oh, don't kill her! Don't do that!"

"Kill? Who said anything about killing? I would kill *him* if he was here; but not her. When you want to get revenge on a woman you don't kill her—bosh! you go for her looks. You slit her nostrils—you notch her ears like a sow's!"[4]

"By God, that's—"

"Keep your opinion to yourself! It will be safest for you. I'll tie her to the bed. If she bleeds to death, is that my fault? I'll not cry, if she does. My friend, you'll help in this thing—for *my* sake—that's why you're here—I mightn't be able alone. If you flinch, I'll kill you. Do you understand that? And if I have to kill you, I'll kill her—and then I reckon nobody'll ever know much about who done this business."

"Well, if it's got to be done, let's get at it. The quicker the better—I'm all in a shiver."

"Do it *now*? And company there? Look here—I'll get suspicious of you, first thing you know. No—we'll wait till the lights are out—there's no hurry."

Huck felt that a silence was going to ensue—a thing still more awful than any amount of murderous talk; so he held his breath and stepped gingerly back; planted his foot carefully and firmly, after balancing, one-legged, in a precarious way and almost toppling over,

3. Jailed (slang).
4. Female hog.

first on one side and then on the other. He took another step back, with the same elaboration and the same risks; then another and another, and—a twig snapped under his foot! His breath stopped and he listened. There was no sound—the stillness was perfect. His gratitude was measureless. Now he turned in his tracks, between the walls of sumach bushes—turned himself as carefully as if he were a ship—and then stepped quickly but cautiously along. When he emerged at the quarry he felt secure, and so he picked up his nimble heels and flew. Down, down he sped, till he reached the Welchman's. He banged at the door, and presently the heads of the old man and his two stalwart sons were thrust from windows.

"What's the row there? Who's banging? What do you want?"

"Let me in—quick! I'll tell everything."

"Why who are you?"

"Huckleberry Finn—quick, let me in!"

"Huckleberry Finn, indeed! It ain't a name to open many doors, I judge! But let him in, lads, and let's see what's the trouble."

"Please don't ever tell I told you," were Huck's first words when he got in. "Please don't—I'd be killed, sure—but the widow's been good friends to me sometimes, and I want to tell—I *will* tell if you'll promise you won't ever say it was me."

"By George he *has* got something to tell, or he wouldn't act so!" exclaimed the old man; "out with it and nobody here'll ever tell, lad."

Three minutes later the old man and his sons, well armed, were up the hill, and just entering the sumach path on tip-toe, their weapons in their hands. Huck accompanied them no further. He hid behind a great bowlder and fell to listening. There was a lagging, anxious silence, and then all of a sudden there was an explosion of firearms and a cry.

Huck waited for no particulars. He sprang away and sped down the hill as fast as his legs could carry him.

Chapter XXX.

As the earliest suspicion of dawn appeared on Sunday morning, Huck came groping up the hill and rapped gently at the old Welchman's door. The inmates were asleep but it was a sleep that was set on a hair-trigger, on account of the exciting episode of the night. A call came from a window—

"Who's there!"

Huck's scared voice answered in a low tone:

"Do please let me in! It's only Huck Finn!"

"It's a name that can open this door night or day, lad!—and wel-come!"

These were strange words to the vagabond boy's ears, and the pleasantest he had ever heard. He could not recollect that the closing word had ever been applied in his case before. The door was quickly unlocked, and he entered. Huck was given a seat and the old man and his brace[5] of tall sons speedily dressed themselves.

"Now my boy I hope you're good and hungry, because breakfast will be ready as soon as the sun's up, and we'll have a piping hot one, too—make yourself easy about that! I and the boys hoped you'd turn up and stop here last night."

"I was awful scared," said Huck, "and I run. I took out when the pistols went off, and I didn't stop for three mile. I've come now becuz I wanted to know about it, you know; and I come before daylight becuz I didn't want to run acrost them devils, even if they was dead."

"Well, poor chap, you do look as if you'd had a hard night of it—but there's a bed here for you when you've had your breakfast. No, they ain't dead, lad—we are sorry enough for that. You see we knew right where to put our hands on them, by your description; so we crept along on tip-toe till we got within fifteen feet of them—dark as a cellar that sumach path was—and just then I found I was going to sneeze. It was the meanest kind of luck! I tried to keep it back, but no use—'twas bound to come, and it did come! I was in the lead, with my pistol raised, and when the sneeze started those scoundrels a-rustling to get out of the path, I sung out, 'Fire, boys!' and blazed away at the place where the rustling was. So did the boys. But they were off in a jiffy, those villains, and we after them, down through the woods. I judge we never touched them. They fired a shot apiece as they started, but their bullets whizzed by and didn't do us any harm. As soon as we lost the sound of their feet we quit chasing, and went down and stirred up the constables. They got a posse together, and went off to guard the river bank, and as soon as it is light the sheriff and a gang are going to beat up the woods. My boys will be with them presently. I wish we had some sort of description of those rascals—'twould help a good deal. But you couldn't see what they were like, in the dark, lad, I suppose?"

"O, yes, I saw them down town and follered them."

"Splendid! Describe them—describe them, my boy!"

"One's the old deef and dumb Spaniard that's ben around here once or twice, and t'other's a mean looking ragged—"

"That's enough, lad, we know the men! Happened on them in the

5. Pair.

woods back of the widow's one day, and they slunk away. Off with you, boys, and tell the sheriff—get your breakfast to-morrow morning!"

The Welchman's sons departed at once. As they were leaving the room Huck sprang up and exclaimed:

"Oh, please don't tell *any*body it was me that blowed on them! Oh, please!"

"All right if you say it, Huck, but you ought to have the credit of what you did."

"Oh, no, no! Please don't tell!"

When the young men were gone, the old Welchman said—

"They won't tell—and I won't. But why don't you want it known?"

Huck would not explain, further than to say that he already knew too much about one of those men and would not have the man know that he knew anything against him for the whole world—he would be killed for knowing it, sure.

The old man promised secrecy once more, and said:

"How did you come to follow these fellows, lad? Were they looking suspicious?"

Huck was silent while he framed a duly cautious reply. Then he said:

"Well, you see, I'm a kind of a hard lot,—least everybody says so, and I don't see nothing agin it—and sometimes I can't sleep much, on accounts of thinking about it and sort of trying to strike out a new way of doing. That was the way of it last night. I couldn't sleep, and so I come along up street 'bout midnight, a-turning it all over, and when I got to that old shackly brick store by the Temperance Tavern, I backed up agin the wall to have another think. Well, just then along comes these two chaps slipping along close by me, with something under their arm and I reckoned they'd stole it. One was a-smoking, and t'other one wanted a light; so they stopped right before me and the cigars lit up their faces and I see that the big one was the deef and dumb Spaniard, by his white whiskers and the patch on his eye, and t'other one was a rusty, ragged looking devil."

"Could you see the rags by the light of the cigars?"

This staggered Huck for a moment. Then he said:

"Well, I don't know—but somehow it seems as if I did."

"Then they went on, and you—"

"Follered 'em—yes. That was it. I wanted to see what was up— they sneaked along so. I dogged 'em to the widder's stile, and stood in the dark and heard the ragged one beg for the widder, and the Spaniard swear he'd spile her looks just as I told you and your two—"

"What! The *deaf and dumb* man said all that!"

Huck had made another terrible mistake! He was trying his best to keep the old man from getting the faintest hint of who the Spaniard might be, and yet his tongue seemed determined to get him into trouble in spite of all he could do. He made several efforts to creep out of his scrape, but the old man's eye was upon him and he made blunder after blunder. Presently the Welchman said:

"My boy, don't be afraid of me. I wouldn't hurt a hair of your head for all the world. No—I'd protect you—I'd protect you. This Spaniard is not deaf and dumb; you've let that slip without intending it; you can't cover that up now. You know something about that Spaniard that you want to keep dark. Now trust me—tell me what it is, and trust me—I won't betray you."

Huck looked into the old man's honest eyes a moment, then bent over and whispered in his ear—

" 'Tain't a Spaniard—it's Injun Joe!"

The Welchman almost jumped out of his chair. In a moment he said:

"It's all plain enough, now. When you talked about notching ears and slitting noses I judged that that was your own embellishment, because white men don't take that sort of revenge. But an Injun! That's a different matter, altogether."

During breakfast the talk went on, and in the course of it the old man said that the last thing which he and his sons had done, before going to bed, was to get a lantern and examine the stile and its vicinity for marks of blood. They found none, but captured a bulky bundle of—

"Of WHAT?"

If the words had been lightning they could not have leaped with a more stunning suddenness from Huck's blanched lips. His eyes were staring wide, now, and his breath suspended—waiting for the answer. The Welchman started—stared in return—three seconds— five seconds—ten—then replied—

"Of burglar's tools. Why what's the *matter* with you?"

Huck sank back, panting gently, but deeply, unutterably grateful. The Welchman eyed him gravely, curiously—and presently said—

"Yes, burglar's tools. That appears to relieve you a good deal. But what did give you that turn? What were *you* expecting we'd found?"

Huck was in a close place—the inquiring eye was upon him—he would have given anything for material for a plausible answer—nothing suggested itself—the inquiring eye was boring deeper and deeper—a senseless reply offered—there was no time to weigh it, so at a venture he uttered it—feebly:

"Sunday-school books, maybe."

Poor Huck was too distressed to smile, but the old man laughed loud and joyously, shook up the details of his anatomy from head to foot, and ended by saying that such a laugh was money in a man's pocket, because it cut down the doctor's bills like everything. Then he added:

"Poor old chap, you're white and jaded—you ain't well a bit—no wonder you're a little flighty and off your balance. But you'll come out of it. Rest and sleep will fetch you all right, I hope."

Huck was irritated to think he had been such a goose and betrayed such a suspicious excitement, for he had dropped the idea that the parcel brought from the tavern was the treasure, as soon as he had heard the talk at the widow's stile. He had only *thought* it was not the treasure, however—he had not known that it wasn't—and so the suggestion of a captured bundle was too much for his self-possession. But on the whole he felt glad the little episode had happened, for now he knew beyond all question that that bundle was not *the* bundle, and so his mind was at rest and exceedingly comfortable. In fact everything seemed to be drifting just in the right direction, now; the treasure must be still in No. 2, the men would be captured and jailed that day, and he and Tom could seize the gold that night without any trouble or any fear of interruption.

Just as breakfast was completed there was a knock at the door. Huck jumped for a hiding place, for he had no mind to be connected even remotely with the late event. The Welchman admitted several ladies and gentlemen, among them the widow Douglas, and noticed that groups of citzens were climbing the hill—to stare at the stile. So the news had spread.

The Welchman had to tell the story of the night to the visitors. The widow's gratitude for her preservation was outspoken.

"Don't say a word about it, madam. There's another that you're more beholden to than you are to me and my boys, maybe, but he don't allow me to tell his name. We wouldn't ever have been there but for him."

Of course this excited a curiosity so vast that it almost belittled the main matter—but the Welchman allowed it to eat into the vitals of his visitors, and through them be transmitted to the whole town, for he refused to part with his secret. When all else had been learned, the widow said:

"I went to sleep reading in bed and slept straight through all that noise. Why didn't you come and wake me?"

"We judged it warn't worth while. Those fellows warn't likely to come again—they hadn't any tools left to work with, and what was the use of waking you up and scaring you to death? My three negro men stood guard at your house all the rest of the night. They've just come back."

More visitors came, and the story had to be told and re-told for a couple of hours more.

There was no Sabbath school during day-school vacation, but everybody was early at church. The stirring event was well canvassed. News came that not a sign of the two villains had been yet discovered. When the sermon was finished, Judge Thatcher's wife dropped alongside of Mrs. Harper as she moved down the aisle with the crowd and said:

"Is my Becky going to sleep all day? I just expected she would be tired to death."

"Your Becky?"

"Yes,"—with a startled look,—"didn't she stay with you last night?"

"Why, no."

Mrs. Thatcher turned pale, and sank into a pew, just as aunt Polly, talking briskly with a friend, passed by. Aunt Polly said:

"Good morning, Mrs. Thatcher. Good morning Mrs. Harper. I've got a boy that's turned up missing. I reckon my Tom staid at your house last night—one of you. And now he's afraid to come to church. I've got to settle with him."

Mrs. Thatcher shook her head feebly and turned paler than ever.

"He didn't stay with us," said Mrs. Harper, beginning to look uneasy. A marked anxiety came into Aunt Polly's face.

"Joe Harper, have you seen my Tom this morning?"

"No'm."

"When did you see him last?"

Joe tried to remember, but was not sure he could say. The people had stopped moving out of church. Whispers passed along, and a boding uneasiness took possession of every countenance. Children were anxiously questioned, and young teachers. They all said they had not noticed whether Tom and Becky were on board the ferryboat on the homeward trip; it was dark; no one thought of inquiring if any one was missing. One young man finally blurted out his fear that they were still in the cave! Mrs. Thatcher swooned away. Aunt Polly fell to crying and wringing her hands.

The alarm swept from lip to lip, from group to group, from street to street, and within five minutes the bells were wildly clanging and the whole town was up! The Cardiff Hill episode sank into instant insignificance, the burglars were forgotten, horses were saddled, skiffs were manned, the ferry boat ordered out, and before the horror was half an hour old, two hundred men were pouring down highroad and river toward the cave.

All the long afternoon the village seemed empty and dead. Many women visited Aunt Polly and Mrs. Thatcher and tried to comfort them. They cried with them, too, and that was still better than words. All the tedious night the town waited for news; but when the morning dawned at last, all the word that came was, "Send more candles—and send food." Mrs. Thatcher was almost crazed; and aunt Polly also. Judge Thatcher sent messages of hope and encouragement from the cave, but they conveyed no real cheer.

The old Welchman came home toward daylight, spattered with candle grease, smeared with clay, and almost worn out. He found Huck still in the bed that had been provided for him, and delirious with fever. The physicians were all at the cave, so the widow Douglas came and took charge of the patient. She said she would do her best by him, because, whether he was good, bad, or indifferent, he was the Lord's, and nothing that was the Lord's was a thing to be neglected. The Welchman said Huck had good spots in him, and the widow said—

"You can depend on it. That's the Lord's mark. He don't leave it off. He never does. Puts it somewhere on every creature that comes from his hands."

Early in the forenoon parties of jaded men began to straggle into the village, but the strongest of the citizens continued searching. All the news that could be gained was that remotenesses of the cavern were being ransacked that had never been visited before; that every corner and crevice was going to be thoroughly searched; that wherever one wandered through the maze of passages, lights were to be seen flitting hither and thither in the distance, and shoutings and pistol shots sent their hollow reverberations to the ear down the sombre aisles. In one place, far from the section usually traversed by tourists, the names "BECKY & TOM" had been found traced upon the rocky wall with candle smoke, and near at hand a grease-soiled bit of ribbon. Mrs. Thatcher recognized the ribbon and cried over it. She said it was the last relic she should ever have of her child; and that no other memorial of her could ever be so precious, because this one parted latest from the living body before the awful death came. Some said that now and then, in the cave, a far-away speck of light would glimmer, and then a glorious shout would burst forth and a score of men go trooping down the echoing aisle—and then a sickening disappointment always followed; the children were not there; it was only a searcher's light.

Three dreadful days and nights dragged their tedious hours along, and the village sank into a hopeless stupor. No one had heart for anything. The accidental discovery, just made, that the proprietor of the Temperance Tavern kept liquor on his premises, scarcely fluttered the public pulse, tremendous as the fact was. In a lucid interval, Huck feebly led up to the subject of taverns, and finally asked—dimly dreading the worst—if anything had been discovered at the Temperance Tavern since he had been ill?

"Yes," said the widow.

Huck started up in bed, wild-eyed:

"What! What was it?"

"Liquor!—and the place has been shut up. Lie down, child—what a turn you did give me!"

"Only tell me one thing—only just one—please! Was it Tom Sawyer that found it?"

The widow burst into tears.

"Hush, hush, child, hush! I've told you before, you must *not* talk. You are very, very sick!"

Then nothing but liquor had been found; there would have been a great pow-wow if it had been the gold. So the treasure was gone forever—gone forever! But what could she be crying about? Curious that she should cry.

These thoughts worked their dim way through Huck's mind, and under the weariness they gave him he fell asleep. The widow said to herself:

"There—he's asleep, poor wreck. Tom Sawyer find it! Pity but somebody could find Tom Sawyer! Ah, there ain't many left, now, that's got hope enough, or strength enough, either, to go on searching."

Chapter XXXI.

Now to return to Tom and Becky's share in the pic-nic. They tripped along the murky aisles with the rest of the company, visiting the familiar wonders of the cave—wonders dubbed with rather over-descriptive names, such as "The Drawing Room," "The Cathedral," "Aladdin's Palace," and so on. Presently the hide-and-seek frolicking began, and Tom and Becky engaged in it with zeal until the exertion began to grow a trifle wearisome; then they wandered down a sinuous avenue holding their candles aloft and reading the tangled web-work of names, dates, post-office addresses and mottoes with which the rocky walls had been frescoed[6] (in candle smoke.) Still drifting along and talking, they scarcely noticed that they were now in a part of the cave whose walls were not frescoed. They smoked their own names under an overhanging shelf and moved on. Presently they came to a place where a little stream of water, trickling over a ledge and carrying a limestone sediment with it, had, in the slow-dragging ages, formed a laced and ruffled Niagara in gleaming and imperishable stone. Tom squeezed his small body behind it in order to illuminate it for Becky's gratification. He found that it curtained a sort of steep natural stairway which was enclosed between narrow walls, and at once the ambition to be a discoverer seized him. Becky responded to his call, and they made a smoke-mark for future guidance, and

6. Painted, as if on plaster.

started upon their quest. They wound this way and that, far down into the secret depths of the cave, made another mark, and branched off in search of novelties to tell the upper world about. In one place they found a spacious cavern, from whose ceiling depended a multitude of shining stalactites[7] of the length and circumference of a man's leg; they walked all about it, wondering and admiring, and presently left it by one of the numerous passages that opened into it. This shortly brought them to a bewitching spring, whose basin was encrusted with a frost work of glittering crystals; it was in the midst of a cavern whose walls were supported by many fantastic pillars which had been formed by the joining of great stalactites and stalagmites[8] together, the result of the ceaseless water-drip of centuries. Under the roof vast knots of bats had packed themselves together, thousands in a bunch; the lights disturbed the creatures and they came flocking down by hundreds, squeaking and darting furiously at the candles. Tom knew their ways and the danger of this sort of conduct. He seized Becky's hand and hurried her into the first corridor that offered; and none too soon, for a bat struck Becky's light out with its wing while she was passing out of the cavern. The bats chased the children a good distance; but the fugitives plunged into every new passage that offered, and at last got rid of the perilous things. Tom found a subterranean lake, shortly, which stretched its dim length away until its shape was lost in the shadows. He wanted to explore its borders, but concluded that it would be best to sit down and rest a while, first. Now, for the first time, the deep stillness of the place laid a clammy hand upon the spirits of the children. Becky said—

"Why, I didn't notice, but it seems ever so long since I heard any of the others."

"Come to think, Becky, we are away down below them—and I don't know how far away north, or south, or east, or whichever it is. We couldn't hear them here."

Becky grew apprehensive.

"I wonder how long we've been down here, Tom. We better start back."

"Yes, I reckon we better. P'raps we better."

"Can you find the way, Tom? It's all a mixed-up crookedness to me."

"I reckon I could find it—but then the bats. If they put both our candles out it will be an awful fix. Let's try some other way, so as not to go through there."

"Well. But I hope we won't get lost. It would be so awful!" and the child shuddered at the thought of the dreadful possibilities.

7. Limestone deposits hanging from the roof of a cave.
8. Limestone deposits built up from the floor of a cave.

They started through a corridor, and traversed it in silence a long way, glancing at each new opening, to see if there was anything familiar about the look of it; but they were all strange. Every time Tom made an examination, Becky would watch his face for an encouraging sign, and he would say cheerily—

"Oh, it's all right. This ain't the one, but we'll come to it right away!"

But he felt less and less hopeful with each failure, and presently began to turn off into diverging avenues at sheer random, in the desperate hope of finding the one that was wanted. He still said it was "all right," but there was such a leaden dread at his heart, that the words had lost their ring and sounded just as if he had said, "All is lost!" Becky clung to his side in an anguish of fear, and tried hard to keep back the tears, but they would come. At last she said:

"O, Tom, never mind the bats, let's go back that way! We seem to get worse and worse off all the time."

Tom stopped.

"Listen!" said he.

Profound silence; silence so deep that even their breathings were conspicuous in the hush. Tom shouted. The call went echoing down the empty aisles and died out in the distance in a faint sound that resembled a ripple of mocking laughter.

"Oh, don't do it again, Tom, it is too horrid," said Becky.

"It is horrid, but I better, Becky; they *might* hear us, you know;" and he shouted again.

The "might" was even a chillier horror than the ghostly laughter, it so confessed a perishing hope. The children stood still and listened; but there was no result. Tom turned upon the back track at once, and hurried his steps. It was but a little while before a certain indecision in his manner revealed another fearful fact to Becky—he could not find his way back!

"O, Tom, you didn't make any marks!"

"Becky I was such a fool! Such a fool! I never thought we might want to come back! No—I can't find the way. It's all mixed up."

"Tom, Tom, we're lost! we're lost! We never never can get out of this awful place! O, why *did* we ever leave the others!"

She sank to the ground and burst into such a frenzy of crying that Tom was appalled with the idea that she might die, or lose her reason. He sat down by her and put his arms around her; she buried her face in his bosom, she clung to him, she poured out her terrors, her unavailing regrets, and the far echoes turned them all to jeering laughter. Tom begged her to pluck up hope again, and she said she could not. He fell to blaming and abusing himself for getting her into this miserable situation; this had a better effect. She said she would try to hope again, she would get up and follow wherever he might lead if only he would not talk like that any more. For he was no more to blame than she, she said.

So they moved on, again—aimlessly—simply at random—all they could do was to move, keep moving. For a little while, hope made a show of reviving—not with any reason to back it, but only because it is its nature to revive when the spring has not been taken out of it by age and familiarity with failure.

By and by Tom took Becky's candle and blew it out. This economy meant so much! Words were not needed. Becky understood, and her hope died again. She knew that Tom had a whole candle and three or four pieces in his pockets—yet he must economise.

By and by, fatigue began to assert its claims; the children tried to pay no attention, for it was dreadful to think of sitting down when time was grown to be so precious; moving, in some direction, in any direction, was at least progress and might bear fruit; but to sit down was to invite death and shorten its pursuit.

At last Becky's frail limbs refused to carry her farther. She sat down. Tom rested with her, and they talked of home, and the friends there, and the comfortable beds and above all, the light! Becky cried, and Tom tried to think of some way of comforting her, but all his encouragements were grown threadbare with use, and sounded like sarcasms. Fatigue bore so heavily upon Becky that she drowsed off to sleep. Tom was grateful. He sat looking into her drawn face and saw it grow smooth and natural under the influence of pleasant dreams; and by and by a smile dawned and rested there. The peaceful face reflected somewhat of peace and healing into his own spirit, and his thoughts wandered away to bygone times and dreamy memories. While he was deep in his musings, Becky woke up with a breezy little laugh—but it was stricken dead upon her lips, and a groan followed it.

"Oh, how *could* I sleep! I wish I never, never had waked! No! No, I don't, Tom! Don't look so! I won't say it again."

"I'm glad you've slept, Becky; you'll feel rested, now, and we'll find the way out."

"We can try, Tom; but I've seen such a beautiful country in my dream. I reckon we are going there."

"Maybe not, maybe not. Cheer up, Becky, and let's go on trying."

They rose up and wandered along, hand in hand and hopeless. They tried to estimate how long they had been in the cave, but all they knew was that it seemed days and weeks, and yet it was plain that this could not be, for their candles were not gone yet.

A long time after this—they could not tell how long—Tom said they must go softly and listen for dripping water—they must find a spring. They found one presently, and Tom said it was time to rest again. Both were cruelly tired, yet Becky said she thought she could go a little farther. She was surprised to hear Tom dissent. She could not understand it. They sat down, and Tom fastened his candle to the wall in front of them with some clay. Thought was soon busy; nothing was said for some time. Then Becky broke the silence:

"Tom, I am so hungry!"

Tom took something out of his pocket.

"Do you remember this?" said he.

Becky almost smiled.

"It's our wedding cake, Tom."

"Yes—I wish it was as big as a barrel, for it's all we've got."

"I saved it from the pic-nic for us to dream on, Tom, the way grown-up people do with wedding cake—but it'll be our—"

She dropped the sentence where it was. Tom divided the cake and Becky ate with good appetite, while Tom nibbled at his moiety.[9] There was abundance of cold water to finish the feast with. By and by Becky suggested that they move on again. Tom was silent a moment. Then he said:

"Becky, can you bear it if I tell you something?"

Becky's face paled, but she said she thought she could.

"Well then, Becky, we must stay here, where there's water to drink. That little piece is our last candle!"

Becky gave loose to tears and wailings. Tom did what he could to comfort her but with little effect. At length Becky said:

"Tom!"

"Well, Becky?"

"They'll miss us and hunt for us!"

"Yes, they will! Certainly they will!"

"Maybe they're hunting for us now, Tom?"

"Why I reckon maybe they are. I hope they are."

"When would they miss us, Tom?"

"When they get back to the boat, I reckon."

"Tom, it might be dark, then—would they notice we hadn't come?"

"I don't know. But anyway, your mother would miss you as soon as they got home."

A frightened look in Becky's face brought Tom to his senses and he saw that he had made a blunder. Becky was not to have gone home that night! The children became silent and thoughtful. In a moment a new burst of grief from Becky showed Tom that the thing in his mind had struck hers also—that the Sabbath morning might be half spent before Mrs. Thatcher discovered that Becky was not at Mrs. Harper's.

The children fastened their eyes upon their bit of candle and watched it melt slowly and pitilessly away; saw the half inch of wick

9. Half.

stand alone at last; saw the feeble flame rise and fall, rise and fall, climb the thin column of smoke, linger at its top a moment, and then—the horror of utter darkness reigned!

How long afterward it was that Becky came to a slow consciousness that she was crying in Tom's arms, neither could tell. All that they knew was, that after what seemed a mighty stretch of time, both awoke out of a dead stupor of sleep and resumed their miseries once more. Tom said it might be Sunday, now—maybe Monday. He tried to get Becky to talk, but her sorrows were too oppressive, all her hopes were gone. Tom said that they must have been missed long ago, and no doubt the search was going on. He would shout, and maybe some one would come. He tried it; but in the darkness the distant echoes sounded so hideously that he tried it no more.

The hours wasted away, and hunger came to torment the captives again. A portion of Tom's half of the cake was left; they divided and ate it. But they seemed hungrier than before. The poor morsel of food only whetted desire.

By and by Tom said:

"*Sh!* Did you hear that?"

Both held their breath and listened. There was a sound like the faintest, far-off shout. Instantly Tom answered it, and leading Becky by the hand, started groping down the corridor in its direction. Presently he listened again; again the sound was heard, and apparently a little nearer.

"It's them!" said Tom; "they're coming! Come along, Becky—we're all right now!"

The joy of the prisoners was almost overwhelming. Their speed was slow, however, because pitfalls were somewhat common, and had to be guarded against. They shortly came to one and had to stop. It might be three feet deep, it might be a hundred—there was no passing it, at any rate. Tom got down on his breast and reached as far down as he could. No bottom. They must stay there and wait until the searchers came. They listened; evidently the distant shoutings were growing more distant! a moment or two more and they had gone altogether. The heart-sinking misery of it! Tom whooped until he was hoarse, but it was of no use. He talked hopefully to Becky; but an age of anxious waiting passed and no sounds came again.

The children groped their way back to the spring. The weary time dragged on; they slept again, and awoke famished and woe-stricken. Tom believed it must be Tuesday by this time.

Now an idea struck him. There were some side passages near at hand. It would be better to explore some of these than bear the weight of the heavy time in idleness. He took a kite-line from his pocket, tied it to a projection, and he and Becky started, Tom in the lead, unwinding the line as he groped along. At the end of twenty steps the corridor ended in a "jumping-off place." Tom got down on his knees and felt below, and then as far around the corner as he could reach with his hands conveniently; he made an effort to stretch yet a little further to the right, and at that moment, not twenty yards away, a human hand, holding a candle, appeared from behind a rock! Tom lifted up a glorious shout, and instantly that hand was followed by the body it belonged to—Injun Joe's! Tom was paralyzed; he could not move. He was vastly gratified, the next moment, to see the "Spaniard" take to his heels and get himself out of sight. Tom wondered that Joe had not recognized his voice and come over and killed him for testifying in court. But the echoes must have disguised the voice. Without doubt, that was it, he reasoned. Tom's fright weakened every muscle in his body. He said to himself that if he had strength enough to get back to the spring he would stay there, and nothing should tempt him to run the risk of meeting Injun Joe again. He was careful to keep from Becky what it was he had seen. He told her he had only shouted "for luck."

But hunger and wretchedness rise superior to fears in the long run. Another tedious wait at the spring and another long sleep brought changes. The children awoke tortured with a raging hunger. Tom believed it must be Wednesday or Thursday or even Friday or Saturday, now, and that the search had been given over. He proposed to explore another passage. He felt willing to risk Injun Joe and all other terrors. But Becky was very weak. She had sunk into a dreary apathy and would not be roused. She said she would wait, now, where she was, and die—it would not be long. She told Tom to go with the kite-line and explore if he chose; but she implored him to come back every little while and speak to her; and she made him promise that when the awful time came, he would stay by her and hold her hand until all was over.

Tom kissed her, with a choking sensation in his throat, and made a show of being confident of finding the searchers or an escape from the cave; then he took the kite-line in his hand and went groping down one of the passages on his hands and knees, distressed with hunger and sick with bodings of coming doom.

Chapter XXXII.

TUESDAY afternoon came, and waned to the twilight. The village of St. Petersburg still mourned. The lost children had not been found. Public prayers had been offered up for them, and many and many a private prayer that had the petitioner's whole heart in it; but still no good news came from the cave. The majority of the searchers had given up the quest and gone back to their daily avocations,[1] saying that it was plain the children could never be found. Mrs. Thatcher was very ill, and a great part of the time delirious. People said it was heart-breaking to hear her call her child, and raise her head and listen a whole minute at a time, then lay it wearily down again with a moan. Aunt Polly had drooped into a settled melancholy, and her gray hair had grown almost white. The village went to its rest on Tuesday night, sad and forlorn.

Away in the middle of the night a wild peal burst from the village bells, and in a moment the streets were swarming with frantic half-clad people, who shouted, "Turn out! turn out! they're found! they're found!" Tin pans and horns were added to the din, the population massed itself and moved toward the river, met the children coming in an open carriage drawn by shouting citizens, thronged around it, joined its homeward march, and swept magnificently up the main street roaring huzzah after huzzah!

The village was illuminated; nobody went to bed again; it was the greatest night the little town had ever seen. During the first half hour a procession of villagers filed through Judge Thatcher's house, seized the saved ones and kissed them, squeezed Mrs. Thatcher's hand, tried to speak but couldn't—and drifted out raining tears all over the place.

Aunt Polly's happiness was complete, and Mrs. Thatcher's nearly so. It would be complete, however, as soon as the messenger dispatched with the great news to the cave should get the word to her husband. Tom lay upon a sofa with an eager auditory[2] about him and told the history of the wonderful adventure, putting in many striking additions to adorn it withal; and closed with a description of how he left Becky and went on an exploring expedition; how he followed two avenues as far as his kite-line would reach; how he followed a third to the fullest stretch of the kite-line, and was about to turn back when he glimpsed a far-off speck that looked like daylight; dropped the line and groped toward it, pushed his head and shoulders through a small hole and saw the broad Mississippi rolling by! And if it had only happened to be night he would not have seen that speck of daylight and would not have explored that passage any more! He told how he went back for Becky and broke the good news and she told him not to fret her with such stuff, for she was tired, and knew she was going to die, and wanted to. He described how he labored with her and convinced her; and how she almost died for joy when she had groped to where she actually saw the blue speck of daylight; how he pushed his way out at the hole and then helped her

1. Occupations, hobbies.
2. Audience.

out; how they sat there and cried for gladness; how some men came along in a skiff and Tom hailed them and told them their situation and their famished condition; how the men didn't believe the wild tale at first, "because," said they, "you are five miles down the river below the valley the cave is in"—then took them aboard, rowed to a house, gave them supper, made them rest till two or three hours after dark and then brought them home.

Before day-dawn, Judge Thatcher and the handful of searchers with him were tracked out, in the cave, by the twine clews they had strung behind them, and informed of the great news.

Three days and nights of toil and hunger in the cave were not to be shaken off at once, as Tom and Becky soon discovered. They were bedridden all of Wednesday and Thursday, and seemed to grow more and more tired and worn, all the time. Tom got about, a little, on Thursday, was down town Friday, and nearly as whole as ever Saturday; but Becky did not leave her room until Sunday, and then she looked as if she had passed through a wasting illness.

Tom learned of Huck's sickness and went to see him on Friday, but could not be admitted to the bedroom; neither could he on Saturday or Sunday. He was admitted daily after that, but was warned to keep still about his adventure and introduce no exciting topic. The widow Douglas staid by to see that he obeyed. At home Tom learned of the Cardiff Hill event; also that the "ragged man's" body had eventually been found in the river near the ferry landing; he had been drowned while trying to escape, perhaps.

About a fortnight after Tom's rescue from the cave, he started off to visit Huck, who had grown plenty strong enough, now, to hear exciting talk, and Tom had some that would interest him, he thought. Judge Thatcher's house was on Tom's way, and he stopped to see Becky. The Judge and some friends set Tom to talking, and some one asked him ironically if he wouldn't like to go to the cave again. Tom said yes, he thought he wouldn't mind it. The Judge said:

"Well, there are others just like you, Tom, I've not the least doubt. But we have taken care of that. Nobody will get lost in that cave any more."

"Why?"

"Because I had its big door sheathed with boiler iron two weeks ago, and triple-locked—and I've got the keys."

Tom turned as white as a sheet.

"What's the matter, boy! Here, run, somebody! Fetch a glass of water!"

The water was brought and thrown into Tom's face.

"Ah, now you're all right. What was the matter with you, Tom?"

"Oh, Judge, Injun Joe's in the cave!"

Chapter XXXIII.

WITHIN a few minutes the news had spread, and a dozen skiff-loads of men were on their way to McDougal's cave, and the ferry-boat, well filled with passengers, soon followed. Tom Sawyer was in the skiff that bore Judge Thatcher.

When the cave door was unlocked, a sorrowful sight presented itself in the dim twilight of the place. Injun Joe lay stretched upon the ground, dead, with his face close to the crack of the door, as if his longing eyes had been fixed, to the latest moment, upon the light and the cheer of the free world outside. Tom was touched, for he knew by his own experience how this wretch had suffered. His pity was moved, but nevertheless he felt an abounding sense of relief and security, now, which revealed to him in a degree which he had not fully appreciated before, how vast a weight of dread had been lying upon him since the day he lifted his voice against this bloody-minded outcast.

Injun Joe's bowie knife lay close by, its blade broken in two. The great foundation-beam of the door had been chipped and hacked through, with tedious labor; useless labor, too, it was, for the native rock formed a sill outside it, and upon that stubborn material the knife had wrought no effect; the only damage done was to the knife itself. But if there had been no stony obstruction there the labor would have been useless still, for if the beam had been wholly cut away Injun Joe could not have squeezed his body under the door, and he knew it. So he had only hacked that place in order to be doing something—in order to pass the weary time—in order to employ his tortured faculties. Ordinarily one could find half a dozen bits of candle stuck around in the crevices of this vestibule, left there by tourists; but there were none now. The prisoner had searched them out and eaten them. He had also contrived to catch a few bats, and these, also, he had eaten, leaving only their claws. The poor unfortunate had starved to death. In one place near at hand, a stalagmite had been slowly growing up from the ground for ages, builded by the water-drip from a stalactite overhead. The captive had broken off the stalagmite, and upon the stump had placed a stone, wherein he had scooped a shallow hollow to catch the precious drop that fell once in every three minutes with the dreary regularity of a clock-tick—a dessert spoonful once in four and twenty hours. That drop was falling when the Pyramids were new; when Troy fell; when the foundations of Rome were laid; when Christ was crucified; when the Conqueror created the British empire; when Columbus sailed; when the massacre at Lexington was "news." It is falling now; it will still be falling when all these things shall have sunk down the afternoon of history, and the twilight of tradition, and been swallowed up in the thick night of oblivion. Has everything a purpose and a mission? Did this drop fall patiently during five thousand years to be ready for this flitting human insect's need? and has it another important object to accomplish ten thousand years to come? No matter. It is many and many a year since the hapless half-breed scooped out the stone to catch the priceless drops, but to this day the tourist stares longest at that pathetic stone and that slow dropping water when he comes to see the wonders of McDougal's cave. Injun Joe's Cup stands first in the list of the cavern's marvels; even "Aladdin's Palace" cannot rival it.

Injun Joe was buried near the mouth of the cave; and people flocked there in boats and wagons from the town and from all the farms and hamlets for seven miles around; they brought their children, and all sorts of provisions, and confessed that they had had almost as satisfactory a time at the funeral as they could have had at the hanging.

This funeral stopped the further growth of one thing—the petition to the Governor for Injun Joe's pardon. The petition had been largely signed; many tearful and eloquent meetings had been held, and a committee of sappy women been appointed to go in deep mourning and wail around the governor, and implore him to be a merciful ass and trample his duty under foot. Injun Joe was believed to have killed five citizens of the village, but what of that? If he had been Satan himself there would have been plenty of weaklings ready to scribble their names to a pardon-petition, and drip a tear on it from their permanently impaired and leaky water-works.

The morning after the funeral Tom took Huck to a private place to have an important talk. Huck had learned all about Tom's adventure from the Welchman and the widow Douglas, by this time, but Tom said he reckoned there was one thing they had not told him; that thing was what he wanted to talk about now. Huck's face saddened. He said:

"I know what it is. You got into No. 2 and never found anything but whisky. Nobody told me it was you; but I just knowed it must 'a' ben you, soon as I heard 'bout that whisky business; and I knowed you hadn't got the money becuz you'd 'a' got at me some way or other and told me even if you was mum to everybody else. Tom, something's always told me we'd never get holt of that swag."

"Why Huck, I never told on that tavern-keeper. You know his tavern was all right the Saturday I went to the pic-nic. Don't you remember you was to watch there that night?"

"Oh, yes! Why it seems 'bout a year ago. It was that very night that I follered Injun Joe to the widder's."

"You followed him?"

"Yes—but you keep mum. I reckon Injun Joe's left friends behind him, and I don't want 'em souring on me and doing me mean tricks. If it hadn't ben for me he'd be down in Texas now, all right."

Then Huck told his entire adventure in confidence to Tom, who had only heard of the Welchmen's part of it before.

"Well," said Huck, presently, coming back to the main question, "whoever nipped the whisky in No. 2, nipped the money too, I reckon—anyways it's a goner for us, Tom."

"Huck, that money wasn't ever in No. 2!"

"What!" Huck searched his comrade's face keenly. "Tom, have you got on the track of that money again?"

"Huck, it's in the cave!"

Huck's eyes blazed.

"Say it again, Tom!"

"The money's in the cave!"

"Tom,—honest injun, now—is it fun, or earnest?"

"Earnest, Huck—just as earnest as ever I was in my life. Will you go in there with me and help get it out?"

"I bet I will! I will if it's where we can blaze our way to it and not get lost."

"Huck, we can do that without the least little bit of trouble in the world."

"Good as wheat! What makes you think the money's—"

"Huck, you just wait till we get in there. If we don't find it I'll agree to give you my drum and everything I've got in the world. I will, by jings."

"All right—it's a whiz.³ When do you say?"

"Right now, if you say it. Are you strong enough?"

"Is it far in the cave? I ben on my pins a little, three or four days, now, but I can't walk more'n a mile, Tom—least I don't think I could."

"It's about five mile into there the way anybody but me would go, Huck, but there's a mighty short cut that they don't anybody but me know about. Huck, I'll take you right to it in a skiff. I'll float the skiff down there, and I'll pull it back again all by myself. You needn't ever turn your hand over."

"Less start right off, Tom."

"All right. We want some bread and meat, and our pipes, and a little bag or two, and two or three kite-strings, and some of these new fangled things they call lucifer matches.⁴ I tell you many's the time I wished I had some when I was in there before."

A trifle after noon the boys borrowed a small skiff from a citizen

3. Agreement, bargain.
4. Friction matches.

who was absent, and got under way at once. When they were several miles below "Cave Hollow," Tom said:

"Now you see this bluff here looks all alike all the way down from the cave hollow—no houses, no wood-yards, bushes all alike. But do you see that white place up yonder where there's been a land-slide? Well that's one of my marks. We'll get ashore, now."

They landed.

"Now Huck, where we're a-standing you could touch that hole I got out of with a fishing-pole. See if you can find it."

Huck searched all the place about, and found nothing. Tom proudly marched into a thick clump of sumach bushes and said—

"Here you are! Look at it, Huck; it's the snuggest hole in this country. You just keep mum about it. All along I've been wanting to be a robber, but I knew I'd got to have a thing like this, and where to run across it was the bother. We've got it now, and we'll keep it quiet, only we'll let Joe Harper and Ben Rogers in—because of course there's got to be a Gang, or else there wouldn't be any style about it. Tom Sawyer's Gang—it sounds splendid, don't it, Huck?"

"Well, it just does, Tom. And who'll we rob?"

"Oh, most anybody. Waylay people—that's mostly the way."

"And kill them?"

"No—not always. Hive them in the cave till they raise a ransom."

"What's a ransom?"

"Money. You make them raise all they can, off'n their friends; and after you've kept them a year, if it ain't raised then you kill them. That's the general way. Only you don't kill the women. You shut up the women, but you don't kill them. They're always beautiful and rich, and awfully scared. You take their watches and things, but you always take your hat off and talk polite. They ain't anybody as polite as robbers—you'll see that in any book. Well the women get to loving you, and after they've been in the cave a week or two weeks they stop crying and after that you couldn't get them to leave. If you drove them out they'd turn right around and come back. It's so in all the books."

"Why it's real bully, Tom. I b'lieve it's better'n to be a pirate."

"Yes, it's better in some ways, because it's close to home and circuses and all that."

By this time everything was ready and the boys entered the hole, Tom in the lead. They toiled their way to the farther end of the tunnel, then made their spliced kite-strings fast and moved on. A few steps brought them to the spring and Tom felt a shudder quiver all through him. He showed Huck the fragment of candle-wick perched on a lump of clay against the wall, and described how he and Becky had watched the flame struggle and expire.

The boys began to quiet down to whispers, now, for the stillness and gloom of the place oppressed their spirits. They went on, and presently entered and followed Tom's other corridor until they reached the "jumping-off place." The candles revealed the fact that it was not really a precipice, but only a steep clay hill twenty or thirty feet high. Tom whispered—

"Now I'll show you something, Huck."

He held his candle aloft and said—

"Look as far around the corner as you can. Do you see that? There—on the big rock over yonder—done with candle smoke."

"Tom, it's a *cross!*"

"*Now* where's your Number Two? *'Under the cross,'* hey? Right yonder's where I saw Injun Joe poke up his candle, Huck!"

Huck stared at the mystic sign a while, and then said with a shaky voice—

"Tom, less git out of here!"

"What! and leave the treasure?"

"Yes—leave it. Injun Joe's ghost is round about there, certain."

"No it ain't, Huck, no it ain't. It would ha'nt the place where he died—away out at the mouth of the cave—five mile from here."

"No, Tom, it wouldn't. It would hang round the money. I know the ways of ghosts, and so do you."

Tom began to fear that Huck was right. Misgivings gathered in his mind. But presently an idea occurred to him—

"Looky here, Huck, what fools we're making of ourselves! Injun Joe's ghost ain't a going to come around where there's a cross!"

The point was well taken. It had its effect.

"Tom I didn't think of that. But that's so. It's luck for us, that cross is. I reckon we'll climb down there and have a hunt for that box."

Tom went first, cutting rude steps in the clay hill as he descended. Huck followed. Four avenues opened out of the small cavern which the great rock stood in. The boys examined three of them with no result. They found a small recess in the one nearest the base of the rock, with a pallet of blankets spread down in it; also an old suspender, some bacon rhind, and the well gnawed bones of two or three fowls. But there was no money box. The lads searched and researched this place, but in vain. Tom said:

"He said *under* the cross. Well, this comes nearest to being under the cross. It can't be under the rock itself, because that sets solid on the ground."

They searched everywhere once more, and then sat down discouraged. Huck could suggest nothing. By and by Tom said:

"Looky here, Huck, there's footprints and some candle grease on the clay about one side of this rock, but not on the other sides. Now what's that for? I bet you the money *is* under the rock. I'm going to dig in the clay."

"That ain't no bad notion, Tom!" said Huck with animation.

Tom's "real Barlow" was out at once, and he had not dug four inches before he struck wood.

"Hey, Huck!—you hear that?"

Huck began to dig and scratch now. Some boards were soon uncovered and removed. They had concealed a natural chasm which led under the rock. Tom got into this and held his candle as far under the rock as he could, but said he could not see to the end of the rift. He proposed to explore. He stooped and passed under; the narrow way descended gradually. He followed its winding course, first to the right, then to the left, Huck at his heels. Tom turned a short curve, by and by, and exclaimed—

"My goodness, Huck, looky here!"

It was the treasure box, sure enough, occupying a snug little cavern, along with an empty powder keg, a couple of guns in leather cases, two or three pairs of old moccasins, a leather belt, and some other rubbish well soaked with the water-drip.

"Got it at last!" said Huck, plowing among the tarnished coins with his hand. "My, but we're rich, Tom!"

"Huck, I always reckoned we'd get it. It's just too good to believe, but we *have* got it, sure! Say—let's not fool around here. Let's snake[5] it out. Lemme see if I can lift the box."

It weighed about fifty pounds. Tom could lift it, after an awkward fashion, but could not carry it conveniently.

"I thought so," he said; "*they* carried it like it was heavy, that day at the ha'nted house. I noticed that. I reckon I was right to think of fetching the little bags along."

The money was soon in the bags and the boys took it up to the cross-rock.

"Now less fetch the guns and things," said Huck.

"No, Huck—leave them there. They're just the tricks to have when we go to robbing. We'll keep them there all the time, and we'll hold our orgies[6] there, too. It's an awful snug place for orgies."

"What's orgies?"

"*I* dono. But robbers always have orgies, and of course we've got to have them, too. Come along, Huck, we've been in here a long time. It's getting late, I reckon. I'm hungry, too. We'll eat and smoke when we get to the skiff."

They presently emerged into the clump of sumach bushes, looked warily out, found the coast clear, and were soon lunching and smok-

5. Drag.
6. Wild, drunken parties.

ing in the skiff. As the sun dipped toward the horizon they pushed out and got under way. Tom skimmed up the shore through the long twilight, chatting cheerily with Huck, and landed shortly after dark.

"Now Huck," said Tom, "we'll hide the money in the loft of the widow's wood-shed, and I'll come up in the morning and we'll count it and divide, and then we'll hunt up a place out in the woods for it where it will be safe. Just you lay quiet here and watch the stuff till I run and hook Benny Taylor's little wagon; I won't be gone a minute."

He disappeared, and presently returned with the wagon, put the two small sacks into it, threw some old rags on top of them, and started off, dragging his cargo behind him. When the boys reached the Welchman's house, they stopped to rest. Just as they were about to move on, the Welchman stepped out and said:

"Hallo, who's that?"

"Huck and Tom Sawyer."

"Good! Come along with me, boys, you are keeping everybody waiting. Here—hurry up, trot ahead—I'll haul the wagon for you. Why, it's not as light as it might be. Got bricks in it?—or old metal?"

"Old metal," said Tom.

"I judged so; the boys in this town will take more trouble and fool away more time, hunting up six bits worth of old iron to sell to the foundry than they would to make twice the money at regular work. But that's human nature—hurry along, hurry along!"

The boys wanted to know what the hurry was about.

"Never mind; you'll see, when we get to the widow Douglas's."

Huck said with some apprehension—for he was long used to being falsely accused—

"Mr. Jones, *we* haven't been doing nothing."

The Welchman laughed.

"Well, I don't know, Huck, my boy. I don't know about that. Ain't you and the widow good friends?"

"Yes. Well, she's ben good friends to me, any ways."

"All right, then. What do you want to be afraid for?"

This question was not entirely answered in Huck's slow mind before he found himself pushed, along with Tom, into Mrs. Douglas's drawing room. Mr. Jones left the wagon near the door and followed.

The place was grandly lighted, and everybody that was of any consequence in the village was there. The Thatchers were there, the Harpers, the Rogerses, Aunt Polly, Sid, Mary, the minister, the editor, and a great many more, and all dressed in their best. The widow received the boys as heartily as any one could well receive two such looking beings. They were covered with clay and candle grease. Aunt Polly blushed crimson with humiliation, and frowned and shook her head at Tom. Nobody suffered half as much as the two boys did, however. Mr. Jones said:

"Tom wasn't at home, yet, so I gave him up; but I stumbled on him and Huck right at my door, and so I just brought them along in a hurry."

"And you did just right," said the widow:—"Come with me, boys."

She took them to a bed chamber and said:

"Now wash and dress yourselves. Here are two new suits of clothes—shirts, socks, everything complete. They're Huck's—no, no thanks Huck—Mr. Jones bought one and I the other. But they'll fit both of you. Get into them. We'll wait—come down when you are slicked up enough."

Then she left.

Chapter XXXIV.

HUCK said:

"Tom, we can slope,[7] if we can find a rope. The window ain't high from the ground."

"Shucks, what do you want to slope for?"

"Well I ain't used to that kind of a crowd. I can't stand it. I ain't going down there, Tom."

"O, bother! It ain't anything. I don't mind it a bit. I'll take care of you."

Sid appeared.

"Tom," said he, "Auntie has been waiting for you all the afternoon. Mary got your Sunday clothes ready, and everybody's been fretting about you. Say—ain't this grease and clay, on your clothes?"

"Now Mr. Siddy, you jist 'tend to your own business. What's all this blow-out about, anyway?"

"It's one of the widow's parties that she's always having. This time it's for the Welchman and his sons, on account of that scrape they helped her out of the other night. And say—I can tell you something, if you want to know."

"Well, what?"

"Why old Mr. Jones is going to try to spring something on the people here to-night, but I overheard him tell auntie to-day about it, as a secret, but I reckon it's not much of a secret *now*. Everybody knows—the widow, too, for all she tries to let on she don't. Oh, Mr. Jones was bound Huck should be here—couldn't get along with his grand secret without Huck, you know!"

"Secret about what, Sid?"

"About Huck tracking the robbers to the widow's. I reckon Mr.

7. Leave suddenly.

Jones was going to make a grand time over his surprise, but I bet you it will drop pretty flat."

Sid chuckled in a very contented and satisfied way.

"Sid, was it you that told?"

"O, never mind who it was. *Somebody* told—that's enough."

"Sid, there's only one person in this town mean enough to do that, and that's you. If you had been in Huck's place you'd 'a' sneaked down the hill and never told anybody on the robbers. You can't do any but mean things, and you can't bear to see anybody praised for doing good ones. There—no thanks, as the widow says"—and Tom cuffed Sid's ears and helped him to the door with several kicks. "Now go and tell auntie if you dare—and to-morrow you'll catch it!"

Some minutes later the widow's guests were at the supper table, and a dozen children were propped up at little side tables in the same room, after the fashion of that country and that day. At the proper time Mr. Jones made his little speech, in which he thanked the widow for the honor she was doing himself and his sons, but said that there was another person whose modesty—

And so forth and so on. He sprung his secret about Huck's share in the adventure in the finest dramatic manner he was master of, but the surprise it occasioned was largely counterfeit and not as clamorous and effusive as it might have been under happier circumstances. However, the widow made a pretty fair show of astonishment, and heaped so many compliments and so much gratitude upon Huck that he almost forgot the nearly intolerable discomfort of his new clothes in the entirely intolerable discomfort of being set up as a target for everybody's gaze and everybody's laudations.[8]

The widow said she meant to give Huck a home under her roof and have him educated; and that when she could spare the money she would start him in business in a modest way. Tom's chance was come. He said:

"Huck don't need it. Huck's rich!"

Nothing but a heavy strain upon the good manners of the company kept back the due and proper complimentary laugh at this pleasant joke. But the silence was a little awkward. Tom broke it—

"Huck's got money. Maybe you don't believe it, but he's got lots of it. Oh, you needn't smile—I reckon I can show you. You just wait a minute."

Tom ran out the doors. The company looked at each other with a perplexed interest—and inquiringly at Huck, who was tongue-tied.

"Sid, what ails Tom?" said Aunt Polly. "He—well, there ain't ever any making of that boy out. I never—"

Tom entered, struggling with the weight of his sacks, and Aunt

8. Praise.

Polly did not finish her sentence. Tom poured the mass of yellow coin upon the table and said—

"There—what did I tell you? Half of it's Huck's and half of it's mine!"

The spectacle took the general breath away. All gazed, nobody spoke for a moment. Then there was a unanimous call for an explanation. Tom said he could furnish it, and he did. The tale was long, but brim full of interest. There was scarcely an interruption from any one to break the charm of its flow. When he had finished, Mr. Jones said—

"I thought I had fixed up a little surprise for this occasion, but it don't amount to anything now. This one makes it sing mighty small, I'm willing to allow."

The money was counted. The sum amounted to a little over twelve thousand dollars. It was more than any one present had ever seen at one time before, though several persons were there who were worth considerably more than that in property.

Chapter XXXV.

THE reader may rest satisfied that Tom's and Huck's windfall made a mighty stir in the poor little village of St. Petersburg. So vast a sum, all in actual cash, seemed next to incredible. It was talked about, gloated over, glorified, until the reason of many of the citizens tottered under the strain of the unhealthy excitement. Every "haunted" house in St. Petersburg and the neighboring villages was dissected, plank by plank, and its foundations dug up and ransacked for hidden treasure—and not by boys, but men—pretty grave, unromantic men, too, some of them. Wherever Tom and Huck appeared they were courted, admired, stared at. The boys were not able to remember that their remarks had possessed weight before; but now their sayings were treasured and repeated; everything they did seemed somehow to be regarded as remarkable; they had evidently lost the power of doing and saying commonplace things; moreover, their past history was raked up and discovered to bear marks of conspicuous originality. The village paper published biographical sketches of the boys.

The widow Douglas put Huck's money out at six per cent., and Judge Thatcher did the same with Tom's at aunt Polly's request. Each lad had an income, now, that was simply prodigious—a dollar for every week-day in the year and half of the Sundays. It was just what the minister got—no, it was what he was promised—he generally couldn't collect it. A dollar and a quarter a week would board, lodge and school a boy in those old simple days—and clothe him and wash him, too, for that matter.

Judge Thatcher had conceived a great opinion of Tom. He said that no commonplace boy would ever have got his daughter out of the cave. When Becky told her father, in strict confidence, how Tom had taken her whipping at school, the Judge was visibly moved; and when she pleaded grace for the mighty lie which Tom had told in order to shift that whipping from her shoulders to his own, the Judge said with a fine outburst that it was a noble, a generous, a magnanimous lie—a lie that was worthy to hold up its head and march down through history breast to breast with George Washington's lauded Truth about the hatchet![9] Becky thought her father had never looked so tall and so superb as when he walked the floor and stamped his foot and said that. She went straight off and told Tom about it.

Judge Thatcher hoped to see Tom a great lawyer or a great soldier some day. He said he meant to look to it that Tom should be admitted to the National military academy and afterwards trained in the best law school in the country, in order that he might be ready for either career or both.

Huck Finn's wealth and the fact that he was now under the widow Douglas's protection, introduced him into society—no, dragged him into it, hurled him into it—and his sufferings were almost more than he could bear. The widow's servants kept him clean and neat, combed and brushed, and they bedded him nightly in unsympathetic sheets that had not one little spot or stain which he could press to his heart and know for a friend. He had to eat with knife and fork; he had to use napkin, cup and plate; he had to learn his book, he had to go to church; he had to talk so properly that speech was become insipid in his mouth; whithersoever he turned, the bars and shackles of civilization shut him in and bound him hand and foot.

He bravely bore his miseries three weeks, and then one day turned up missing. For forty-eight hours the widow hunted for him everywhere in great distress. The public were profoundly concerned; they searched high and low, they dragged the river for his body. Early the third morning Tom Sawyer wisely went poking among some old empty hogsheads down behind the abandoned slaughter-house, and in one of them he found the refugee. Huck had slept there; he had just breakfasted upon some stolen odds and ends of food, and was lying off, now, in comfort with his pipe. He was unkempt, uncombed, and clad in the same old ruin of rags that had made him picturesque in the days when he was free and happy. Tom routed him out, told him the trouble he had been causing, and urged him to go home. Huck's face lost its tranquil content, and took a melancholy cast. He said:

9. According to Mason Weems's popular 1806 biography, the young George Washington admitted to chopping down a cherry tree with his hatchet, rather than tell a lie. Weems invented the story. "Magnanimous": grandly generous.

"Don't talk about it, Tom. I've tried it, and it don't work; it don't work, Tom. It ain't for me; I ain't used to it. The widder's good to me, and friendly; but I can't stand them ways. She makes me git up just at the same time every morning; she makes me wash, they comb me all to thunder; she won't let me sleep in the wood-shed; I got to wear them blamed clothes that just smothers me, Tom; they don't seem to any air git through 'em, somehow; and they're so rotten nice that I can't set down, nor lay down, nor roll around anywhers; I hain't slid on a cellar-door for—well, it 'pears to be years; I got to go to church and sweat and sweat—I hate them ornery sermons! I can't ketch a fly in there, I can't chaw,[1] I got to wear shoes all Sunday. The widder eats by a bell; she goes to bed by a bell; she gits up by a bell—everything's so awful reg'lar a body can't stand it."

"Well, everybody does that way, Huck."

"Tom, it don't make no difference. I ain't everybody, and I can't *stand* it. It's awful to be tied up so. And grub comes too easy—I don't take no interest in vittles,[2] that way. I got to ask, to go a-fishing; I got to ask, to go in a-swimming—dern'd if I hain't got to ask to do everything. Well, I'd got to talk so nice it wasn't no comfort—I'd got to go up in the attic and rip out a while, every day, to git a taste in my mouth, or I'd a died, Tom. The widder wouldn't let me smoke; she wouldn't let me yell, she wouldn't let me gape,[3] nor stretch, nor scratch, before folks—" [Then with a spasm of special irritation and injury],—"And dad fetch it, she prayed all the time! I never *see* such a woman! I *had* to shove, Tom—I just had to. And besides, that school's going to open, and I'd a had to go to it—well, I wouldn't stand *that*, Tom. Lookyhere, Tom, being rich ain't what it's cracked up to be. It's just worry and worry, and sweat and sweat, and a-wishing you was dead all the time. Now these clothes suits me, and this bar'l suits me, and I ain't ever going to shake 'em any more. Tom, I wouldn't ever got into all this trouble if it hadn't 'a' been for that money; now you just take my sheer of it along with yourn, and gimme a ten-center sometimes—not many times, becuz I along don't give a dern for a thing 'thout it's tollable hard to git—and you go and beg off for me with the widder."

"Oh, Huck, you know I can't do that. 'Tain't fair; and besides if you'll try this thing just a while longer you'll come to like it."

"Like it! Yes—the way I'd like a hot stove if I was to set on it long enough. No, Tom, I won't be rich, and I won't live in them cussed smothery houses. I like the woods, and the river, and hogsheads, and I'll stick to 'em, too. Blame it all! just as we'd got guns, and a cave,

---

1. Chew tobacco (dialect).
2. I.e., Victuals, food (dialect).
3. Yawn.

and all just fixed to rob, here this dern foolishness has got to come up and spile it all!"

Tom saw his opportunity—

"Lookyhere, Huck, being rich ain't going to keep me back from turning robber."

"No! Oh, good-licks, are you in real dead-wood earnest, Tom?"

"Just as dead earnest as I'm a sitting here. But Huck, we can't let you into the gang if you ain't respectable, you know."

Huck's joy was quenched.

"Can't let me in, Tom? Didn't you let me go for a pirate?"

"Yes, but that's different. A robber is more high-toned than what a pirate is—as a general thing. In most countries they 're awful high up in the nobility—dukes and such."

"Now Tom, hain't you always ben friendly to me? You wouldn't shet me out, would you, Tom? You wouldn't do that, now, *would* you, Tom?"

"Huck, I wouldn't want to, and I *don't* want to—but what would people say? Why they'd say, 'Mph! Tom Sawyer's Gang! pretty low characters in it!' They'd mean you, Huck. You wouldn't like that, and I wouldn't."

Huck was silent for some time, engaged in a mental struggle. Finally he said:

"Well, I'll go back to the widder for a month and tackle it and see if I can come to stand it, if you'll let me b'long to the gang, Tom."

"All right, Huck, it's a whiz! Come along, old chap, and I'll ask the widow to let up on you a little, Huck."

"Will you Tom—now will you? That's good. If she'll let up on some of the roughest things, I'll smoke private and cuss private, and crowd through or bust. When you going to start the gang and turn robbers?"

"Oh, right off. We'll get the boys together and have the initiation to-night, maybe."

"Have the which?"

"Have the initiation."

"What's that?"

"It's to swear to stand by one another, and never tell the gang's secrets, even if you're chopped all to flinders, and kill anybody and all his family that hurts one of the gang."

"That's gay—that's mighty gay, Tom, I tell you."

"Well I bet it is. And all that swearing's got to be done at midnight, in the lonesomest, awfulest place you can find—a ha'nted house is the best, but they're all ripped up now."

"Well, midnight's good, anyway, Tom."

"Yes, so it is. And you've got to swear on a coffin, and sign it with blood."

"Now that's something *like!* Why it's a million times bullier than pirating. I'll stick to the widder till I rot, Tom; and if I git to be a reglar ripper of a robber, and everybody talking 'bout it, I reckon she'll be proud she snaked me in out of the wet."

Conclusion.

So endeth this chronicle. It being strictly a history of a *boy,* it must stop here; the story could not go much further without becoming the history of a *man*. When one writes a novel about grown people, he knows exactly where to stop—that is, with a marriage; but when he writes of juveniles, he must stop where he best can.

Most of the characters that perform in this book still live, and are prosperous and happy. Some day it may seem worth while to take up the story of the younger ones again and see what sort of men and women they turned out to be; therefore it will be wisest not to reveal any of that part of their lives at present.

The end.

A Note on the Text

The text of this edition is that of the first American edition, published in December 1876 by the American Publishing Company of Hartford, generally considered the most authoritative of the editions published in Twain's lifetime. Obvious errors and inconsistencies have been silently corrected. I have, for instance, retained spellings that were accepted variants in the nineteenth century, such as "lappel" for *lapel* and "sumach" for *sumac*, yet I have changed such typographical errors as "wierd" to "weird," "your'e" to "you're," "posssble" to "possible," and the two instances of "St. Petersburgh" to the more commonly used "St. Petersburg." Where the patterns are less clear, though, the inconsistencies remain: thus the reader will find both "Aunt Polly" and "aunt Polly," both "Widow Douglas" and "widow Douglas"; and sometimes interjections and direct address are set off by commas, sometimes not. I have also made more than two hundred additional changes to bring the text closer to Twain's original manuscript, a process facilitated by the publication of a facsimile of the holograph manuscript, with an introduction by Paul Baender, by University Publications of America and Georgetown University Library (1982, 2 vols.). The most notable of these is a change recommended by Robert H. Hirst, general editor of the Mark Twain Project: "hopes" was a typesetter's misreading of "bodies," in Chapter X. And like many recent editors I have changed "rode" (a relic of a deleted passage in which Tom was riding a broomstick horse) to "went" in Chapter III, in agreement with Twain's revisions in the secretarial copy of the manuscript.

Textual Variants

The following chart lists the substantive ways in which the current edition differs from the first U.S. edition of 1876 and from the text carefully edited by John C. Gerber, Paul Baender, and Terry Firkins for the Iowa Center for Textual Studies (University of California Press, 1980). I have omitted from the chart many differences in punctuation, case, font, and spacing, and some changes in spelling. The 1982 column lists the nineteen changes made to the 1980 text for the more authoritative version edited by Paul Baender for the Mark Twain Library edition (University of California Press, 1982); I am indebted to Robert H. Hirst's "Note on the Text" (272–74). I am likewise indebted to the 1980 edition (533–40, 545–54) for the fullest listings of variants among the holograph manuscript, the secretarial copy, the first English edition, the first U.S. edition, and subsequent nineteenth-century editions.

2007	1876	1980	1982
Pic-nic (9.8)	Pic-nie (xiii.12)	Pic-nic (viii.30)	
them, (11.8)	them (17.9)	them (39.7)	them, (1.10)
around (11.37)	round (18.26)	around (40.14)	
Consound (13.34)	Confound (21.7)	Consound (42.16)	
Petersburg (14.16)	Petersburgh (21.29)	Petersburg (43.3)	
and (14.20)	and (21.32)	and yet (43.7)	
Get (15.24)	Go (23.17)	Get (44.18)	
sheep (15.41)	sheep (24.4)	a sheep (44.35)	
gwyne (17.28)	gwine (27.15)	gwyne (46.31)	
s'sh't (19.9)	s'h't (29.24)	s'sh't (48.20)	
to see (21.25)	at seeing (33.16–17)	to see (51.9)	
¶ "Mayn't (21.27)	[no ¶] "Mayn't (33.19)	¶ "Mayn't (51.12)	
around (21.38)	round (34.9)	around (51.22)	

173

2007	1876	1980	1982
you're (21.39)	your'e (34.9)	you're (51.23)	
around (22.18)	round (35.1)	around (52.12)	
around (23.23)	round (37.2)	around (53.20)	
went (23.31)	rode (37.9)	went (53.27)	
what 're (24.11)	what 'er (37.30)	what're (54.13)	what 're (22.15)
owdacious (24.15)	audacious (38.2)	owdacious (54.17)	
wet, and his poor hands still forever, (24.29–30)	wet, (38.23)	wet, and his poor hands still forever, (54.31)	
o'clock, (25.16)	o'clock (40.1)	o'clock (55.23)	o'clock, (24.17)
"Poor—" (26.20)	"Poor"—(43.5)	"Poor—" (57.17)	
And he was (28.6)	He was (45.4)	And he was (59.12)	
of (28.18)	of of (45.17)	of (59.24)	
Superinten-dent (29.3)	Superin-dant (46.16)	Superinten-dent (60.16)	
the application (29.6)	application (46.18)	the application (60.18)	
breast (29.18)	heart (46.29)	breast (60.30)	
mien (29.41)	mein (48.2)	mien (61.15)	
¶ And (30.12)	[no ¶] And (48.13)	¶ And (61.28)	
verses then (33.5)	verses (51.29)	verses then (64.37)	
button (33.11)	button hole (52.1)	button (65.4)	
Douglas (33.33)	Douglass (54.1)	Douglas (66.11)	
fight (34.26)	fight (55.5)	fought (67.12)	
sail (34.26)	sail (55.5)	sailed (67.12)	
¶ By (39.29)	[no ¶] By (63.7)	¶ By (73.21)	
Petersburg (40.27)	Petersburgh (64.21)	Petersburg (74.22)	
Cert'nly (41.15)	Certainly (65.19)	Cert'nly (75.14)	
warts (41.36)	warfs (66.5)	warts (75.35)	
Joe (42.6)	Jo (66.16)	Joe (76.10)	

2007	1876	1980	1982
ben (42.6)	been (66.17)	been (76.10)	ben (50.26)
Coonville (42.6)	Coonville (66.17)	Constantinople (76.10–11)	
a saying (42.26)	saying (67.3)	a-saying (76.31)	
Saturday. (42.29)	Saturday. (67.8)	Saturday, Huck. (76.34)	
Say— (42.42)	Say— (67.24)	Say, Huck, (77.9)	
[no ¶] Tom's (46.11)	[no ¶] Tom's (72.19)	¶ Tom's (81.11)	
"Like? (48.17)	"Like?" (75.20)	"Like? (83.34)	
the apron (49.5)	her apron (76.18)	the apron (84.29–30)	
Lawrence—" (49.20)	Lawrence"— (76.32)	Lawrence—" (85.8)	
kept com-pressed (51.3)	compressed (80.14)	kept com-pressed (87.26)	
came (51.8)	come (80.18)	came (88.1)	
all brown (51.27)	brown (81.3)	all brown (88.19)	
away, (53.3)	away. (83.4)	away, (90.2)	
are (53.12)	art (83.12)	are (90.10)	
perceptible (54.22)	preceptible (85.14)	perceptible (92.8)	
Aunt (54.25)	Aunt (85.19)	aunt (92.11)	Aunt (70.21)
S'cat (54.36)	Scat (86.10)	S'cat (92.22)	
in. There (55.12)	in, there (86.30)	in. There (93.4)	
ensconced (55.22)	ensconsced (87.7)	ensconced (93.14)	
devils, (56.40)	devils (89.1)	devils (94.33)	devils, (74.7)
hiding place. (57.2)	hiding-place." (89.4)	hiding place. (94.36)	
year (57.29)	years (89.30)	year (95.25)	
dead (58.38)	as dead (91.9)	dead (96.36)	
accounts (58.41)	account (91.11)	accounts (97.1)	
agreed. (60.29)	agreed. (95.1)	agreed, Huck (99.27)	
t'other (63.6)	'tother (97.29)	t'other (102.17)	
bodies (63.20)	hopes (98.9)	hopes (102.31)	bodies (82.31)

2007	1876	1980	1982
whipporwill (63.29)	whippoorwill (99.3)	whipporwill (103.2)	
gray (64.14)	grey (99.28)	gray (103.28)	
vengeful (64.20)	revengeful (100.1)	vengeful (103.35)	
hookey (64.23)	hooky (100.4)	hookey (103.38)	
Who?" (65.29)	Who?" (102.31)	Who? (106.4)	Who?" (87.16)
[no ¶] They (66.29)	¶ They (104.26)	[no ¶] They (107.11)	
quickly (67.17)	quick (105.20)	quickly (108.2)	
phrenological (68.26)	phreneological (108.6)	phrenological (109.17)	
mustn't (70.6)	musn't (109.30)	mustn't (111.5)	
into (70.9)	in (110.1)	into (111.8)	
perceptible (71.8)	preceptible (111.21)	perceptible (112.9)	
possible (71.35)	posssble (112.12)	possible (112.35)	
two- (74.32)	two (116.32)	two (117.7)	two- (102.2)
ruther (75.40)	rather (119.4)	ruther (118.16)	
provision (79.2)	provisions (123.21)	provision (122.36)	
Mrs. (83.6)	Mrs (130.4)	Mrs. (128.18)	
up, (83.13)	up! (130.10)	up, (128.25)	
away.— (83.16)	away,— (130.12)	away. (128.28)	
them that (87.41)	them (137.27)	them that (133.35)	
away (88.17)	way (138.13)	away (134.17)	
down there (88.19–20)	down (138.15)	down there (134.19–20)	
Joe. (88.34)	Joe, (138.29)	Joe. (134.33)	
lip (89.15)	lips (139.29)	lip (135.21)	
weird (89.38)	wierd (140.18)	weird (136.5)	
lightnings (90.22)	lightning (141.19)	lightnings (136.33)	
¶ "Praise (94.18)	[no ¶] "Praise (147.4)	¶ "Praise (141.28)	
town (94.36)	the town (148.8)	town (142.4)	

2007	1876	1980	1982
seized (97.10)	siezed (152.2)	seized (144.35)	
lip (99.11)	lips (154.29)	lip (147.8)	
things—and (99.44)	things—and (156.2)	things; (148.1)	
Island (101.21)	island (159.8)	Island (150.20)	
Girls' (104.17)	Girl's (163.23)	Girls' (154.35)	
longer, (104.20)	longer (163.25)	longer (155.1)	longer, (149.11)
late; there (105.18)	late. There (164.29)	late; there (156.4)	
¶ "I (106.1)	[no ¶] "I (165.26)	¶ "I (156.32)	
seized (107.34)	siezed (169.29)	seized (159.25)	
sermon; (108.29)	sermom; (171.14)	sermon; (160.20)	
A MISSOURI MAIDEN'S FAREWELL TO ALA-BAMA. (109.22)	A MISSOURI MAIDEN'S FAREWELL TO ALABAMA. (172.4)	A MISSOURI MAIDEN'S FAREWELL TO ALABAMA. (161.11)	A MISSOURI MAIDEN'S FARE-WELL TO ALABAMA. (157.24)
A VISION. (110.4)	A VISION. (172.26)	A VISION. (161.33)	A VISION. (158.6)
down (111.10)	and down (174.22)	down (162.37)	
[no ¶] The funeral (112.9)	¶ The funeral (177.10)	[no ¶] The funeral (164.22)	
his fears (114.3)	fears (181.9)	his fears (167.5)	
solitry (114.17)	solitary (182.6)	solitry (167.19)	
ben (115.20)	been (183.19)	been (168.34)	ben (168.4)
[no ¶] Daily (118.40)	¶ Daily (190.15)	[no ¶] Daily (173.22)	
St. (119.7)	St (190.24)	St. (173.30)	
¶ "Where'll (119.26)	[no ¶] "Where'll (191.19)	¶ "Where'll (175.12)	
hy'rogliphics (120.5)	hy'roglyhics (192.21)	hy'rogliphics (175.30)	
do. (121.36)	do. (194.30)	do, Tom. (177.33)	

2007	1876	1980	1982
either. (123.30)	either. (197.10)	either, Huck. (179.34)	
doorstep, (124.17)	doorsteps, (198.7)	doorstep, (180.27)	
weird (125.41)	wierd (201.14)	weird (182.27)	
deef (126.29)	deaf (202.8)	deef (183.20)	
serape (126.33)	*serapè* (202.12)	*serape* (183.24)	
debris (129.39)	*débris* (206.26)	debris (187.7)	
"Revenge? (130.24)	"Revenge?" (207.26)	"Revenge? (187.33)	
one (131.32)	once (210.2)	one (189.11)	
day time, (135.9)	day time, (216.9)	daytime, Huck, (193.31)	
pic-nic (135.21)	picnic (217.17)	pic-nic (194.9)	
produced (136.40)	procured (219.18)	produced (195.37)	
high up (136.42)	up (219.19)	high up (196.2)	
aisles (137.13)	isles (220.2)	aisles (196.17)	
lapsed (139.9)	elapsed (222.30)	lapsed (198.19)	
the millionth (139.19)	a millionth (223.6)	the millionth (198.29)	
sow's (139.27)	sow (223.14)	sow's (198.37)	
bowlder (140.27)	bowlder (225.8)	boulder (200.4)	
Do please (140.40)	Please (226.13)	Do please (201.8)	
deef (141.40)	deaf (228.7)	deef (202.17)	
deef (142.32)	deaf (229.2)	deef (203.13)	
you (144.6)	you out (230.33)	you (204.36)	
climbing (144.24)	climbing up (231.15)	climbing (205.15)	
wouldn't ever (144.30)	wouldn't (231.21)	wouldn't ever (205.21)	
one thing (147.3)	just one thing (235.21)	one thing (208.13)	
¶ "Hush (147.6)	[no ¶] "Hush (235.24)	¶ "Hush (208.16)	
before, (147.6)	before, (235.24)	before (208.16)	before, (221.8)
seized (148.17)	siezed (238.3)	seized (210.7)	

2007	1876	1980	1982
child (148.43)	girl (239.16)	child (210.32)	
in the (149.9)	in (239.24)	in the (211.4)	
never never (149.35)	never (240.20)	never never (211.30)	
¶ A long (150.42)	[no ¶] A long (242.7)	¶ A long (213.6)	
go (151.1)	go on (242.10)	go (213.9)	
she said she thought (151.19)	she thought (243.2)	she said she thought (213.28)	
fall, rise and fall, (152.1)	fall, (243.26)	fall, rise and fall, (214.14)	
gratified, (153.8)	gratified (245.8)	gratified (215.29)	gratified, (230.36)
believed (153.21)	believed that (246.8)	believed (216.4)	
seized (154.19)	siezed (248.10)	seized (217.24)	
said yes, (155.32)	said (250.31)	said yes, (219.8)	
town (157.13)	towns (254.30)	town (221.23)	
¶ "Tom (163.16)	[no ¶] "Tom (264.3)	¶ "Tom (229.3)	
Oh, Mr. (163.37)	Mr. (265.8)	Oh, Mr. (229.23)	
cent., (165.35)	cent., (269.5)	cent, (232.17)	cent., (254.26)
'pears (167.9)	'pears (270.24)	pears (234.6)	'pears (257.1)
in, (168.10)	in, (272.17)	in. (235.8)	in, (258.26)
they 're (168.12)	they're (272.19)	they're (235.10)	they 're (258.28)
The end. (169.15)	THE END. (275.10)	The end. (237.11)	

BACKGROUNDS AND CONTEXTS

The Adventures of Tom Sawyer (1876) is partly autobiographical, as excerpts from Mark Twain's autobiography and an 1870 letter make clear. An anonymous account of the cave near Hannibal likewise suggests the extent to which Twain drew on his own experiences, as, in their way, do E. Anthony Rotundo's insights into boy culture of the nineteenth century, K. Patrick Ober's observations on Perry Davis's Pain-Killer, and Robert Jackson's sketch of the national positioning of nineteenth-century Missouri. Twain's and Eli Rapp's accounts of schooling suggest additional ways in which Twain drew on—and at times reworked—his own experiences and observations. The pieces on dissection provide background on Dr. Robinson's interest in graverobbing. In writing his novel Twain was also responding to other literary works, reacting against moralizing tales, such as those he had parodied in his stories of good and bad little boys, and showing how the legend of Robin Hood could fire a boy's imagination. An 1868 draft of what has since been called the "Boy's Manuscript," not published in Twain's lifetime, rehearsed themes that would reappear in *Tom Sawyer*. His exchange of letters with William Dean Howells in 1875–76 provides insight into Twain's process of revising the novel, a process further elucidated by Bernard DeVoto. An 1887 letter, unsent, provides a later comment by Twain on *Tom Sawyer*.

Biographical Backgrounds

MARK TWAIN

[Autobiography]†

Chapter 5

* * *

FROM SUSY'S BIOGRAPHY.[1]

> Clara and I are sure that papa played the trick on Grandma, about the whipping, that is related in "The Adventures of Tom Sayer"; "Hand me that switch." The switch hovered in the air, the peril was desperate—"My, look behind you Aunt!" The old lady whirled around and snatched her skirts out of danger. The lad fled on the instant, scrambling up the high board fence and disappeared over it.

Susy and Clara were quite right about that.

Then Susy says:

> And we know papa played "Hookey" all the time. And how readily would papa pretend to be dying so as not to have to go to school!

These revelations and exposures are searching, but they are just. If I am as transparent to other people as I was to Susy, I have wasted much effort in this life.

* * *

My mother had a good deal of trouble with me, but I think she enjoyed it. She had none at all with my brother Henry, who was two years younger than I, and I think that the unbroken monotony of his goodness and truthfulness and obedience would have been a burden

---

† From *Chapters from My Autobiography* in *North American Review* no. 602 (2 November 1906): 838–42; no. 610 (1 March 1907): 454–55, 457; no. 614 (3 May 1907): 4–6; no. 620 (2 August 1907): 692–93, 695; no. 623 (October 1907): 164–66; and *Life on the Mississippi* (1883; reprint, New York: Harper & Brothers, 1904), 413.
1. Penned by Twain's daughter Susy (1872–1896) when she was thirteen [Editor's note].

to her but for the relief and variety which I furnished in the other direction. I was a tonic. I was valuable to her. I never thought of it before, but now I see it. I never knew Henry to do a vicious thing toward me, or toward any one else—but he frequently did righteous ones that cost me as heavily. It was his duty to report me, when I needed reporting and neglected to do it myself, and he was very faithful in discharging that duty. He is "Sid" in "Tom Sawyer." But Sid was not Henry. Henry was a very much finer and better boy than ever Sid was.

It was Henry who called my mother's attention to the fact that the thread with which she had sewed my collar together to keep me from going in swimming, had changed color. My mother would not have discovered it but for that, and she was manifestly piqued when she recognized that that prominent bit of circumstantial evidence had escaped her sharp eye. That detail probably added a detail to my punishment. It is human. We generally visit our shortcomings on somebody else when there is a possible excuse for it—but no matter, I took it out of Henry. There is always compensation for such as are unjustly used. I often took it out of him—sometimes as an advance payment for something which I hadn't yet done. These were occasions when the opportunity was too strong a temptation, and I had to draw on the future. I did not need to copy this idea from my mother, and probably didn't. Still she wrought upon that principle upon occasion.

If the incident of the broken sugar-bowl is in "Tom Sawyer"—I don't remember whether it is or not—that is an example of it. Henry never stole sugar. He took it openly from the bowl. His mother knew he wouldn't take sugar when she wasn't looking, but she had her doubts about me. Not exactly doubts, either. She knew very well I *would*. One day when she was not present, Henry took sugar from her prized and precious old English sugar-bowl, which was an heirloom in the family—and he managed to break the bowl. It was the first time I had ever had a chance to tell anything on him, and I was inexpressibly glad. I told him I was going to tell on him, but he was not disturbed. When my mother came in and saw the bowl lying on the floor in fragments, she was speechless for a minute. I allowed that silence to work; I judged it would increase the effect. I was waiting for her to ask "Who did that?"—so that I could fetch out my news. But it was an error of calculation. When she got through with her silence she didn't ask anything about it—she merely gave me a crack on the skull with her thimble that I felt all the way down to my heels. Then I broke out with my injured innocence, expecting to make her very sorry that she had punished the wrong one. I expected her to do something remorseful and pathetic. I told her that I was not the one—it was Henry. But there was no upheaval. She said, without emotion, "It's all right. It isn't any matter. You deserve it for something you've done that I didn't know about; and if you haven't done it, why then you deserve it for something that you are going to do, that I sha'n't hear about."

There was a stairway outside the house, which led up to the rear part of the second story. One day Henry was sent on an errand, and he took a tin bucket along. I knew he would have to ascend those stairs, so I went up and locked the door on the inside, and came down into the garden, which had been newly ploughed and was rich in choice firm clods of black mold. I gathered a generous equipment of these, and ambushed him. I waited till he had climbed the stairs and was near the landing and couldn't escape. Then I bombarded him with clods, which he warded off with his tin bucket the best he could, but without much success, for I was a good marksman. The clods smashing against the weather-boarding fetched my mother out to see what was the matter, and I tried to explain that I was amusing Henry. Both of them were after me in a minute, but I knew the way over that high board fence and escaped for that time. After an hour or two, when I ventured back, there was no one around and I thought the incident was closed. But it was not. Henry was ambushing me. With an unusually competent aim for him, he landed a stone on the side of my head which raised a bump there that felt like the Matterhorn. I carried it to my mother straightway for sympathy, but she was not strongly moved. It seemed to be her idea that incidents like this would eventually reform me if I harvested enough of them. So the matter was only educational. I had had a sterner view of it than that, before.

It was not right to give the cat the "Pain-Killer"; I realize it now. I would not repeat it in these days. But in those "Tom Sawyer" days it was a great and sincere satisfaction to me to see Peter perform under its influence—and if actions *do* speak as loud as words, he took as much interest in it as I did. It was a most detestable medicine, Perry Davis's Pain-Killer. Mr. Pavey's negro man, who was a person of good judgment and considerable curiosity, wanted to sample it, and I let him. It was his opinion that it was made of hell-fire.

Those were the cholera days of '49. The people along the Mississippi were paralyzed with fright. Those who could run away, did it. And many died of fright in the flight. Fright killed three persons where the cholera killed one. Those who couldn't flee kept themselves drenched with cholera preventives, and my mother chose Perry Davis's Pain-Killer for me. She was not distressed about herself. She avoided that kind of preventive. But she made me promise to take a teaspoonful of Pain-Killer every day. Originally it was my intention to keep the promise, but at that time I didn't know as much about Pain-Killer as I knew after my first experiment with it. She didn't watch Henry's bottle—she could trust Henry. But she marked my bottle with a pencil, on the label, every day, and examined it to see if the teaspoonful had been removed. The floor was not carpeted. It had cracks in it, and I fed the Pain-Killer to the cracks with very good results—no cholera occurred down below.

It was upon one of these occasions that that friendly cat came waving his tail and supplicating for Pain-Killer—which he got—and then went into those hysterics which ended with his colliding with all the furniture in the room and finally going out of the open window and carrying the flower-pots with him, just in time for my mother to arrive and look over her glasses in petrified astonishment and say, "What in the world is the matter with Peter?"

I don't remember what my explanation was, but if it is recorded in that book it may not be the right one.

*   *   *

Chapter 13

*   *   *

In my schoolboy days I had no aversion to slavery. I was not aware that there was anything wrong about it. No one arraigned it in my hearing; the local papers said nothing against it; the local pulpit taught us that God approved it, that it was a holy thing, and that the doubter need only look in the Bible if he wished to settle his mind— and then the texts were read aloud to us to make the matter sure; if the slaves themselves had an aversion to slavery they were wise and said nothing. In Hannibal we seldom saw a slave misused; on the farm,[2] never.

There was, however, one small incident of my boyhood days which touched this matter, and it must have meant a good deal to me or it would not have stayed in my memory, clear and sharp, vivid and shadowless, all these slow-drifting years. We had a little slave boy whom we had hired from some one, there in Hannibal. He was from the Eastern Shore of Maryland, and had been brought away from his family and his friends, half-way across the American continent, and sold. He was a cheery spirit, innocent and gentle, and the noisiest creature that ever was, perhaps. All day long he was singing, whistling, yelling, whooping, laughing—it was maddening, devastating, unendurable. At last, one day, I lost all my temper, and went raging to my mother, and said Sandy had been singing for an hour without a single break, and I couldn't stand it, and *wouldn't* she please shut him up. The tears came into her eyes, and her lip trembled, and she said something like this—

2. Twain's aunt and uncle's farm, near Florida, Missouri [Editor's note].

"Poor thing, when he sings, it shows that he is not remembering, and that comforts me; but when he is still, I am afraid he is thinking, and I cannot bear it. He will never see his mother again; if he can sing, I must not hinder it, but be thankful for it. If you were older, you would understand me; then that friendless child's noise would make you glad."

It was a simple speech, and made up of small words, but it went home, and Sandy's noise was not a trouble to me any more. She never used large words, but she had a natural gift for making small ones do effective work. She lived to reach the neighborhood of ninety years, and was capable with her tongue to the last—especially when a meanness or an injustice roused her spirit. She has come handy to me several times in my books, where she figures as Tom Sawyer's "Aunt Polly." I fitted her out with a dialect, and tried to think up other improvements for her, but did not find any. I used Sandy once, also; it was in "Tom Sawyer"; I tried to get him to whitewash the fence, but it did not work. I do not remember what name I called him by in the book.

* * *

I think she [my mother] was never in the cave in her life; but everybody else went there. Many excursion parties came from considerable distances up and down the river to visit the cave. It was miles in extent, and was a tangled wilderness of narrow and lofty clefts and passages. It was an easy place to get lost in; anybody could do it—including the bats. I got lost in it myself, along with a lady, and our last candle burned down to almost nothing before we glimpsed the search-party's lights winding about in the distance.

"Injun Joe" the half-breed got lost in there once, and would have starved to death if the bats had run short. But there was no chance of that; there were myriads of them. He told me all his story. In the book called "Tom Sawyer" I starved him entirely to death in the cave, but that was in the interest of art; it never happened. "General" Gaines, who was our first town drunkard before Jimmy Finn got the place, was lost in there for the space of a week, and finally pushed his handkerchief out of a hole in a hilltop near Saverton, several miles down the river from the cave's mouth, and somebody saw it and dug him out. There is nothing the matter with his statistics except the handkerchief. I knew him for years, and he hadn't any. But it could have been his nose. That would attract attention.

* * *

Chapter 17

* * *

A boy's life is not all comedy; much of the tragic enters into it. The drunken tramp—mentioned in "Tom Sawyer" or "Huck Finn"— who was burned up in the village jail, lay upon my conscience a hundred nights afterward and filled them with hideous dreams— dreams in which I saw his appealing face as I had seen it in the pathetic reality, pressed against the window-bars, with the red hell glowing behind him—a face which seemed to say to me, "If you had not give me the matches, this would not have happened; you are responsible for my death." I was *not* responsible for it, for I had meant him no harm, but only good, when I let him have the matches; but no matter, mine was a trained Presbyterian conscience, and knew but the one duty—to hunt and harry its slave upon all pretexts and on all occasions; particularly when there was no sense or reason in it. The tramp—who was to blame—suffered ten minutes; I, who was not to blame, suffered three months.

* * *

Then there was the case of the young California emigrant who got drunk and proposed to raid the "Welshman's house" all alone one dark and threatening night.[3] This house stood half-way up Holliday's Hill ("Cardiff" Hill), and its sole occupants were a poor but quite respectable widow and her young and blameless daughter. The invading ruffian woke the whole village with his ribald yells and coarse challenges and obscenities. I went up there with a comrade— John Briggs, I think—to look and listen. The figure of the man was dimly visible; the women were on their porch, but not visible in the deep shadow of its roof, but we heard the elder woman's voice. She had loaded an old musket with slugs, and she warned the man that if he stayed where he was while she counted ten it would cost him his life. She began to count, slowly: he began to laugh. He stopped laughing at "six"; then through the deep stillness, in a steady voice, followed the rest of the tale: "seven . . . eight . . . nine"—a long pause, we holding our breath—"ten!" A red spout of flame gushed out into the night, and the man dropped, with his breast riddled to rags. Then the rain and the thunder burst loose and the waiting town swarmed up the hill in the glare of the lightning like an invasion of ants. Those people saw the rest; I had had my share and was satisfied. I went home to dream, and was not disappointed.

* * *

3. Used in "Huck Finn," I think [Twain's note, not altogether correct].

Chapter 21

*   *   *

* * *Once he [my father] tried to reform Injun Joe. * * * It was a failure, and we boys were glad. For Injun Joe, drunk, was interesting and a benefaction to us, but Injun Joe, sober, was a dreary spectacle. We watched my father's experiments upon him with a good deal of anxiety, but it came out all right and we were satisfied. Injun Joe got drunk oftener than before, and became intolerably interesting.

I think that in "Tom Sawyer" I starved Injun Joe to death in the cave. But that may have been to meet the exigencies of romantic literature. I can't remember now whether the real Injun Joe died in the cave or out of it, but I do remember that the news of his death reached me at a most unhappy time—that is to say, just at bedtime on a summer night when a prodigious storm of thunder and lightning accompanied by a deluging rain that turned the streets and lanes into rivers, caused me to repent and resolve to lead a better life. I can remember those awful thunder-bursts and the white glare of the lightning yet, and the wild lashing of the rain against the window-panes. By my teachings I perfectly well knew what all that wild riot was for—Satan had come to get Injun Joe. I had no shadow of doubt about it. It was the proper thing when a person like Injun Joe was required in the under world, and I should have thought it strange and unaccountable if Satan had come for him in a less impressive way. With every glare of lightning I shrivelled and shrunk together in mortal terror, and in the interval of black darkness that followed I poured out my lamentings over my lost condition, and my supplications for just one more chance, with an energy and feeling and sincerity quite foreign to my nature.

But in the morning I saw that it was a false alarm and concluded to resume business at the old stand and wait for another reminder.

*   *   *

* * *I remember Dawson's schoolhouse perfectly. If I wanted to describe it I could save myself the trouble by conveying the description of it to these pages from "Tom Sawyer." I can remember the drowsy and inviting summer sounds that used to float in through the open windows from that distant boy-Paradise, Cardiff Hill (Holliday's Hill), and mingle with the murmurs of the studying pupils and make them the more dreary by the contrast. I remember Andy Fuqua, the oldest pupil—a man of twenty-five. I remember the youngest pupil, Nannie Owsley, a child of seven. I remember George Robards, eighteen or twenty years old, the only pupil who studied Latin. I remember—in some cases vividly, in others vaguely—the

rest of the twenty-five boys and girls. I remember Mr. Dawson very
well. I remember his boy, Theodore, who was as good as he could
be. In fact, he was inordinately good, extravagantly good, offensively
good, detestably good—and he had pop-eyes—and I would have
drowned him if I had had a chance.* * *

*   *   *

Chapter 23

*   *   *

* * *Richmond, the stone mason, * * * was a very kindly and con-
siderate Sunday-school teacher, and patient and compassionate, so
he was the favorite teacher with us little chaps. In that school they
had slender oblong pasteboard blue tickets, each with a verse from
the Testament printed on it, and you could get a blue ticket by reciting two verses. By reciting five verses you could get three blue tickets,
and you could trade these at the bookcase and borrow a book for a
week. I was under Mr. Richmond's spiritual care every now and then
for two or three years, and he was never hard upon me. I always
recited the same five verses every Sunday. He was always satisfied
with the performance. He never seemed to notice that these were
the same five foolish virgins that he had been hearing about every
Sunday for months. I always got my tickets and exchanged them for
a book. They were pretty dreary books, for there was not a bad boy
in the entire bookcase. They were *all* good boys and good girls and
drearily uninteresting, but they were better society than none, and I
was glad to have their company and disapprove of it.

Twenty years ago Mr. Richmond had become possessed of Tom
Sawyer's cave in the hills three miles from town, and had made a
tourist-resort of it. In 1849 when the gold-seekers were streaming
through our little town of Hannibal, many of our grown men got the
gold fever, and I think that all the boys had it. On the Saturday
holidays in summer-time we used to borrow skiffs whose owners
were not present and go down the river three miles to the cave hollow
(Missourian for "valley"), and there we staked out claims and pretended to dig gold, panning out half a dollar a day at first; two or
three times as much, later, and by and by whole fortunes, as our
imaginations became inured to the work. Stupid and unprophetic
lads! We were doing this in play and never suspecting. Why, that
cave hollow and all the adjacent hills were made of gold! But we did
not know it. We took it for dirt. We left its rich secret in its own
peaceful possession and grew up in poverty and went wandering
about the world struggling for bread—and this because we had not
the gift of prophecy. That region was all dirt and rocks to us, yet all

it needed was to be ground up and scientifically handled and it was gold. That is to say, the whole region was a cement-mine—and they make the finest kind of Portland cement there now, five thousand barrels a day, with a plant that cost $2,000,000.

*   *   *

Life on the Mississippi

There is an interesting cave a mile or two below Hannibal, among the bluffs. * * * In my time the person who then owned it turned it into a mausoleum for his daughter, aged fourteen. The body of this poor child was put into a copper cylinder filled with alcohol, and this was suspended in one of the dismal avenues of the cave. The top of the cylinder was removable; and it was said to be a common thing for the baser order of tourists to drag the dead face into view and examine it and comment upon it.

MARK TWAIN

Letter to Will Bowen, 6 February 1870†

My First, & Oldest & Dearest Friend,

My heart goes out to you just the same as ever! Your letter has stirred me to the bottom. The fountains of my great deep are broken up & I have rained reminiscences for four & twenty hours. The old life has swept before me like a panorama; the old days have trooped by in their old glory, again; the old faces have looked out of the mists of the past; old footsteps have sounded in my listening ears; old hands have clasped mine, old voices have greeted me, & the songs I loved ages & ages ago have come wailing down the centuries! Heavens what eternities have swung their hoary cycles about us since those days were new!—Since we tore down Dick Hardy's stable; since you had the measles & I went to your house purposely to catch them; since Henry Beebe kept that envied slaughter-house, & Joe Craig sold him cats to kill in it; since old General Gaines used to say, "Whoop! Bow your neck & spread!;" since Jimmy Finn was town drunkard & we stole his dinner while he slept in the vat & fed it to the hogs in order to keep them still till we could mount them & have a ride; since Clint Levering was drowned; since we taught that one-

† Reprinted from *Mark Twain's Letters*, vol. 4, 1870–1871, ed. Victor Fischer and Michael B. Frank (Berkeley: University of California Press, 1995), 50–51. Indications of Twain's insertions and deletions are omitted. Will Bowen was Twain's childhood friend.

legged nigger, Higgins, to offend Bill League's dignity by hailing him in public with his exasperating "Hello, League!"—since we used to undress & play Robin Hood in our shirt-tails, with lath swords, in the woods on Holliday's Hill on those long summer days; since we used to go in swimming above the still-house branch—& at mighty intervals wandered on vagrant fishing excursions clear up to "the Bay," & wondered what was curtained away in the great world beyond that remote point; since I jumped overboard from the ferry boat in the middle of the river that stormy day to get my hat, & swam two or three miles after it (& *got* it,) while all the town collected on the wharf & for an hour or so looked out across the angry waste of "white-caps" toward where people said Sam. Clemens was last seen before he went down; since we got up a rebellion against Miss Newcomb, under Ed. Stevens' leadership, (to force her to let us all go over to Miss Torry's side of the schoolroom,) & gallantly "sassed" Laura Hawkins when she came out the third time to call us in, & then afterward marched in in threatening & bloodthirsty array,—& meekly yielded, & took each his little thrashing, & resumed his old seat entirely "reconstructed;" since we used to indulge in that very peculiar performance on that old bench outside the school-house to drive good old Bill Brown crazy while he was eating his dinner; since we used to remain at school at noon & go hungry, in order to persecute Bill Brown in all possible ways—poor old Bill, who *could* be driven to such extremity of vindictiveness as to call us "You *infernal* fools!" & chase us round & round the school-house—& yet who never had the heart to hurt us when he caught us, & who always loved us & always took our part when the big boys wanted to thrash us; since we used to lay in wait for Bill Pitts at the pump & whale him; (I saw him two or three years ago, & was awful polite to his six feet two, & mentioned no reminiscences); since we used to be in Dave Garth's class in Sunday school & on week-days stole his leaf tobacco to run our miniature tobacco presses with; since Owsley shot Smar; since Ben Hawkins shot off his finger; since we accidentally burned up that poor fellow in the calaboose; since we used to shoot spool cannons, & cannons made of keys, while that envied & hated Henry Beebe drowned out our poor little pop-guns with his booming brazen little artillery on wheels; since Laura Hawkins was my sweetheart——

*   *   *

The Cave at Hannibal†

In all the works on physical geography which have fallen under our notice, not one makes the least mention of the

WONDERFUL FORMATION

near Hannibal, Missouri, although thousands upon thousands have visited it, and it has been known for at least fifty years, and every visitor has gone away wondering and questioning why the world has not heard more about it. It is a cave only second in depth (and perhaps first, for it has never been fully explored,) to any in the world. A day spent not long since in traversing its endless galleries was filled with astonishment and wonder.

THE ENTRANCE

to this cavern is about two miles below Hannibal and one half mile west of the Mississippi River. The opening, which is fifteen or twenty feet high and about ten feet broad, is probably fifty feet above the level of the river, and faces toward the north. In company with a small party, members of the press, and a guide, we entered this opening into the bowels of the earth, carrying our torches high above our heads. This

MAIN GALLERY,

near the entrance, varies from ten to twenty feet in height, and comes together over the top in an acute arch. The walls all through the covering are a soft white sand stone. In some places the gallery was so narrow that we had to turn sidewise to pass. The guide rushed on at a fearful rate of speed, and the first word we heard from him was, "Look out for the 'wells.' You don't want to fall into them." Sure enough, right in front of us were two round holes, very like a well, indeed, but they had no water in them.

After going at a rapid pace for some time, the hall sometimes wider and sometimes narrower, we came upon the

"DEVIL'S BACKBONE,"

so the guide said. He must have had a huge one, if this ever belonged to him. It is petrified now into solid limestone, is about forty feet long, and lies in the middle of the hall, with a pathway on each side, and has, indeed, aside from its size, a close resemblance to a spinal column. After making an examination of his Majesty's lost vertebrae, we started on. The next thing that attracted our attention was a corridor running at right angles with the one we were following. Here we held a consultation which course to choose, and finally decided to take the right hand, deeply regretting that we could not spend a month in this wonder of the world, so as to see it all. The guide said we would have to take a month longer time than that, if we wanted

† Letter to the Editor, *St. Louis Democrat*, 7 April 1874, 2.

to see it all, for a party once spent a month in the cave and did not find the end of half the galleries. He pointed to some arrows on the corners of the galleries under which was written "out," and said that it was that party which had put those signs all through the cave as far as it had been explored. Starting down this gallery toward the west (that was the last we knew about the points of the compass) we soon came to

A GRAND ROOM

fully fifty feet high and two hundred feet long. Overhead, fastened to the ceiling, were ten thousand glistening diamonds which sparkled in the light of our torches like stars in a midnight sky.

Turning to one side we saw a low opening, perhaps two feet high, and the "Missionary of the Chicago *Times*" on his knees trying to crawl through. He came back complaining that the cuticle had disappeared from his knees (perhaps he was unaccustomed to the position). The next feat he tried was to climb up the side of the cavern and knock down some of the crystals which were sparkling being on the walls and dome. When he was almost lost to sight among the ledges above, we heard a fearful cry of

"BATS! BATS!"

And, looking above, sure enough, there they were by the thousand. Expressing great surprise to the guide, at the number, he said "that there were none here in comparison with "Bat Alley," where they were so thick that one could hardly wade through them." We did not go to "Bat Alley."

Passing along this gallery for some distance where it became somewhat narrower, we saw a finger of lime-stone full fifty feet long, fastened at one end to the roof, and stretching out unsupported. The stone all around it was very soft sand-stone, so soft that we could write on it with the large end of our pencils.

As we passed along huge bowlders blocked up the way, and

GALLERIES SHOT OFF IN EVERY DIRECTION.

Several of these had names written on them, and their length given in figures, as for example: Low passage, 125 yards; Fleming avenue (named after one of the exploring party mentioned above), 4,900 yards. Traveling on and on we came at last to a large room, around the sides of which there were a regular series of shelves. There was no name on it. We called it the dry goods store.

The next place that attracted our attention was

MYSTIC FOUNTAIN,

a beautiful side grotto, in the back part of which the water was constantly and silently dripping down. In most places the walls and ceiling are perfectly dry.

Leaving Mystic Fountain, we wandered off into

ROGUE'S GALLERY,

which had many dark-looking side passages and mysterious hiding places, and ends in a long, narrow fissure in the rock, fifty feet high and fourteen inches wide. Near the end of this gallery the guide picked up an indelible pencil which some one had dropped.

Striking off into some of the side passages, we soon found ourselves in a very large opening, with a smooth, clean bottom, which is known as No. 10.

Everywhere in the cavern, the walls and every accessible place on the ceiling, was

COVERED WITH NAMES.

There are thousands upon thousands of these autographs. Among them are A. Lincoln, 1834, and Mark Twain. By the way, Mr. Clemens used to reside in Hannibal.

ROBBERS' DEN,

a room 500 feet long, and fifty feet wide, is a cosy place, and in early days was a nice retreat for criminals. Horrible stories are told about it. We passed the mouth of a gallery labeled Lost Gallery. The guide informed us that several attempts had been made to explore it, but as yet no one had succeeded in finding a terminus to it.* * *

* * *

* * *Turning about we started off in another direction, finding many strange formations. In some places arches were thrown across, touching at no place except upon the two points where they rested. Huge galleries shot off in every direction. We would sometimes pass a dozen in as many minutes. Some were almost closed with fallen rocks. At last the guide informed us that he could lead us no farther; that from there on we would know just as much as he did. We left him at the crossing of two galleries and started out on exploring expeditions of our own, being careful not to get out of hailing distance.

At last we started out, by a different way from the one by which we came in, and visited the Grotto of the Nymphs, Fairies' Retreat, etc., etc. In one place we saw some beautiful stalactites and stalagmites, in another a beautiful spring, which the guide said they could never get a string long enough to reach the bottom; we at last, perfectly exhausted, reached daylight once more.

A THOUSAND WEIRD TALES

are told about the cave. It is strange that some enterprising storyteller has not seized upon it as the locality of some blood and thunder novel. Unknown as it seems at present to be, it is nevertheless, and always will be, one of the wonders of the world.

Nineteenth-Century Education

MARK TWAIN

Miss Clapp's School†

By authority of an invitation from Hon. Wm. M. Gillespie, member of the House Committee on Colleges and Common Schools, I accompanied that statesman on an unofficial visit to the excellent school of Miss Clapp and Mrs. Cutler, this afternoon. The air was soft and balmy—the sky was cloudless and serene—the odor of flowers floated upon the idle breeze—the glory of the sun descended like a benediction upon mountain and meadow and plain—the wind blew like the very devil, and the day was generally disagreeable.

*　*　*

The present school is a credit both to the teachers and the town. It now numbers about forty pupils, I should think, and is well and systematically conducted. The exercises this afternoon were of a character not likely to be unfamiliar to the free American citizen who has a fair recollection of how he used to pass his Friday afternoons in the days of his youth. The tactics have undergone some changes, but these variations are not important. In former times a fellow took his place in the luminous spelling class in the full consciousness that if he spelled cat with a "k," or indulged in any other little orthographical eccentricities of a similar nature, he would be degraded to the foot or sent to his seat; whereas, he keeps his place in the ranks now, in such cases, and his punishment is simply to " 'bout face." Johnny Eaves stuck to his first position, to-day, long after the balance of the class had rounded to, but he subsequently succumbed to the word "nape," which he persisted in ravishing of its final vowel. There was nothing irregular about that. Your rightly constructed schoolboy will spell a multitude of hard words without hesitating once, and then lose his grip and miss fire on the easiest one in the book.

---

† "Letter from Mark Twain: Miss Clapp's School," *Territorial Enterprise* (Virginia City, Nevada), 19–20 January 1864. Reprinted from *Early Tales and Sketches*, Vol. 1, 1851–1864, ed. Edgar Marquess Branch and Robert H. Hirst (Berkeley: University of California Press, 1979), 334–38.

The fashion of reading selections of prose and poetry remains the same; and so does the youthful manner of doing that sort of thing. Some pupils read poetry with graceful ease and correct expression, and others place the rising and falling inflection at measured intervals, as if they had learned the lesson on a "see-saw;" but then they go undulating through a stanza with such an air of unctuous satisfaction, that it is a comfort to be around when they are at it.

> "The boy—stoo-dawn—the bur—ning deck—
> When-sawl—but *him* had fled—
> The flames—that shook—the battle—zreck—
> Shone round—him *o'er*—the dead."[1]

That is the old-fashioned *impressive* style—stately, slow-moving and solemn. It is in vogue yet among scholars of tender age. It always will be. Ever since Mrs. Hemans wrote that verse, it has suited the pleasure of juveniles to emphasize the word "him," and lay atrocious stress upon that other word "o'er," whether she liked it or not; and I am prepared to believe that they will continue this practice unto the end of time, and with the same indifference to Mrs. Hemans' opinions about it, or any body's else.

They sing in school, now-a-days, which is an improvement upon the ancient regime; and they don't catch flies and throw spit-balls at the teacher, as they used to do in my time—which is another improvement, in a general way. Neither do the boys and girls keep a sharp look-out on each other's shortcomings and report the same at headquarters, as was a custom of by-gone centuries.* * *

The "compositions" read to-day were as exactly like the compositions I used to hear read in our school as one baby's nose is exactly like all other babies' noses. I mean the old principal ear-marks were all there: the cutting to the bone of the subject with the very first gash, without any preliminary foolishness in the way of a gorgeous introductory; the inevitable and persevering tautology; the brief, monosyllabic sentences (beginning, as a very general thing, with the pronoun "I"); the penchant for presenting rigid, uncompromising facts for the consideration of the hearer, rather than ornamental fancies; the depending for the success of the composition upon its general merits, without tacking artificial aids to the end of it, in the shape of deductions, or conclusions, or clap-trap climaxes, albeit their absence sometimes imparts to these essays the semblance of having come to an end before they were finished—of arriving at full speed at a jumping-off place and going suddenly overboard, as it were, leaving a sensation such as one feels when he stumbles without previous warning upon that infernal "To be Continued" in the midst

1. From "Casabianca" by Felicia Hemans (1793–1835) [Editor's note].

of a thrilling magazine story. I know there are other styles of school compositions, but these are the characteristics of the style which I have in my eye at present. I do not know why this one has particularly suggested itself to my mind, unless the literary effort of one of the boys there to-day left with me an unusually vivid impression. It ran something in this wise:

COMPOSITION

"I like horses. Where we lived before we came here, we used to have a cutter and horses. We used to ride in it. I like winter. I like snow. I used to have a pony all to myself, where I used to live before I came here. Once it drifted a good deal—very deep—and when it stopped I went out and got in it."

That was all. There was no climax to it, except the spasmodic bow which the tautological little student jerked at the school as he closed his labors.

Two remarkably good compositions were read. Miss P.'s was much the best of these—but aside from its marked literary excellence, it possessed another merit which was peculiarly gratifying to my feelings just at that time. Because it took the conceit out of young Gillespie as completely as perspiration takes the starch out of a shirt-collar. In his insufferable vanity, that feeble member of the House of Representatives had been assuming imposing attitudes, and beaming upon the pupils with an expression of benignant imbecility which was calculated to inspire them with the conviction that there was only one guest of any consequence in the house. Therefore, it was an unspeakable relief to me to see him forced to shed his dignity. Concerning the composition, however. After detailing the countless pleasures which had fallen to her lot during the holidays, the authoress finished with a proviso, in substance as follows—I have forgotten the precise language: "But I have no cheerful reminiscences of Christmas. It was dreary, monotonous and insipid to the last degree. Mr. Gillespie called early, and remained the greater part of the day!" You should have seen the blooming Gillespie wilt when that literary bombshell fell in his camp! The charm of the thing lay in the fact that the last naive sentence was the only suggestion offered in the way of accounting for the dismal character of the occasion. However, to my mind it was sufficient—entirely sufficient.

*   *   *

ELI M. RAPP

The Old-Time School-Discipline†

The discipline of this school, as recalled, was similar to the discipline of other schools in those times. Severity in a teacher was held to be a virtue rather than the contrary. A muscular clash between teacher and older pupils was not infrequent, and the master who lacked courage or athletic vigor met with ignominious disaster. * * * Parents were uneasy if the master were backward in applying the rod, and inferred that the children could not be learning much. Obedience was the rule in almost every household, and disobedience was a disgrace. Between teacher and parent there was perfect concord. If an unruly urchin was severely "thrashed," there was no complaint and no protest by any one. A bunch of apple- or birch-twigs was, as a matter of course, an indispensable requisite of this school. * * * The dunce-stool is still recalled—a bench four feet high and about three feet long. It was called "riding the jackass" and considered a most disgraceful and dreaded punishment. The victim was an object of ridicule to the whole school. A severe flogging was always preferred to this mode of punishment. O corporal punishment! How many pitiable, miserable subterfuges have been contrived to avoid thy name, when the "real" thing would have been much more effective and, I think, more respectable.

† From "The Eight-Cornered School House at Sinking Spring," *Transactions of the Historical Society of Berks County* 2–3 (1905–09): 222. Rapp interviewed ten adults who had been students "sixty and seventy years ago."

Nineteenth-Century Medicine

JOHN DRAPER

Dissection of the Dead†

* * *

At the foundation of all true medical knowledge, and without which there can be neither physician nor surgeon, is the study of Anatomy. This, which reveals to us the construction of our own bodies, is the only method by which we can reason intelligently respecting the causes of disease, or determine upon methods of cure. He who attempts the practice of medicine without this indispensable preliminary, is an imposter. Yet, there is but one means by which that knowledge can be perfectly obtained—it is by the dissection of the dead.

The public demands that the medical institutions shall furnish it with accomplished physicians; yet, it has set its face against the only means of doing this; it discountenances the study of Anatomy. This sentiment prevails in every part of the United States, both in the cities and in remote country places. Some luckless medical student, caught in the act of a midnight invasion of the grave, is marched off incontinently to the county jail, with his pick-axe, shovel, and sack. He may bless his stars that the walls are thick, and the gratings small, for a mob is howling at the outside. Some country college, conspicuous in its remoteness, is suspected by the populace of teaching Anatomy. It is soon torn to the ground, and the Professors flee for their lives. These are not imaginary cases, but realities, which have occurred again and again, and of which the names and dates could be, without difficulty, supplied.

* * *

† From *New-York Daily Times*, 18 October 1853, 2. In this lecture at the opening exercises of the Medical Department of the University of New York (New York University), Dr. John Draper addresses the anomaly that the state of New York required physicians to learn anatomy but, like most other states, made it illegal for them to obtain cadavers for that study.

The people of the State of New-York have directed by law, that Anatomy shall be taught in their Medical Colleges; they have assigned the conditions under which they authorize a distinction—the Diploma of Doctor of Medicine—to be given, one of which is a knowledge of Anatomy. Even more than this—they have quite recently, descending in an unusual way to particular details, directed by a general law that the science shall be taught by a Demonstrator, whose fee shall be five dollars from every student. And yet, by another law, they have declared that whoever shall be convicted of dissecting the dead shall be sent to the State Prison. Oh! people of New-York, what kind of legislation do you call that! It is no excuse for you that your neighbors of Pennsylvania or other States have stultified themselves in the same way.

*   *   *

Practical Anatomy is to be defended, by the advantages arising to the living from its cultivation. Far beyond all other means, it aids in diminishing the amount of human misery, by enabling us to overcome or mitigate the diseases to which we are incident; and in proportion as the structure of the body is better known, so are the chances of relief the better. An ignorant man, whose watch has stopped, tries, in vain, to set it agoing, by shaking and jolting; but the skillful artist who understands its various parts, examines the complicated mechanism, and applies the necessary adjustment. And so with the physician. The knowledge he has acquired, by the examination of the dead, he brings to the bedside of the sick. The tables of mortality show how striking is the result. In all great cities, and indeed wherever there is an intelligent practice of medicine, and registers of mortality are kept, we recognize, from period to period, an increase in the chances of life. I am not wrong in ascribing this improvement to the more thorough preparation which physicians receive, and the steady advance of their art.* * *

*   *   *

When I look at the bills of mortality of this City, and see that sometimes nearly two hundred infants die in one week, and the majority of them among the poor; when I extend my view to a wider scale, and find that there are strong reasons for believing that the male portion of the Irish Catholic emigration dies out in less than six years, I am appalled at such results. The public works of the United States consume each year more human life than the bloodiest European campaign.* * *

*   *   *

The illustration I have been drawing from the dreadful loss of emigrant life in the United States is only one out of many that might have been presented. Reasons just as forcible might be applied to every rank of society, for there is no exemption from disease. Especially in those cases which require the skill of the surgeon does the necessity of anatomical knowledge become conspicuous. Does any one of us certainly know that before to-morrow he may not require that skill to tie an artery or to amputate a limb? Speaking as I do now, in the presence of the first living surgeons, is there any necessity for me to enforce this precept? They will bear their testimony that their art cannot exist except upon anatomy as its basis, and that just in proportion as the surgeon is skillful, so must his knowledge of anatomy be profound.

* * *

It was a profound sense of the advantage which would accrue to suffering humanity, doubtless suggested by such reflections as those we have been entertaining, which first led the Greek kings of Egypt to break through the practices of all antiquity, and especially through the religious sentiment of the country they ruled over, in directing the Professors of the Medical College at Alexandria to dissect the dead and prepare treatises setting forth the internal construction of man. * * * The lapse of nearly seventeen hundred years, and perhaps the surreptitious researches of the physicians of the fourteenth century, began to suggest the necessity of revising what had thus been derived from remote antiquity. With liberal views, the Papal Governments set an example to Europe, and Italy became distinguished at once as the fountain of anatomical knowledge.* * *

It was my intention to have given you a few thoughts on what might be termed the religious view of this matter; though, standing here a mere medical professor, perhaps I might have stepped from my right position in so doing. And, after all, where is the necessity? It is enough that I fall back on the fact I have just mentioned. Whatever our religious sentiments may be, Protestant or Catholic, we shall surely all agree in this, that they who thus first sanctified practical anatomy before Europe, deliberated when they took that course. Yet they did it in an age not only of acute theological discussion, but of the deepest feeling: it was done in view of the solemn services of the dead. It was done with the consent of men of the largest understanding, the highest philanthropy, and whose sincere piety no one can question. All that I could say in this respect, sinks into insignificance when compared with the discussions which must of necessity have taken place among those able men who looked at the matter in every light, and in the face of semi-barbarian but profoundly religious

Europe, lent their great authority to the conclusion, that it is lawful to dissect the dead.

* * *

If my voice could be heard in the Legislature of New-York, I would address an appeal to it, not only in the name of the colleges and of the body of physicians, but also in the name of humanity. I would call on those able men, to whom are committed our interests, to remove from the statute-book laws which were repudiated in Europe even in the dark ages. I would ask them if there be any reason why we should stand behind Massachusetts or Michigan in an enlightened policy. * * * To one scrupulous from conscientious motives, I would point out the authority that has been given by both the chief divisions of the Christian Church, Protestant and Catholic. To another, timid for fear of popular prejudice, I would show that those who are to be mainly profited are the poor. Of what avail are all our munificent provisions for the destitute, if we deny the only means by which surgeons can be skillful? Our Hospitals and Alms-Houses cannot accompany the emigrant on his lonely way; but let us make sure as far as legislation can do it, that wherever sickness may surprise him a good physician shall be at hand. To provide that good physician, is a matter of philanthropy, charity, and State concern—not a party question. It is one of those things in which, whatever our political opinions may be, we have all the same interest. Disease invades all our families in turn, and takes away one member after another. In turn we have all to come under obligations to that medical skill, the acquisition of which is threatened with punishment. Is it well that laws should exist, which men in every condition in life, poor and rich, the governors and the governed, unanimously agree must be broken? I would earnestly enforce my appeal, by asking, Is it right as between man and man, that you should put this profession in such an attitude, when there is not one of you who would receive a medical adviser except you knew that he had again and again broken this law?

* * *

[The Case against Dissection]†

The sacredness of the human body—or the respect due to the human remains—is it a prejudice, a relic of the times when men did not think, a blind superstition at war with science, with philosophy, with our truest secular good? or has it a deep ground in the reason, as

† From "Editor's Table," *Harper's New Monthly Magazine* 8.57 (April 1854): 690–93. All notes are the editor's.

well as in the purest moral and religious sentiments of our nature?* * *

The fact is beyond all doubt. There ever has been in all places, in all ages, among all classes and conditions of mankind, a deep-feeling in respect to the remains of our earthly mortality. The human body, on the departure of the spirit from it, has never been regarded in the same light as other matter. Nor has this been merely a tender association of ideas, such as would be caused by any object intimately connected with our recollections of departed friends. It has a deeper ground. The body is not like a picture, a book, a garment, or any thing else that once *belonged* to the deceased, and which recalls him vividly to our remembrance. It is something more than a belonging, a property, an association. Philosophy and psychology may protest against the thought, but still they can never do away the deep planted feeling, that in those cold, and motionless, and speechless relics there is still remaining something of the former selfhood.* * *

* * *

We can not help thinking that the necessities of medical science have been greatly overrated. Even where the want is conceded, the benefits may be purchased too dear. Better that the causes of some bodily diseases remain concealed, than that the knowledge of them be obtained at the sacrifice of some of the best feelings of the soul. But admitting the force of every plea, may we not ask—is there not in many cases, in most cases perhaps, an unfeeling waste? A very scientific Professor once told us that in one of our Medical Colleges, the number of subjects obtained for dissection in one course of winter lectures amounted to upward of forty, and this he spoke of as a very insufficient supply. Carry out the ratio to the numerous medical colleges in our city and land, and the number of graves disturbed, and human bodies desecrated, every year, must be reckoned by thousands. We would be cautious here in treating of a matter which, it may be said, the writer does not professionally understand; but must it not strike almost every unprofessional mind in the same light? Why this apparently enormous waste? Why must the human body be dissected over and over again ten thousand times, not so much for the discovery of new truths—for that is not even alleged as the ground in most cases—but to explain old and well known truths to every new class of students? May there not be made most accurate anatomical representations by means of drawings, by preparations in wax, and other modes that might be mentioned, reserving dissections for those cases alone, where the parts are too minute, and the action too microscopical to be set forth by any such methods? Can not a knowledge of the general anatomy be given unless a man is cut up every time the class comes before the lecturer? These

questions may perhaps betray ignorance of the subject in some
respects, but of the ordinary workings of human nature all intelligent
men are alike judges, and upon the minds of such the conviction
will press itself, that the hardening effect of these scientific butch-
eries—we mean to use the term in no more offensive sense than if
we were applying it to the worthy citizens who supply us with animal
food—must produce an indifference, a recklessness, which not only
leads to the waste of which complaint is made, but actually comes
to believe it indispensable?* * *

It does no hurt to the dead. Nothing can be weaker than this
common argument; nothing could show a more inadequate appre-
ciation of the real merits of the great question involved. It does no
hurt to the dead, but it does an immense injury to the living. We
refer not now to the more immediate pain given to the sensibilities.
Severe as this is, there is an evil far greater in what may be styled
the demoralizing consequences that must flow from the loss of that
reverence which has ever been connected with all that reminds us
of the departed. It is the tendency to mar, and, in time, wholly to
destroy, a feeling most intimately associated with all that goes to
make life serious, rational, and religious. It breaks up the sympathies
which unite us with the dead and thus tend more than all things else
to preserve the past as well as present brotherhood of the race. An
increasing indifference to the grave and its sacred contents must
produce a state of mind at war, in feeling, if not in abstract dogma,
with some of the most solemn revelations of Scripture. We do not
make enough of the resurrection in our modern theology. If there is
any thing in Christianity fundamental it is this. The New Testament
not obscurely teaches, that a most important part of Christ's work
was "the redemption of the body" as well as of the soul.* * *

* * *

But not to trespass farther upon the domain of theology, it is in
this great truth we see the reason of this special reverence for the
human body. It is not like any other portion of matter. It undergoes
dissolution, but yet there is a mysterious preservation of a surviving
identity. It is true the dissecting knife of the lecturer, and the after
combustion of the janitor, do no more than hasten a process which
is going on more slowly in the earth; every body understands that as
well as those who would present it as their profoundest argument;
but, as far as the associations and feelings are concerned, the difference is immense. In the one case there come up to the mind,
calmly, seriously, impressively, the ideas of rest, of seclusion, of
divine guardianship, of a silent waiting for the great day of deliver-
ance from the dominion of death and Hades;[1] with the other we

1. The underworld, hell.

connect, and we can not help connecting, the ideas of ignominy, of vile abuse, of irreverence, of irreligion.* * *

Now what a contrast to all this religious feeling, so tender, so melancholy, and yet so full of moral health to the soul—what a contrast, we say, to these blessed influences that come to us from the grave in connection with the doctrine of the resurrection, is presented by the scenes and associations of a dissecting room—the sacred human body, the once loved form, the former temple of a loving spirit, thus lying mangled, debased, deformed, made the subject of unfeeling remark by some cold materializing lecturer, and exposed to the rude gaze, and ruder hands of hardened, and it may be, licentious students.

Must it not be demoralizing? We are fully aware of the strength of the opposing plea, and, on the score of utility, would admit the difficulty of fully answering it. Science, it is said, must have its subjects as well as its books! We would treat with all fairness the honorable and useful men who present the claim. But there is, certainly, another side to the picture; there are other evils; there are other utilities; and if they come in conflict, we are compelled to strike a balance between the higher and the lower—between those that relate to the body's health and those that belong to the spiritual hygieia,[2] or the soul's truest good.

*   *   *

But why such apprehensions, some may say; it is only the bodies of the unknown that are required—the poor, the lost, the unclaimed, the forfeited by crime. But this in fact is one of the harshest features of the measure. The poor have not only feelings like the rich, but often these are their only treasure. The poor think more of death— they have more to remind them of it—than their wealthy brethren; and this may account for the fact that these classes are ever more alarmed at the thought of sepulchral violation than those "who fare sumptuously every day."[3]* * *

*   *   *

We can only give the general aspects of this question. The medical profession, it is said, must have subjects. If so, let them be content with the fewest possible; let the most serious wisdom among us be exercised in providing the means with the least sacrifice of feeling, the least of moral detriment; and then let the necessary duty be ever discharged with all the devout reverence of a high and religious trust.

*   *   *

2. Health (after the Greek goddess of health).
3. In Luke 16.19–26, Jesus tells a parable contrasting the heavenly rewards that go to a beggar and to a rich man who "fared sumptuously every day."

[The Page That Becky Tore?]†

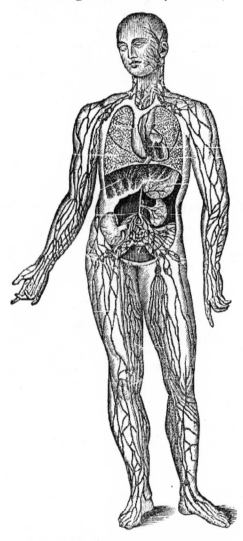

† Frontispiece, *A Treatise on Anatomy, Physiology, and Hygiene*, by Calvin Cutter (Boston: Mussey, 1855). Courtesy of the Marion B. Gebbie, class of 1901, Archives & Special Collections, Madeleine Clark Wallace Library, Wheaton College, Norton, Massachusetts. Alan Gribben, author of *Mark Twain's Library: A Reconstruction* (1980, update forthcoming) informs me that there is evidence Twain may have owned an 1848 edition of Cutter's *Anatomy and Physiology*; its frontispiece is identical to the one in Cutter's 1855 volume.

K. PATRICK OBER

Fire in a Liquid Form†

* * *

Jane Clemens[1] was not the only American who came to put her trust in Perry Davis's Pain-Killer as her family's preventative against cholera. Davis was a schemer and con man of renown, the epitome of the "get rich quick" entrepreneur of the nineteenth century who had mastered the art of translating the health concerns of the population into large sums of money for himself. Born in Dartmouth, Massachusetts, in 1791, Davis was initially trained as a shoemaker. According to his own account, which he undoubtedly embellished for public consumption, he developed a severe respiratory infection in December 1839. His multitude of symptoms included a bad cough, a sore stomach, a poor appetite, night sweats, "piles of the worst kind," and a canker in his mouth. He felt driven to develop a medicine to save himself from the grave, and he was apparently successful in doing so. He decided to name his creation "Pain-Killer" because, reasonably enough, it had killed all of his pains. Davis moved to Providence, Rhode Island, and started a business to manufacture and distribute Pain-Killer. He was an aggressive self-promoter, and his name and picture were on every label.

While making a batch of the Pain-Killer in 1844, so the story goes, Davis sustained severe burns to his face and arms from an explosion of alcohol (which was the major ingredient in his invention). He claimed to have cured his own burns by applying the Pain-Killer, and he further claimed that the Pain-Killer "gave immediate relief" (a most unlikely consequence of pouring alcohol and cayenne pepper onto a burn).[2]

Perry Davis's Pain-Killer was similar to the many other patent medicines in that it contained a considerable quantity of alcohol, an ingredient that was the basis for much of the popularity of such products. Davis used the drama of the explosion to his marketing advantage by hiring an artist to create a drawing of his engulfment in flames. The picture, which was widely publicized, showed a huge

† Reprinted from *Mark Twain and Medicine: "Any Mummery Will Cure"* by K. Patrick Ober by permission of the University of Missouri Press. Copyright © 2003 by the Curators of the University of Missouri. All notes are Ober's unless otherwise indicated.
1. Mother of Samuel Clemens (Mark Twain) [Editor's note].
2. A batch of the Pain-Killer was mixed up by combining 5 gallons of alcohol with 2¼ pounds of gum myrrh, 10 ounces of capsicum (the active ingredient of cayenne pepper), 8 ounces of gum opium, 6 ounces of gum benzoin, and 3 ounces of gum fuiaic (Stewart H. Holbrook, *The Golden Age of Quackery* [New York: Macmillan, 1959], 152–53).

can exploding, and the text referred to "Alcohol" with a large "A" (lest there was any question about what the purchaser was *really* getting when he bought the Pain-Killer). Using the defense that the alcohol content was medicinal, Davis proclaimed disingenuously that the Pain-Killer was "a stimulant that will not destroy the soul by creating a taste for liquor." Davis, who contributed money to the temperance movement, stated (with a pride that was either hypocritical or self-deceiving) that the Pain-Killer "has saved many a soul from a drunkard's grave."[3]

The popularity of the Pain-Killer and similar patent medicines was undoubtedly related to their considerable content of alcohol, just as the widespread appeal of other patent medicines was due to their opiate content. Information about the content of the different patent medicines was not typically shared with the general public, as the trademark on the medicines allowed their manufacturing process and contents to be kept secret. However, there can be little question that the secret ingredients of the patent medicines contributed greatly to their appeal. For example, the fact that Shiloh's Cure for Consumption was fortified with heroin undoubtedly broadened its market to include many citizens who were nonconsumptive. Kopp's Baby Friend was made of sweetened water and morphine and was advertised as the perfect way to calm down babies. It is not likely that many mothers realized that Mrs. Winslow's Soothing Syrup for teething babies also derived most of its soothing action from its morphine content (one testimonial bragged that the syrup "makes 'em lay like the dead 'til mornin' ").

Alcohol was the most predictable solvent, however, and it seemed to become increasingly popular as a constituent of patent therapies as the temperance movement gained momentum. Dr. Kilmer's Swamp Root, touted for its utility in treating occult kidney disease, had a 10.5 percent alcohol content in addition to its 46.5 percent sugar content. Parker's True Tonic was marketed as a reliable cure for alcoholism, and undoubtedly many daughters and wives were impressed by how effectively this tonic discouraged their wayward men from going out and getting drunk, especially when it was taken on a regular basis. (If they had realized that the True Tonic had a 41.6 percent alcohol content, they might have been somewhat less pleased.) Eventually, Americans purchased more alcohol (excluding the sales of ales and beer) in the form of patent medicines than they bought by legal purchase from licensed liquor vendors,[4] and for a while the federal government even considered licensing patent medicine dealers as liquor vendors. The fact that Perry Davis's Pain-

3. Ibid., 155.
4. Ibid., 15.

Killer was nothing more than a spiced-up alcoholic beverage was undoubtedly a major factor in its widespread popularity. It does seem reasonable to assume, however, that Jane Clemens was naively unaware of its ingredients, and that her own purchases were based on her belief in its claims as a "medicinal" product that would protect her family's health.

The rapid and widespread use of the Pain-Killer is a testimony to Perry Davis's ability as a salesman. The Pain-Killer had been invented in the eastern United States in 1840, but due to its successful promotion it had found its way to Hannibal by 1849 (just in time to help Jane Clemens in her effort to protect her family from the cholera epidemic). Even though it was advertised as a multipurpose remedy, Davis specifically emphasized the Pain-Killer's effectiveness in treating cholera. In his drive to make a buck, he understood the value in playing off the greatest fears of the general population. As he later recounted the successful story of his invention, Davis was particularly proud of the recognition achieved by the Pain-Killer as a nostrum for "the dreaded cholera." He bragged about how the Pain-Killer "was suddenly brought into general notice by the astonishing cures it effected of this terrible disease."[5] Perry Davis's widespread advertisements for the Pain-Killer were found in Hannibal newspapers of 1849.[6] Known Hannibal advertisements of the era promoted the Pain-Killer for external use in the treatment of bruises, sores, and burns,"[7] but Clemens's numerous references to its fiery potency when ingested are consistent with its marketing as a substance that could be used either internally or externally.

Jane Clemens, always eager to employ the newest and the best in medical therapeutics, made the decision to use the Pain-Killer as a cholera preventative for her family. With alcohol as its major constituent, and additional ingredients that included camphor and cayenne pepper, each fiery dose of Perry Davis's Pain-Killer was unforgettable to its users, and Samuel Clemens's childhood memories of the remedy were not particularly fond ones, as he recalled in his *Autobiography*: "It was a most detestable medicine, Perry Davis's

5. Ibid., 154. In truth, when Dr. William McPheeters was systematically trying to find an effective cholera antidote, the first treatment he rejected was one recommended by a Dr. Cartwright of St. Louis that consisted of calomel, capsicum, and camphor. "This compound, instead of arresting the disease, was found to be positively prejudicial," McPheeters discovered. He determined that most of the problems from the Cartwright remedy could be attributed to the capsicum, which in many instances increased the severity of the gastritis. McPheeters abandoned the use of capsicum as "worse than useless" in the treatment of cholera ("Epidemic of Cholera in St. Louis in 1849," in *A History of Medicine in Missouri*, by E. J. Goodwin [St. Louis: W. L. Smith, 1905], 89), even as Perry Davis was actively promoting his capsicum-laden Pain-Killer as the world's best cholera treatment.
6. Mark Twain, *Early Tales and Sketches, vol. 1, 1851–1864*, ed. Edgar Marquess Branch and Robert H. Hirst (Berkeley: University of California Press, 1979), 470–71.
7. Dixon Wecter, *Sam Clemens of Hannibal* (Boston: Houghton Mifflin, 1952), 213–14.

Pain-Killer. Mr. Pavey's negro man, who was a person of good judg-ment and considerable curiosity, wanted to sample it, and I let him. It was his opinion that it was made of hell-fire."[8]

Clemens's early experience with the Pain-Killer was memorable enough that he found a place for it in his fiction, where it burned with similar intensity when Aunt Polly dosed Tom with it in *The Adventures of Tom Sawyer.* * * *

*   *   *

8. *Mark Twain's Own Autobiography: The Chapters from the* North American Review, ed. Michael J. Kiskis (Madison: University of Wisconsin Press, 1990), 53.

Social and Regional Contexts

E. ANTHONY ROTUNDO

Boy Culture†

In 1853, a popular etiquette writer called Mrs. Manners launched an angry attack on the boys of America. "Why is it," she asked, "that there must be a period in the lives of boys when they should be spoken of as 'disagreeable cubs'? Why is a gentle, polite boy such a rarity?" She continued her assault in that tone of embattled hauteur so common to etiquette writers: "If your parents are willing for you to be the 'Goths and Vandals' of society, I shall protest against it. You have been outlaws long enough, and now I beg you will observe the rules."[1]

For all her wounded righteousness, Mrs. Manners expressed a widely shared view. Source after source described boys as "wild" and "careless," as "primitive savages" full of "animal spirits." They were commonly compared to Indians and African tribesmen. One writer even called them a race unto themselves—"the race of boys."[2] * * *

* * *

Technically, of course, boy culture was really a subculture—distinct, oppositional, but intimately related to the larger culture of which it was a part. Boys shuttled constantly in and out of this world of theirs, home and then back again. Their experiences with boy culture helped to prepare them in many ways for life in the adult spheres that surrounded them. Boy culture, then, was not the only world that a young male inhabited, nor was it the only one that left its mark on him. Still, within its carefully set boundaries, boy culture was surprisingly free of adult intervention—it gave a youngster his first exhilarating taste of independence and made a lasting imprint on his character.

---

† From *American Manhood*, by E. Anthony Rotundo. Copyright © 1993 by Basic Books, A Division of HarperCollins Publishers, Inc. Reprinted by permission of Basic Books, a member of Perseus Books, L.L.C. All notes are Rotundo's.

1. Mrs. Manners, *At Home and Abroad; or How to Behave* (New York, 1853), 40–41.
2. The phrase is from Charles Dudley Warner, *Being a Boy* (Boston, 1897 [1877]), 66–67, but similar imagery appears throughout the source material.* * *

To be sure, this was not the first time historically that Northern boys had been free from supervision. Perpetual supervision of *any* child is impossible. But the circumstances of boys' lives in the nine-teenth century freed them from adult oversight for long periods of time in the company of other boys, and this was different from the colonial experience. In the villages of New England during the 1600s and 1700s, a boy past the age of six was given responsibility for the first time. He began to help his father with farm work, which put him in the company of another generation and not among his male peers. His father did give him independent chores to do, but they tended to be solitary activities like tending livestock or running errands to other farms. Of course, boys did gather and play in colo-nial New England, but circumstances made it hard for them to come together on a regular basis in the absence of adults. They lacked the independence and cohesion as a group that boys developed in the nineteenth century.[3]

These later generations of the 1800s spent more time in the peer world of schoolhouse and schoolyard. Middle-class boys were needed less to do the work of the family. They were increasingly isolated from males of the older generation. A growing proportion of them lived in large towns and cities, which brought them in contact with a denser mass of peers. And, in a world where autonomy had become a male virtue, there were positive reasons to give boys time and space of their own. In sum, the conditions were ripe in the nineteenth century for a coherent, independent boys' world.

Nineteenth-century boys lived a different sort of life in the years before boy culture opened up to them—a life so different from what came later that it bears special notice here. Until the age of six or so, boys were enmeshed in a domestic world of brothers, sisters, and cousins. They rarely strayed from the presence of watchful adults.[4] Mothers kept an especially keen eye on their children during these early years, for popular thinking held that this was the phase of life when the basis was laid for good character. Thus, for his first five to seven years, a boy's adult companions were female and his environ-ment was one of tender affection and moral rigor.[5] By the time that

---

3. John Demos, *A Little Commonwealth: Family Life in Plymouth Colony* (New York, 1970), 131–44; Ross Beales, "In Search of the Historical Child: Miniature Adulthood and Youth in Colonial America," *American Quarterly*, 27 (1975).

4. Edward Everett Hale, *A New England Boyhood* (Boston, 1964 [1893]), 22–23, 31.

5. E. Anthony Rotundo, "Manhood in America: The Northern Middle Class, 1770–1920" (Ph.D. diss., Brandeis Univ., 1982), 180–97, 347–56; Nancy F. Cott, *The Bonds of Wom-anhood: "Woman's Sphere" in New England, 1780–1835* (New Haven, Conn., 1977), 44–47, 57–60, 84–92; Mary Ryan, *The Cradle of the Middle Class: The Family in Oneida County, New York, 1790–1865* (New York, 1981), 157–65.

boys reached the age of three or four, their mothers were beginning to complain about their rowdy, insolent ways.[6] But however much they rebelled, these little boys were still embedded in a feminine world.

The clothing that boys wore during their early years served as a vivid symbol of their feminization: they dressed in the same loose-fitting gowns that their sisters wore.* * *

Finally, at about age six, Northern boys cut loose from these social and physical restraints.[7] Although they would continue to live for many years in the woman's world of the home, they were now inhabitants of an alternate world as well.[8] * * * For those who lived in small towns, the neighboring orchards, fields, and forests provided a natural habitat for boy culture.[9] By contrast, indoors was alien territory. A parlor, a dining room, almost any place with a nice carpet, repelled boy culture. Boys did sometimes carve out their own turf within the house—usually in the attic, where dirt, noise, and physical activity created fewer problems than in the clean, placid lower floors. And the house was not the only indoor space that was alien. Boy culture languished in the school and in the church, and it never even approached the offices and countinghouses where middle-class fathers worked.[1]

* * *As they broke away from the constant restriction of home, boys also shed forever the gowns and petticoats of younger days. Suddenly, the differences between themselves and their sisters—so long discouraged by the rules and habits of the home—seemed to be encouraged and even underscored.[2] For their sisters were still enveloped by the moral and physical confinements of domesticity and by the gowns and petticoats that were its visible emblems. With

6. James R. McGovern, *Yankee Family* (New Orleans, 1975), 73; Ryan, 162; Mrs. Manners, 40.
7. This approximate age is based on several pieces of evidence: Henry Dwight Sedgwick, *Memoirs of an Epicurean* (New York, 1942), 43; Daniel Carter Beard, *Hardly a Man Is Now Alive: The Autobiography of Dan Beard* (New York, 1939), 79; Hale, 16–17; Kenneth S. Lynn, *William Dean Howells: An American Life* (New York, 1970), 43.
8. Gender segregation was not unique to middle-class Victorian children.* * *
9. The "city states" quotation is from Henry Seidel Canby, *The Age of Confidence: Life in the Nineties* (New York, 1934), 35; see also 42–46; Lewis Wallace, *Lew Wallace: An Autobiography* (New York, 1906), 55; Sedgwick, 31; Lynn, 42; Howard Doughty, *Francis Parkman* (Cambridge, Mass., 1983 [1962]), 14–15.
1. For instance, Hale, 45, 53–54, 57–59.
2. There is a danger of overstating the similarities between girls' and boys' lives before age six. They were given different toys to play with (McGovern, 73), and mothers were kept keenly aware of the different worlds for which they were raising their toddlers (James Barnard Blake diary, Aug. 3, 1851, American Antiquarian Society; Kirk Jeffrey, "Family History: The Middle-Class American Family in the Urban Context, 1830–1870" [Ph.D. diss., Stanford Univ., 1972], 202–3), so that they must have treated their children differently according to sex. Still, the early domestic life of boys zealously discouraged basic "male" virtues like aggression and self-assertion in favor of "feminine" kindness and submission.

great clarity a boy saw that female meant fettered and male meant free.[3]

Boys, of course, were not absolutely free any more than the girls were literally chained. Indeed, their worlds of play and sociability overlapped at many points. At play, girls shared the yard with their brothers, and on rainy days boys cohabited attics and odd rooms with their sisters. Girls and boys enjoyed many of the same games, such as hide-and-seek and tag, and they pursued some of the same outdoor activities, such as sledding and skating. But their social worlds and their peer cultures were distinct. Boys had a freedom to roam that girls lacked. Physical aggression drove boys' activity in a way that was not acceptable for girls. The activities of both sexes mixed competition with collaboration, but the boys placed a stronger emphasis on their rivalries and the girls stressed their cooperation more heavily. Most importantly, the social worlds of boys and girls had different relationships with the world of adults of the same sex. Boy culture was independent of men and often antagonistic toward them. Girls' common culture was interdependent with that of women and even shared much of the same physical space. There was continuity, if not always amity, between the worlds of female generations.[4] The same was not true for men and boys. The nineteenth-century emphasis on male autonomy encouraged a gap between generations of males.

Boy Culture: Games and Pastimes

Boys now enjoyed the liberty of trousers and the independence of the great outdoors. More than that, they were beyond the reach of adult supervision for hours at a time. Boys were suddenly free to pursue a range of activities that would have been difficult if not impossible in the domestic world. The physical activities that had been hindered in early boyhood now became particular passions. Hiking, exploring, swimming, rowing, and horseback riding took on special meaning for boys newly liberated from domestic confinement.[5]

---

3. Beard, 76; Philip Greven, Jr., *The Protestant Temperament: Patterns of Child-Rearing, Religious Experience, and Self in Early America* (New York, 1977), 45–46.
4. On girls' play and common culture, see Henrietta Dana Skinner, *An Echo from Parnassus: Being Girlhood Memories of Longfellow and His Friends* (New York, 1928), 87–111, 175–81; Mary Starbuck, *My House and I: A Chronicle of Nantucket* (Boston, 1929), esp. 212, 215; Lucy Larcom, *A New England Girlhood* (New York, 1961 [1889]), 17–117. On the interdependence of girls and women, see Carroll Smith-Rosenberg, "The Female World of Love and Ritual: Relations between Women in Nineteenth-Century America," *Signs*, 1 (1975), 14–19.
5. Alphonso David Rockwell, *Rambling Recollections: An Autobiography* (New York, 1920), 30–31, 56; Wallace, 55, 121; Beard, 203; Ray Stannard Baker, *Native American: The Book of My Youth* (New York, 1941), 85; Hale, 40, 88, 151; Warner, 49; Doughty, 14–15;

*   *   *

While boys pursued these pastimes for the simple pleasure of exercise, they engaged in many other activities that set them head to
head in hostile combat. Friends fought or wrestled for the fun of it,
while other boys goaded playmates unwillingly into fights with each
other. * * * One of the bonds that held boy culture together was the
pain that youngsters inflicted on each other.

If boys posed a danger to one another, they were downright lethal
to small animals. Boys especially enjoyed hunting birds and squirrels,
and they did a good deal of trapping as well. There were several
reasons for hunting's great appeal. In the rural North of the nineteenth century, the gun and the rod were still emblems of the male
duty to feed one's family. The hunt, in that way, was associated with
the power and status of grown men.[6] Yet city boys—given the opportunity to hunt—took the same lusty pleasure in it that their country
cousins did. They just liked the challenge of the kill. Another practice
that links the hunting habit to the violent tendencies of boy culture
is the extravagant sadism that youngsters sometimes showed when
they killed their prey. Boys turned woodchuck trapping into woodchuck torture, and they often killed insects simply to inflict suffering.
While the boyish interest in hunting and fishing reflected in some
part a remnant of earlier manly duties, it was also related to the
pleasure that boys took in fighting and even stoning one another.[7]

Not all of boys' play was so openly violent or so freeform. Popular
boys' games such as marbles, tag, blindman's buff, leapfrog, and tug-
of-war demanded physical skill, and most involved exercise and competition as well. An informal, prehistoric form of football mixed
elements of tag, rugby, soccer, and the modern gridiron game with
a large dose of free-for-all mayhem. There were also a number of
variants on the current sport of baseball. What united these varied
pastimes in contrast to modern games was a lack of elaborate rules
and complicated strategies. Spontaneous exercise and excitement
were more important than elaborate expertise in boys' games of the
nineteenth century.[8] Other pastimes were more personally expressive. Games that developed on the spur of the moment or that grew
slowly within the context of a friendship or a gang revealed many of
the preoccupations of boy culture. A favorite subject in these impro-

Wheaton J. Lane, *Commodore Vanderbilt: An Epic of the Steam Age* (New York, 1942),
11, 13, 162.

6. John Mack Faragher, *Women and Men on the Overland Trail* (New Haven, Conn., 1979),
135–36.

7. Hale, 55, 151; Warner, 127–28; Doughty, 14–15; Lynn, 45.

8. Beard, 92, 110; Hale, 23, 200–201; James Lovett, *Old Boston Boys and the Games They
Played* (Boston, 1906); William Wells Newell, *Games and Songs of American Children*
(New York, 1883).

vised games was warfare. Sometimes, the young combatants took on the roles of the knights they read about in books, while during the Civil War they played the soldiers of their own time.[9]

The most popular variant on these war games seemed to be the struggle between settlers and Indians. In this case, the boys were often inspired by the stories of people they knew or by the local folklore about ancestral generations.[1] One revealing aspect of these games involved the choosing of sides. By race and sometimes by ancestry, the boys were kin to the settlers. Yet there is no indication that any stigma attached to playing an Indian. Indeed, the boys relished the role of the Indian—assumed by them all to be more barbarous and aggressive—as much as they did the role of the settler.[2] These settler-and-Indian games allowed boys to enter and imagine roles that were played by real adult males.* * *

* * *

Above all, the pastimes favored by Northern boys set their world in sharp contrast to the domestic, female world—the world from which they emerged as little boys and to which they returned every evening. Where women's sphere offered kindness, morality, nurture, and a gentle spirit, the boys' world countered with energy, self-assertion, noise, and a frequent resort to violence. The physical explosiveness and the willingness to inflict pain contrasted so sharply with the values of the home that they suggest a dialogue in actions between the values of the two spheres—as if a boy's aggressive impulses, so relentlessly opposed at home, sought extreme forms of release outside it; then, with stricken consciences, the boys came home for further lessons in self-restraint. The two worlds seemed almost to thrive on their opposition to each other. Boys, though they valued both worlds deeply, often complained about the confinement of home. The world that they created just beyond the reach of domesticity gave them a space for expressive play and a sense of freedom from the women's world that had nurtured them early in boyhood—and that welcomed them home every night.

* * *

9. Ellery H. Clark, *Reminiscences of an Athlete: Twenty Years on Track and Field* (Boston, 1911), 6; Beard, 102–3; Wallace, 22.
1. The boys' games of settlers and Indians were inspired not only by folklore but also by their reading. Cooper's *Leatherstocking Tales* was especially important in this regard (see Wallace, 54, and Canby, 192). Cowboys did not enter into these games until the final years of the century—the white men who fought Indians were called "the settlers" in the games of nineteenth-century boys.
2. Warner, 89–91; Beard, 92; Clark, 6.

The Values of Boy Culture

* * *

Physical prowess and the various forms of courage were uppermost among the qualities that boys valued, but there were also others that they expected of each other. Boys demanded loyalty between friends and loyalty of the individual to the group. Their concept of the faithful friend closely resembled the code of fidelity that links comrades at arms. The true test of this loyalty came at moments when one boy was threatened and the other came to his aid.* * *

Boy Culture and Adult Authority

One of boy culture's most striking features was its independence from close adult supervision. This autonomy existed, however, within well-defined boundaries of place and time. Many adults tried to influence what went on within boy culture even though they did not supervise it.* * *

Of all the forces that threatened the borders of boy culture, the most pervasive was the community at large. The confrontations between youngsters and their communities came usually over minor acts of vandalism. The reasons for these social collisions varied. Acts of trespass and petty theft often grew out of the blithe disregard that boys had for private property. They refused to recognize the lines that separated one adult's possessions from another's.[3] At other times, it was the very knowledge of possible trouble with adults that led to vandalism. Boys, after all, were constantly daring each other to perform dangerous acts. And since a confrontation with authority was one kind of danger, risking that confrontation was a way to prove one's bravery.[4] Thus, the pleasure in raiding a garden or an orchard came from the adventure as much as the fruit, and youthful mischief-makers made a sport of avoiding officers of the law and irate property owners.

Sometimes an angry private citizen took it upon himself to fight petty youth crime in his community, but doing so made him a handsome target for another form of boyish malfeasance—the prank. One Ohio man—a "strait-laced Presbyterian farmer . . . who often rebuked the boys for their escapades"—paid for his opposition to vandalism when he found a ghastly battered corpse in his barn one morning. Although a frightened inspection showed that the corpse was a carefully prepared dummy, the episode had given the local boys an effective way to express their resentment of the farmer.[5]

3. Hale, 37; Wallace, 55; John Doane Barnard journal, Essex Institute, 3–4; Canby, 43–44.
4. Beard, 78.
5. Beard, 73–74.

Pranks, however, were more than just acts of vengeance. They reversed men's and boy's roles, giving younger males the power to disrupt the lives of older males and forcing the elders to do their boyish bidding. There was, for example, a Connecticut doctor who made a favorite target for the local boys. The "queerest man of the town," he had only one eye, spoke in a high falsetto, and possessed the strange habit of dismounting from his horse every time he saw a stone in the road. This made him an easy victim for pranks, as the boys scattered stones in his path and then watched with delight as he got off his horse to throw them away. The boys had found an exciting way to attack the dignity of an adult.[6]

* * *

Outgrowing Boy Culture

* * *

In spite of these vague age boundaries, there were a few important events that marked the end of boyhood for many youngsters. These often had to do with leaving home or taking a first clerkship or full-time job.* * *

* * *A teenager also brought his time in boy culture to a close when he took his first strides toward another signpost of manhood—marriage. The journey toward marriage began with the dawning interest of pubescent boys in the opposite sex.[7] As boys developed an interest in girls, the customs and habits of boy culture started to lose their luster. Daniel Beard recalled in his autobiography the ways in which his outlook changed when an attractive new girl arrived in town: "Suddenly marbles became a childish game which made knuckles grimy and chapped. . . . Prisoner's base was good enough sport but it mussed one's clothes." The rhymes and rituals of boy-hood now "seemed absurd instead of natural" while the services at church took on a new interest. Daniel suddenly began to appear in public with his face clean and his hair neatly combed.[8]

* * *

6. Rockwell, 35–36.* * *
7. The average age of puberty for boys in this era was about sixteen (Joseph Kett, *Rites of Passage: Adolescence in America, 1790 to the Present* [New York, 1977], 44).
8. Beard, 199.

ROBERT JACKSON

[Mark Twain's Missouri]†

* * *

The complicated, often contradictory identities of the Missouri of Twain's youth are almost entirely ignored in criticism of his work [, which focuses on "what might be called the more prevalent national thesis, emerging from a clearly and consciously national gaze"].[1] * * * Critics variously refer to the state as part of the North, the South, and the West—everywhere, it seems, except the East where Twain settled in adult life—often to suit their purposes in the advancement of a specific argument. * * * But even when this kind of rhetorical appropriation on the part of many critics is exposed, it must be admitted that Missouri, approached as a regional construction, has indeed predisposed itself to such uncertainties, both geographically and culturally.

Missouri had always been a home for slavery, and its entry into the Union wrought havoc for the latitudinal symmetry of the country's North/South division. The clearest and most literal expression of this disorder came in 1820 with what would become known as the Missouri Compromise. The compromise attempted to deal with slavery in two ways that appear almost ridiculous in their contradiction to one another. First, national leaders agreed that the southern border of Missouri would forever—that is, as the nation edged farther to the West—demarcate the limits of slavery: all new states north of the border would be admitted as free states, and those to the south would be slave states. Second, and rather absurdly from a strictly geometric surveying perspective, Missouri itself was constituted as a slave state, and thus bulged out on the north side of the slave border. This exception would allow Maine to enter the Union as a free state at the same time, and thus preserve the tenuous balance of power between North and South in Congress.

As a political act, the compromise seemed to suit everyone in power, at least for the time being. As a cultural act, it served only to illustrate the diverse nation's irreconcilable and messy realities which no single leader or group could resolve, and which, indeed, the very constitution of the national government appears to have

† From "The Emergence of Mark Twain's Missouri: Regional Theory and *Adventures of Huckleberry Finn,*" *Southern Literary Journal* 35.1 (Fall 2002): 47–69. Copyright © 2002 by the *Southern Literary Journal* and the University of North Carolina at Chapel Hill Department of English. Reprinted with permission. All notes are Jackson's unless otherwise indicated.

1. See Henry Nash Smith, ed., *Mark Twain: A Collection of Critical Essays* (Englewood Cliffs: Prentice-Hall, 1963), for a representative survey of critical treatments of this space.

been inadequate to confront. Of course, the compromise was successful only as a temporary measure, delaying the crisis that would culminate, forty years later, in the Civil War. Missouri's role in this kind of temporary compromise, the uniqueness of its geographic placement before and after the 1820 national remapping, and the singularity of its particular cultural identities that made such an internally contradictory act of legislation desirable or even possible, testify to the complexity native to the state and its relationship to the nation as a whole.

Most Missourians did not own any slaves during Twain's youth, and those who did generally had no more than one or two. By 1850, only those with a sentimental attachment to the institution or to individual slaves had resisted the lucrative opportunities to sell slaves to planters in the Deep South. There was little plantation culture in Missouri, with the minor exception of a few counties north of the Missouri River in the central part of the state and along the upper Mississippi River (which included Twain's boyhood homes); thus the southern half of Missouri, with generally inferior soil and hillier, rockier terrain in the Ozarks area, was in a crucial cultural sense the least "southern" part of the state. During the years just before the Civil War, slaves accounted for a mere ten percent of the state's population, a figure far lower than in Deep South states. In addition, the population growth of the state during Twain's youth included vast numbers of anti-slavery German immigrants and pragmatic New England business families, important waves that followed earlier settlements by the slaveholding (or at least pro-slavery) Virginians, Kentuckians, and Tennesseeans of which Twain's own family had been a part.[2] These groups further complicated Missouri's sentiments about slavery, forging new industrial and political alliances and producing increasingly complex and diverse visions of the state's future. This does not suggest that most people acted or even spoke out against slavery, but simply that the simmering ambiguity of the state during Twain's early youth should not be grouped clumsily with the

2. Twain's father, John Marshall Clemens, was born in Virginia in 1798 and lived in Kentucky and Tennessee from 1809 to 1835. Jane Lampton Clemens, Twain's mother, was born in 1803 in Lexington, Kentucky, like her husband into a family of refugees from Virginia. Both regarded themselves as heirs, at least culturally, to Old Virginia aristocratic gentry, despite the ongoing inability of John Clemens to provide the financial resources necessary for such a lifestyle. The family's resettlement to Florida, Missouri, in 1835 (a few months before Twain's birth), and their later move to Hannibal, were motivated primarily by dire economic circumstances. In this sense the Clemens family was typical of many southern transplants in Missouri, people who retained many of the values of the Old South, including pro-slavery sympathies, but had difficulty preserving the balance of their southern culture in the more complex and economically challenging frontier society west of the Mississippi. And while both the Clemens and Lampton families had owned slaves in the South, and Twain himself grew up in the care of a household slave named Jennie until he was six years old (at which point his father sold her, much to his son's despair, to settle debts), the Clemens family in Missouri never accumulated the kind of wealth that would have enabled them to own a large number of slaves and sustain an aristocratic life.

much more confrontational secessionism of Deep South states like Louisiana, Mississippi, and Alabama.

A brief glance at the "supercharged atmosphere" of the cultural and political life in St. Louis during this period, and increasingly in the later 1850s, gives the impression of an almost guerrilla chaos.[3] With countless ideological factions, several competing political machines, a citizenry of diverse origins and languages, a vigorous and prolific local press with perspectives and languages as various as its readers, and an explosive business economy with interests in farming, industry, and river and railroad trades, the only thing absent during this period was any kind of consensus on key cultural and political questions. Twain's travels during his early years as a riverboat pilot enabled him to witness much of this culture firsthand, and to view it alongside the more polar regional distinctions of the industrial North upriver and the southern plantation culture of the lower Mississippi. This experience may also have left him with an increasingly problematic sense of his own place, his own kind of border status, in a national context that was seeking more and more to define itself in the strictly binary terms of northern unionism or southern secessionism.

In its own moment of crisis, finally, a deeply fractious Missouri remained loyal to the North during the Civil War, with economic motives and fears about the risks of war taking precedence over the state's historical connection to slavery. During the war itself, the state provided the setting for countless local skirmishes, often highly intramural in nature, including many among hardy civilians who distrusted their neighbors. The state never gained anything like the single-minded momentum that expressed the fervor and decisiveness of less ambivalent states on both sides of the Mason-Dixon Line.

Missourians had spread their votes widely among the four presidential candidates in 1860, with the moderate, or, as some charged, absurdly contradictory, Stephen Douglas carrying the state by a narrow margin. Abraham Lincoln's unconditional Unionism, perhaps too absolute a stance in such a state, won him a mere eleven percent of the statewide vote and last place in Missouri. In effect, what historian James Neal Primm says about the inestimably consequential 1860 elections may be applied more generally to the state's identity and overall history during this period: "Missourians had chosen the middle ground."[4]

The "middle ground" here is indeed a paradoxical conception. It

---

3. James Neal Primm, *Lion of the Valley: St. Louis, Missouri, 1764–1980* (1980; St. Louis: Missouri Historical Society Press, 1998), 227. See Primm's Chapter 7, "For the Union," for an excellent general account of the city and state during the Civil War era.
4. James Neal Primm, "Missouri, St. Louis, and the Secession Crisis," *Germans for a Free Missouri: Translations from the St. Louis Radical Press, 1857–1862*, trans. Steven Rowan (Columbia: University of Missouri Press, 1983), 13.

is a construction that is both central and devoid of precise location; both centered and, somehow, lacking a firm center. The phrase seems to express aptly Missouri's desire to maintain the status quo in its public affairs, and to suggest that its individuals would rather negotiate each new moment improvisationally, as they had no doubt been doing all along, without recourse to a histrionic, potentially cataclysmic confrontation of national armies. This suggests, for my purposes here, that the Missouri of this period, with all its historical and geographic uniqueness, may be considered as a distinct region in the cultural life of the larger nation.

Mark Twain's own behavior during the war was notoriously erratic and, to say the least, improvisational; it may be summarized as a series of failed attempts to participate in the increasingly public or collective national culture, followed each time by a kind of ritualistic, and very personal, escape from such developments: a lighting out, of sorts.[5] Without endowing Missouri with a wholly deterministic power over the identities of its residents, Twain's behavior does seem quite consistent with his native region's own erratic, often contradictory character. Dissatisfied with each and every single voice in the increasingly partisan crisis, the indecisive Twain seems that much more representative of the very culture within which and against which he is struggling for his own identity and humanity. Considered in this way, Twain's literary persona, traditionally canonized, quite publicly and nationally, for its typically and consummately "American" character, can be seen as a most revealing, ironic marvel in its own right.

*   *   *

5. In 1861, for example, Twain briefly joined an irregular militia that was loosely allied with the Confederacy—before lighting out for Nevada [Editor's note].

Literary Contexts

MARK TWAIN

The Story of the Bad Little Boy
Who Didn't Come to Grief†

Once there was a bad little boy, whose name was Jim—though, if you will notice, you will find that bad little boys are nearly always called James in your Sunday-school books. It was very strange, but still it was true, that this one was called Jim.

He didn't have any sick mother, either—a sick mother who was pious and had the consumption, and would be glad to lie down in the grave and be at rest, but for the strong love she bore her boy, and the anxiety she felt that the world would be harsh and cold towards him when she was gone. Most bad boys in the Sunday books are named James, and have sick mothers, who teach them to say, "Now I lay me down," etc., and sing them to sleep with sweet plaintive voices, and then kiss them good-night, and kneel down by the bedside and weep. But it was different with this fellow. He was named Jim, and there wasn't any thing the matter with his mother—no consumption, or any thing of that kind. She was rather stout than otherwise, and she was not pious; moreover, she was not anxious on Jim's account. She said if he were to break his neck, it wouldn't be much loss. She always spanked Jim to sleep, and she never kissed him good-night; on the contrary, she boxed his ears when she was ready to leave him.

Once this little bad boy stole the key of the pantry and slipped in there and helped himself to some jam, and filled up the vessel with tar, so that his mother would never know the difference; but all at once a terrible feeling didn't come over him, and something didn't seem to whisper to him, "Is it right to disobey my mother? Isn't it sinful to do this? Where do bad little boys go who gobble up their

---

† This parody of Sunday-school stories first appeared under the title "The Story of the Bad Little Boy That Bore a Charmed Life" and the heading "The Christmas Fireside" in the *Californian*, 23 December 1865. Reprinted from Twain's *The Celebrated Jumping Frog of Calaveras County, and Other Sketches* (New York: C. H. Webb, 1867), 60–66. All notes are the editor's.

good kind mother's jam?" and then he didn't kneel down all alone and promise never to be wicked any more, and rise up with a light, happy heart, and go and tell his mother all about it, and beg her forgiveness, and be blessed by her with tears of pride and thankfulness in her eyes. No; that is the way with all other bad boys in the books; but it happened otherwise with this Jim, strangely enough. He ate that jam, and said it was bully, in his sinful, vulgar way; and he put in the tar, and said that was bully also, and laughed, and observed that "the old woman would get up and snort" when she found it out; and when she did find it out, he denied knowing any thing about it, and she whipped him severely, and he did the crying himself. Every thing about this boy was curious—every thing turned out differently with him from the way it does to the bad Jameses in the books.

Once he climbed up in Farmer Acorn's apple-tree to steal apples, and the limb didn't break, and he didn't fall and break his arm, and get torn by the farmer's great dog, and then languish on a sick bed for weeks, and repent and become good. Oh! no; he stole as many apples as he wanted, and came down all right; and he was all ready for the dog, too, and knocked him endways with a rock when he came to tear him. It was very strange—nothing like it ever happened in those mild little books with marbled backs, and with pictures in them of men with swallow-tailed coats, and bell-crowned hats, and pantaloons that are short in the legs, and women with the waists of their dresses under their arms and no hoops on. Nothing like it in any of the Sunday-school books.

Once he stole the teacher's penknife, and when he was afraid it would be found out, and he would get whipped, he slipped it into George Wilson's cap—poor Widow Wilson's son, the moral boy, the good little boy of the village, who always obeyed his mother, and never told an untruth, and was fond of his lessons and infatuated with Sunday-school. And when the knife dropped from the cap, and poor George hung his head and blushed, as if in conscious guilt, and the grieved teacher charged the theft upon him, and was just in the very act of bringing the switch down upon his trembling shoulders, a white-haired improbable justice of the peace did not suddenly appear in their midst and strike an attitude and say, "spare this noble boy—there stands the cowering culprit! I was passing the school-door at recess, and, unseen myself, I saw the theft committed!" And then Jim didn't get whaled, and the venerable justice didn't read the tearful school a homily, and take George by the hand and say such a boy deserved to be exalted, and then tell him to come and make his home with him, and sweep out the office, and make fires, and run errands, and chop wood, and study law, and help his wife to do household labors, and have all the balance of the time to play, and get forty cents a month, and be happy. No; it would have happened that way in the books, but it didn't happen that way to Jim. No meddling old clam of a justice dropped in to make trouble, and so the model boy George got threshed, and Jim was glad of it; because, you know, Jim hated moral boys. Jim said he was "down on them milk-sops." Such was the coarse language of this bad, neglected boy.

But the strangest things that ever happened to Jim was the time he went boating on Sunday and didn't get drowned, and that other time that he got caught out in the storm when he was fishing on Sunday, and didn't get struck by lightning. Why, you might look, and look, and look through the Sunday-school books, from now till next Christmas, and you would never come across any thing like this. Oh! no; you would find that all the bad boys who go boating on Sunday invariably get drowned; and all the bad boys who get caught out in storms, when they are fishing on Sunday, infallibly get struck by lightning. Boats with bad boys in them always upset on Sunday, and it always storms when bad boys go fishing on the Sabbath. How this Jim ever escaped is a mystery to me.

This Jim bore a charmed life—that must have been the way of it. Nothing could hurt him. He even gave the elephant in the menagerie a plug of tobacco, and the elephant didn't knock the top of his head off with his trunk. He browsed around the cupboard after essence of peppermint, and didn't make a mistake and drink aqua fortis.[1] He stole his father's gun and went hunting on the Sabbath, and didn't shoot three or four of his fingers off. He struck his little sister on the temple with his fist when he was angry, and she didn't linger in pain through long summer days, and die with sweet words of forgiveness upon her lips that redoubled the anguish of his breaking heart. No; she got over it. He ran off and went to sea at last, and didn't come back and find himself sad and alone in the world, his loved ones sleeping in the quiet churchyard, and the vine-embowered home of his boyhood tumbled down and gone to decay. Ah! no; he came home as drunk as a piper, and got into the station-house[2] the first thing.

And he grew up, and married, and raised a large family, and brained them all with an ax one night, and got wealthy by all manner of cheating and rascality; and now he is the infernalest wickedest scoundrel in his native village, and is universally respected, and belongs to the Legislature.

So you see there never was a bad James in the Sunday-school books that had such a streak of luck as this sinful Jim with the charmed life.

1. Nitric acid.
2. Police station.

MARK TWAIN

The Story of the Good Little Boy
Who Did Not Prosper†

[The following has been written at the instance of several literary friends, who thought that if the history of "The Bad Little Boy who Did not Come to Grief" (a moral sketch which I published five or six years ago) was worthy of preservation several weeks in print, a fair and unprejudiced companion-piece to it would deserve a similar immortality.—EDITOR MEMORANDA.]

Once there was a good little boy by the name of Jacob Blivens. He always obeyed his parents, no matter how absurd and unreasonable their demands were; and he always learned his book, and never was late at Sabbath school. He would not play hookey, even when his sober judgment told him it was the most profitable thing he could do. None of the other boys could ever make that boy out, he acted so strangely. He wouldn't lie, no matter how convenient it was. He just said it was wrong to lie, and that was sufficient for him. And he was so honest that he was simply ridiculous. The curious ways that that Jacob had surpassed everything. He wouldn't play marbles on Sunday, he wouldn't rob birds' nests, he wouldn't give hot pennies to organ-grinders' monkeys; he didn't seem to take any interest in any kind of rational amusement. So the other boys used to try to reason it out and come to an understanding of him, but they couldn't arrive at any satisfactory conclusion; as I said before, they could only figure out a sort of vague idea that he was "afflicted," and so they took him under their protection, and never allowed any harm to come to him.

This good little boy read all the Sunday-school books; they were his greatest delight. This was the whole secret of it. He believed in the good little boys they put in the Sunday-school books; he had every confidence in them. He longed to come across one of them alive, once; but he never did. They all died before his time, maybe. Whenever he read about a particularly good one, he turned over quickly to the end to see what became of him, because he wanted to travel thousands of miles and gaze on him; but it wasn't any use; that good little boy always died in the last chapter, and there was a picture of the funeral, with all his relations and the Sunday-school children standing around the grave in pantaloons that were too short, and bonnets that were too large, and everybody crying into hand-

† From *The Galaxy* 9.5 (May 1870): 724–26. The "Editor Memoranda" are Twain's.

kerchiefs that had as much as a yard and a half of stuff in them. He was always headed off in this way. He never could see one of those good little boys, on account of his always dying in the last chapter.

Jacob had a noble ambition to be put in a Sunday-school book. He wanted to be put in, with pictures representing him gloriously declining to lie to his mother, and she weeping for joy about it; and pictures representing him standing on the doorstep giving a penny to a poor beggar-woman with six children, and telling her to spend it freely, but not to be extravagant, because extravagance is a sin; and pictures of him magnanimously refusing to tell on the bad boy who always lay in wait for him around the corner, as he came from school, and welted him over the head with a lath, and then chased him home, saying "Hi! hi!" as he proceeded. That was the ambition of young Jacob Blivens. He wished to be put in a Sunday-school book. It made him feel a little uncomfortable sometimes when he reflected that the good little boys always died. He loved to live, you know, and this was the most unpleasant feature about being a Sunday-school-book boy. He knew it was not healthy to be good. He knew it was more fatal than consumption to be so supernaturally good as the boys in the books were; he knew that none of them had ever been able to stand it long, and it pained him to think that if they put him in a book he wouldn't ever see it, or even if they did get the book out before he died, it wouldn't be popular without any picture of his funeral in the back part of it. It couldn't be much of a Sunday-school book that couldn't tell about the advice he gave to the community when he was dying. So, at last, of course he had to make up his mind to do the best he could under the circumstances— to live right, and hang on as long as he could, and have his dying speech all ready when his time came.

But somehow, nothing ever went right with this good little boy; nothing ever turned out with him the way it turned out with the good little boys in the books. They always had a good time, and the bad boys had the broken legs; but in his case there was a screw loose somewhere, and it all happened just the other way. When he found Jim Blake stealing apples and went under the tree to read to him about the bad little boy who fell out of a neighbor's apple tree, and broke his arm, Jim fell out of the tree too, but he fell on *him*, and broke *his* arm, and Jim wasn't hurt at all. Jacob couldn't understand that. There wasn't anything in the books like it.

And once, when some bad boys pushed a blind man over in the mud, and Jacob ran to help him up and receive his blessing, the blind man did not give him any blessing at all, but whacked him over the head with his stick and said he would like to catch him shoving *him* again and then pretending to help him up. This was not in accordance with any of the books. Jacob looked them all over to see.

One thing that Jacob wanted to do was to find a lame dog that hadn't any place to stay, and was hungry and persecuted, and bring him home and pet him and have that dog's imperishable gratitude. And at last he found one, and was happy; and he brought him home and fed him, but when he was going to pet him the dog flew at him and tore all the clothes off him except those that were in front, and made a spectacle of him that was astonishing. He examined authorities, but he could not understand the matter. It was of the same breed of dogs that was in the books, but it acted very differently. Whatever this boy did, he got into trouble. The very things the boys in the books got rewarded for turned out to be about the most unprofitable things he could invest in.

Once when he was on his way to Sunday school he saw some bad boys starting off pleasuring in a sail-boat. He was filled with consternation, because he knew from his reading that boys who went sailing on Sunday invariably got drowned. So he ran out on a raft to warn them, but a log turned with him and slid him into the river. A man got him out pretty soon, and the doctor pumped the water out of him and gave him a fresh start with his bellows, but he caught cold and lay sick abed nine weeks. But the most unaccountable thing about it was that the bad boys in the boat had a good time all day, and then reached home alive and well, in the most surprising manner. Jacob Blivens said there was nothing like these things in the books. He was perfectly dumbfounded.

When he got well he was a little discouraged, but he resolved to keep on trying, anyhow. He knew that so far his experiences wouldn't do to go in a book, but he hadn't yet reached the allotted term of life for good little boys, and he hoped to be able to make a record yet, if he could hold on till his time was fully up. If everything else failed, he had his dying speech to fall back on.

He examined his authorities, and found that it was now time for him to go to sea as a cabin boy. He called on a ship captain and made his application, and when the captain asked for his recommendations he proudly drew out a tract and pointed to the words: "To Jacob Blivens, from his affectionate teacher." But the captain was a coarse, vulgar man, and he said, "Oh, that be blowed! that wasn't any proof that he knew how to wash dishes or handle a slush-bucket, and he guessed he didn't want him." This was altogether the most extraordinary thing that ever had happened to Jacob in all his life. A compliment from a teacher, on a tract, had never failed to move the tenderest emotions of ship captains and open the way to all offices of honor and profit in their gift—it never had in any book that ever he had read. He could hardly believe his senses.

This boy always had a hard time of it. Nothing ever came out according to the authorities with him. At last, one day, when he was around hunting up bad little boys to admonish, he found a lot of them in the old iron foundry fixing up a little joke on fourteen or fifteen dogs, which they had tied together in long procession and were going to ornament with empty nitro-glycerine cans made fast to their tails. Jacob's heart was touched. He sat down on one of those cans—for he never minded grease when duty was before him—and he took hold of the foremost dog by the collar, and turned his reproving eye upon wicked Tom Jones. But just at that moment Alderman McWelter, full of wrath, stepped in. All the bad boys ran away; but Jacob Blivens rose in conscious innocence and began one of those stately little Sunday-school-book speeches which always commence with "Oh, Sir!" in dead opposition to the fact that no boy, good or bad, ever starts a remark with "Oh, Sir!" But the Alderman never waited to hear the rest. He took Jacob Blivens by the ear and turned him around, and hit him a whack in the rear with the flat of his hand; and in an instant that good little boy shot out through the roof and soared away toward the sun, with the fragments of those fifteen dogs stringing after him like the tail of a kite. And there wasn't a sign of that Alderman or that old iron foundry left on the face of the earth; and as for young Jacob Blivens, he never got a chance to make his last dying speech after all his trouble fixing it up, unless he made it to the birds; because, although the bulk of him came down all right in a tree-top in an adjoining county, the rest of him was apportioned around among four townships, and so they had to hold five inquests on him to find out whether he was dead or not, and how it occurred. You never saw a boy scattered so.[1]

Thus perished the good little boy who did the best he could, but didn't come out according to the books. Every boy who ever did as he did prospered, except him. His case is truly remarkable. It will probably never be accounted for.

STEPHEN PERCY [JOSEPH CUNDALL]

From Robin Hood and His Merry Foresters†

Tales of Robin Hood and his merry foresters were the delight of my boyhood.

1. This catastrophe is borrowed (without the unknown but most ingenious owner's permission) from a stray newspaper item, and trimmed up and altered to fit Jacob Blivens, who stood sadly in need of a doom that would send him out of the world with *éclat*—EDITOR MEMORANDA.
† (London: Tilt and Bogue, 1841), 1–3, 8–9, 44–47, 78–80, 85–86, 144–46, 151–53. Alan Gribben cites this source for Twain in "How Tom Sawyer Played Robin Hood 'by the Book,'" *English Language Notes* 13.3 (March 1976): 201–4. All notes are the editor's.

Many an hour which my school-fellows spent in games of cricket or leap-frog, I passed happily away in the rustic arbour that we had built in the corner of our play-ground, deeply intent upon a volume of old ballads that chance had thrown before me. Sometimes a companion or two, weary of the sport in which they had been engaged, would join me in my retreat, and ask me to read aloud; and seldom would they leave me till the school-bell warned us that it was time to return to our duties.

*   *   *

Though many years have since glided away, I can recall these pleasures most vividly. Well do I recollect the youth who shared my bed,[1] and who in school hours sat next me on the first form; and well do I remember, as we sauntered together one bright summer's evening through the shrubbery that encircled our play-ground, his asking me to tell him some tale of Robin Hood. Willingly I complied.* * *

*   *   *

"More than six hundred years ago, in the reigns of King Henry the Second and Richard Cœur de Lion,[2] there lived in the northern part of England a most famous outlaw, named Robin Hood.* * *

*   *   *

"Robin Hood and his followers all dressed themselves in cloth of Lincoln green, and generally wore a scarlet cap upon their heads. Each man was armed with a dagger and a short basket-hilted sword, and carried a long bow in his hand, while a quiver filled with arrows a cloth-yard long hung at his back. The captain, besides wearing a better cloth than his men, always carried with him a bugle horn, whose notes he taught his followers to distinguish at a most incredible distance.

*   *   *

"[From the branches of a tree, Robin Hood observes the sheriff of Nottingham pass with a band of men and then strikes out to find his own men.] On his way he was obliged to cross the high road, where a stranger arrested his steps.

" 'Hast thou seen the sheriff of Nottingham in the forest?' he inquired.

---

1. It was common in the early nineteenth century, when beds were relatively scarce, for schoolmates to share a bed, likewise for siblings.
2. Richard I of England (1157–1199, reigned 1189–99), also called the Lion Hearted. Henry II (1133–1189) reigned 1154–89.

" 'Aye, my good fellow, and with a fine band at his tail,' replied Robin Hood. 'Art thou seeking him?'

" 'Not him,' returned the stranger, who was a bold yeoman,[3] dressed in a coat of the untanned skin of some wild beast, and who carried a bow in his hand, and a sword and dagger at his side. 'I seek not the sheriff, but him whom he seeks.'

" 'And who may that be?' said the forester, at the same time forming a pretty shrewd guess.

" 'A man they call Robin Hood,' answered the stranger. 'If thou canst show me where he is, this purse shall be thine;' and taking a well-filled leathern bag from his girdle, he rattled the contents together.

" 'Come with me, my friend, and thou shalt soon see Robin Hood,' returned the outlaw. 'But thou hast a brave bow; wilt thou not try thy skill with me in archery?' The stranger at once consented. Robin Hood with his dagger cut down the branch of a tree, and fixing it in the earth, suspended upon the top a little garland, which he entwined with the long grass. The archers took their station at the distance of three hundred yards, and the stranger drew the first bow. His arrow flew past the mark far too high. The outlaw next bent his weapon, and shot within an inch or two of the stick. Again the yeoman essayed; and this time his shaft flew straight and passed through the garland; but Robin Hood stepped up boldly, and drawing his arrow to the very head, shot it with such vehemence that it clave the branch into two pieces, and still flew onwards for some yards.

" 'Give me thy hand,' cried the stranger,—'thou'rt the bravest bowman I've seen for many a day, an thy heart be as true as thy aim, thou art a better man than Robin Hood. What name bearest thou?'

" 'Nay—first tell me thine,' replied Robin, 'and then by my faith I will answer thee.'

" 'They call me Guy of Gisborne,' rejoined the yeoman. 'I'm one of the king's rangers; and am sworn to take that outlawed traitor, Robin Hood.'

" 'He's no traitor, sirrah,' returned the forester angrily; 'and cares as much for thee as for the beast whose skin thou wearest. I am that outlaw whom thou seek'st,—I am Robin Hood:' and in a moment his drawn sword was in his hand.

" 'That's for thee then,' cried the yeoman, striking fiercely. 'Five hundred pounds are set upon thine head, and if I get it not I'll lose mine own.'

"Robin Hood intercepted the intended blow, and fought skillfully with his fiery and more athletic antagonist, who poured down an

---

3. Attendant to a nobleman or king; assistant to a sheriff; farmer.

incessant shower of strokes upon him. Once the bold outlaw fell; but recovering himself sufficiently to place a foot upon the earth, he thrust his sword at the ranger, and as he drew back to avoid it, Robin Hood sprung up, and with one sudden back-handed stroke slew poor Guy of Gisborne upon the spot.* * *

* * *

"[Later the bishop of Hereford and his retinue encounter what appear to be shepherds, roasting venison. He tells his guards to seize them for killing the king's deer—deer roaming in the king's forest.]

" 'Mercy! mercy! good bishop,' cried one of the shepherds; 'surely it beseemeth not thy holy office to take away the lives of so many innocent peasants.'

" 'Guards, seize these villains,' cried the prelate, indignant at the presumption of the serf;—'away with them to York,—they shall be strung on the highest gibbet in the city.' The armed horsemen turned not over-willingly against the offenders, and endeavoured to seize them, but with a loud laugh they darted among the trees, where the steeds could not possibly follow. Presently the shepherd who had begged for mercy pulled from under his frock a little bugle-horn, and blew a short call upon it. The bishop and his retinue started with affright, and had already begun to urge on their horses, when they found themselves surrounded on every side by archers, dressed in green, with bows drawn in their hands.

" 'Mercy! mercy!' cried the bishop in great trepidation at the sight of fifty or more arrows ready to pierce him through. 'Have mercy upon an unfortunate traveller.'

" 'Fear not, good father,' replied Robin Hood, who was the shepherd that had before spoken; 'we do but crave thy worshipful company to dine with us under the green-wood tree, and then, when thou hast paid the forest toll, thou shalt depart in safety;' and, stepping into the road, the bold outlaw laid one hand upon the embossed bridle of the bishop's steed, and held the stirrup with the other.

" 'Oh! that we had but gone the outer road,' groaned the bishop to his holy brother; 'we should have avoided these limbs of the evil one.'

" 'Nay, nay reverend father,' cried Robin Hood, laughing at the poor bishop's rueful countenance; 'call us not by so bad a name. We do but take from the rich to administer to the necessities of the poor and if we do now and then slay a fat buck or two, our good king will never know his loss. But dismount, holy sir; and do ye, my friends, come likewise; right merry shall we be with such a jovial company.'* * *

*   *   *

"[After the feast] At Robin Hood's bidding, * * * two young men again took the bishop upon their shoulders, and bore him to the spot where his steed and those of his retinue were fastened. They placed him upon his saddle, with his face to the animal's tail, and giving it him instead of the bridle, they pricked the creature with their daggers, and started it off at full gallop, the terrified rider clinging both with hands and knees to its back. The dean, the armed horsemen, and the servants were allowed to follow their superior in peace; but the sumpter[4] mules and their burdens were detained as payment for the feast that had been given to their owners.

*   *   *

"[Later Sir Rychard of Wierysdale, an ally of Robin Hood, is captured by the sheriff of Nottingham, and his lady seeks help from Robin.]

" 'God save thee, good Robin Hood,' said the lady as the forester advanced; 'grant me thine aid, and that quickly. Thine enemy, the sheriff, hath bound my dear husband, and led him captive to Nottingham.'

"The outlaw replied by setting his bugle-horn to his lips, and sounding a shrill blast, it was answered from every side, and seven-score men soon gathered round him.

" 'Busk ye, my merry men,' he cried to them. 'To the rescue of the knight of Wierysdale. That double villain, the sheriff of Nottingham, hath bound him. He that will not fight for our good friend is no longer follower of mine.'

"The men gave a loud shout to prove their readiness, and their captain, bidding the lady be of good cheer, and await the issue in her castle, darted through the woods. The foresters followed him in a crowd close upon his heels; neither hedge nor stream stopped their progress; they leaped over every obstacle, and in two hours reached the town of Nottingham. They were just in time. The gaoler was even at the moment unbarring the gates of the castle to admit the prisoner, and the sheriff was unfastening the bonds by which he was held to his horse. At the appearance of the outlaws a loud cry was raised by the astonished inhabitants, and the sheriff leaped into his saddle. He had but a small force at hand, quite insufficient to oppose the assailants, and seizing his prisoner's bridle rein, he attempted to fly;—'twas too late. An arrow from the bow of the foremost outlaw pierced his brain, and he fell headlong from his steed. His attendants were routed, and the knight of Wierysdale was recaptured. Robin

4. Animal carrying a burden.

Hood himself cut his bonds with a dagger, and after raising a loud shout of victory, he and his gallant foresters retired to Wierysdale, where they received the warm thanks of the lady of the castle, and after partaking of a glorious feast, they returned to their wonted abodes in merry Sherwood.

*   *   *

"[Robin Hood is then in disfavor with King Richard but, after an archery competition, is pardoned—as long as he and his men become royal archers.]

"Here, it is said, our brave hero assumed his title of earl of Huntingdon, and lived in most noble style; but soon growing tired of the confinement of the court, he asked permission to revisit the merry woods. The king granted him seven days, but when Robin Hood breathed the delightful air of Sherwood, and heard the songs of the sweet birds, he could not tear himself away. He ranged through many a well-known thicket and oft-frequented lawn, and in the ecstacy of his delight he set his bugle horn to his mouth, and made the old trees re-echo with the blast. To his great astonishment it was replied to, and four-score youths bounded towards him. Several had deserted him in London, and many who were at first disbanded had returned to their favourite haunts, and Robin Hood was again acknowledged as the leader of a forest band. Little John and Will Scarlet soon learned the intelligence, and with all speed joined him with the rest.

"King Richard was enraged; he sent a renowned knight with two hundred soldiers to capture the rebellious outlaw, and a desperate fight took place upon a plain in Sherwood forest. It lasted from sunrise to sun-set, but neither party could boast of victory, and the knight lost many of his men. Robin Hood himself was wounded by an arrow, and was obliged to be taken to Kirkleys Nunnery, where he was treacherously suffered to bleed to death by the prioress. As he found his end approaching he called Little John to him. 'Carry me into the woods, I entreat thee,' he said to him:

> " 'And give me my bent bow in my hand,
>   And a broad arrow I'll let flee;
> And where this arrow is taken up
>   There shall my grave digged be.'

"The outlaw shot his last bow. His shaft flew feebly to a short distance, and fell beneath an oak. He leaned back into the arms of his faithful attendant—and died. His wish was complied with; and a stone was placed upon the green sod to mark the last resting-place of the brave Robin Hood; it bore this inscription:—

'Here, underneath this little stone,
Lies Robert, Earl of Huntingdon.
Ne'er archer was as he so good;
And people called him 'Robin Hood.'
Such outlaws as he and his men
Will England never see again."

*   *   *

Composing the Book

MARK TWAIN

Boy's Manuscript†

[two manuscript pages (about 300 words) missing]

me that put the apple there. I don't know how long I waited, but it was very long. I didn't mind it, because I was fixing up what I was going to say, and so it was delicious. First I thought I would call her Dear Amy, though I was a little afraid; but soon I got used to it and it was beautiful. Then I changed it to Sweet Amy—which was better—and then I changed it again, to Darling Amy—which was bliss. When I got it all fixed at last, I was going to say, "Darling Amy, if you found an apple on the doorstep, which I think you did find one there, it was *me* that done it, and I hope you'll think of me sometimes, if you can—only a little"—and I said that over ever so many times and got it all by heart so I could say it right off without ever thinking at all. And directly I saw a blue ribbon and a white frock—my heart began to beat again and my head began to swim and I began to choke—it got worse and worse the closer she came—and so, just in time I jumped behind the lumber and she went by. I only had the strength to sing out "Apples!" and then I shinned it through the lumber yard and hid. How I did wish she knew my voice! And then I got chicken-hearted and all in a tremble for fear she *did* know it. But I got easy after a while, when I came to remember that she didn't know *me*, and so perhaps she wouldn't know my voice either. When I said my prayers at night, I prayed for her. And I prayed the good God not to let the apple make her sick, and to bless her every way for the sake of Christ the Lord. And then I tried to go to sleep but I was troubled about Jimmy Riley, though she don't know him, and I said the first chance I got I would lick him again. Which I will.

† The text for "Boy's Manuscript" (1868) is from *Huck Finn and Tom Sawyer among the Indians,* by Mark Twain, ed. Dahlia Armon, Walter Blair, Paul Baender, William M. Gibson, and Franklin R. Rogers (Berkeley: University of California Press, 1989), 1–19. Courtesy of the Mark Twain Foundation (chief representative: Richard A. Watson, of Chamberlain, Willi, Ouchterloney, & Watson, 575 Eighth Ave., 16th Floor, New York, NY 10018). Brackets in the main text are Twain's. All notes are the editor's, except the one marked "M. T."

Tuesday.—I played hookey yesterday morning, and stayed around about her street pretending I wasn't doing it for anything, but I was looking out sideways at her window all the time, because I was sure I knew which one it was—and when people came along I turned away and sneaked off a piece when they looked at me, because I was dead sure from the way they looked that they knew what I was up to—but I watched out, and when they had got far away I went back again. Once I saw part of a dress flutter in that window, and O, how I felt! I was so happy as long as it was in sight—and so awful miserable when it went away—and *so* happy again when it came back. I could have staid there a year. Once I was watching it so close I didn't notice, and kept getting further and further out in the street, till a man hollered "Hi!" and nearly ran over me with his wagon. I wished he had, because then I would have been crippled and they would have carried me into her house all bloody and busted up, and she would have cried, and I would have been per-fectly happy, because I would have had to stay there till I got well, which I wish I never *would* get well. But by and bye it turned out that that was the nigger chambermaid fluttering her dress at the window, and then I felt so down-hearted I wished I had never found it out. But I know which is her window now, because she came to it all of a sudden, and I thought my heart, was going to burst with happiness—but I turned my back and pretended I didn't know she was there, and I went to shouting at some boys (there wasn't any in sight,) and "show-ing off" all I could. But when I sort of glanced around to see if she was taking notice of me she was gone—and then I wished I hadn't been such a fool, and had looked at her when I had a chance. Maybe she thought I was cold towards her? It made me feel awful to think of it. Our torchlight procession came off last night. There was nearly eleven of us, and we had a lantern. It was splendid. It was John Wagner's uncle's lantern. I walked right alongside of John Wagner all the evening. Once he let me carry the lantern myself a little piece. Not when we were going by *her* house, but if she was where she could see us she could see easy enough that I knowed the boy that had the lantern. It was the best torchlight procession the boys ever got up—all the boys said so. I only wish I could find out what she thinks of it. I got them to go by her house four times. They didn't want to go, because it is in a back street, but I hired them with marbles. I had twenty-two commas and a white alley[1] when I started out, but I went home dead broke. Suppose I grieved any? No. I said I didn't mind any expense when her happiness was concerned. I shouted all the time we were going by her house, and ordered the procession around lively, and so I don't make any doubt but she

1. Kinds of marbles.

thinks I was the captain of it—that is, if she knows me and my voice.
I expect she does. I've got acquainted with her brother Tom, and I
expect he tells her about me. I'm always hanging around him, and
giving him things, and following him home and waiting outside the
gate for him. I gave him a fish-hook yesterday; and last night I
showed him my sore toe where I stumped it—and to-day I let him
take my tooth that was pulled out New-Year's to show to his mother.
I hope *she* seen it. I was a-playing for that, anyway. How awful it is
to meet her father and mother! They seem like kings and queens to
me. And her brother Tom—I can hardly understand how it can be—
but he can hug her and kiss her whenever he wants to. I wish I was
her brother. But it can't be, I don't reckon.

Wednesday.—I don't take any pleasure, nights, now, but carrying
on with the boys out in the street before her house, and talking loud
and shouting, so she can hear me and know I'm there. And after
school I go by about three times, all in a flutter and afraid to hardly
glance over, and always letting on that I am in an awful hurry—going
after the doctor or something. But about the fourth time I only get
in sight of the house, and then I weaken—because I am afraid the
people in the houses along will know what I am about. I am all the
time wishing that a wild bull or an Injun would get after her so I
could save her, but somehow it don't happen so. It happens so in
the books, but it don't seem to happen so to me. After I go to bed, I
think all the time of big boys insulting her and me a-licking them.
Here lately, sometimes I feel ever so happy, and then again, and
dreadful often, too, I feel mighty bad. *Then* I don't take any interest
in anything. I don't care for apples, I don't care for molasses candy,
swinging on the gate don't do me no good, and even sliding on the
cellar door don't seem like it used to did. I just go around hankering
after something I don't know what. I've put away my kite. I don't
care for kites now. I saw the cat pull the tail off of it without a pang.
I don't seem to want to go in a-swimming, even when Ma don't allow
me to. I don't try to catch flies any more. I don't take any interest in
flies. Even when they light right where I could nab them easy, I don't
pay any attention to them. And I don't take any interest in property.
To-day I took everything out of my pockets, and looked at them—
and the very things I thought the most of I don't think the least about
now. There was a ball, and a top, and a piece of chalk, and two fish
hooks, and a buckskin string, and a long piece of twine, and two slate
pencils, and a sure-enough china, and three white alleys, and a spool
cannon, and a wooden soldier with his leg broke, and a real Barlow,
and a hunk of maple sugar, and a jewsharp, and a dead frog, and a
jaybird's egg, and a door knob, and a glass thing that's broke off of
the top of a decanter (I traded two fish-hooks and a tin injun for it,)

and a penny, and a potato-gun, and two grasshoppers which their legs was pulled off, and a spectacle glass, and a picture of Adam and Eve without a rag. I took them all up stairs and put them away. And I know I shall never care anything about property any more. I had all that trouble accumulating a fortune, and now I am not as happy as I was when I was poor. Joe Baldwin's cat is dead, and they are expecting me to go to the funeral, but I shall not go. I don't take any interest in funerals any more. I don't wish to do anything but just go off by myself and think of *her*. I wish I was dead—that is what I wish I was. Then maybe she would be sorry.

Friday.—My mother don't understand it. And I can't tell her. She worries about me, and asks me if I'm sick, and where it hurts me— and I have to say that I ain't sick and nothing don't hurt me, but she says she knows better, because it's the measles. So she gave me ipecac, and calomel,[2] and all that sort of stuff and made me awful sick. And I had to go to bed, and she gave me a mug of hot sage tea and a mug of hot saffron tea, and covered me up with blankets and said that that would sweat me and bring it to the surface. I suffered. But I couldn't tell her. Then she said I had bile. And so she gave me some warm salt water and I heaved up everything that was in me. But she wasn't satisfied. She said there wasn't any bile in that. So she gave me two blue mass pills, and after that a tumbler of Epsom salts[3] to work them off—which it did work them off. I felt that what was left of me was dying, but still I couldn't tell. The measles wouldn't come to the surface and so it wasn't measles; there wasn't any bile, and so it wasn't bile. Then she said she was stumped—but there was *some thing* the matter, and so there was nothing to do but tackle it in a sort of a *general* way. I was too weak and miserable to care much. And so she put bottles of hot water to my feet, and socks full of hot ashes on my breast, and a poultice on my head. But they didn't work, and so she gave me some rhubarb to regulate my bowels, and put a mustard plaster[4] on my back. But at last she said she was satisfied it wasn't a cold on the chest. It must be general stagnation of the blood, and then I knew what was coming. But I couldn't tell, and so, with *her* name on my lips I delivered myself up and went through the water treatment—douche, sitz, wet-sheet and shower-bath[5] (awful,) and came out all weak, and sick, and played out. Does *she*—ah, no, she knows nothing of it. And all the time that I lay suffering, I did

2. Nineteenth-century medicines. Ipecac is still used to induce vomiting; calomel is no longer used to enhance excretion because it contains mercury, a poison.
3. Taken internally or externally.
4. Poultices and plasters were applied externally.
5. Versions of the mid-nineteenth-century water cure. A douche was a kind of shower. A sitz-bath entailed sitting in a tub.

so want to hear somebody only mention her name—and I hated them because they thought of everything else to please me but that. And when at last somebody *did* mention it my face and my eyes lit up so that my mother clasped her hands and said: "Thanks, O thanks, the pills are operating!"

Saturday Night.—This was a blessed day. Mrs. Johnson came to call and as she passed through the hall I saw—O, I like to jumped out of bed!—I saw the flash of a little red dress, and I knew who was in it. Mrs. Johnson is her aunt. And when they came in with Ma to see me I was perfectly happy. I was perfectly happy but I was afraid to look at her except when she was not looking at me. Ma said I had been very sick, but was looking ever so much better now. Mrs. Johnson said it was a dangerous time, because children got hold of so much fruit. Now she said Amy found an apple [I started,] on the doorstep [Oh!] last Sunday, [Oh, geeminy, the very, very one!] and ate it all up, [Bless her heart!] and it gave her the colic. [Dern that apple!] And so *she* had been sick, too, poor dear, and it was her Billy that did it—though she couldn't know that, of course. I wanted to take her in my arms and tell her all about it and ask her to forgive me, but I was afraid to even speak to her. But she had suffered for my sake, and I was happy. By and bye she came near the bed and looked at me with her big blue eyes, and never flinched. It gave me some spunk. Then she said:

"What's your name?—Eddie, or Joe?"

I said, "It ain't neither—it's Billy."

"Billy what?"

"Billy Rogers."

"Has your sister got a doll?"

"I ain't got any sister."

"It ain't a pretty name I don't think—much."

"Which?"

"Why Billy Rogers—Rogers ain't, but Billy is. Did you ever see two cats fighting?—*I* have."

"Well I reckon I have. I've *made* 'em fight. More'n a thousand times. I've fit 'em over close-lines, and in boxes, and under barrels— every way. But the most fun is to tie fire-crackers to their tails and see 'em scatter for home. Your name's Amy, ain't it?—and you're eight years old, ain't you?"

"Yes, I'll be *nine*, ten months and a half from now, and I've got two dolls, and one of 'em can cry and the other's got its head broke and all the sawdust is out of its legs—it don't make no difference, though—I've give all its dresses to the other. Is this the first time you ever been sick?"

"*No!* I've had the scarlet fever and the mumps, and the hoop'n cough, and ever so many things. H'mph! *I* don't consider it anything to be sick."

"My mother don't, either. She's been sick maybe a thousand times—and once, would you believe it, they thought she was going to die."

"They *always* think I'm going to die. The doctors always gives me up and has the family crying and snuffling round here. But I only think it's bully."

"Bully is naughty, my mother says, and she don't 'low Tom to say it. Who do you go to school to?"

"Peg-leg Bliven. That's what the boys calls him, cause he's got a cork leg."

"Goody! I'm going to him, too."

"Oh, *that's* bul—. I like that. When?"

"To-morrow. Will you play with me?"

"You bet!"

Then Mrs. Johnson called her and she said "Good-bye, Billy"— she called me Billy—and then she went away and left me *so* happy. And she gave me a chunk of molasses candy, and I put it next my heart, and it got warm and stuck, and it won't come off, and I can't get my shirt off, but I don't mind it. I'm only glad. But won't I be out of this and at school Monday? I should *think* so.

Thursday.—They've been plaguing us. We've been playing together three days, and to-day I asked her if she would be my little wife and she said she would, and just then Jim Riley and Bob Sawyer jumped up from behind the fence where they'd been listening, and begun to holler at the other scholars and told them all about it. So she went away crying, and I felt bad enough to cry myself. I licked Jim Riley, and Bob Sawyer licked me, and Jo Bryant licked Sawyer, and Peg-leg licked all of us. But nothing could make me happy. I was too dreadful miserable on account of seeing her cry.

Friday.—She didn't come to school this morning, and I felt awful. I couldn't study, I couldn't do anything. I got a black mark because I couldn't tell if a man had five apples and divided them equally among himself and gave the rest away, how much it was—or something like that. I didn't know how many parts of speech there was, and I didn't care. I was head of the spelling class and I spellt baker with two k's and got turned down foot. I got lathered for drawing a picture of her on the slate, though it looked more like women's hoops with a hatchet on top than it looked like her. But I didn't care for sufferings. Bill Williams bent a pin and I set down on it, but I never even squirmed. Jake Warner hit me with a spit-ball, but I never took any notice of it. The world was all dark to me. The first hour that morning was awful. Something told me she wouldn't be there. I don't know what, but *something* told me. And my heart sunk away down when I looked among all the girls and didn't find her. No matter what was going on, that first hour, I was watching the door. I wouldn't hear the teacher sometimes, and then I got scolded. I kept on hoping and hoping—and starting, a little, every time the door opened—till it was no use—she wasn't coming. And when she came in the afternoon, it was all bright again. But she passed by me and never even looked at me. I felt so bad. I tried to catch her eye, but I couldn't. She always looked the other way. At last she set up close to Jimmy Riley and whispered to him a long, long time—five minutes, I should think. I wished that I could die right in my tracks. And I said to myself I would lick Jim Riley till he couldn't stand. Presently she looked at me—for the first time—but she didn't smile. She laid something as far as she could toward the end of the bench and motioned that it was for me. Soon as the teacher turned I rushed there and got it. It was wrote on a piece of copy-book, and so the first line wasn't hers. This is the letter:

"*Time and Tide wait for no Man.*

"mister william rogers i do not love you dont come about me any more i will not speak to you"

I cried all the afternoon, nearly, and I hated her. She passed by me two or three times, but I never noticed her. At recess I licked three of the boys and put my arms round May Warner's neck, and *she* saw me do it, too, and she didn't play with anybody at all. Once she came near me and said very low, "*Billy, I—I'm sorry.*" But I went away and wouldn't look at her. But pretty soon I was sorry myself. I was scared, then. I jumped up and ran, but school was just taking in and she was already gone to her seat. I thought what a fool I was; and I wished it was to do over again, I wouldn't go away. She had said she was sorry—*and I wouldn't notice her.* I wished the house would fall on me. I felt so mean for treating her so when she wanted to be friendly. How I did wish I could catch her eye!—I would look a look that she would understand. But she never, never looked at me. She sat with her head down, looking sad, poor thing. She never spoke but once during the afternoon, and then it was to that hateful Jim Riley. *I* will pay him for this conduct.

Saturday.—Going home from school Friday evening, she went with the girls all around her, and though I walked on the outside, and talked loud, and ran ahead sometimes, and cavorted around, and said all sorts of funny things that made the other girls laugh, *she* wouldn't laugh, and wouldn't take any notice of me at all. At her gate I was close enough to her to touch her, and she knew it, but she wouldn't look around, but just went straight in and straight to the door, without ever turning. And Oh, how I felt! I said the world was a mean, sad place, and had nothing for me to love or care for in it— and life, life was only misery. It was then that it first came into my head to take my life. I don't know why I wanted to do that, except that I thought it would make her feel sorry. I liked that, but then she could only feel sorry a little while, because she would forget it, but I would be dead for always. I did not like that. If she would be sorry as long as I would be dead, it would be different. But anyway, I felt so dreadful that I said at last that it was better to die than to live. So I wrote a letter like this:

"*Darling Amy*

"I take my pen in hand to inform you that I am in good health and hope these fiew lines will find you injoying the same god's blessing I love you. I cannot live and see you hate me and talk to that Jim riley which I will lick every time I ketch him and have done so already I do not wish to live any more as we must part. I will pisen myself when I am done writing this and that is the last you will ever see of your poor Billy forever. I enclose my tooth which was pulled out newyears, keep it always to remember me by, I wish it was larger. Your dyeing BILLY ROGERS."

I directed it to her and took it and put it under her father's door. Then I looked up at her window a long time, and prayed that she might be forgiven for what I was going to do—and then cried and kissed the ground where she used to step out at the door, and took a pinch of the dirt and put it next my heart where the candy was, and started away to die. But I had forgotten to get any poison. Something else had to be done. I went down to the river, but it would not do, for I remembered that there was no place there but was over my head. I went home and thought I would jump off of the kitchen, but every time, just I had clumb nearly to the eaves I slipped and fell, and it was plain to be seen that it was dangerous—so I gave up that plan. I thought of hanging, and started up stairs, because I knew where there was a new bed-cord, but I recollected my father telling me if he ever caught me meddling with that bed-cord he would thrash me in an inch of my life—and so I had to give *that* up. So there was nothing for it but poison. I found a bottle in the closet, labeled laudanum on one side and castor oil on the other. I didn't know which it was, but I drank it all. I think it was oil. I was dreadful sick all night, and not constipated, my mother says, and this morning I had lost all interest in things, and didn't care whether I lived or died. But Oh, by nine o'clock *she* was here, and came right in—how my heart did beat and my face flush when I saw her dress go by the window!—she came right in and came right up to the bed, before

Ma, and kissed me, and the tears were in her eyes, and she said, "Oh, Billy, how *could* you be so naughty!—and Bingo is going to die, too, because another dog's bit him behind and all over, and Oh, I shan't have *any*body to love!"—and she cried and cried. But I told her I was not going to die and *I* would love her, always—and then her face brightened up, and she laughed and clapped her hands and said now as Ma was gone out, we'd talk all about it. So I kissed her and she kissed me, and she promised to be my little wife and love me forever and never love anybody else; and I promised just the same to her. And then I asked her if she had any plans, and she said No, she hadn't thought of that—no doubt I could plan everything. I said I could, and it would be my place, being the husband, to always plan and direct, and look out for her, and protect her all the time. She said that was right. But I said she could make suggestions—she *ought* to say what kind of a house she would rather live in. So she said she would prefer to have a little cosy cottage, with vines running over the windows and a four-story brick attached where she could receive company and give parties—that was all. And we talked a long time about what profession I had better follow. I wished to be a pirate, but she said that would be horrid. I said there was nothing horrid about it—it was grand. She said pirates killed people. I said of course they did—what would you have a pirate do?—it's in his line. She said, But just think of the blood! I said I loved blood and carnage. She shuddered. She said, well, perhaps it was best, and she hoped I would be great. Great! I said, where was there ever a pirate that *wasn't* great? Look at Capt. Kydd—look at Morgan—look at Gibbs— look at the noble Lafitte—look at the Black Avenger of the Spanish Main![6]—names that 'll never die. That pleased her, and so she said, let it be so. And then we talked about what *she* should do. She wanted to keep a milliner shop, because then she could have all the fine clothes she wanted; and on Sundays, when the shop was closed, she would be a teacher in Sunday-school. And she said I could help her teach her class Sundays when I was in port. So it was all fixed that as soon as ever we grow up we'll be married, and I am to be a pirate and she's to keep a milliner shop. Oh, it is splendid. I wish we were grown up now. Time does drag along so! But won't it be glorious! I will be away a long time cruising, and then some Sunday morning I'll step into Sunday School with my long black hair, and my slouch hat with a plume in it, and my long sword and high boots and splen- did belt and red satin doublet and breeches, and my black flag with scull and cross-bones on it, and all the children will say, "Look—

---

6. A pirate tale by Ned Buntline (1847). Captain (William) Kidd, Sir Henry Morgan, Charles Gibbs, and Jean Lafitte were pirates of the previous two centuries.

look—that's Rogers the pirate!" Oh, I wish time would move along faster.

Tuesday.—I was disgraced in school before her yesterday. These long summer days are awful. I *couldn't* study. I couldn't think of anything but being free and far away on the bounding billow. I hate school, anyway. It is *so* dull. I sat looking out of the window and listening to the buzz, buzz, buzzing of the scholars learning their lessons, till I was drowsy and did want to be out of that place so much. I could see idle boys playing on the hill-side, and catching butterflies whose fathers ain't able to send them to school, and I wondered what *I* had done that God should pick me out more than any other boy and give me a father able to send me to school. But *I* never could have any luck. There wasn't anything I could do to pass off the time. I caught some flies, but I got tired of that. I couldn't see Amy, because they've moved her seat. I got mad looking out of the window at those boys. By and bye, my chum, Bill Bowen, he bought a louse from Archy Thompson—he's got millions of them—bought him for a white alley and put him on the slate in front of him on the desk and begun to stir him up with a pin. He made him travel a while in one direction, and then he headed him off and made him go some other way. It was glorious fun. I wanted one, but I hadn't any white alley. Bill kept him a-moving—this way—that way—every way—and I did wish I could get a chance at him myself, and I begged for it. Well, Bill made a mark down the middle of the slate, and he says,

"Now when he is on my side, *I'll* stir him up—and I'll try to keep him from getting over the line, but if he *does* get over it, then *you* can stir him up as long as he's over there."

So he kept stirring him up, and two or three times he was so near getting over the line that I was in a perfect fever; but Bill always headed him off again. But at last he got on the line and all Bill could do he couldn't turn him—he made a dead set to come over, and presently over he *did* come, head over heels, upside down, a-reaching for things and a-clawing the air with all his hands! I snatched a pin out of my jacket and begun to waltz him around, and I made him git up and git—it was splendid fun—but at last, I kept him on my side so long that Bill couldn't stand it any longer, he was so excited, and he reached out to stir him up himself. I told him to let him alone, and behave himself. He said he wouldn't. I said

"You've got to—he's on my side, now, and you haven't got any right to punch him."

He said, "I haven't, haven't I? By George he's *my* louse—I bought him for a white alley, and I'll do just as I blame please with him!"

And then I felt somebody nip me by the ear, and I saw a hand nip

Bill by the ear. It was Peg-leg the schoolmaster. He had sneaked up behind, just in his natural mean way, and seen it all and heard it all, and we had been so taken up with our circus that we hadn't noticed that the buzzing was all still and the scholars watching Peg-leg and us. He took us up to his throne by the ears and thrashed us good, and Amy saw it all. I felt so mean that I sneaked away from school without speaking to her, and at night when I said my prayers I prayed that I might be taken away from school and kept at home until I was old enough to be a pirate.[7]

Tuesday Week.—For six whole days she has been gone to the country. The first three days, I played hookey all the time, and got licked for it as much as a dozen times. But I didn't care. I was desperate. I didn't care for anything. Last Saturday was the day for the battle between our school and Hog Davis's school (that is the boys's name for their teacher). I'm captain of a company of the littlest boys in our school. I came on the ground without any paper hat and without any wooden sword, and with my jacket on my arm. The Colonel said I was a fool—said I had kept both armies waiting for me a half an hour, and now to come looking like that—and I better not let the General see me. I said him and the General both could lump it if they didn't like it. Then he put me under arrest—under arrest of that Jim Riley—and I just licked Jim Riley and got *out* of arrest—and then I waltzed into Hog Davis's infant department and the way I made the fur fly was awful. I wished Amy could see me then. We drove the whole army over the hill and down by the slaughter house and lathered them good, and then they surrendered till next Saturday. I was made a lieutenant-colonel for desperate conduct in the field and now I am almost the youngest lieutenant-colonel we've got. I reckon I ain't no slouch. We've got thirty-two officers and fourteen men in our army, and we can take that Hog Davis crowd and do for them any time, even if they *have* got two more men than we have, and eleven more officers. But nobody knew what made me fight so—nobody but two or three, I guess. They never thought of Amy. Going home, Wart Hopkins overtook me (that's his nickname—because he's all over warts). He'd been out to the cross-roads burying a bean that he'd bloodied with a wart to make them go away and he was going home, now. I was in business with him once, and we had fell out. We had a circus and both of us wanted to be clown, and he wouldn't give up. He was always contrary that way. And he wanted to do the zam, and *I* wanted to do the zam (which the zam means the zampillerostation), and there it was again. He knocked a barrel from under me when I was a-standing on my head one night, and

7. Every detail of the above incident is strictly true, as I have excellent reason to remember—
   [M.T.

once when we were playing Jack the Giant-Killer I tripped his stilts
up and pretty near broke him in two. We charged two pins admission
for big boys and one pin for little ones—and when we came to divide
up he wanted to shove off all the pins on me that hadn't any heads
on. That was the kind of a boy he was—always mean. He always tied
the little boys' clothes when they went in a-swimming. I was with
him in the nigger-show business once, too, and he wanted to be
bones all the time himself. He would sneak around and nip marbles
with his toes and carry them off when the boys were playing knucks,
or anything like that; and when he was playing himself he always
poked or he always hunched. He always throwed his nutshells under
some small boy's bench in school and let him get lammed. He used
to put shoemaker's wax in the teacher's seat and then play hookey
and let some other fellow catch it. I hated Wart Hopkins. But now he
was in the same fix as myself, and I did want somebody to talk to *so*
bad, who was in that fix. He loved Susan Hawkins and she was gone
to the country too. I could see he was suffering, and he could see I
was. I wanted to talk, and he wanted to talk, though we hadn't spoken
for a long, long time. Both of us was full. So he said let bygones be
bygones—let's make up and be good friends, because we'd ought to
be, fixed as we were. I just overflowed, and took him around the neck
and went to crying, and he took me around the neck and went to crying, and we were perfectly happy because we were so miserable
together. And I said I would always love him and Susan, and he said
he would always love me and Amy—beautiful, beautiful Amy, he
called her, which made me feel good and proud; but not quite so
beautiful as Susan, he said, and I said it was a lie and he said I was
another and a fighting one and darsn't take it up; and I hit him and he
hit me back, and then we had a fight and rolled down a gulley into the
mud and gouged and bit and hit and scratched, and neither of us was
whipped; and then we got out and commenced it all over again and
he put a chip on his shoulder and dared me to knock it off and I did,
and so we had it again, and then he went home and I went home, and
Ma asked me how I got my clothes all tore off and was so ragged and
bloody and bruised up, and I told her I fell down, and then she black-
snaked me and I was all right. And the very next day I got a letter from
Amy! Mrs. Johnson brought it to me. It said:

"mister william rogers dear billy i have took on so i am all Wore out
a crying becos i Want to see you so bad the cat has got kittens but it
Dont make me happy i Want to see you all the Hens lays eggs excep
the old Rooster and mother and me Went to church Sunday and had
hooklebeary pie for Dinner i think of you Always and love you no
more from your amy at present   AMY."

I read it over and over and over again, and kissed it, and studied
out new meanings in it, and carried it to bed with me and read it

again first thing in the morning. And I did feel so delicious I wanted to lay there and think of her hours and hours and never get up. But they made me. The first chance I got I wrote to her, and this is it:

"*Darling Amy*

"I have had lots of fights and I love you all the same. I have changed my dog which his name was Bull and now his name is Amy. I think its splendid and so does he I reckon because he always comes when I call him *Amy* though he'd come anyhow ruther than be walloped, which I *would* wallop him if he didn't. I send you my picture. The things on the lower side are the legs, the head is on the other end, the horable thing which its got in its hand is you though not so pretty by a long sight. I didn't mean to put only one eye in your face but there wasnt room. I have been thinking sometimes I'll be a pirate and sometimes I'll keep grocery on account of candy   And I would like ever so much to be a brigadire General or a deck hand on a steamboat because they have fun you know and go everywheres. But a fellow cant be everything I dont reckon. I have traded off my sunday school book and Ma's hatchet for a pup and I reckon I'm going to ketch it, maybe. Its a good pup though. It nipped a chicken yesterday and goes around raising cain all the time. I love you to destruction Amy and I can't live if you dont come back. I had the branch dammed up beautiful for water-mills, but I dont care for water mills when you are away so I traded the dam to Jo Whipple for a squirt gun though if you was here I wouldnt give a dam for a squirt gun because we could have water mills. So no more from your own true love.

> My pen is bad my ink is pale
> Roses is red the violets blue
> But my love for you shall never change.

> WILLIAM T. ROGERS.

"P.S. I learnt that poetry from Sarah Mackleroy—its beautiful."

Tuesday Fortnight.—I'm thankful that I'm free. I've come to myself. I'll never love another girl again. There's no dependence in them. If I was going to hunt up a wife I would just go in amongst a crowd of girls and say

> "Eggs, cheese, butter, bread,
> Stick, stock, stone—DEAD!"

and take the one it lit on just the same as if I was choosing up for fox or baste or three-cornered cat or hide'n'whoop[8] or anything like that. I'd get along just as well as by selecting them out and falling in

---

8. Games of tag, ball, and hiding.

love with them the way I did with—with—I can't write her name, for the tears *will* come. But she has treated me Shameful. The first thing she did when she got back from the country was to begin to object to me being a pirate—because some of her kin is down on pirates I reckon—though *she* said it was because I would be away from home so much. A likely story, indeed—if she knowed anything about pirates she'd know that they go and come just whenever they please, which other people can't. Well I'll be a pirate now, in spite of all the girls in the world. And next she didn't want me to be a deck hand on a steamboat, or else it was a judge she didn't want me to be, because one of them wasn't respectable, she didn't know which—some more bosh from relations I reckon. And then she said she didn't want to keep a milliner shop, she wanted to clerk in a toy-shop, and have an open barouche and she'd like me to sell peanuts and papers on the railroad so she could ride without it costing anything.

"What!" I said, "and not be a pirate at all?"

She said yes. I was disgusted. I told her so. Then she cried, and said I didn't love her, and wouldn't do anything to please her, and wanted to break her heart and have some other girl when she was dead, and then I cried, too, and told her I *did* love her, and nobody but her, and I'd do anything she wanted me to and I was sorry, Oh, so sorry. But she shook her head, and pouted—and I begged again, and she turned her back—and I went on pleading and she wouldn't answer—only pouted—and at last when I was getting mad, she slammed the jewsharp, and the tin locomotive and the spool cannon and everything I'd given her, on the floor, and flourished out mad and crying like sin, and said I was a mean, good-for-nothing thing and I might go and *be* a pirate and welcome!—*she* never wanted to see me any more! And I was mad and crying, too, and I said By George I *would* be a pirate, and an awful bloody one, too, or my name warn't Bill Rogers!

And so it's all over between us. But now that it *is* all over, I feel mighty, mighty bad. The whole school knowed we were engaged, and they think it strange to see us flirting with other boys and girls, but we can't help that. I flirt with other girls, but I don't care anything about them. And I see her lip quiver sometimes and the tears come in her eyes when she looks my way when she's flirting with some other boy—and then I do *want* to rush there and grab her in my arms and be friends again!

Saturday.—I am happy again, and forever, this time. I've seen her! I've seen the girl that is my doom. I shall die if I cannot get her. The first time I looked at her I fell in love with her. She looked at me twice in church yesterday, and Oh how I felt! She was with her mother and her brother. When they came out of church I followed them, and twice she looked back and smiled, and I would have smiled too, but there was a tall young man by my side and I was afraid he would notice. At last she dropped a leaf of a flower—rose geranium Ma calls it—and I could see by the way she looked that she meant it for me, and when I stooped to pick it up the tall young man stooped too. I got it, but I felt awful sheepish, and I think he did, too, because he blushed. He asked me for it, and I had to give it to him, though I'd rather given him my bleeding heart, but I pinched off just a little piece and kept it, and shall keep it forever. Oh, she is *so* lovely! And she loves me. I know it. I could see it, easy. Her name's Laura Miller. She's nineteen years old, Christmas. I never, never, never will part with *this* one! NEVER.

MARK TWAIN AND WILLIAM DEAN HOWELLS

Correspondence on *The Adventures of Tom Sawyer*†

Twain to Howells, 21 June 1875, after Howells visited Twain

*   *   *

Thank you ever so much for the praises you give the story.[1] I am going to take into serious consideration all you have said, & then make up my mind by & by. Since there is no plot to the thing, it is likely to follow its own drift, & so is as likely to drift into manhood

---

†   The 1875 letters are from *Mark Twain's Letters*, vol. 6, 1874–1875, ed. Michael B. Frank and Harriet Elinor Smith (Berkeley: University of California Press, 2002), 497, 503–4, 506, 509, 510, 595; indications of Twain's insertions and deletions are omitted. Courtesy of the Mark Twain Foundation (chief representative: Richard A. Watson, of Chamberlain, Willi, Ouchterloney, & Watson, 575 Eighth Ave., 16th Floor, New York, NY 10018). The sentence from the 4 January 1876 letter is from *Life in Letters of William Dean Howells*, ed. Mildred Howells (Garden City: Doubleday, 1928), 1: 216. The 18 January 1876, 3 April 1876, 26 April 1876, and 8 September 1887 letters: from *Mark Twain's Letters*, ed. Albert Bigelow Paine (New York: Harper, 1917), 1:272–73, 274–75, 277, 2:476–77 (bracketed corrections from *Mark Twain-Howells Letters: The Correspondence of Samuel L. Clemens and William D. Howells, 1872–1910*, ed. Henry Nash Smith and William M. Gibson [Cambridge: Belknap–Harvard University Press, 1960], 1:121, 122, 132). The first seven words of the 19 January 1876 letter are from Smith and Gibson, 1:124; the next thirty-three from Paine, *Letters*, 1:274; the remainder from *Mark Twain: A Biography*, by Albert Bigelow Paine (New York: Harper, 1912), 1:549. All notes are the editor's.
    William Dean Howells was both Twain's friend and, as the editor of the *Atlantic Monthly* (1871–81), among other things, the most influential cultural gatekeeper in the late-nineteenth-century United States. For Bernard DeVoto's discussion of the changes Twain made in response to Howells' suggestions see pp. 260–62 herein.

1.   A partial draft of *The Adventures of Tom Sawyer*, which Howells must have looked at on his visit.

as anywhere—I won't interpose. If I only had the Mississippi book[2]
written, I would surely venture this story in the Atlantic. But I'll
see—I'll think the whole thing over.

*   *   *

Howells to Twain, 3 July 1875

*   *   *

—You must be thinking well of the notion of giving us that story.
I really feel very much interested in your making that your chief
work; you wont have such another chance; don't waste it on a **boy,**
and don't hurry the writing for the sake of making a book. Take your
time, and deliberately advertise by Atlantic publication. Mr. Houghton has his back up, and says he would like to catch any newspaper
copying it.[3]

*   *   *

Twain to Howells, 5 July 1875

I have finished the story & didn't take the chap beyond boyhood.
I believe it would be fatal to do it in any shape but autobiographi-
cally—like Gil Blas.[4] I perhaps made a mistake in not writing it in
the first person. If I went on, now, & took him into manhood, he
would just be like all the one-horse men in literature & the reader
would conceive a hearty contempt for him. It is *not* a boy's book, at
all. It will only be read by adults. It is only written for adults.

Moreover, the book is plenty long enough, as it stands. It is about
900 pages of MS., & may be 1000 when I shall have finished "working up" vague places; so it would make from 130 to 150 pages of the
Atlantic—about what the Foregone Conclusion[5] made, isn't it?

I would dearly like to see it in the Atlantic, but I doubt if it would
pay the publishers to buy the privilege, or me to sell it. Bret Harte
has sold his novel (same size as mine, I should say) to Scribner's
Monthly for $6,500 (publication to begin in September, I think,) &
he gets a royalty of 7½ per cent from Bliss[6] in book form afterward.
He gets a royalty of ten per cent on it in England (issued in serial

2. "Old Times on the Mississippi," then being serialized in the *Atlantic*, later to become part
   of *Life on the Mississippi* (1883).
3. At issue is whether a serialized appearance in the *Atlantic Monthly* would help book sales
   or harm them, if newspapers reprinted chapters, a common practice at the time. Henry
   Oscar Houghton, publisher of the *Atlantic*.
4. In Alain-René Lesage's *Gil Blas de Santillane* (1715–35).
5. Title of a novel by Howells, serialized in the *Atlantic Monthly* in 1874.
6. Elisha Bliss, publisher of *The Adventures of Tom Sawyer*.

numbers) & the same royalty on it in book form afterward, & is to receive an advance payment of five hundred pounds the day the first No. of the serial appears. If I could do as well, here & there, with mine, it might possibly pay me, but I seriously doubt it—though it is likely I could do better in England than Bret, who is not widely known there.

You see I take a vile, mercenary view of things—but then my household expenses are something almost ghastly.

By & by I shall take a boy of twelve & run him on through life (in the first person) but not Tom Sawyer—he would not be a good character for it.

I wish you would promise to read the MS of Tom Sawyer some time, & see if you don't really decide that I am right in closing with him as a boy—& point out the most glaring defects for me. It is a tremendous favor to ask, & I expect you to refuse, & would be ashamed to expect you to do otherwise. But the thing has been so many months in my mind that it seems a relief to snake it out. I don't know any other person whose judgment I could venture to take fully & entirely. Don't hesitate about saying no, for I know how your time is taxed, & I would have honest need to blush if you said yes.

* * *

Howells to Twain, 6 July 1875

Send on your Ms. when it's ready. You've no idea what I may ask you to do for **me** some day. I'm sorry that you can't do it for the Atlantic, but I succumb. Perhaps you'll do Boy No. 2 for us.

* * *

Twain to Howells, 13 July 1875

Just as soon as you consented I realized all the atrocity of my request, & straightway blushed & weakened. I telegraphed my theatrical agent to come here & carry off the MS & copy it.

But I will gladly send it to you if you will do as follows: dramatize it if you perceive that you can, & take, for your remuneration, half of the first $6,000 which I receive for its representation on the stage. You could alter the plot entirely, if you chose. I would help in the work, most cheerfully, after you had arranged the plot. I have my eye upon two young girls who can play "Tom" & "Huck." I believe a good deal of a drama can be made of it. Come—can't you tackle this in the odd hours of your vacation?—or later, if you prefer?

*   *   *

Howells to Twain, 19 July 1875

It's very pleasant to have you propose my working in any sort of concert with you; and if the $3000 were no temptation, it **is** a temptation to think of trying to do you a favor. But I couldn't do it, and if I could, it wouldn't be a favor to dramatize your story. In fact I don't see how anybody can do that but yourself. * * *

*   *   *

Howells to Twain, 21 November 1875

*   *   *

—I finished reading Tom Sawyer a week ago, sitting up till one A.M., to get to the end, simply because it was impossible to leave off. It's altogether the best boy's story I ever read. It will be an immense success. But I think you ought to treat it explicitly *as* a boy's story. Grown-ups will enjoy it just as much if you do; and if you should put it forth as a study of boy character from the grown-up point of view, you'd give the wrong key to it.—I have made some corrections and suggestions in faltering pencil, which you'll have to look for. They're almost all in the first third. When you fairly swing off, you had better be let alone.—The adventures are enchanting. I wish *I* had been on that island. The treasure-hunting, the loss in the cave—it's all exciting and splendid. I shouldn't think of publishing this story serially. Give me a hint when it's to be out, and I'll start the sheep to jumping in the right places.

—I don't seem to think I like the last chapter. I believe I would cut that.

*   *   *

Twain to Howells, 23 November 1875

*   *   *

It is glorious news that you like Tom Sawyer so well. I mean to see to it that your review of it shall have plenty of time to appear before the other notices. Mrs. Clemens decides with you that the book should issue as a book for boys, pure & simple—and so do I. It is surely the correct idea. As to that last chapter, I think of just leaving it off & adding nothing in its place. Something told me that the book was done when I got to that point—& so the strong temp-

tation to put Huck's life at the widow's into detail instead of gener-
alizing it in a paragraph, was resisted.[7]* * *

*   *   *

Howells to Twain, 4 January 1876

*   *   *

* * *The more I think back over your boy-book the more I like it.

*   *   *

Twain to Howells, 18 January 1876

Thanks, and ever so many, for the good opinion of Tom Sawyer.
Williams has made about 300 [200] rattling pictures for it—some of
them very dainty. Poor devil, what a genius he has and how he does
murder it with rum. He takes a book of mine, and without suggestion
from anybody builds no end of pictures just from his reading of it.

There was never a man in the world so grateful to another as I
was to you day before yesterday, when I sat down (in still rather
wretched health) to set myself to the dreary and hateful task of making final revision of Tom Sawyer, and discovered, upon opening the
package of MS that your pencil marks were scattered all along. This
was splendid, and swept away all labor. Instead of *reading* the MS,
I simply hunted out the pencil marks and made the emendations
which they suggested. I reduced the boy battle to a curt paragraph;
I finally concluded to cut the Sunday school speech down to the first
two sentences, leaving no suggestion of satire, since the book is to
be for boys and girls; I tamed the various obscenities until I judged
that they no longer carried offense. So, at a single sitting I began
and finished a revision which I had supposed would occupy 3 or 4
days and leave me mentally and physically fagged out at the end. I
was careful not to inflict the MS upon you until I had thoroughly
and painstakingly revised it. Therefore, the only faults left were those
that would discover themselves to others, not me—and these you
had pointed out.

There was one expression which perhaps you overlooked. When
Huck is complaining to Tom of the rigorous system in vogue at the
widow's, he says the servants harass him with all manner of compulsory decencies, and he winds up by saying: "and they comb me

7. Bernard DeVoto, in *Mark Twain at Work* (Cambridge: Harvard University Press, 1942),
11, suggests that Twain substituted the current "Conclusion" for a final chapter that is
now lost.

all to hell." (No exclamation point.) Long ago, when I read that to Mrs. Clemens, she made no comment; another time I created occasion to read that chapter to her aunt and mother (both sensitive and loyal subjects of the kingdom of heaven, so to speak) and *they* let it pass. I was glad, for it was the most natural remark in the world for that boy to make (and he had been allowed few privileges of speech in the book;) when I saw that you, too, had let it go without protest, I was glad, and afraid, too—afraid you hadn't observed it. Did you? And did you question the propriety of it? Since the book is now professedly and confessedly a boy's and girl's book, that darn [dern] word bothers me some, nights, but it never did until I had ceased to regard the volume as being for adults.

* * *

Howells to Twain, 19 January 1876

* * *

As to the point in your book: I'd have that swearing out in an instant. I suppose I didn't notice it because the locution was so familiar to my Western sense, and so exactly the thing that Huck would say. But it won't do for the children.

* * *

Twain to Howells, 3 April 1876

It is a splendid notice,[8] and will embolden weak-kneed journalistic admirers to speak out, and will modify or shut up the unfriendly. To "fear God and dread the Sunday school" exactly described that old feeling which I used to have, but I couldn't have formulated it. I want to enclose one of the illustrations in this letter, if I do not forget it. Of course the book is to be elaborately illustrated, and I think that many of the pictures are considerably above the American average, in conception if not in execution.

* * *

Twain to Howells, 26 April 1876

* * *

Bliss made a failure in the matter of getting Tom Sawyer ready on time—the engravers assisting, as usual. I went down to see how

---

8. Howells's review of *Tom Sawyer*, *Atlantic Monthly*, May 1876, 621–22 (see pp. 265–66 herein).

much of a delay there was going to be, and found that the man had not even put a canvasser on, or issued an advertisement yet—in fact, that the electrotypes[9] would not all be done for a month! But of course the main fact [trouble] was that no canvassing had been done—because a subscription harvest is *before* publication, (not *after*, when people have discovered how bad one's book is.)[1]

Well, yesterday I put in the Courant[2] an editorial paragraph stating that Tom Sawyer is "ready to issue, but publication is put off in order to secure English copyright by simultaneous publication there and here. The English edition is unavoidably delayed."

You see, part of that is true. Very well. When I observed that my "Sketches" had dropped from a sale of 6 or 7000 a month down to 1200 a month, I said "*this* ain't no time to be publishing books; therefore, let Tom lie still till Autumn, Mr. Bliss, and make a holiday book of him to beguile the young people withal."

* * *

I shall print items occasionally, still further delaying Tom, till I ease him down to Autumn without shock to the waiting world.

* * *

Unmailed letter from Twain to the manager of a theatrical company proposing to dramatize The Adventures of Tom Sawyer, *8 September 1887*

* * *

Dear Sir,—And so it has got around to you, at last; and you also have "taken the liberty." You are No. 1365. When 1364 sweeter and better people, including the author, have "tried" to dramatize Tom Sawyer and did not arrive, what sort of show do you suppose you stand? That is a book, dear sir, which cannot be dramatized. One might as well try to dramatize any other hymn. Tom Sawyer is simply a hymn, put into prose form to give it a worldly air.

* * *

9. Metal plates used in printing.
1. Twain published *Tom Sawyer* and other novels by subscription—salesmen went door to door, selling it in advance.
2. Hartford *Daily Courant*.

BERNARD DeVOTO

[Revisions Inspired by Howells]†

* * *

Most of Howells's suggestions can still be made out in the margins of the amanuensis copy.[1] Mark seems to have adopted all of them, but there are fewer than the letters suggest. At the end of Chapter III, Howells writes, "Don't like this chapter much. The sham fight is too long. Tom is either too old for that or too young for [word or words lost]. Don't like the chaps in [word or words lost]." Obediently Mark cuts some three hundred words from the sham battle, much to its improvement. (He missed one word, however, which remained a meaningless vestige in all editions of the book till 1939. Tom rode a broomstick horse in that battle, and later he made it "cavort" in front of Becky's house. At his final departure the text has hitherto inexplicably read, "Finally he rode home reluctantly with his poor head full of visions.") Mr. Walters's speech in Sunday school has been improved by its reduction. A speech of Joe Harper's before the venture in piracy has been cleared of burlesque. Howells objects to "cussedness" as a Yankee expression and Mark makes it "Old Scratch." Howells checks Alfred Temple's "Aw—what a long tail our cat's got" (which Mark had already substituted for "Aw—go blow your nose") and it comes out "Aw—take a walk." Where Tom now says, in the next speech, that he will "bounce a rock off'n your head," Howells has objected, soundly, to "mash your mouth." There are perhaps a half-dozen further stylistic changes, as where Tom's "throes of bliss" on receiving the Barlow knife become a "convulsion of delight," and where his original intention to "gloom the air with a lurid lie" is altered to "take refuge in a lie." But more interesting and important are the mild "obscenities" that Mark mentions in his letter.

Howells cannot be charged with the change of "the devil" to "Satan" toward the end of the book nor (I think—the copy is not clear) with the softening of "foul slop" to "water" where the Thatcher's maid drenched the adoring Tom, whose "reeking" garments are then made merely "drenched." Mark had also softened Injun Joe's intentions toward the Widow Douglas. His original explanation that to get revenge on a woman "you cut her nose off—and her ears" had been altered to "you slit her nostrils—you notch her

† From *Mark Twain at Work* (Cambridge, Mass.: Harvard University Press), 12–14, 16, 17–18, Copyright © 1942 by the President and Fellows of Harvard College, Copyright © 1970 by Helen Vicar DeVoto. Reprinted by permission of the publisher. Brackets in the main text are DeVoto's.

1. Secretarial copy of the original manuscript [Editor's note].

ears" when the amanuensis copy was made, and where Huck now tells the Welshman that he heard "the Spaniard swear he'd spile her looks" he originally added "and cut her ears off." Perhaps Olivia Clemens or Mark's children had shrunk from these expressions, though more likely it was Mark's own nerves that flinched. But Howells's nerves required further alterations.

The poodle which relieves the suffering of the congregation by sitting down on a pinchbug now goes "sailing up the aisle" and no more; but originally he sailed up that aisle "with his tail shut down like a hasp." Howells writes in the margin, "Awfully good but a little too dirty," and an amusing phrase goes out. Much more important, by far the most important change anywhere in the manuscript is the modification of Chapter XX. Here, in the margin opposite Becky Thatcher's stolen glimpse of "a human figure, stark naked" in Mr. Dobbins's textbook of anatomy, Howells writes, "I should be afraid of this picture incident," and so cancels one of the truest moments of childhood in the manuscript. Reproached by Becky for sneaking up on her, Tom had originally said, "How could *I* know it wasn't a nice book? I didn't know girls ever—." Becky's apprehension of being whipped carried a postscript, "But that isn't anything—it ain't *half*. You'll tell everybody about the picture, and O, O, *O!*" Meditating on what a curious kind of fool a girl is, Tom was originally permitted to think:

> But that picture—is—well, now it ain't so curious she feels bad about that. No . . . [Mark's punctuation] No, I reckon it ain't. Suppose she was Mary and Alf Temple had caught her looking at such a picture as that and went around telling. She'd feel—well, I'd lick him. I bet I would. [Then, farther toward the end of the soliloquy] Then Dobbins will tell his wife about the picture. [Note the information that Dobbins is married.]

And Becky was originally permitted to think, "He'll tell the scholars about that hateful picture—maybe he's told some of them before now."

*   *   *

Before this essay no one, I think, had noticed the softening of Chapter XX, but Howells's remaining modification has become famous. Curiously enough, he missed the offense when he read the manuscript. He did encounter in Huck's passionate grievance against the Widow Douglas, "she'd gag when I spit," and that had to go, but he passed "they comb me all to hell" without questioning it. But Mark had already spent some concern on the phrase—writing "hell," then changing it to "thunder," and finally restoring the dreadful word—and demanded judgment from his arbiter.* * *

* * *

Mark's own changes in the manuscript are usually stylistic and always for the best. It is interesting to discover that Injun Joe's companion in the grave-robbing was originally Old Man Finn. He became Muff Potter, no doubt, to prevent Huck's oath from putting his father's life in jeopardy. And there is one deletion which not only suggests that there was another intermediate stage of the book but also makes one thankful that, though Mark was tempted, he found grace to resist the kind of extravaganza that defaces the last quarter of *Huckleberry Finn*. At the end of Chapter III, Tom, saddened by Aunt Polly's cruelty, goes down to the river, where he sits on a raft in the darkness, takes out his wilted flower, and thinks of Becky with the melancholy that made Burton diagnose love as a neurosis. And "at last," the text says, "he rose up sighing and departed in the darkness." Until Mark crossed out the passage, the manuscript went on, "A dimly defined, stalwart figure emerged from behind a bundle of shingles upon the raft, muttering 'There's something desperate breeding here,' and then dropped stealthily into the boy's wake." There is no telling what wild notion was in Mark's mind but he was beginning to burlesque a passage already strained to the breaking-point and, remembering such passages elsewhere that he did not strike out, one is overjoyed to see heavy ink cancelling this one in time.

* * *

CRITICISM

[WILLIAM DEAN HOWELLS]†

[Review]

Mr. Aldrich has studied the life of A Bad Boy as the pleasant reprobate led it in a quiet old New England town twenty-five or thirty years ago, where in spite of the natural outlawry of boyhood he was more or less part of a settled order of things, and was hemmed in, to some measure, by the traditions of an established civilization. Mr. Clemens, on the contrary, has taken the boy of the Southwest for the hero of his new book, and has presented him with a fidelity to circumstance which loses no charm by being realistic in the highest degree, and which gives incomparably the best picture of life in that region as yet known to fiction. The town where Tom Sawyer was born and brought up is some such idle, shabby little Mississippi River town as Mr. Clemens has so well described in his piloting reminiscences, but Tom belongs to the better sort of people in it, and has been bred to fear God and dread the Sunday-school according to the strictest rite of the faiths that have characterized all the respectability of the West. His subjection in these respects does not so deeply affect his inherent tendencies but that he makes himself a beloved burden to the poor, tender-hearted old aunt who brings him up with his orphan brother and sister, and struggles vainly with his manifold sins, actual and imaginary. The limitations of his transgressions are nicely and artistically traced. He is mischievous, but not vicious; he is ready for almost any depredation that involves the danger and honor of adventure, but profanity he knows may provoke a thunderbolt upon the heart of the blasphemer, and he almost never swears; he resorts to any stratagem to keep out of school, but he is not a downright liar, except upon terms of after shame and remorse that make his falsehood bitter to him. He is cruel, as all children are, but chiefly because he is ignorant; he is not mean, but there are very definite bounds to his generosity; and his courage is the Indian sort, full of prudence and mindful of retreat as one of the conditions of prolonged hostilities. In a word, he is a boy, and merely and exactly an ordinary boy on the moral side. What makes him delightful to the reader is that on the imaginative side he is very much more, and though every boy has wild and fantastic dreams, this boy cannot rest till he has somehow realized them. Till he has actually run off with two other boys in the character of buccaneer, and lived for a week on an island in the Mississippi, he has lived in vain; and this passage

† Review of *The Adventures of Tom Sawyer*, from *Atlantic Monthly* 37.223 (May 1876): 621–22. The U.S. publication of *Tom Sawyer* was delayed until December 1876, so Howells's review was very much an advance notice. All notes are the editor's.

is but the prelude to more thrilling adventures, in which he finds
hidden treasures, traces the bandits to their cave, and is himself lost
in its recesses. The local material and the incidents with which his
career is worked up are excellent, and throughout there is scrupulous
regard for the boy's point of view in reference to his surroundings
and himself, which shows how rapidly Mr. Clemens has grown as an
artist. We do not remember anything in which this propriety is vio-
lated, and its preservation adds immensely to the grown-up reader's
satisfaction in the amusing and exciting story. There is a boy's love-
affair, but it is never treated otherwise than as a boy's love-affair.
When the half-breed has murdered the young doctor, Tom and his
friend, Huckleberry Finn, are really, in their boyish terror and superstition, going to let the poor old town-drunkard be hanged for the
crime, till the terror of that becomes unendurable. The story is a
wonderful study of the boy-mind, which inhabits a world quite distinct from that in which he is bodily present with his elders, and in
this lies its great charm and its universality, for boy-nature, however
human-nature varies, is the same everywhere.

The tale is very dramatically wrought, and the subordinate characters are treated with the same graphic force that sets Tom alive
before us. The worthless vagabond, Huck Finn, is entirely delightful
throughout, and in his promised reform his identity is respected: he
will lead a decent life in order that he may one day be thought worthy
to become a member of that gang of robbers which Tom is to orga-
nize. Tom's aunt is excellent, with her kind heart's sorrow and secret
pride in Tom; and so is his sister Mary, one of those good girls who
are born to usefulness and charity and forbearance and unvarying
rectitude. Many village people and local notables are introduced in
well-conceived character; the whole little town lives in the reader's
sense, with its religiousness, its lawlessness, its droll social distinctions, its civilization qualified by its slave-holding, and its traditions
of the wilder West which has passed away. The picture will be
instructive to those who have fancied the whole Southwest a sort of
vast Pike County,[1] and have not conceived of a sober and serious
and orderly contrast to the sort of life that has come to represent the
Southwest in literature. Mr. William M. Baker gives a notion of this
in this stories, and Mr. Clemens has again enforced the fact here in
a book full of entertaining character, and of the greatest artistic sincerity.

Tom Brown and Tom Bailey[2] are, among boys in books, alone
deserving to be named with Tom Sawyer.

---

1. Characterized by uncouth frontier humor, as in John Hay's *Pike County Ballads* (1871).
2. Tom Brown is featured in Thomas Hughes's *Tom Brown's Schooldays* (1857), Tom Bailey
   in Thomas Bailey Aldrich's *The Story of a Bad Boy* (1870).

HAMLIN L. HILL

The Composition and the Structure of *Tom Sawyer*†

The structure of *The Adventures of Tom Sawyer* has for some time marked a point of divergence among Twain scholars. Walter Blair's study "On the Structure of *Tom Sawyer*" suggested that the book was organized as the story of a boy's maturation, presented to the reader through four lines of action—the Tom and Becky story, the Muff Potter story, the Jackson's Island adventure, and the Injun Joe story—each of which begins with an immature act and ends with a relatively mature act by Tom.[1] Blair's interpretation has been accepted by Dixon Wecter, who agreed that "Tom and Huck grow visibly as we follow them,"[2] by Gladys Bellamy,[3] and E. H. Long.[4] But it has been ignored by DeLancey Ferguson, who claimed that "*Tom Sawyer,* in short, grew as grows the grass; it was not art at all, but it was life."[5] It was disclaimed by Alexander Cowie, who stated that *Tom Sawyer* "lives in small units, which when added up (not arranged) equal the sum of boyhood experience."[6] And most recently, Roger Asselineau dismissed Blair's hypothesis as a mere tour de force when he suggested, "This attempt at introducing logic and order into a book which had been rather desultorily composed was interesting, but not fully convincing. Such *a posteriori* conclusions, however tempting, smacked of artificiality and could only contain a measure of truth."[7]

These, then, are the two poles: that *Tom Sawyer* has a narrative plan and exhibits what was for Twain a high degree of literary crafts-manship; or that it is a ragbag of memories, thrown together at random with little or no thought to order or structure. My suggestion is that the original manuscript, now in the Riggs Memorial Library of Georgetown University, Washington, D.C.,[8] holds the solution to the

† From *American Literature*, Volume 32, No. 4, pp. 379–392. Copyright © 1961, Duke University Press. All rights reserved. Used by permission of the publisher. All notes are Hill's unless otherwise indicated.

1. Walter Blair, "On the Structure of *Tom Sawyer*," *Modern Philology*, XXXVII, 75–88 (August, 1939).
2. "Mark Twain," *Literary History of the United States,* ed. Robert E. Spiller *et al.* (New York, 1953), p. 930.
3. *Mark Twain as a Literary Artist* (Norman, 1950), pp. 334–335.
4. *Mark Twain Handbook* (New York, 1957), pp. 316–318.
5. *Mark Twain: Man and Legend* (Indianapolis, 1943), p. 176.
6. *The Rise of the American Novel* (New York, 1948), p. 609.
7. *The Literary Reputation of Mark Twain from 1910 to 1950* (Paris, 1954), p. 58.
8. I am grateful to Mr. Joseph Jeffs of the Riggs Memorial Library for making a microfilm of the manuscript available to me. I also thank the Mark Twain Estate for granting permission to quote previously unpublished notations in the manuscript, which are copyright 1959, by the Mark Twain Company.

problem of the book's structure and that a more intensive examination of it than DeVoto made in *Mark Twain at Work*[9] provides the secret of Mark Twain's methods of composition of *Tom Sawyer*.

I

Twain's own statements about the book's composition support the "ragbag" theory. He began work on *Tom Sawyer* itself, as distinguished from its several precursors,[1] probably in the summer of 1874. By September 4, he "had worked myself out, pumped myself dry,"[2] so he put the manuscript aside until the spring or summer of 1875, and on July 5, 1875, announced its completion.[3] Years later, he described the crisis which presumably came in September, 1874:

> At page 400 of my manuscript the story made a sudden and determined halt and refused to proceed another step. Day after day it still refused. I was disappointed, distressed and immeasurably astonished, for I knew quite well that the tale was not finished and I could not understand why I was not able to go on with it. The reason was very simple—my tank had run dry; it was empty; the stock of materials in it was exhausted; the story could not go on without materials; it could not be wrought out of nothing.[4]

And Brander Matthews, reporting a discussion with Twain, confirmed this haphazard method of composition:

> He began the composition of "Tom Sawyer" with certain of his boyish recollections in mind, writing on and on until he had utilized them all, whereupon he put his manuscript aside and ceased to think about it, except in so far as he might recall from time to time, and more or less unconsciously, other recollections of those early days. Sooner or later he would return to his work and make use of memories he had recaptured in the interval.[5]

The manuscript provides many examples of this plot development through recollection and association.

While writing or reading over the early parts of *Tom Sawyer*, Twain apparently remembered ideas and incidents from his earlier writings

9. Bernard DeVoto, *Mark Twain at Work* (Cambridge, Mass., 1942), pp. 3–18. Cited hereafter as MTAW.
1. See MTAW, pp. 3–9.
2. *Mark Twain's Letters*, ed. Albert B. Paine (New York, 1917), p. 224.
3. *Ibid.*, p. 258.
4. *Mark Twain in Eruption*, ed. Bernard DeVoto (New York, 1940), p. 197.
5. Brander Matthews, *The Tocsin of Revolt and Other Essays* (New York, 1922), p. 265.

or his own boyhood which he felt might be of use to him later. Accordingly, he wrote notes and suggestions in the margins of his manuscript, mentioning material which would either be utilized later in the book or be discarded.[6] A few of these notations are so cryptic that I have been unable to identify them: "The dead cigar man" on manuscript page 210, "The old whistler" on page 85, and "Silver moons" on page 322. But in most cases his intention is perfectly clear.

Among the marginal reminders which Twain discarded was the name of a steamboat, the *City of Hartford*, which he wrote on manuscript page 89, opposite the Sunday school superintendent's speech (Chapter IV). Evidently his first thought was to utilize an anecdote from his May, 1870, "Memoranda" column for this speech. The episode went thus:

> "Just about the close of that long, hard winter," said the Sunday-school superintendent, "as I was wending toward my duties one brilliant Sabbath morning, I glanced down toward the levee, and there lay the City of Hartford!—no mistake about it, there she was, puffing and panting, after her long pilgrimage through the ice. . . . I should have to instruct empty benches, sure; the youngsters would all be off welcoming the first steamboat of the season. You can imagine how surprised I was when I opened the door and saw half the benches full! My gratitude was free, large, and sincere. I resolved that they should not find me unappreciative. I said: 'Boys, what renewed assurance it gives me of your affection. I confess that I said to myself, as I came along and saw that the City of Hartford was in—'
>
> " '*No! But is she, though!*'
>
> "And as quick as any flash of lightning I stood in the presence of empty benches! I had brought them the news myself."[7]

In the margin of a page for Chapter VIII (MS p. 210), he wrote "Rolling the rock," a reference to the Holliday's Hill episode which he had utilized in *The Innocents Abroad* (Chapter LVIII) and which he rejected for *Tom Sawyer*. And three pages later Twain noted, "candy-pull," apparently toying with the idea of having "Jim Wolfe

---

6. DeVoto (MTAW, p. 6) mentions only one of these many marginal notations, the one on the first page of the manuscript: "Put in thing from Boy-lecture." The reference was probably to a lecture Twain proposed for the 1871–1872 lecture season. In the *American Publisher,* a magazine published by the American Publishing Company, Twain's publisher, and edited by Orion Clemens, Twain's brother, Orion revealed, "We have the pleasure to announce that Mark Twain will lecture in New England during the ensuing fall, and later, in the Western States. The subject is not yet decided upon. He has *two* new lectures, one an appeal in behalf of Boy's Rights, and one entitled simply 'D.L.H.' " (*American Publisher,* I, 4, July, 1871).

7. Memoranda," *Galaxy,* IX, 726 (May, 1870), reprinted in *Mark Twain at Your Fingertips,* ed. Caroline T. Harnsberger (New York, 1948), pp. 30–31.

and the Cats" make an appearance in the book.[8] He also suggested to himself on page 464, "Becky had the measles," and "Joe drowned." One suggestion which was not eliminated entirely but was greatly altered in the book appeared on manuscript page 161: "burnt up the old sot." The story recalled the time that Clemens gave a tramp some matches which "the old sot" used to burn up the jail and himself, and Twain referred to it in *Life on the Mississippi* and the *Autobiography*[9] as well as *Tom Sawyer*. The character corresponding to the tramp was Muff Potter, and Tom did smuggle "small comforts" to Muff in jail and was bothered with nightmares, just as young Sam Clemens was in 1853. But since burning Muff Potter would have made it necessary to omit the trial chapter, Twain used only those portions of the story which we find in the book.

Some of the marginal notations bore fruit immediately. On page 15 Twain wrote "coppers" and on page 19 mentioned that the "new boy" whom Tom was challenging "took two broad coppers out of his pocket and held them out with derision" (Chapter i). On page 409 he wrote "storm" and on page 432 began describing the storm on Jackson's Island (Chapter xvi).

Several of the notes were not incorporated into the manuscript until much later. In the margin of a page of Chapter viii (MS p. 209), he wrote, "Cadets of Temp.," a suggestion for including material which would appear in Chapter xxii of the book. On the next page, 210, he wrote, "Learning to smoke" and "Burying pet bird or cat." The first note was amplified in Chapter xvi, where Huck instructs Tom and Joe Harper in the art of smoking; and the other received brief mention in Chapter xxii: "He drifted listlessly down the street & found Jim Hollis acting as Judge in a juvenile court that was trying a cat for murder, in the presence of her victim, a bird" (MS p. B-12).

In another hand, probably Mrs. Clemens's, there was a note on page 160 (Chapter vi) which read, "Take of[f] his wig with a cat." Twain himself reiterated the suggestion on page 573 (Chapter xxiii, but written before the graduation ceremony chapter), noting "(Dropping cat)."[1] Finally, in Chapter xxi, the humorist incorporated the

8. "Jim Wolfe and the Cats" was frequently reprinted. According to Merle Johnson, *A Bibliography of Mark Twain* (New York, 1935), p. 229, it appeared in the *Californian*, the New York *Sunday Mercury*, the "Buyer's Manual of 1872," "Beecher's Readings and Recitations," and in book form in *Mark Twain's Speeches* (New York, 1910), pp. 262–264, and *Mark Twain's Autobiography*, ed. Albert B. Paine (New York, 1924), I, 135–138.

9. *Life on the Mississippi*, Chapter lvi, and *Autobiography*, I, 130–131. See Dixon Wecter, *Sam Clemens of Hannibal* (Boston, 1952), pp. 253–256, for a succinct account of the actual incident.

1. This and one other note of Livy's, considered below, are the only comments I have found in the manuscript which are by his wife; neither smacks of censorship. Mr. Fred Anderson, curator of the Mark Twain Papers, has suggested that since the language of these two notes does not sound like Mrs. Clemens, she may well have written them at her husband's dictation, perhaps while they were reading the manuscript aloud together. [Robert H.

incident of lowering a cat from the ceiling to remove the schoolmaster's wig.

Incidentally, the graduation chapter, although it utilized these notes, was greatly assisted by a book Twain possessed: *The Pastor's Story and Other Pieces; or Prose and Poetry* by Mary Ann Harris Gay, of which seven editions were published between 1858 and 1871.[2] It was this author and this book which Twain acknowledged in his note at the end of the graduation chapter: "The pretended 'compositions' quoted in this chapter are taken without alteration from a volume entitled 'Prose and Poetry, by a Western Lady'—but they are exactly and precisely after the school-girl pattern and hence are much happier than any mere imitations could be." The elocutions in this chapter, "Is This, Then, Life?," "A Missouri Maiden's Farewell to Alabama," and "A Vision," were not, then, as Dixon Wecter suggested,[3] Twain's own satiric efforts. On the contrary, the humorist pasted actual pages torn from Mary Ann Gay's book in his manuscript. His page A-14 (547–548) is actually pages 31 and 32 of her selection, "Is This, Then, Life?" His pages A-16 (550) and A-17 (551) are her pages 118 and 119, "Farewell to Alabama," written, her footnote explained, in imitation of Mr. Tyrone Power's "Farewell to America." And finally, Twain's page A-19 (553) was her pages 189 and 190, "A Vision."

All this material supports the theory that *Tom Sawyer* was structureless. The author's own statements suggested that he wrote those memories of his childhood which came to mind, waited until he remembered some more, and then added them to his manuscript. The marginal notations show that as he wrote he thought of other incidents by association and made his notes to keep them in mind. In one instance the associative link between the material he was writing and the marginal note is apparent. On page 209 he was describing Tom Sawyer's daydream of returning to St. Petersburg as a pirate wearing a "crimson sash." A red sash was the enticement which the author could not resist as a boy when joining the Cadets of Temperance, and, remembering this, he wrote the "Cadets of Temp." note in his margin. This was sheer opportunism, but it was the way he collected the material for the book—from immediate memory and from brief notes in his margins which he would later expand.[4]

Hirst, general editor of the Mark Twain Project, assures me that these notes are not in Olivia Clemens's hand but in Twain's own—Editor's note.]

2. See L. H. Wright, *American Fiction, 1851–1875* (San Marino, 1957), p. 131.

3. Wecter, *Sam Clemens of Hannibal*, p. 257, speaks of saccharine poetry "which he later satirized in *Tom Sawyer*, when at school exercises a 'slim, melancholy girl' arose and recited 'A Missouri Maiden's Farewell to Alabama.' "

4. On at least one occasion, however, Twain wrote some separate notes relating to his book.

II

On the other hand, some of the material in the manuscript supports the "maturation" theory. In the margin of manuscript page 276, in the hand I believe is Mrs. Clemens's, there appeared, "Tom licked for Becky." Twain repeated the suggestion on page 464: "T takes B's whipping." And in Chapter xx, he expanded the note into one of the chapters which Blair suggests are crucial,[5] delaying the use of his wife's note until fairly late in the book. Conversely, he manipulated the Cadets of Temperance episode to emphasize Tom's immaturity. He first mentioned the Cadets of Temperance in a brief paragraph of a letter for the *Alta California*:

> . . . And they started militia companies, and Sons of Temperance and Cadets of Temperance. Hannibal always had a weakness for the Temperance cause. I joined the cause myself, although they didn't allow a boy to smoke, or drink or swear, but I thought I never could be truly happy till I wore one of those stunning red scarfs and walked in procession when a distinguished citizen died. I stood it four months, but never an infernal distinguished citizen died during the whole time; and when they finally pronounced old Doctor Norton convalescent (a man I had been depending on for seven or eight weeks,) I just drew out. I drew out in disgust, and pretty much all the distinguished citizens in the camp died within the next three weeks.[6]

In the Aldis Collection of the Yale University Library there is a single page of notes for the graveyard scene:

Potter & Dr.
    objects to job
    quarrell [*sic*]
    fight
    Potter knocked down with Tom's
shovel.
    Joe rushed in & stabs Dr.
    Potter insensible
    Joe will bury Dr in Tom's hole &
will make Potter think *he* is accessory.
    Finds treasure—goes & hides it
—returns & finds P up.
    No use to bury body, for Potter
thinks *he* did it.
    When boys leave, they carry their
tools with them & will never tell.
    Somewhere previously it is
said Joe lives in the cave.

Since Injun Joe has been substituted for Pap Finn (who originally played this part in the manuscript [see MTAW, p. 17]), and since the graveyard and the treasure scenes have been combined, this was probably a note for a lecture or a dramatization.

5. "On the Structure of *Tom Sawyer*," pp. 84–87.
6. *Mark Twain's Travels with Mr. Brown*, ed. Franklin Walker and G. Ezra Dane (New York, 1940), p. 146.

In *Tom Sawyer* (Chapter XXII), the material was almost as short:

> Tom joined the new order of Cadets of Temperance, being attracted by the showy character of their "regalia." He promised to abstain from smoking, chewing, and profanity as long as he remained a member. Now he found out a new thing—namely, that to promise not to do a thing is the surest way in the world to make a body want to go and do that very thing. Tom soon found himself tormented with a desire to drink and swear; the desire grew to be so intense that nothing but the hope of a chance to display himself in his red sash kept him from withdrawing from the order. Fourth of July was coming; but he soon gave that up—gave it up before he had worn his shackles over forty-eight hours—and fixed his hopes upon old Judge Frazer, justice of the peace, who was apparently on his death-bed and would have a big public funeral, since he was so high an official. During three days Tom was deeply concerned about the Judge's condition and hungry for news of it. Sometimes his hopes ran high—so high that he would venture to get out his regalia and practice before the looking-glass. But the Judge had a most discouraging way of fluctuating. At last he was pronounced upon the mend—and then convalescent. Tom was disgusted; and felt a sense of injury, too. He handed in his resignation at once— and that night the Judge suffered a relapse and died. Tom resolved that he would never trust a man like that again.

The four months of membership were shortened to less than a week in *Tom Sawyer*, making Tom much less steadfast than young Clemens. And the overwhelming desire to drink and swear made Tom much more irresolute and immature. Both changes tended to emphasize the boy's inability to abide by his decisions at this point in the book.

But the most important support for Blair's interpretation occurs on the first page of the manuscript. Here Twain wrote a long note, never before discussed, which merits careful study:

> 1, Boyhood & youth; 2 y & early manh; 3 the Battle of Life in many lands; 4 (age 37 to [40?],) return & meet grown babies & toothless old drivelers who were the grandees of his boyhood. The Adored Unknown a [illegible] faded old maid & full of rasping, puritanical vinegar piety.

This outline was written, if not before he began the book, before he reached page 169 of his manuscript. Before that page, the "new girl" was referred to as "the Adored Unknown" (Chapter III of the published book). And on that page the name "Becky Thatcher" appeared for the first time (Chapter VI). If Becky had been "christened" when Twain wrote this outline, it seems likely that he would have used her

name in it. The marginal note represents, then, a very early if not
the earliest plan for the plot of the new novel. The book was to be
in four parts, clearly progressing from boyhood to maturity and ending with Tom's return to St. Petersburg and a puritanical Becky. The
"return" idea was a recurrent one, appearing in Twain's notebooks
several times.[7] Rudimentary though it is, this outline assumes enormous importance, for the only "theme" it conveys is one of the maturation of a person from boyhood to manhood. It is obviously crucial
to determine exactly when this plan was discarded, because if Twain
composed the book by this formula the "maturation" theory stands
vindicated.

Even after the book was finished, Twain was uncertain about the
wisdom of having stopped with Tom's youth. "I have finished the
story and didn't take the chap beyond boyhood," he told Howells.
"See if you don't really decide that I am right in closing with him as
a boy."[8] But the decision to alter the original outline was not made
until after September 4, 1874, and perhaps as late as the spring of
1875.

Page 403 of the manuscript, where the change is noticeable,
appears toward the end of Chapter xv. Tom, Joe Harper, and Huck
have run away to Jackson's Island to become pirates. Joe and Huck,
homesick and ready to return to St. Petersburg, have been "withered
with derision" by Tom, who has no desire to go back to civilization.
The cannons on the ferry boat have failed to bring up the boys' bodies. Just as in *Huckleberry Finn*, the stage has been set, the devices
prepared, for an imminent departure. After the other boys go to
sleep, Tom scrawls a note to Joe Harper on a piece of sycamore bark
and leaves it, together with his "schoolboy treasures of almost inestimable value." This leavetaking from Joe thus sounds much more
final than would be necessary merely for Tom to deliver a note to
his aunt. Tom writes another note for Aunt Polly, returns to his home
in St. Petersburg, and at page 403 is standing over his sleeping aunt.

Preparations were thus made for Tom to begin his "Battle of Life
in many lands," to leave both St. Petersburg and his comrades who
were about to return there. But Mark Twain's manuscript shows that
he pondered the wisdom of having Tom depart. Aware that a critical
point in the story was at hand, he sprinkled the page with signs of
his indecision. Deliberating what course to take, he wrote at the top
margin, "Sid is to find and steal that scroll," and "He is to show the
scroll in proof of his intent." In the left margin, he wrote two further
lines and cancelled them. Across the page itself he wrote, "No, he

7. See MTAW, p. 49, and *Mark Twain's Notebook*, ed. Albert B. Paine (New York, 1935),
p. 212.
8. *Mark Twain's Letters*, pp. 258–259. See also his letter of June 21, 1875, to Howells
(MTAW, p. 10, n. 2). [See pp. 253–54 herein—Editor's note.]

leaves the bark there, & Sid gets it." Then he suggested, "He forgets to leave the bark." This was the point at which he had "pumped myself dry"[9] and found that "at page 400 of my manuscript the story made a sudden and determined halt and refused to proceed another step."[1]

If the note was merely to contain the message, "We ain't dead—we are only off playing pirates," the author's ruminations over what would happen to it were completely out of proportion. If Tom left Jackson's Island to deliver this message and then return, the bequest of his proudest possessions to Joe Harper was equally absurd. If, as one of the notes suggested, he was to forget to leave the scroll after swimming part of the river and sneaking under his aunt's bed, he would be completely unbelievable. But if the bark was to contain a farewell message to Aunt Polly and was to be stolen by Sid, this scene might prepare for Tom's return at age thirty-seven to St. Petersburg. Though the possible development of the plot is conjectural, it is plausible to suggest an identification scene, perhaps a court trial, in which the stolen bark would be the crucial evidence.[2] Almost literally, the piece of bark with a scrawled message separated the reader from something very similar to *Adventures of Huckleberry Finn*; the scroll of sycamore bark became the key to the further progress of *Tom Sawyer* that the resurrected raft would later be in Twain's masterpiece.[3] Used in one way, the plot would continue on the course Twain outlined on the first page of his manuscript; used in another, the direction of the novel would be altered.

Twain chose not to have Tom start his travels. The boy returns the scroll to his jacket pocket, where Aunt Polly discovers it a few chapters later. It was undoubtedly after he made his decision that he also turned back to page 401 and inserted a paragraph: "This was Wednesday night. If the OVER [then on the back of the page] bodies continued missing until Sunday, all hope would be given over, & the funeral would be preached on that morning. Tom shuddered." *Now* the stage was set for the boys' return to their own funeral.

In several places the author reminded himself marginally to insert Aunt Polly's discovery of the message: on page 409 he jotted down, "The piece of bark at Aunt Polly's," and on page 464, "Aunt P's bark." Finally, on manuscript page 512 he related her discovery of the scroll

9. Sept. 4, 1874, *Mark Twain's Letters*, p. 224.
1. *Mark Twain in Eruption*, p. 197.
2. Court trials with surprise witnesses and sensational evidence were the ingredients of one of Mark Twain's favorite plots. They occurred in "Ah Sin," "Simon Wheeler, the Amateur Detective," and several of the trials analyzed in D. M. McKeithan, *Court Trials in Mark Twain and Other Essays* (The Hague, 1958), pp. 10–114.
3. See Walter Blair, "When Was *Huckleberry Finn* Written?" *American Literature*, XXX, 1–25 (March, 1958), and Henry Nash Smith, "Introduction," *Adventures of Huckleberry Finn* (Boston, 1958), p. ix.

and rounded off the awkward solution of that problem. He never explained Tom's similar message to Joe or his strange bequest of his "treasures" to his friend. Whether from expediency, indifference, or, most likely, the realization that Tom Sawyer was not the boy to send off on the "Battle of Life in many lands," Twain decided not to start Tom's journeying. Evidence that he realized Tom's shortcomings for such a role is offered by his own statement to Howells that "by and by I shall take a boy of twelve and run him on through life (in the first person) but not Tom Sawyer—he would not be a good character for it."[4] The decision committed him to center the book in his protagonist's boyhood in St. Petersburg.

Even though Twain thus determined the direction of his plot on manuscript page 403, the second half of the book gave him some problems in organization. For two hundred pages, beginning at manuscript page 533 and therefore in the late spring and summer of 1875, he juggled and rearranged his chapters extensively. For the two hundred pages following page 533 the manuscript is paginated thus (brackets indicating cancelled page numbers):

		A-1	to	A-24		
		B-1	to	B-13		
	[534]	573	to	[642]	694	
[535]	[643]	695	to	[345]	[653]	705
	[654]	706	to	[669]	721	

The two inserts, A-1 to A-24 and B-1 to B-13, related the graduation ceremonies and the Cadets of Temperance episode (Chapters xxi and xxii). The latter chapter may have been composed separately when the author wrote a note about it the previous fall; but since a marginal note referring to the graduation chapter occurred at page 573, that material must have been composed after the note (in Chapter xxiii) was written. Obviously neither insert was placed in its present position until after Twain had written beyond them to page 722 (Chapter xxx). The third section listed above contained Chapters xxiii through the first paragraph of xxix. The fourth contained eleven pages of Chapter xxix relating some preliminary details about the picnic. The final section related the last paragraphs of Chapter xxix, those concerning Huck, Injun Joe, and Widow Douglas. From the pagination it appears that Twain originally intended the picnic section to follow the scene in which Tom took Becky's whipping.[5] Then Muff Potter's trial was substituted. While writing of the aftereffects

---

4. *Mark Twain's Letters*, p. 259.
5. The first three pages of the picnic material were originally numbered "535" to "537." The next eight pages were "338" to "345." The two-hundred-page drop in pagination was apparently inadvertent. There is no indication in the manuscript that this material might have belonged at page 338; Twain was making preparations for the picnic in Chapter xviii, ms pp. 487–490.

of Muff's trial, Twain cancelled a passage which was to lead to the capture or death of Injun Joe. In Chapter xxiv, just before the final sentence of the published book, he wrote regarding Tom's apprehension of Injun Joe's revenge: "But Providence lifts even a boy's burden when it begins to get too heavy for him. The angel sent to attend to Tom's was an old back-country farmer named Ezra Ward, who had been a schoolmate of Aunt Polly's so many. . . ." The page (ms p. 600) ended and Twain discarded whatever other pages carried the idea further. Ezra Ward became an enigma, the only clue to his intended function in the story being the cryptic marginal note, "Brick pile." At this spot, probably, Twain replaced whatever plan he had for Injun Joe with the "buried treasure" chapters culminating in Joe's death in the cave. For he began writing the treasure chapters (xxv–xxix) immediately after cancelling the "Ezra Ward" material. These chapters then followed the trial chapter, and the beginning of the picnic was placed in Chapter xxix. At this point, apparently realizing the climactic possibilities of the cave chapters, Twain placed the two sections on the graduation exercises and on the Cadets of Temperance between the whipping scene and Potter's trial. This manipulation of material which was written more or less at random was accurately described by Brander Matthews:

> When at last he became convinced that he had made his profit out of every possible reminiscence, he went over what he had written with great care, adjusting the several instalments one to the other, sometimes transposing a chapter or two and sometimes writing into the earlier chapters the necessary preparation for adventures in the later chapters unforeseen when he was engaged on the beginnings of the book.[6]

Furthermore, this rearrangement of his material tends to support the theory that Twain was working with the deliberate intention of showing Tom's maturation. The school graduation depicting the high jinks at the expense of the school master and the painfully amateurish orations, and the Cadets of Temperance material revealing a youthful, irresolute Tom Sawyer were inserted in a relatively early spot in the manuscript, forcing three of the four chapters which Blair suggests are crucial into later positions.[7] The trial of Muff Potter was followed by the treasure chapters which portrayed a superstitious and fanciful pair of boys, and before this line of action was completed in Chapter xxix by "showing Huck conquering fear to rescue the widow,"[8] the author inserted some preliminary paragraphs originat-

6. Matthews, p. 266.
7. "On the Structure of *Tom Sawyer*," p. 87: "And well in the second half of the book, in a series of chapters—xx, xxiii, xxix, xxxii—come those crucial situations in which he acts more like a grownup than like an irresponsible boy."
8. *Ibid.*, p. 85.

ing the picnic scene, paragraphs which had originally been intended
for Chapter XXI. Next came Huck's bravery (MS pp. 706–721), com-
pleting the Injun Joe line of action. Finally the picnic material developed into the adventures in the cave, which not only completed the
Tom and Becky line of action but also showed Tom at his most
manly. Though terms like *maturation*, *boyhood*, *youth*, and *early manhood* are ambiguous and ill-defined, nevertheless the rearranging of
these climactic chapters allowed Twain to present Tom in a group
of critical situations toward the end of the book where maturer judgment and courage were vital. These events required a Tom Sawyer
who was nowhere apparent in the idyllic first half of the book.

III

In composing *Tom Sawyer*, then, Twain faced and solved two problems. First, when he was about half way through his manuscript, he
paused at a crucial point and determined to keep his story centered
in youth in St. Petersburg. An early scheme had included taking Tom
on a "Battle of Life in many lands," and the moment for his departure
was reached on manuscript page 403. Even though he altered the
structure of the novel then, the author was nevertheless progressing
through several stages of childhood mentioned in his outline, a pro-
gression which would be, as Blair observed, a "working out in fictional form . . . of a boy's maturing."[9]

Then in 1875, in the second half of the book, Twain very deliberately shifted his chapters so that climactic actions were placed
after childish and immature incidents. Though the various anecdotes
and episodes which he mentioned in his margins came to him cha-
otically and without formal significance, the humorist's selectivity
and rearrangement of the material provided him with the structure
he envisioned, roughly, in his early outline of the book. The marginal
notations were identical with the working notes of *Huckleberry Finn*:
though they were a ragbag of memories, the book which resulted was
not structureless.

The manuscript of *Tom Sawyer* thus provides convincing evidence
to corroborate Blair's interpretation of the book. The original outline
indicated that it was begun with a definite structure in the author's
mind. And the rearrangement of the later material shows that,
instead of growing "as grows the grass," the book was considerably
altered to conform to a bisected version of the outline when Twain
determined to keep it, as he stated in the "Conclusion," "strictly a
history of a *boy* . . . the story could not go much further without
becoming the history of a *man*."

9. *Ibid.*, p. 84.

JUDITH FETTERLEY

The Sanctioned Rebel†

One of the major rhythms of *The Adventures of Tom Sawyer* is established in its opening lines: " 'Tom!' No answer. 'Tom!' No answer. 'What's gone with that boy, I wonder? You, TOM!' "[1] Much of the action of the novel is a variation on this theme of looking for Tom, for in the world of St. Petersburg the boy, Tom, is central. It is he who creates the major occasions for the town, and the emotional arcs of the book are described by his being lost or found. When Tom is thought lost, the town is in dismay; when he is found, it rejoices:

> The alarm swept from lip to lip, from group to group, from street to street, and within five minutes the bells were wildly clanging and the whole town was up! The Cardiff Hill episode sank into instant insignificance, the burglars were forgotten, horses were saddled, skiffs were manned, the ferryboat ordered out, and before the horror was half an hour old two hundred men were pouring down highroad and river toward the cave (p. 248).

> *

> Away in the middle of the night a wild peal burst from the village bells and in a moment the streets were swarming with frantic half-clad people, who shouted, "Turn out! turn out! they're found! they're found!" Tin pans and horns were added to the din, the population massed itself and moved toward the river, met the children coming in an open carriage drawn by shouting citizens, thronged around it, joined its homeward march, and swept magnificently up the main street roaring huzzah after huzzah! (pp. 263–64).

The world of St. Petersburg is dull and sleepy, and its arch enemy is the boredom which lies at its heart, making it so sensation-hungry that everything that happens is greeted as an entertainment. Thus the discovery of Dr. Robinson's murder constitutes a local holiday for which school is dismissed. Thus the town turns out to fill the church as never before for the spectacle of a triple funeral. Thus the trial of Muff Potter is the biggest entertainment of the summer; and when Tom finally decides to testify at the trial, he does so as much

---

† From *Studies in the Novel*, v. 3, no. 3, Fall 1971. Copyright © 1971 by North Texas State University. Reprinted by permission of the publisher. All notes are Fetterley's.
1. Samuel L. Clemens, *The Adventures of Tom Sawyer* in *The Writings of Mark Twain*, Definitive Edition (New York: Gabriel Wells, 1922–25), VIII, 1. Subsequent references will be to this edition of *Tom Sawyer* and will be included in parentheses in the text.

out of a sense of what is dramatically appropriate and will improve the show as he does out of a tormented conscience.

The boredom which lies at the heart of St. Petersburg is most fully pictured in the scenes which take place in the Sunday school and church the first Sunday of the novel. The dreadful monotony of Sunday school text, of prayer and sermon, the painful rigidity of never-varying rituals, symbolized by the superintendent's clothes—"a fence that compelled a straight lookout ahead, and a turning of the whole body when a side view was required" (p. 35)—is relieved only by a few paper wads, an occasional scuffle, a fly to be caught. The world of St. Petersburg is trapped into boredom by its own hypocrisy, by its refusal to admit how dull and uninteresting the things which it professes to value really are. It is against this background that Tom's centrality to St. Petersburg can be understood. He provides life, interest, amusement; he is a master entertainer with a bug for every occasion. No wonder St. Petersburg is always looking for Tom.

One of the central scenes which defines this aspect of the inter-relation of Tom and his society is the moment in church when Tom discovers and releases his pinch bug. Tom's boredom has reached painful proportions; the momentary flicker of interest aroused by the image of the little child leading the lion and lamb before the hosts at Judgment Day has faded. Then he remembers his pinch bug, a "treasure" of the first order. He takes it out, it bites him, and he flips it on the floor. Immediately the congregation stirs itself; at last something is happening. A few minutes later a poodle which is the very image of the congregation, bored and sleepy, comes along and, like the congregation, begins to take an interest in the bug and to play with it. But after awhile he forgets about the bug and in starting to go to sleep, sits on it, whereupon it promptly bites him and sends him tearing around the church and ultimately out a window. "Tom Sawyer went home quite cheerful, thinking to himself that there was some satisfaction about divine service when there was a bit of variety in it" (p. 49). He has provided a brilliant entertainment and won the thanks of the congregation, for his act has not only amused them but has made it impossible for church to continue.

The other center of boredom in this world is school, and once again Tom has a bug to relieve him. Tom is bored to a point almost beyond endurance when he sticks his hand in his pocket and discovers the tick he has just purchased from Huck Finn: "his face lit up with a glow of gratitude that was prayer" (p. 65). His comrade, Joe Harper, as painfully bored as Tom, greets the tick and its promise of pleasure "deeply and gratefully" (p. 66). The language which describes the discovery of the tick is an impressive index of the boredom of school. But again the boys are not the only ones bored. The schoolmaster, Mr. Dobbins, is asleep when Tom comes in and only wakes up long enough to switch him. Tom's tick and his play with it become equally the source of the schoolmaster's interest: "He had contemplated a good part of the performance before he contributed his bit of variety to it" (p. 67). The switching is part of the complex game which the boys and adults play in order to make school bearable. It is the mode by which the teacher is allowed to save face and keep on professing his interest in school. It in no way prevents Tom from continuing to create interest through his pranks, for, unlike the world of Dickens, the switching in Tom's world leaves neither psychological nor physical scars. It is, indeed, the mark of the boys' success in gaining attention and creating interest; it is a modest form of showing off for both boys and teacher. The relationship between the adults and children in this novel is deeply symbiotic.

Tom's interactions with Aunt Polly develop another dimension of this relationship. Aunt Polly, like the rest of St. Petersburg, loves Tom, because he makes her laugh and gives variety to her life. But Aunt Polly expresses her affection for Tom by constantly rapping him on the head with her thimble, setting traps to catch him in lies, carping at him for being bad and breaking her heart, and enforcing labor on his holidays. She never comes out and openly says what Tom means to her until she thinks he is dead. In part, Aunt Polly is a victim of her own hypocrisy and unreality. She refuses to take account of the split which she everywhere expresses between her heart and her conscience, with its conception of duty. Thus she is never free to say what she truly feels. But this is really a very small part of the psychology behind Aunt Polly's actions. Tom knows that Aunt Polly's thimble on his head, like Dobbins's switching, is an index of the place he holds in her heart; thus he worries only when she does not rap him. But much more important, Tom knows that it is her resistance, her posture of disapproval, which creates his pleasure.

The fact that the boys' world of pranks is no fun without the existence of an adult world to prohibit them is made clear in a number of scenes in the story. When school is finally over and vacation finally comes, there is nothing Tom wants to do. What has happened to the lure of Cardiff Hill, which called to him so irresistibly through the schoolroom window? Clearly "hooky" is one thing and vacation another. When the boys run off to Jackson's Island everything is bully for the first day or so, but pretty soon they lose interest in going naked and sleeping out in the open and swimming whenever they want, because, as Joe says, "Swimming's no good. I don't seem to care for it, somehow, when there ain't anybody to say I shan't go in" (p. 138). But perhaps the most famous instance of this principle is the whitewashing episode, which casts Tom in the role of discovering it as a great law of human nature. The success of Tom's strategy rests

on his intuitive discovery that people want to do what they are forbidden to. In order to change whitewashing from hard labor into the
one thing the boys are mad to do Tom has only to present it as
something he cannot allow them to do, an art requiring special skill
which only he possesses, a task which he is under strict orders to
perform only himself without help from anyone else. By means of
this tactic Tom not only gets the boys to do the whitewashing for
him; he gets them to pay him for the privilege.

The Adventures of Tom Sawyer is steeped in the rhythm of this
relationship between adults and children. The delight of midnight
trips is in creeping out of the window in answer to a secret signal
and in defiance of an adult stricture. The pleasure of Huck Finn's
society, like the attractiveness of his state, lies in its being forbidden.
When Huck first enters the book, it is this angle from which he is
viewed. Thus he is described as a "romantic outcast," a phrase which
defines the point of view on him as Tom's. There is at this point no
hint of what Huck's life might be like either from his point of view
or the narrator's. The strong implication, however, is that the joys of
his existence are imaginary, a product of prohibition. Huck is introduced in the book in great part as an element in Mark Twain's creation of the dynamic between pleasure and prohibition in the mind
of Tom Sawyer. And Mark Twain's achievement in creating this
dynamic in *The Adventures of Tom Sawyer* prepares us for Tom's
passion for creating obstacles at the end of *Huckleberry Finn*. It is
part and parcel of his conception of pleasure. If the adults have failed
to fulfill their part of the game and provide difficulties for Tom to
overcome, then he will simply have to play both parts and create the
obstacles himself. That a new mode of pleasure has been discovered
to the reader in the process of Huck's adventures is not Tom's fault;
he is doing only what he thinks is expected of him.

II

Tom entertains his world and in return it provides the structures
which make his pleasure possible and heaps on him all the attention
he could possibly desire. The relationship between Tom and his community is remarkably positive and indeed it is so throughout the
book. There are, however, aspects to this relationship which are a
little darker than those so far discussed and which bring us to a
further understanding of Tom's character, an understanding which
begins to explain what happens to Tom in *Adventures of Huckleberry
Finn*.

Tom's actions in the first half of *Tom Sawyer* are a series of entertainments, but they are also a series of exposures which reveal the
absurdity and hypocrisy of his world. One of the basic hypocrisies

which Tom exposes early in the book is that which lies behind the phrase "virtue rewarded." By "virtue" the community means hard, dull, stupid work and by "reward" it means a sense of pleasure and achievement in doing this hard, dull, stupid work. The exposure begins when Tom, having completed his whitewashing assignment, presents himself to Aunt Polly and reports that he is done. When she has assured herself that he is not lying, she proceeds to reward him with a choice apple and a "lecture upon the added value and flavor a treat took to itself when it came without sin through virtuous effort" (p. 21). The scene which precedes Aunt Polly's lecture has, of course, made a shambles of her premise. People do not enjoy what they work for; they enjoy what they play at. The "added value and flavor" of a treat come not through "virtuous effort" but through being told you cannot have it. But Aunt Polly herself no more acts on the basis of her scripture than Tom, for what she is now calling "virtuous effort" was just a few pages before hard work and punishment, something she would have to force Tom to do. The explosion of Aunt Polly's myth of human behavior, however, is built right into this scene: "And while she closed with a happy Scriptural flourish, he 'hooked' a doughnut" (p. 21).

The exposure of the hypocrisy of "virtue rewarded" continues in the scene in Sunday school in chapter 4. A certain kind of virtue is indeed rewarded in this incident but not exactly the kind the authorities pretend they wish to recognize. Outside the church on Sunday morning, Tom trades all the wealth he has gotten from selling whitewashing privileges the previous afternoon for Bible tickets. The exchange is certainly justified in Tom's eyes, for the opportunity to be called up in front of the entire Sunday school world to receive a Bible fulfills his ever-present dream of being the center of attention. But the tactic by which Tom wins his way to the Bible marks the absurdity of the terms of Judge Thatcher's presentation and expresses the absurdity of the "virtue rewarded" premise behind it:

> "That's it! That's a good boy. Fine boy. Fine, manly little fellow. Two thousand verses is a great many—very, very great many. And you never can be sorry for the trouble you took to learn them; for knowledge is worth more than anything there is in the world; it's what makes great men and good men; you'll be a great man and a good man yourself, someday, Thomas. . . . And you wouldn't take any money for those two thousand verses—no indeed you wouldn't" (pp. 40–41).

But Tom's exposure is made possible by the hypocrisy built into the situation and reflected in Judge Thatcher's speech. If the knowledge was its own reward, a thing which one would not take any money for, there would be no need for the bait of tickets yellow, red, and blue, and the Bible whose purchase they add up to. The very existence of these tickets defines the fact that no one would learn those verses without at least the dim possibility of having a moment of glory for it. All Tom does is to carry the implications of St. Petersburg Christianity to their logical conclusion, and thus there is a certain justice in his particular virtue being rewarded.

Tom's most dramatic exposure, however, occurs when he stages his own funeral and resurrection, for the situation he creates invites the adults to indulge in the hypocrisy of remorse:

> "But it's *so* hard—oh, it's so hard! Only last Saturday my Joe busted a firecracker right under my nose and I knocked him sprawling. Little did I know then how soon—Oh, if it was to do over again I'd hug him and bless him for it."
>
> "Yes, yes, yes, I know just how you feel, Mrs. Harper, I know just exactly how you feel. No longer than yesterday noon, my Tom took and filled the cat full of Pain-killer, and I did think the cretur would tear the house down. And God forgive me, I cracked Tom's head with my thimble, poor boy, poor dead boy" (pp. 131–32).

The situations which Aunt Polly and Mrs. Harper remember are such as to make clear the nature of their remorse. The absurdity of claiming you would hug a boy who has just set off a firecracker under your nose is patent. It could only happen if one had knowledge at the time of something that was to happen later. As this is impossible, so the formulations are absurd and unreal, a fact made quite clear when the boys return and thimble crackings and cuffings continue. The remorse is an emotional indulgence which ultimately has the effect of making the mourners feel good about themselves, because it implies that their actions are no real index of their hearts.

Tom's appearance at his own funeral exposes the hypocrisy at the heart of the adult's lament. His entrance is perfectly timed to accomplish this exposure with maximum effect. At just the moment when the minister has moved the entire congregation to tears and is himself openly weeping over the angelic picture he has created of the boys, Tom appears in all his bedraggled and mischievous reality. The illusion that the minister has created and the congregation conspired in is exploded and the unreality at the heart of the funeral exposed. As James Cox has noted, "Tom's joke, his play funeral, provides the ultimate definition of what the 'sincere' funeral was to have been for the town in the first place—an entertainment! A tearful, lugubrious, and hackneyed production in which each of the participants was fully working up his part—but an entertainment nonetheless."[2]

---

2. *Mark Twain: The Fate of Humor* (Princeton: Princeton Univ. Press, 1966), p. 140.

The adults are sufficiently happy to get the boys back that they do not mind being exposed as ridiculous. The potential humiliation of the scene is averted by the singing of "Old Hundred" and the final note is one of reconciliation and joy. But it has been a tight situation for a moment. Tom's series of exposures has culminated in something particularly egregious, for it is far harder to be exposed as an emotional hypocrite than a moral one. What is it that allows Tom to get away with this exposure? The answer lies in the discovery of a further dimension to the symbiotic relationship between Tom and the adults of St. Petersburg.

A number of critics who have written on *The Adventures of Tom Sawyer* have discussed the book in terms of its relation to the convention of Bad Boy literature which appeared in the United States, particularly after the Civil War.[3] Books built around the character of the Bad Boy sprang up as a reaction against an inundation of highly moralistic juvenile fiction. This fiction pictured and exalted an unreal creature who was totally good and spent all his time in memorizing the Bible and going to church and taking care of his mother, and who reaped the rewards of this earth and then those of heaven. It also pictured an evil child who stole apples, lied to his mother, played hooky, and was eventually hanged. It was against the background of this absurdity that the Bad Boy books arose. Their hero, while called a Bad Boy to make clear that he is not the Good Boy of the moralistic fiction, is in fact just a real human boy, whose pranks, jokes, and rascalities are the natural result of his energy and healthiness. The Bad Boy is not really bad, only "mischievous," and it is clear that when he grows up he will be a pillar of the community. The implication behind this literature is clear: socially useful adults develop only from real boys who have shown some life as children. The rascality of such children is not negative; rather it is understood and affirmed as a stage they must go through on their way to becoming useful adults; it is indeed the indication that they will, in fact, become useful adults.

The Adventures of Tom Sawyer is a paradigm of the Bad Boy convention, and its structure and hero can be most clearly understood in its terms. There has been considerable critical debate on the structure of *Tom Sawyer* since Walter Blair published, in 1939, his article, "On the Structure of *Tom Sawyer*."[4] His thesis, most recently supported by Hamlin Hill, Robert Reagan, and Albert Stone,[5] claims

---

3. The following are most important: Walter Blair, "On the Structure of *Tom Sawyer*," *MP*, 37 (1939), 75–88; John Hinz, "Huck and Pluck: 'Bad' Boys in American Fiction," *SAQ*, 51 (1952), 120–29; Jim Hunter, "Mark Twain and the Boy-Book in 19th-Century America," *CE*, 24 (1963), 430–38; Albert E. Stone, *The Innocent Eye: Childhood in Mark Twain's Imagination* (New Haven: Yale Univ. Press, 1961), pp. 58–90.
4. *MP*, 37 (1939), 75–88.
5. Hamlin Hill, "The Composition and the Structure of *Tom Sawyer*," *AL*, 32 (1961), 379–

that the book enacts Tom's growth from callow, unworthy childhood to worthy maturity. Blair defined four major narrative strands in the story: "the story of Tom and Becky, the story of Tom and Muff Potter, the Jackson's Island episode, and the series of happenings (which might be called the Injun Joe story) leading to the discovery of the treasure."[6] Each of these strands, according to Blair, "is initiated by a characteristic and typically boyish action. The love story begins with Tom's childishly fickle desertion of his fiancée, Amy Lawrence; the Potter narrative with the superstitious trip to the graveyard; the Jackson's Island episode with the adolescent revolt of the boy against Aunt Polly, and Tom's youthful ambition to be a pirate; the Injun Joe story with the juvenile search for buried treasure."[7]

Three of these strands, however, "are climaxed by a characteristic and mature sort of action, a sort of action, moreover, directly opposed to the initial action. Tom chivalrously takes Becky's punishment and faithfully helps her in the cave; he defies boyish superstition and courageously testifies for Muff Potter; he forgets a childish antipathy and shows mature concern for his aunt's uneasiness about him."[8] The Injun Joe story for Blair was "the least useful of the four so far as showing Tom's maturing is concerned."[9] But surely there is no need for this reservation, for in Blair's terms Tom's pity on discovering Injun Joe's death is a mature act, replacing his self-centered and seemingly callous earlier response. But, of course, the problem with Blair's analysis is precisely in the terms, for while he has accurately described a pattern in the book he has, I feel, inaccurately evaluated its meaning. Blair assumes certain actions to be "mature" and positive and other actions to be "immature" and negative without ever establishing the grounds for his classification and valuation. The closest he comes is to say that Tom's actions are mature because each of them "eventuates in an expression of adult approval."[1] In fact, the basis of Blair's thesis, and of the essays of those who support him, lies in the claim that Tom's progress in the book is a movement from bad to good and that this movement is defined as such by the changing reaction of the adult community to him. But clearly the adults in *Tom Sawyer* are in all essentials like the children: "Mr. Walters fell to 'showing off'. . . . The librarian 'showed off'. . . . The young lady teachers 'showed off'. . . . The little girls 'showed off' . . . and the little boys 'showed off'. . . . And above it all the great man sat and beamed a majestic judicial smile upon all the house, and

---

92; Robert Reagan, *Unpromising Heroes: Mark Twain and His Characters* (Berkeley: Univ. of California Press, 1966), pp. 117–21; Stone, pp. 78–89.
6. Blair, p. 84.
7. Ibid.
8. Ibid., pp. 84–85.
9. Ibid., p. 85.
1. Ibid.

warmed himself in the sun of his own grandeur—for he was 'showing off,' too" (p. 38). Indeed, the very "search for buried treasure," which Blair labels as "juvenile," is, upon Tom's success, taken up by every adult in St. Petersburg. If, in fact, the adults are in any way different from the children, the difference does not make them more positive than the children but more negative. The children admit, after all, that they are showing off to gain attention but the adults have to pretend that they are doing something else. The children are honest; the adults are hypocrites, a point which Tom's actions make again and again. Thus it hardly makes sense to assume that they provide the yardstick which charts a growth from something negative to something positive. In fact, it hardly seems accurate to describe Tom's change in the book as one of growth in this sense at all. One has only to compare the tone of the end of the book with that of the beginning to feel this. Indeed, in commenting on this ending, Blair does an about-face and finds that Tom's "adult" behavior in talking to Huck Finn means that he has "gone over to the side of the enemy."[2]

What Blair is responding to at the end of his article is Mark Twain's vision of the meaning of Bad Boy fiction as dramatized in *The Adventures of Tom Sawyer*. The structure of *Tom Sawyer* is at once an embodiment and an exposure of this convention and it takes its shape from the dynamics of the interaction between child and adult which lie behind the convention. Since the Bad Boy is just a natural child marked for the future as a solid, respectable citizen, he is the agent through whom the community can gain a temporary release from the boredom and rigidity of their codes and beliefs, a release which is dramatized in the conventional scene in which the Bad Boy licks the overly pious, unnatural Good Boy. But the Bad Boy does not hold any values which are at root different from those of the community, nor does he really intend to expose the hypocrisy of the values which the community holds and which the Good Boy is simply exaggerating. The Bad Boy is a rebel in that he temporarily flaunts and outrages the community, but he is a sanctioned rebel, because his rebellion is limited in time and intention; his rebellion is a stage which has respectability at its other end. The community wants, in fact demands, this rebellion, because it provides excitement and release, and because the ultimate assimilation of the rebellion constitutes a powerful affirmation of their values. The convention of the Bad Boy and the books that express it represent the form of rebellion without the reality, titillation without threat. They channel rebellion by confining it to a stage and sanctioning that stage, and ultimately they transform rebellion into affirmation.

2. Ibid., p. 88.

The structure of *Tom Sawyer* is a perfect embodiment of this pattern. In the early part of the book Tom is consistently outrageous. He lies and steals and plays hooky as a matter of course. He hobnobs with Huck Finn against the express prohibition of the adults. He sneaks out at midnight to join the outcast in his adventure to the graveyard. There he watches a murder and makes no move to reveal the murderer. His early actions constitute a series of exposures, which culminates in his appearance at his own funeral. This is the height of Tom's rebellion and outrageousness, for in threatening to make the congregation look ridiculous in front of each other, in threatening to humiliate them, he pushes against the limits of what is sanctioned. Dignity is salvaged by the singing of "Old Hundred" but Tom's rebellion has reached its peak and from this point on his pattern of action changes.

In the first major scene after the resurrection episode, Tom is discovered in the ultimately approvable role, one which embodies to the highest possible degree the values of the community: he saves Becky not simply from the public humiliation of a whipping but from having to admit to herself or anyone else an interest in sex. He is here cast in the role of the true Southern gentleman. Such action clearly neutralizes the threat posed by his funeral and makes clear which side he is on. From this point on Tom adopts conventional values more and more explicitly. He becomes society's detective and exposes its murderer; indirectly he brings the murderer to bay and ultimately he kills him. He gets money and makes clear that he intends to invest it and make capital. In an extension of his role toward Becky, he saves her life and thus further adopts the conventional masculine role of protector of womanhood. In the final scene of the book, Tom, who began by longing for Huck's outcast state and by cordially hating along with him the confinements of clothes and schools, becomes the advocate of civilization, the adult who seeks to channel and transform the rebellion which threatens the community. As Henry Nash Smith has observed, "Mark Twain has written the Sunday-school story about the Good Little Boy Who Succeeded all over again with only a slight change in the hero's make-up and costume."[3] Thus Smith succinctly defines the essential similarity of the Bad Boy convention to the Good Boy literature which it was presumably attacking. And thus he succinctly defines the nature of Tom Sawyer's character and rebellion and the source of Mark Twain's final attitude toward Tom.

---

3. *Mark Twain: The Development of a Writer* (Cambridge, Mass: Harvard Univ. Press, 1962), p. 89.

III

In spite of the negative undercurrents of the action and structure of *The Adventures of Tom Sawyer*, negative in terms both of Tom's relation to his community and of the narrator's and reader's attitude toward Tom, the tone of the novel is essentially genial and the character of Tom Sawyer emerges as essentially positive. Thus Robert Reagan is moved to call *Tom Sawyer* "the most amiable of all Mark Twain's novels,"[4] and Kenneth Lynn remarks, "Of all Twain's major fictions, *Tom Sawyer* is the only one in which an initiation ends neither in flight nor in catastrophe, but in serene and joyous acceptance."[5] For indeed the focus of *The Adventures of Tom Sawyer* is on the harmony between Tom and his community and on the satisfactions of the symbiotic relationship between them. Further, all Tom's characteristics are ultimately placed within this context and are made positive by it. Thus Tom's egotism, his overriding passion to be the center of attention, and his insistence on masterminding every action constitute the mode by which he both provides pleasure for the community and becomes useful to them. It is his egotism, his desire to be the center of attention, which leads him to create the situations which entertain and release them; it is equally these characteristics which in great part move him to testify for Muff Potter at the trial and to take Becky's whipping.

Of course, there are negative overtones to his character. His self-pity with its undercurrent of revenge and aggression, issuing in the desire to make people suffer for what they have done to him; his capacity to subordinate his sense of others' feelings to his desire for an effect; his insistence on things being done according to the rules—a characteristic which links him to the hypocrisy and rigidity which he is otherwise engaged in exploding and looks forward to what he will become in *Huckleberry Finn*; his genius in manipulating people—all of these qualities are present in Tom in *The Adventures of Tom Sawyer*. But they are either secondary and muted or they are transformed by the way they operate in the particular situation of this book. For, again, the focus of *The Adventures of Tom Sawyer* is on the pleasures of the relationship between Tom and his community, which is in essence the relationship between the entertainer and his audience. And in this study of the entertainer, his genius is the joy of his audience, and the necessary egotism, selfishness, and aggressiveness of his character are exculpated by this fact.

It is only at the very end of the book that the tone toward Tom becomes noticeably negative and we feel the presence of some new attitude, some new perspective. What we feel, of course, is the birth

4. Reagan, p. 116.
5. *Mark Twain and Southwestern Humor* (Boston: Little, Brown, 1959), p. 196.

of *Adventures of Huckleberry Finn*, for the change in attitude toward Tom is intimately connected with the discovery of Huck Finn. It is only very late in *Tom Sawyer*, when Huck is separated from Tom by the necessities of the plot, that the possibilities of his character are discovered. It is only then that Huck is discovered as a voice, and a mask, and a point of view, one which will define Tom Sawyer differently and crystallize the perceptions about him which dominate the end of the book. What is wrong with the ending of *The Adventures of Tom Sawyer* is that it is the beginning of *Adventures of Huckleberry Finn* and *Huckleberry Finn* is a quite different book and in it Tom Sawyer is a quite different character.

ALAN GRIBBEN

Boy Books, Bad Boy Books, and *The Adventures of Tom Sawyer*†

Tom Sawyer's impudence sorely tried the patience of the fictional villagers of St. Petersburg, and during recent decades he has proved even more annoying for literary critics. In contrast to the stature of his universally acclaimed companion, Huckleberry Finn, Tom Sawyer's reputation has noticeably sagged over the years. The problem for most critics is that Mark Twain did not restrict Tom's horseplay to *The Adventures of Tom Sawyer* (1876); he reintroduced Tom's boyish frivolity in the opening and closing chapters of *Adventures of Huckleberry Finn* (1885). For the majority of modern-day commentators, the very presence there of Tom—vainglorious, prevaricating, exhibitionistic, domineering, manipulative—"ruins" Huck Finn's marvelous narrative.

Of course Tom Sawyer will always be at a disadvantage in any comparison with his playmate, for in both the first and second book their creator endowed Tom with the trite sensibilities and grandiose visions of a declining Romantic tradition, burlesquing in this literary figure some of the reading that Sam Clemens himself had relished as an adolescent. Most readers will allow Tom Sawyer the right to

† Portions of this revised essay appeared previously in *One Hundred Years of* Huckleberry Finn: *The Boy, His Book, and American Culture*, ed. Robert Sattelmeyer and J. Donald Crowley (Columbia: University of Missouri Press, 1985), 149–70, and in *South Central Review* 5 (Winter 1988): 15–21. Reprinted from *One Hundred Years of* Huckleberry Finn, ed. Sattelmeyer and Crowley by permission of the University of Missouri Press. Copyright © 1985 by the Curators of the University of Missouri. Reprinted from "Manipulating a Genre: *Huckleberry Finn* as Boy Book" by permission of *South Central Review*. All notes are Gribben's.

make believe and play pranks in his own book,[1] but Jesse Bier is typical in characterizing him in *Adventures of Huckleberry Finn* as "the biggest little con man of them all. . . . At his worst, . . . he is a self-deceiver, over-romanticizing and falsifying all experience, bathing in sentimentality, and living a constant lie of style and substance."[2] Judith Fetterley asserts that Tom Sawyer "becomes a creature of delusion" in *Huckleberry Finn*, in which "the action of the novel works to expose the hypocrisy of Tom Sawyer who . . . enacts cruelty after cruelty."[3] Jeffrey Steinbrink laments that "Tom is at the beginning and especially the end of Huck's book, making himself available to our hearty contempt," adding that "Tom seems, like the duke, to be a con-man accustomed to furthering his own interests at the expense of others."[4] Critical opinion is so united on this score that only a few commentators have mounted any defense of Tom Sawyer as a fictional character, most notably Richard Hill.[5] Nearly all other critics agree that to dislike the "Evasion" episodes of *Huckleberry Finn* is to deplore Tom Sawyer as an embarrassment to the stature of his originator and to the artistic masterpiece in which Tom interferes as a definite blemish.[6]

1. A number of twentieth-century scholars endeavored to make the case that Tom Sawyer displays signs of maturing in *The Adventures of Tom Sawyer*—for example, Walter Blair, "On the Structure of *Tom Sawyer*," *Modern Philology* 37 (August 1939): 75–88; reprinted in *Essays on American Humor: Blair Through the Ages*, ed. Hamlin Hill (Madison: University of Wisconsin Press, 1992), 154–64; Barry A. Marks, "Mark Twain's Hymn of Praise," *English Journal* 48 (November 1959): 443–49; Hamlin Hill, "The Composition and the Structure of *Tom Sawyer*," *American Literature* 32 (January 1961): 379–92; Albert E. Stone, Jr., *The Innocent Eye: Childhood in Mark Twain's Imagination* (New Haven: Yale University Press, 1961), 78–89; and Robert Regan, *Unpromising Heroes: Mark Twain and His Characters* (Berkeley: University of California Press, 1966), 117–21. Robert Bray entertainingly summarizes this and related debates in "*Tom Sawyer* Once and for All," *Review* 3 (1981): 77–83.
2. *The Rise and Fall of American Humor* (New York: Holt, Rinehart and Winston, 1968), 132. Likewise A. N. Kaul, *The American Vision: Actual and Ideal Society in Nineteenth-Century Fiction* (New Haven: Yale University Press, 1963), declares: "Tom Sawyer is nowhere else so unsympathetic, and his 'heroism' nowhere so meretricious, as in the concluding chapters of this novel" (304).
3. "Disenchantment: Tom Sawyer in *Huckleberry Finn*," *PMLA* 87 (January 1972): 70, 73.
4. "Who Shot Tom Sawyer?," *American Literary Realism* 35.1 (Fall 2002): 29, 34.
5. "Overreaching: Critical Agenda and the Ending of *Adventures of Huckleberry Finn*," in *Mark Twain among the Scholars: Reconsidering Contemporary Twain Criticism*, ed. Richard Hill and Jim McWilliams (Troy, NY: Whitston, 2002), 67–90. Victor A. Doyno, *Writing Huck Finn: Mark Twain's Creative Process* (Philadelphia: University of Pennsylvania Press, 1991), chooses a position of compromise. While conceding that "Tom dramatizes a particular kind of moral corruption, a combination of subservience to his authorities and absolute, arrogant, disregard for his companions," Doyno nonetheless argues that reintroducing Tom in the last section of *Huckleberry Finn* was a valid "artistic intuition" (164) because his reappearance sets up a masterful "satire on bookish inspirations" (171).
6. Tom Sawyer's characterization becomes all the more vexatious and tiresome for many commentators if Twain's sequels to *Tom Sawyer* and *Huckleberry Finn* are taken into account: *Tom Sawyer: A Play in Four Acts* (written between 1876 and 1884), "Huck Finn and Tom Sawyer among the Indians" (begun in 1884), *Tom Sawyer Abroad* (1894), *Tom Sawyer, Detective* (1896), "Tom Sawyer's Conspiracy" (begun in 1897), and "Tom Sawyer's Gang Plans a Naval Battle" (written around 1900). I do not discuss these inferior works, but their contents generally corroborate my conclusions.

But to understand Tom Sawyer as he behaves in *Adventures of Huckleberry Finn* it is necessary to recall his exertions in *The Adventures of Tom Sawyer*, and to fathom the Tom Sawyer figure in that earlier novel it behooves us to look into the entire "boy book" vogue. Mark Twain's contributions to this type of juvenile fiction have never been in doubt. As one scholar noted, "From the moment of Aunt Polly's first cry ["Tom!"] a new spontaneity and vigor have entered the boy-book."[7] Although *The Adventures of Tom Sawyer* initially had a disappointing sale,[8] the work gradually gained a hold on the American popular imagination. Twain later explained, shrewdly: "I conceive that the right way to write a story for boys is to write it so that it will not only interest boys but will also strongly interest any man *who has ever been a boy*. That immensely *enlarges the audience*."[9] The efficacy of this formula, despite its phrasing in exclusively male terms, is apparent in the public's abiding fondness for Tom Sawyer's escapades, which found permanent reflection in Norman Rockwell's idealized series of Hannibal paintings.

Twain's achievement in creating Tom Sawyer, when set against the reigning literature about boys, was immediately apparent to a reviewer for the *New York Times* who commented in 1877 on salutary differences between Twain's high-spirited youngster and the goody-goody moral characters drawn by Thomas Day (1748–1789): "Had Sandford or Merton ever for a single moment dipped inside of *Tom Sawyer*'s pages, astronomy and physics, with all the musty old farrago of Greek and Latin history, would have been thrown to the dogs. . . . Books for children in former bygone periods were mostly constructed in one monotonous key. Was it not good old Peter Parley [Samuel G. Goodrich, 1793–1860] who in this country first broke loose from conventional trammels, and made American children truly happy? We have certainly gone far beyond Mr. Goodrich's manner." The reviewer went on to praise Mark Twain's ability to re-create "that wild village life which has schooled many a man to self-reliance and energy. Mr. Clemens has a remarkable memory for those peculiarities of American boy-talk which the grown man may have forgotten, but which return to him not unpleasantly."[1]

What that anonymous reviewer was heralding was the rise of what has been termed the *bad boy book*, a movement that began by rebel-

7. Jim Hunter, "Mark Twain and the Boy-Book in 19th-Century America," *College English* 24 (March 1963): 433.
8. Introduction, *The Adventures of Tom Sawyer, Tom Sawyer Abroad, Tom Sawyer, Detective*, ed. John C. Gerber, Paul Baender, and Terry Firkins (Berkeley: University of California Press, 1980), 29.
9. *Mark Twain's Letters*, ed. Albert Bigelow Paine, 2 vols. (New York: Harper, 1917), 2:566. The emphasis is Twain's.
1. Unsigned review, January 13, 1877, 3; reprinted in *Mark Twain: The Critical Heritage*, ed. Frederick Anderson (New York: Barnes & Noble, 1971), 70–71.

ling against the implausible portrayals of behavior in the pages of its
listless predecessors and that (some would say) proceeded to the
point of glorifying with nostalgic reverence the escapades of young
village hooligans. Whereas early Southern humorists such as J. J.
Hooper and G. W. Harris and literary comedians like B. P. Shillaber
and James M. Bailey had produced sketches depicting the shenani-
gans of rascally, two-dimensional youths, most literary historians
date the true advent of the bad boy book from the aptly named *The
Story of a Bad Boy* (1869), whose author, Thomas Bailey Aldrich
(1836–1906), once immensely respected but now scarcely known,
would edit the *Atlantic Monthly* for nearly a decade. The opening
sentences of Aldrich's book announce: "This is the Story of a Bad
Boy. Well, not such a very bad, but a pretty bad boy; and I ought to
know, for I am, or rather I was, that boy myself."[2] As Judith Fetterley
observes, the tradition that followed this example implied that
"socially useful adults develop only from real boys who had shown
some life as children"; moreover, "the Bad Boy is a rebel in that he
temporarily flaunts and outrages the community, but he is a sanctioned rebel, because his rebellion . . . is a stage which has respectability at its other end."[3] Joining Aldrich in reacting against the
Model Boy of such series as those manufactured by Jacob Abbott,
Horatio Alger, Jr., and various Sunday school authors were, in addition to Mark Twain (who had made a gesture in this direction in
1865 with his debunking "Story of the Bad Little Boy Who Didn't
Come to Grief"), writers like Charles Dudley Warner, Robert J. Bur-
dette, Edward Eggleston, George W. Peck, William Dean Howells,
Stephen Crane, Henry A. Shute, William Allen White, and Booth
Tarkington.[4]

The whole phenomenon of the American boy book, of which the
bad boy book forms the most interesting category, embraces a curiously heterogeneous assortment of writings—sentimental autobiography, juvenile romance, quasi-sociological documentary, newspaper
humor, comic farce, literary burlesque—that mainly share a reverence for boyhood, a setting in the past, and a code of behavior alien
to most adults. Thomas Hughes probably sired this particular type
of Victorian nostalgia with his *Tom Brown's School Days* (1857); the
romps of Tom Brown in his native Berks county village and his hazing

---

2. *The Story of a Bad Boy, The Little Violinist, and Other Sketches*, The Writings of Thomas
   Bailey Aldrich, 9 vols. (Boston: Houghton Mifflin, 1897), 7:3. This edition will be quoted
   elsewhere, unless otherwise indicated.
3. "The Sanctioned Rebel," *Studies in the Novel* 3 (Fall 1971): 299, 301.
4. For discussions of the boy book tradition, see Blair, "On the Structure," 375–79; John
   Hinz, "Huck and Pluck: 'Bad' Boys in American Fiction," *SAQ* 51 (1952): 120–29; Stone,
   The Innocent Eye, 62–72 (especially useful); Hunter, "Mark Twain and the Boy-Book,"
   430–38; Fetterley, "Sanctioned Rebel," 299–302; and the most comprehensive overview,
   Marcia Jacobson, *Being a Boy Again: Autobiography and the American Boy Book* (Tuscaloosa: University of Alabama Press, 1994), *passim*.

at the hands of Flashman at Rugby set the tone and established many of the incidents of the successful boy book. Charles Dickens's novels depicting boyhood deprivations, including *Oliver Twist* (1838), *David Copperfield* (1850), and *Great Expectations* (1861), rehearsed the pangs of childhood disappointments and terrors, but cannot be said to have produced the nearly complete formula that Thomas Hughes offered to Thomas Bailey Aldrich.

Since Twain neither began nor ended the boy books, it helps to appreciate his achievements if we read forward and backward in their conventions, especially in Charles Dudley Warner's sentimental recollections of Massachusetts farm-life, *Being a Boy* (1878); George W. Peck's broadly comic sketches, collected in *Peck's Bad Boy and His Pa* (1883) and similar titles; Mark Twain's *Adventures of Huckleberry Finn* (1885); William Dean Howells's wistful and occasionally chilling chronicle of small-town life in Ohio, *A Boy's Town* (1890); Hamlin Garland's *Boy Life on the Prairie* (1899), a record of sensory privilege and cultural martyrdom for a boy transported by ox-cart to the Iowa prairie, there to grow into manhood; Stephen Crane's tales about boyhood in a small town in New York state (many of them collected in *Whilomville Stories* [1900]), poignant with the victories and humiliations of childhood; and Booth Tarkington's drolly perceptive, archly amusing, but irredeemably racist *Penrod* (1914). Taking the fictional and the purely autobiographical works together, what *did* these diverse books by Aldrich, Warner, Twain, Howells, Garland, and others have in common as a literary group? To begin with an obvious feature, one can perceive that in every boy book the normal adult sense of scale, of perspective, is tremendously magnified. Since these are books about children, a village in Ohio or New Hampshire or Missouri becomes equivalent in dimensions and cultural activity to a metropolis as important as London. The basic order of this town—its legal, political, and social codes—can never be fundamentally challenged, as Fetterley has pointed out.[5] The wintertime snowball wars recounted in Warner's *Being a Boy* pay tribute to the random raids of Native American Indians, not the major upheavals of revolutionaries. All the same, the boys in these books are capable of fooling the townspeople and farmers, sometimes causing reacting communities to form into anxious, mindless mobs. A preponderance of the boy books, including Howells's study of his Ohio childhood, insist that to their boys the few surviving bands of unregenerate Native American Indians exemplify the ideal state of existence—bands of savages supposedly able to merge at will with the shadowy forests surrounding sedate villages.[6]

5. "The Sanctioned Rebel," 293–304.
6. See especially Alfred Habegger's incisive study of Howells's *A Boy's Town* in *Gender, Fantasy, and Realism in American Literature* (New York: Columbia University Press, 1982),

Abandoned savagery, however, is what the boys merely long for during a few hours of the day, when they seek to escape the rigors of school or the discipline of family life. The family unit may be the victim of their bloody fantasies, but it is simultaneously a solace and refuge for besieged warriors. Stephen Crane's "His New Mittens" and "The Fight" effectively convey this anomaly, as do Howells's sensitive recollections. Indeed, in virtually every boy book or short story, well-intentioned parents or guardians resume control of the situation at the end, as in Twain's narratives, removing the boy from the environment of his adventures. The endings of Aldrich's and Howells's books do this, for example, and Huckleberry Finn himself is about to be returned to St. Petersburg at the end of his narrative.

Of course, there was only so much that could be portrayed by the dedicated chronicler of boyhood; the possible experiences of a nineteenth-century boy, after all, were inherently limited—his education, siblings, church, chores, gangs, games, pranks, and a few other subjects defined the extent of a boy's permitted activities and illicit aspirations. Again, the cue for potential subject matter often came from Thomas Hughes's account of *Tom Brown's School Days*. In Part II of Hughes's novel, Tom's close friend, George Arthur, lies ill at Rugby with a contagious "fever" for many days, until Tom is finally summoned to his bedside. "Tom remembered a German picture of an angel which he knew; often had he thought how transparent and golden and spirit-like it was; and he shuddered to think how like it Arthur looked."[7] Arthur survives, but another lad, Thompson, sickens and dies at Tom's school, and illnesses would thereafter confine and chasten many American boy-outlaws, who must be nursed by solicitous relatives and visited by anxious chums. Mark Twain traced this convention to the Sunday School books for children, but Hughes's book probably had a large influence in making it a fixture of juvenile literature. Certainly Thomas Bailey Aldrich's character Tom Bailey sets a fine example for his boy book brethren-to-be, reacting to a playmate's death with an alarming collapse: "I was in a forlorn state, physically and mentally. Captain Nutter put me to bed between hot blankets, and sent Kitty Collins for the doctor. I was wandering in my mind, . . . and, in my delirium, I laughed aloud and shouted to my comrades. . . . Towards evening a high fever set in."[8] In other words, Tom Sawyer's feverish swoons that occur in chapters twenty-two ("dead to the world" and "very ill") and thirty-two ("bedridden") of *The Adventures of Tom Sawyer* and that also worry Aunt Sally ("he warn't in his right mind") in chapter forty-two of *Adven-*

139, 215, though in Howells's book the Native Indian and his wilderness are portrayed as vanishing sights, lost causes, a doomed order of natural harmony.

7. *Tom Brown's School Days* (New York: Macmillan, 1884), 305.
8. *The Story of a Bad Boy* (Boston: Houghton Mifflin, 1914), 170–71.

tures of Huckleberry Finn actually were a staple feature of boy books.

Other story patterns also indicate the common heritage of American boy books. Perhaps Dickens's novels about children were partly responsible for the high mortality rate among boys' parents. Frequently, though not always, the primary character is, or becomes, an orphan. Tom Sawyer apparently suffers this fate (his mother is announced as "dead" in chapter one, though his father's fate is never disclosed), and Huck Finn unknowingly joins him when Jim discovers Pap Finn's body midway through Huck's novel. Tom Bailey loses his father to cholera at the end of *The Story of a Bad Boy*, and Tom's days as a Centipedes gang member are ended by his grieving mother's arrival in town and his leaving school.

Gangs such as Tom Bailey's were the preferred form of social structure. In chapter thirteen of *Tom Sawyer* the title character anoints himself The Black Avenger and inveigles Joe Harper and Huck Finn into joining him for a foray on Jackson's Island. Huck Finn joins a bloody-minded boy-gang at the beginning of his book, another way in which both he and Tom resemble the typical boy book protagonists. These gangs never take note of any social distinctions observed by the townspeople. Huck's peers do not discriminate against him, in spite of his outcast status in St. Petersburg, and this basic egalitarianism of boy-comrades is emphasized in virtually every boy book. Thomas Hughes writes, "Squire Brown held . . . that it didn't matter a straw whether his son associated with lords' sons, or ploughmen's sons, provided that they were brave and honest. He himself had played football and gone birds'-nesting with the farmers whom he met at vestry and the labourers who tilled their fields, and so had his father and grandfather with their progenitors. So he encouraged Tom in his intimacy with the boys of the village" (53). William Dean Howells remembered that in childhood "his closest friend was a boy who was probably never willingly at school in his life. . . . Socially, he was as low as the ground under foot, but morally he was as good as any boy in the Boy's Town, and he had no bad impulses" (191). In both *Tom Sawyer* and *Huckleberry Finn*, as in most boy books, there is no rank except what one earns; adult hierarchies count for nothing.

Common, too was the schoolboy "crush" that became a standard bit of comedy in the American boy book, starting with Tom Bailey's mooning over the older and unattainable Miss Nelly Glentworth. Learning in chapter nineteen that she is destined to marry someone much older, young Tom sulks in the manner of Tom Sawyer, indulging in (as Walter Blair noticed[9]) the same morbid fantasies about the advantages of an early death. "I wonder if girls from fifteen to twenty

9. *Mark Twain & Huck Finn* (Berkeley: University of California Press, 1960), 64.

are aware of the glamour they cast over the straggling awkward boys whom they regard and treat as mere children," sighs the narrator (231). Charles Dudley Warner's boy named John stammers out his admiration for Cynthia Rudd and walks her home under the stars from a party. Tom Sawyer's antics for the purpose of catching Becky Thatcher's attention are legendary. He undertakes "gymnastic performances" in front of her house as early as chapter three and in chapter twenty takes a schoolroom whipping on her behalf. Twain's subsequent boy book would intensify and deepen the consequences of this puppy-love infatuation; Huck Finn is truly helpful to Mary Jane Wilks, and his shy affection gives him the courage to save her from embarrassment and financial ruin.

Facing and vanquishing rivals or bullies grew into a standard test of mettle after plucky Tom Brown outwitted and outfought the swaggering Flashman. Aldrich's Tom Bailey must thrash Conway, who "never failed to brush against me, or pull my cap over my eyes . . . I felt it was ordained ages before our birth that we should meet on this planet and fight" (65). Tom Sawyer's novel opens with his obligatory "licking" of a newcomer to St. Petersburg. In Stephen Crane's splendid boy-tale "The Fight" (1900), Johnnie Hedge, forced to win a place for himself in the Whilomville school yard, bloodily defeats both Jimmie Trescott and his leader, Willie Dalzel.

Another thread running through the boy books was the addiction to romance-reading shared by Tom Bailey, Tom Sawyer, and others. Charles Dudley Warner's farmboy John conceals a worn copy of *The Arabian Nights* in the barn, imagining that he "had but to rub the ring and summon a genius [sic], who would feed the calves and pick up chips and bring in wood in a minute."[1] Aldrich's juvenile hero finds a trunk in the garret of his grandfather's house that contains a "collection of novels and romances, embracing the adventures of Baron Trenck, Jack Sheppard, Don Quixote, Gil Blas, and Charlotte Temple—all of which I fed upon like a bookworm"; he also keeps copies of *Robinson Crusoe* and *The Arabian Nights* near his bed (40–41). Twain's Tom Sawyer depends upon the 1840s dime novels of Ned Buntline (E. Z. C. Judson) for his views of pirate life and on Stephen Percy's (Joseph Cundall's) *Robin Hood and His Merry Foresters* (1842) for his notions about the outlaws of Sherwood Forest.[2] This reliance on "authorities" would set the stage for Tom's flaunting of his extensive literary acquaintance in *Huckleberry Finn* (though he often misconstrues them), including Scott, *The Arabian Nights*, Cervantes, Trenck, Cellini, Dumas, Saintine, and Carlyle.

In most boy books, a test of courage involves a large, dangerous

1. *Being a Boy* (Boston: Osgood, 1878), 70.
2. See "How Tom Sawyer Played Robin Hood 'by the Book,' " *English Language Notes* 13 (March 1976): 201–204.

body of water, a sudden, thunderous storm, and a boatload of fool-hardy boys. The expedition in Hamlin Garland's *Boy Life on the Prairie* occurs on Clear Lake, where a storm almost upends the boys' sailboat. In Aldrich's *Story of a Bad Boy*, the boys take their small boat out in the bay to an island. Tom Sawyer, of course, commands a watery expedition midway through his novel: Tom, Huck, and Joe Harper establish a pirate-camp on Jackson's Island that is besieged by a "furious blast," beset by "one blinding flash after another," and subjected to "peal on peal of deafening thunder," but they return to town, triumphant, to witness their own funeral services. Tom and Becky's harrowing ordeal in the labyrinths of McDougal's Cave plays a new variation on these standard trials of stamina and courage—particularly because it pairs a girl with a boy. In *Huckleberry Finn* this ritual "expedition" turns into a full-scale journey rather than a single episode. Mark Twain, by labeling his works as fiction rather than casting them in a purely autobiographical mold—to which the majority of the other entries in this subgenre limited themselves—was able in both *Tom Sawyer* and *Huckleberry Finn* to put the emphasis on the "*Adventures*" promised in his book titles, making the other boy books seem tame by comparison.

At the end of the autobiographical books there is usually an actual departure for college or business or another region (and ultimately, for manhood), as in the books by Hughes, Dickens, Aldrich, Garland, and others. Garland's Lincoln Stewart, for instance, looks back wistfully at his boyhood with a softened, idealized, adult view of his "days of cattle-herding, berrying, hazel-nutting, and all the other now vanished pleasures of boy life on the prairies."[3] Judge Thatcher has intentions of sending Tom Sawyer to both West Point and law school, but the narrator decides he will "endeth this chronicle" before it runs the risk of "becoming the history of a *man*." Likewise Huck Finn wraps up his narrative in the present tense while he is still a boy, another daring decision on Twain's part.

These various features link *The Adventures of Tom Sawyer* and *Adventures of Huckleberry Finn* with the boy book tradition, but it is Aldrich's *Story of a Bad Boy* and Twain's *Tom Sawyer* that have the most in common, in spite of Twain's professed disinterest in Aldrich's book when Fields, Osgood & Company first published it in December 1869. "I have read several books, lately," Clemens casually informed Livy Langdon that month, "but none worth marking, & so I have not marked any. I started to mark the Story of a Bad Boy, but for the life of me I could not admire the volume much."[4] Clemens's

3. *Boy Life on the Prairie*, intro. by B. R. McElderry, Jr. (Lincoln: University of Nebraska Press, 1961), 423.
4. Clemens to Olivia L. Langdon, New Haven, CT, December 27, 1869, in *Mark Twain's*

personal library would contain more than a dozen of Aldrich's books, one of his larger collections of a single writer, and yet, aside from this disparaging remark to his fiancee, no trace of Clemens's ever having owned a copy of *The Story of a Bad Boy* survives. Be that as it may, Aldrich's autobiographical narrative unquestionably made a greater impact on Twain's imagination than he was willing to concede. What pique of chagrin must have seized Mark Twain as he held this small book, written by a man he thus far did not know. Perhaps a sensation of disgust with himself surged through him as he read farther into its pages. For within this work lay incidents that apparently would prompt Mark Twain to value at last the wealth of literary materials lying unclaimed in his recollections of pre-war Hannibal. Pranks that would make Aldrich's Rivermouth boys seem namby-pamby by comparison had been everyday occurrences in river port Hannibal, Twain now remembered. Here in this less-than-great work he suddenly came to terms with the powerful appeal of the materials that Henry Nash Smith called "the Matter of Hannibal." We can hardly blame him for hesitating to show Aldrich's book to the cherished woman who was to read and evaluate all future writings of Mark Twain. Possibly even prior to the serialization of *The Story of a Bad Boy* in *Our Young Folks* magazine he had begun the undated and fragmentary "Boy's Manuscript," his first (if inferior) stab at composing a boy book. During the winter of 1872–73 or soon thereafter Twain began writing in earnest *The Adventures of Tom Sawyer*.[5]

Whether or not Twain wanted to compete in this genre at once, he started sifting his own boyhood for publishable incidents. Biographers have related Twain's marriage in February 1870 to his recovery of the Matter of Hannibal, inferring that the nuptials and the wedding trip somehow released into his conscious memory the recollections that would find fruition in his boy books. But Twain's perusal of Aldrich's story in December 1869 supplies a more tangible explanation than the honeymoon for why Twain "rained reminiscences" about his Hannibal childhood in a famous letter written to his boyhood chum Will Bowen on February 6, 1870.[6] While his new bride was "lying asleep upstairs," Twain wrote that "the old life . . .

Letters, Volume 3, 1869, ed. Victor Fischer and Michael B. Frank (Berkeley: University of California Press, 1992), 440.

5. See *The Adventures of Tom Sawyer, Tom Sawyer Abroad, Tom Sawyer, Detective*, 9, 504–505.

6. *Mark Twain's Letters, Volume 4, 1870–1871*, ed. Victor Fischer and Michael B. Frank (Berkeley: University of California Press, 1995), 50. Marcia Jacobson, *Being a Boy Again*, ascribes the coincidental timing of Twain's letter to "the marriage itself, which committed him to domesticity and life in the East," and to "the constraints of adulthood [that] evidently recalled memories of a freer time" (46).

swept before" him "like a panorama." The lengthy list of boyish hijinks that Twain then catalogued—playing Robin Hood on Holliday's Hill, swimming in the river, making the town think he was drowned—was not only a rehearsal for episodes in *Tom Sawyer*, but also more immediately a responsive tribute to Aldrich's evoking narrative. Twain's benedictory tone in the Bowen letter ("keep your heart fresh & your memory green for the old days that will never come again") betrays his recent encounter with the first American bad boy book. It seems germane that in the previous month, January 1870, the magazine editor who would become Mark Twain's favorite book reviewer, William Dean Howells, had highly commended Aldrich's innovative form of autobiography: "No one else seems to have thought of telling the story of a boy's life, with so great desire to show what a boy's life is, and so little purpose of teaching what it should be; certainly no one else has thought of doing this for the life of an American boy." The book, assured Howells, will give "pleasure . . . to every man that happens to have been a boy."[7]

Most literary histories refer to Aldrich's *The Story of a Bad Boy* as a semi-autobiographical novel about Aldrich's boyhood in Portsmouth, New Hampshire, but it is less a novel than a collection of sketches, and although Portsmouth is the "Rivermouth" in the book, the young protagonist Tom Bailey is constantly aware that he has moved there for his schooling from New Orleans and that his father and mother remain behind in the Deep South. Indeed, his father's dealings periodically take him up the Mississippi River to Natchez, a city with which Clemens had been familiar. Both this Southern background and the conclusion of the book—the early death of Tom's father, and young Tom's consequent leaving school to enter business—paralleled Aldrich's biography (and Clemens's, too). Presumably the book contains fictional episodes, but it reads more nearly like autobiography than fiction: virtually plotless, the narrative simply introduces us to Tom's schoolmates, relates a few of their adventures, closes with Tom's giving up Harvard for a business career in New York City, and sums up the subsequent careers and deaths of Tom's Rivermouth relatives, friends, and teachers.

All the same, it would be difficult to overstate the degree of inspiration that Aldrich's book provided for *Tom Sawyer, Life on the Mississippi*, and *Huckleberry Finn*, or its effect on Clemens's conception of the life he had lived as a youth. In the first place, Aldrich's book opens by identifying the adult persona with the author and the young boy, all in one: "I am, or rather I was, that boy myself." We are already close to the superior adult narrator of *Tom Sawyer*, who in chapter one compares Tom's new discovery about whistling to the elation of

7. Review, *Atlantic Monthly* 25.147 (January 1870): 124.

an astronomer who has spied a new planet, adding, "the reader probably remembers how to do it if he has ever been a boy." The very landscape of Rivermouth must have reawakened Clemens's drowsing recollections of Hannibal environs—Holliday's Hill, the broad brown river, Jackson's Island; Aldrich's narrator recalls in chapter six that "there was always some exciting excursion on foot—a ramble through the pine woods, a visit to the Devil's Pulpit, a high cliff in the neighborhood—or a surreptitious row on the river, involving an exploration of a group of diminutive islands, upon one of which we pitched a tent and played we were the Spanish sailors who got wrecked there years ago."

By midbook, Aldrich's Tom remains divided between two ambitions: to be a classical scholar like his teacher Mr. Grimshaw, "or a circus-rider." Nonetheless, in a passage that notably reminds one of Twain's "The Boy's Ambition," the celebrated first chapter of the "Old Times on the Mississippi" series published in the *Atlantic Monthly* in 1875, Aldrich records, "Every Rivermouth boy looks upon the sea as being in some way mixed up with his destiny. . . . He burns for the time when he shall stand on the quarterdeck of his own ship. . . . He is born a sailor, whatever he may turn out to be afterwards. To own the whole or a portion of a rowboat is his earliest ambition" (chapter fourteen).

Tom Bailey and three friends do acquire a small boat, the *Dolphin*, and on a school holiday they slip away from their families and undertake an expedition to Sandpeep Island, the last of the harbor islands. Aldrich's language resembles that of the amused adult narrator of the "dawn" passage in chapter fourteen of *Tom Sawyer*: "The measured dip of our oars and the drowsy twitterings of the birds seemed to mingle with, rather than break, the enchanted silence that reigned about us. The scent of the new clover comes back to me now, as I recall that delicious morning when we floated away in a fairy boat down a river like a dream!" (*Bad Boy*, chapter fourteen).

But after the boys set up their encampment on Sandpeep Island and make seafood chowder (and Phil Adams smokes his sweet-fern cigars), a tremendous storm overtakes them while they are swimming. "From these threatening masses, seamed at intervals with pale lightning, there now burst a heavy peal of thunder that shook the ground." When the smallest boy in Tom Bailey's group, Binny Wallace, attempts to secure their boat on the beach, he finds himself cast helplessly and oarlessly adrift in the *Dolphin*, and the boys watch in agony as the gale carries the tiny craft far out to sea. Even before Binny Wallace's body washes ashore at Grave Point—where the boys had swum and frolicked—young Bailey experiences torments of remorse that forecast Tom Sawyer's faints and slow recoveries in both of Twain's novels. Tom Bailey's feelings of guilt also resemble

Mark Twain's repentance and distress over the drowning deaths of
Lem Hackett and a boy named Dutchy, tales told in chapter fifty-
four of *Life on the Mississippi* as incidents associated by the narrator
with storms and restless sleep. Tom Bailey recalls after Binny Wallace's disappearance, "How well I remember the funeral, and what
a piteous sight it was afterwards to see his familiar name on a small
headstone in the Old South Burying-Ground" (chapter fourteen).
Twain's imaginative faculty supplied many fresh inventions in Tom
Sawyer's schemes to convince his gang to hide out on an island and
then return to a heroes' welcome at their own funerals, but the con-
gruence of so many elements—the adventurous expeditions, the
remote islands, the group-swimming, the thunderstorms, the real
drowning and the supposed drowning, the Rivermouth boys' genuine
remorse and the villagers' manipulated grief—make for highly sug-
gestive parallels.

One striking passage in *Bad Boy* furnishes indications that
Aldrich's remembrances stimulated Twain's processes of memory
even earlier than the final composition stage of *Tom Sawyer*. Consider Aldrich's description of the bustle attending the approach of a
ship toward the harbor: "In a neglected seaport like Rivermouth the
arrival of a large ship is an event of moment. The prospect of having
twenty or thirty jolly tars let loose on the peaceful town excites divers
emotions among the inhabitants. The small shop-keepers along the
wharves anticipate a thriving trade; the proprietors of the two rival
boarding houses . . . hasten down to the landing to secure lodgers;
and the female population of Anchor Lane turns out to a woman,
for a ship fresh from sea is always full of possible husbands and long-
lost prodigal sons" (chapter fifteen). Could these be sentences that
induced Mark Twain to pen the much-quoted passage in "Old Times
on the Mississippi" (1875) that begins, "Once a day a cheap, gaudy
packet arrived upward from St. Louis, and another downward from
Keokuk"? In Twain's masterful version, "Before these events, the day
was glorious with expectancy; after them, the day was a dead and
empty thing," and he details how dramatically "the scene changes"
when a steamboat heaves into view around the point that turns the
river "into a sort of sea, and withal a very still and brilliant and lonely
one"; "every house and store pours out a human contribution," with
"all . . . hurrying from many quarters to a common centre, the
wharf." Ten minutes later, "the town is dead again."[8]

Mainly, though, Aldrich's book brings to mind Twain's two boy
books. Tom Bailey and Pepper Whitcomb form a friendship adum-
brating Tom Sawyer and Huckleberry Finn's: they rig a twine telegraph between their houses, they share their pocket money, and they

---

8. Included in chapter four of *Life on the Mississippi* (1883).

exchange their secrets—"those amazing secrets which boys have. We met in lonely places by stealth, and parted like conspirators; we could not buy a jackknife or build a kite without throwing an air of mystery and guilt over the transaction." Before revealing one particular secret, Tom Bailey "dragged him for that purpose to a secluded spot in the dark pine woods outside the town" (chapter fifteen).

What, then, can be deduced from this glance at Aldrich's evocative but decidedly minor book? That it built on Thomas Hughes's prototype and anchored the boy book in the United States. That it showed Mark Twain how to make use of the camaraderie, mischief, and games of boyhood. That it perhaps emboldened him to attempt a similar story with an inland (and more Southern) setting. That it tutored him in creating a sentimental, dignified, patronizing adult persona. That it revealed the rich possibilities for adding the superstitions and folkways of children to the quaint customs being explored by local-color writers for the literary monthlies. That it reminded him of such promising material as the strict codes of juvenile fraternities like the Cadets of Temperance, the pangs of blind sexual adoration, the gratification of community acceptance. Truly Aldrich's *Bad Boy* has never been sufficiently accepted as the model inspiriting *Tom Sawyer* and coloring *Life on the Mississippi* and *Huckleberry Finn*, and as the standard work that Twain consciously or unconsciously tried to surpass. Although there are instances where Mark Twain gave public credit to Bret Harte and a few other writers who improved the craftsmanship of his writing, it is fair to say that he was generally reluctant to concede the role of specific books in demonstrating possibilities of plot, incident, and character. There is no question that Mark Twain's techniques surpassed those of *The Story of a Bad Boy*, however. What Aldrich tried to express with heavy-handed sympathy, Twain would communicate with a more colloquial, less condescending tone, and a direct intimacy with his reader; and in *Huckleberry Finn*, of course, he would dispense with the intervening, interpreting adult voice altogether and try a bold experiment that Aldrich could never have conceived.

There is factual evidence that Twain thought rather well of *Bad Boy*; for instance, he included a portion of it, "How We Astonished the Rivermouthians," in the compendium of comic sketches that he edited with William Dean Howells and Charles H. Clark, *Mark Twain's Library of Humor* (1888). That extract tells of the boys' most ambitious practical joke—the nighttime firing of a dozen abandoned cannons along the beach at the outskirts of the town. Tom Bailey is chosen to set the match to the trail of gunpowder. Twain and his coeditors praised Aldrich's "peculiar vein of humor," which is manifest when the startled citizens rush from their homes with lanterns, excitedly conjecturing that their unoffending town is being attacked by spectral ships off the coast. This mass response of the frightened villagers conveys an image of crowd behavior comparable with those occurring in Twain's *Tom Sawyer*, such as the town's search for the missing boys in chapter fourteen and the "two hundred men . . . pouring down . . . toward the cave" to look for Tom and Becky in chapter thirty, as well as the neighborhood abolitionist-scare conclusion to *Huckleberry Finn*. Twain's boys derive satisfaction similar to Tom Bailey's from being the cause of so much commotion and speculation. In Notebook 40 (June 1898), Twain included Tom Bailey's name among the list of famous child characters he thought of assembling for a tale tentatively titled "Creatures of Fiction."[9] And when Aldrich added an epilogue of history and reminiscence in a book called *An Old Town by the Sea* (1893), Twain, beset by financial worries, took time to write to Aldrich on December 6, 1893, testifying that he had stayed up until 3 a.m. reading the slender volume: "Portsmouth was become the town of my childhood," Twain wrote, "with all which that implies & compels. . . . I enjoyed it all—every line of it."[1]

But if Twain partially relied on Aldrich's *The Story of a Bad Boy* as a prototype (and challenge) of sorts for his own boy books, Aldrich himself was equally indebted to a literary work that some critics have been puzzled to find Twain seemingly ignoring. Though Twain apparently owned a copy of Thomas Hughes's *Tom Brown's School Days* (1857),[2] he alluded to it only once in print—in chapter fifteen of *Following the Equator* (1898)—and there confused it with Hughes's less successful sequel, *Tom Brown at Oxford* (1861). Aldrich, on the other hand, openly acknowledged his debt to Hughes, even quoting from *Tom Brown's School Days* in *The Story of a Bad Boy* (regarding the boys' universal code of fighting) and referring to it in chapter ten as "one of the best books ever written for boys."

This cluster of *Tom*-boy books—Thomas Hughes's *Tom Brown's School Days*, the chief influence on Thomas Aldrich's *Bad Boy*, whose hero Tom Bailey was a model of sorts for Tom Sawyer—seems worthy of remark. As a matter of fact, Leslie Fiedler posed the intriguing question of why so many characters named "Tom," as for instance Tom Canty of *The Prince and the Pauper* (1880), appear as half of fictional look-alikes and paired characters in Twain's writings, "and in each a main theme is usurpation."[3] The answer to at least a portion of this conundrum having to do with characters named "Tom" who are taking over someone's rightful place or heritage (as in chapter twelve of *Life on the Mississippi*, where a cub pilot named "Tom" wins a girl's admiration away from young Sam Clemens) can

9. Notebook in the Mark Twain Papers, Bancroft Library, University of California, Berkeley.
1. Letter in the Houghton Library, Harvard University; photocopy in the Mark Twain Papers.
2. Alan Gribben, *Mark Twain's Library: A Reconstruction* (Boston: G. K. Hall, 1980), 338.
3. *Freaks: Myths and Images of the Secret Self* (New York: Simon and Schuster, 1978), 270.

plausibly be traced to the thrill of envy and competitiveness that pulsed through Twain's mind when he first read and grasped the epoch-making achievement of Aldrich's bad boy book. In joining the tradition forged by Thomas Hughes and Thomas Aldrich, Mark Twain calculatedly, defiantly retained the first name of the boy characters, but produced a book that left Aldrich's in its wake and whose literary figures are today far better known on both shores of the Atlantic than the actors in Tom Brown's or Tom Bailey's adventures. One might say that Mark Twain took the dare, by calling his fictional boy "*Tom* Sawyer" and thus placing him squarely in a familial relationship to his celebrated precursors in the boy-book field: if this new cousin was a hit, he would reap the advantages pioneered by his famous namesakes; if he flopped, Tom's very name would give the clue to the inspirations for an unworthy usurper.

Critical commentators overlook an important consideration by writing about Twain's boy books without any reference to their historical and cultural context, and as though Mark Twain invented the bad boy in literature. He did not—he just invented the bad boy as *hero*. Young Tom Bailey had many of the same experiences as Twain's boy characters, but Bailey generally seemed to be a victim—of his comrades' jokes, of adult regulations, of circumstances and fate—rather than a victor. Tom Sawyer vanquishes his enemies and reaps tangible rewards, because his creator drew upon fictional fantasy rather than pure autobiography.

Tom Sawyer's literary status would be more secure if Twain's famous bad boy books were approached the way he originally intended for them to be read, as companion volumes. True, delays interrupted his narration of *Huckleberry Finn* for nearly a decade after its inception, and admittedly the core of that novel, the Huck-and-Jim "raft" section, rises above the artistic level of anything Twain had attempted in his earlier book. But it should always be pointed out that Huck's opening statement in his own novel—"You don't know about me, without you have read a book by the name of 'The Adventures of Tom Sawyer' "—dictates the ideal preparation for every student. If there were more copies in existence of that optional binding of the first edition of *Huckleberry Finn*—volumes in blue cloth that matched the bright blue hue used for *Tom Sawyer*—then perhaps the works would naturally seem like a fictional unit, despite disparities in viewpoint and tone. Viewed jointly, the comical bad boy portions in the two volumes effectually frame Huck's unsentimental, prudent flight downriver, enveloping it between the phantasmagoric conceits of Tom's immature perceptions of literature, family, friendship, and society.

It is too constraining to surmise, as many modern readers do, that Tom Sawyer serves no purpose by appearing in *Huckleberry Finn*.

The brotherless Huck explicitly yearns for (and prefers) Tom's company. Staging his own pretended murder at Pap Finn's cabin, Huck takes pride in his ingenuity in butchering a wild pig to provide a trail of blood; the scheme lacks a satisfying ingredient, however, for Huck immediately muses: "I did wish Tom Sawyer was there, I knowed he would take an interest in this kind of business, and throw in the fancy touches" (41). Is it any wonder that Huck Finn misses Tom, if one considers what Tom Sawyer does for his first-person novel? When the book opens, Tom's presence provides one of the main points of continuity between the earlier book and its successor, helping the reader find his bearings in Huck's unconventional perspective on St. Petersburg. And Huck would never be so appealing or seem so authentic if the officious Tom were not there as an increasingly ludicrous foil. A case could be made, moreover, that Huck is seldom so absolutely in thrall to Tom's bidding in *Adventures of Huckleberry Finn* as most critics assume.[4] Tom in fact yields to Huck's stubbornness on many occasions. On this matter it is well to review, as a reference, the first, indifferent words spoken by Huck in Twain's novel of 1876: "Tom hailed the romantic outcast: 'Hello, Huckleberry!' " whereupon Huck nonchalantly replies, "Hello yourself, and see how you like it" (chapter six). Based on the evidence of what Huck says in his own novel, he chooses to stay around Tom because he finds his stunts and rhetorical skills utterly entertaining. To elevate one of these characters too grandly above the other, or to forget the balance, the elasticity, or the mortising in their relationship, is to leave behind certain subtle effects that Twain achieved in connecting their individual volumes. In many cases, the vilification of Tom Sawyer's traits and role has proceeded too far.

GLENN HENDLER

Masculinity and the Logic of Sympathy in
The Adventures of Tom Sawyer†

The nineteenth century saw major changes in Americans' understanding of the moral and psychological effects of reading. By the

4. As discussed in my " 'I Did Wish Tom Sawyer Was There,' " in Sattelmeyer and Crowley, 169–70.

† A new redaction of "Tom Sawyer's Masculinity," first published in *Arizona Quarterly* 49.4 (Winter 1993): 33–59; revised and reprinted as Chapter 6 of Glenn Hendler's *Public Sentiments: Structures of Feeling in Nineteenth-Century American Literature* (2001), pp. 185–211. Reprinted from *Arizona Quarterly* 49.4 (1993) by permission of the Arizona Board of Regents. And from *Public Sentiments: Structures of Feeling in Nineteenth-Century American Literature*, by Glenn Hendler. Copyright © 2001 by the University of North Carolina Press. Used by permission of the publisher. All notes are Hendler's.

time Mark Twain wrote *The Adventures of Tom Sawyer*, the reception of narrative fiction was generally described using the sentimental vocabulary of *sympathy*. Now nearly synonymous with *pity*, the word *sympathy* referred to a much broader set of emotions and responses; indeed, eighteenth-century moral philosophers, including those whom Twain read enthusiastically and appreciatively, argued that one could define humanity itself by the capacity to sympathize.[1] An eighteenth-century "man of feeling" did not just pity someone experiencing pain or oppression; he was meant to put himself in that person's place, to share the experience of his or her pain. Thus sympathy combined what we today might call "empathy" with an even larger capacity for understanding that is closer to what we mean when we use the word "identification."

Nineteenth-century writers thinking within this sentimental structure of feeling expected readers—especially readers of fiction—to extend themselves imaginatively toward characters who were themselves increasingly depicted as defined by their own capacity to sympathize. This emotional extension was meant to lead not just to a general emotional response, but to a particular kind of transformation and, ultimately, emulation. To put it just a bit too mechanistically: By feeling *for* literary characters as they experienced emotions, we are led to feel *with* them, which leads us to feel *like* them. We are then meant to *act* like these characters, carrying that sympathy for others into the real world by feeling others' emotions and even sensations—especially painful ones—and finally, ideally, acting to relieve their pain.

This logic of sympathy was in a sense circular, especially in cases where that final extension into the real world was omitted or attenuated. But that very circularity helped make it powerfully self-reproducing. It redefined human subjectivity as made up of "sentiments": psychological and emotional states that were simultaneously interior (felt deeply "inside" the person) and exterior (demonstrated through proper, conventional "expressions" of those responses, such as weeping at the depiction of someone else's pain). The most often cited literary examples of these ostensibly selfless or other-oriented affective bonds were the intensely emotional cathexes between characters depicted in the hugely popular sentimental novels written primarily by, for, and about women, novels which occupied a large portion of the literary marketplace during the middle of the nineteenth century.

Sentimentality was not dichotomously gendered in its initial formulation; indeed, the stock figure in eighteenth-century moral phi-

---

1. On Twain's familiarity with Scottish Common Sense philosophy and related writings pertaining to sentimentalism, see Camfield.

losophy was quite explicitly the "man of feeling." However, in part
due to the prominence of female literary sentimentality, by the mid-
nineteenth century sympathy almost always had at least some feminizing connotations even when it was performed and experienced
by men and boys. Didactic fiction for boys was especially liable to
be perceived as feminizing, not only because it was frequently written by women but also because it assumed that its readers would
identify sympathetically in an emulative way that was associated
with women's fiction. Horatio Alger's novels, for instance, were
denounced for their tendency to "emasculate" their readers, even
though they repeatedly emphasize how "frank" and "manly" their boy
heroes are. While later readers of Alger have most often seen his
books as promoting the self-reliance and hard work that could help
a boy rise "from rags to riches," to some readers in the nineteenth
century the forms of sympathy his stories demanded of his readers
looked too much like the identifications provoked by, for instance,
Susan Warner's *The Wide Wide World*. Alger's stories could be read
as feminizing because they aim overtly to evoke the reader's sympathy, because they explicitly ask their readers to emulate their characters, and because their street-boy heroes are rewarded morally and
financially only when they appear to lose themselves in a sympathetic
identification with an even less fortunate boy.[2]

The Adventures of Tom Sawyer presents itself as nearly the antith-
esis of the sentimental novel, and represents its protagonist as indifferent or even hostile to the experience and expression of sympathy.
In place of the selfless, other-oriented feminine protagonist of
women's sentimental fiction, Twain's book asks its readers to identify
with an aggressive, selfish, even self-absorbed boy. Like other protagonists of "bad-boy books," Tom tends toward the mischievous and
mildly sadistic pranks now conventionally attributed to boys; he certainly isn't primarily motivated by the sentimental desire to ease the
pain of others. Where the sentimental heroine is supposed to shrink
from the limelight, Tom takes great pleasure in creating a scene,
often planning his pranks and games with what he calls "the theatrical gorgeousness of the thing" in mind (XV:116). In place of the
transparent emotional honesty and devotion to duty characteristic of
a sentimental heroine, Twain gives us a sly, clever boy whose most
memorable tour-de-force involves tricking his friends into doing his
work for him. *The Adventures of Tom Sawyer* seems in every way
designed to ward off sympathetic identifications, to set itself up as a
resolutely *un*sentimental novel.[3]

2. For an expanded version of this analysis of sympathy and sentimentality, including discussions of sympathy in women's writings and Horatio Alger novels, see Hendler. And on
   masculinity and sentimentality, see Chapman and Hendler, "Introduction."
3. Trensky and Habegger both read the bad-boy figure as a reaction to (implicitly or explicitly

To trace the logic of sympathy in *The Adventures of Tom Sawyer*, then, is to read it against the grain, to focus on aspects of the novel Twain seems to have wanted us to ignore. But for all his efforts to disavow his novel's relation to sentimentalism, sentimentalism's power was by this time so pervasive that even efforts to write against it ended up partaking of its logic. This is not to say that *Tom Sawyer* is a sentimental novel in disguise. But uncovering the sentimental elements in the novel can help us to see how Twain worked out the problems he had taken on by deciding to write a book for boys in a sentimental world: How, in a world where sympathetic identification had feminine connotations, could he construct a young male protagonist who could elicit a strong emotional attachment from his readers (be a "sympathetic character," as we still say) but who could still retain his masculinity?

Creating such a character required some subtle but significant redefinitions of both masculinity and sentimentality. My project here is to trace those redefinitions through Twain's novel. Doing so can get at some interesting contradictions in Twain's novel and some other similar "bad-boy books" written at around the same time, including Thomas Bailey Aldrich's *Story of a Bad Boy* (1869), William Dean Howells's *A Boy's Town* (1890), and Charles Dudley Warner's *Being a Boy* (1877). At the same time, such an exploration can give us a glimpse into shifting understandings of gender and emotion in nineteenth-century American culture. And, as we will see, the way in which sympathetic identification is reworked is not only gendered; it is also sexualized in ways that resonated with nineteenth-century shifts in definitions of sexual desire and identity.

Like many female sentimental writers, Twain fills his fiction with scenes in which other characters observe his protagonist and respond to his actions in ways that are meant to inform the manner in which his readers respond to him. But the relationship Tom has to his observers is quite different from that of the observers of a sentimental heroine, who are characterized by their ability (or lack of ability) to sympathize with her. Tom is extraordinarily skilled at transforming others—sometimes his gang of boys, sometimes the whole town—into audiences for his theatrical spectacles (see Peck). For instance, when he rises in the courtroom to reveal the true murderer of Dr. Robinson, his listeners in the courtroom are spellbound: "Tom began—hesitatingly at first, but as he warmed to his subject his words flowed more and more easily; in a little while every sound ceased but his own voice; every eye fixed itself upon him; with parted

---

female) sentimentality. See also the mocking appropriation of feminine sentimental writings in *Tom Sawyer*, XXI:156–59.

lips and bated breath the audience hung upon his words, taking no note of time, rapt in the ghastly fascinations of the tale. The strain upon pent emotion reached its climax when the boy said . . ." (XXIII: 172). As we see here, Tom's triumphantly theatrical scenes always revolve around a dramatic *self*-display. This is even more clear when he seems to return from the grave, provoking the applause of the entire town.

But while it is clear that Tom's most prominent trait is his desire to attract attention to himself, it is difficult to provide a description of the specific traits that make up that self. In this he is typical of the protagonists of the other bad-boy books of the period, which tend to assert far more emphatically what a boy is *not*, and what a boy does *not* do. A "real boy," writes Twain's friend William Dean Howells, has no love for flowers, never appears in the parlor when his mother has company, nor, most importantly, does he feel or express sympathy. These are all traits of girls, or worse, what he calls "girl-boys." Sympathy differentiates girls from boys, and makes the former inappropriate interpreters of spectacles like the make-believe circus put on by the boys in Howells's book. "[E]ven as spectators [girls] were a little *too* despicable," he writes; "they did not know anything; they had no sense; if a fellow got hurt they cried" (*Boy's Town* 104). Sympathetic identification induced by the display or depiction of suffering, characteristic of women's sentimental novels and didactic children's fiction, is anathema to a "real boy." Instead, "if another boy gets hurt they laugh, because it is funny to see him hop or hear him yell" (*Boy's Town* 209).

Boys, then, respond in exactly the opposite way from girls. When girls cry, boys laugh; when girls invest themselves emotionally, boys distance themselves. This opposition is quite rigorous, leading Howells to "doubt whether small boys understand friendship, or can feel it as they do afterwards, in its tenderness and unselfishness" (*Boy's Town* 209–10). Charles Dudley Warner remarks somewhat sarcastically that the attachments formed in boyhood are "fervent, if not enduring," but he never describes a close friendship between the protagonist and another boy in *Being a Boy* (50). Lacking the capacity for friendship, incessantly disavowing any desire to sympathize with others, boys appear to be atavistically pre-social in these books. Indeed, Howells goes so far as to equate "boy-nature" with "savagery."[4] "Everywhere and always the world of boys is outside of the laws that govern grown-up communities," he says, and a boy obeys his world's unwritten laws "instinctively," like "the far-off savages from whom his customs seem mostly to have come" (*Boy's Town* 67).

4. Habegger discusses the thematization of boys' "savagery" in Howells's novel, arguing that "the central idea in A *Boy's Town* . . . is that boyhood in the life of a man corresponds to savagery in the history of the human race" (213).

Warner seems to have agreed, stating that "[e]very boy who is good for anything is a natural savage" (Warner 150).

Boys' "savagery" and apparent pre-social nature are means by which their world and their character are differentiated from the domestic and feminizing space depicted in sentimental novels and didactic boys' fiction. It is women in general, and mothers in particular, who limit boys' fantasies and threaten to suppress their savagery, to "sivilize" them, as Huck Finn says in Twain's later novel. As Howells writes, "[t]he mother represented the family sovereignty" (*Boy's Town* 104). Other boy-books also envisioned an escape to "savagery" as an alternative to domesticity; Twain's own unfinished *Huck Finn and Tom Sawyer Among the Indians* (1884) is similarly framed.

If boys' responses and reading practices are defined in opposition to those of girls and women, they are just as emphatically opposed to those depicted in more didactic boys' fiction. Unlike the Horatio Alger boy, who thinks of literacy as a sign of virtue, Tom deploys it as an instrumental skill, the value of which can be judged by its consequences rather than its reflection of his moral qualities. Hence Tom expresses no interest in the reading and memorization exercises of his Sunday School until he conceives of the desire to impress Becky Thatcher. Then he trades in the yellow tickets which are meant to signify literate accomplishment but actually represent his profits from tricking his friends into whitewashing a fence. In exchange for his supposed reading, he receives Becky's admiration as well as a Bible, although the latter is withdrawn when his fraud is uncovered. Far more consciously and deliberately than the Alger boy, whose acquisitive desires define him but are usually disavowed, Tom Sawyer uses the apparent virtue of literacy for personal profit.

Like much of the humor in the novel, the parody of the "good boy's" virtuous publicity cuts both ways.[5] For instance, when Tom tries to recite Patrick Henry's "Give me liberty or give me death" speech at a school assembly (XXI:155)—an oration that would have given a more didactic writer for boys an opportunity to associate literacy, republican virtue, and public performance—he is "seized" by a "ghastly stage-fright" and unable to continue. Here Tom's performative nature, which seems designed to demonstrate his cleverness, mastery, and masculine self-possession, serves equally to illustrate the limits of these qualities.

A bad boy like Tom thus seems systematically to negate many of

---

5. Twain lampooned the conventions of sentimental children's fiction in his 1865 "Story of the Bad Little Boy" and 1870 "The Story of the Good Little Boy" by reversing the conclusions the stories would have had in "Sunday-school books." The mischievous boy doesn't die the expected horrific death, but instead grows into a prosperous though still quite "wicked" member of the legislature. The good little boy is accidentally blown up by nitroglycerine, and thus is denied the conventional deathbed speech he has planned for all his life.

the traits valued in nineteenth-century advice books for boys and young men. Boys in bad-boy books are defined as negations so systematically that their creators often claim that they lack any meaningful distinctiveness; as Howells says, "All boys are a good deal alike" (*Boy's Town* 190). More subtly but no less oddly, Twain declares in *Tom Sawyer's* preface that Tom "is a combination of the characteristics of three boys whom I knew, and therefore belongs to the composite order of architecture" ([xvii]).[6] At first glance this seems an innocuous statement of a realistic writer's method of constructing a character, representing a typical but still individualized identity made up of diverse "characteristics." The phrase is part of the novel's claim to verisimilitude—"Huck Finn is drawn from life; Tom Sawyer also, but not from an individual"—and is thus consistent with the bad-boy book's claim to represent the reality of boyhood, in contrast with the idealizations in other writing about boys. Thomas Bailey Aldrich claimed to have invented the term "bad-boy" as a synonym for "real boy" in order to "distinguish [his protagonist] from those faultless young gentlemen who generally figure in narratives of this kind" (3).

But in *A Boy's Town* Howells raises the possibility that a real boy *is* a "composite" or plural subject, and that the subject's origin in multiplicity may not culminate in a larger unity:

> Every boy is two or three boys, or twenty or thirty different kinds of boys in one; he is all the time living many lives and forming many characters; but it is a good thing if he can keep one life and one character when he gets to be a man. He may turn out to be like an onion when he is grown up, and be nothing but hulls, that you keep peeling off, one after another, till you think you have got down to the heart, at last, and then you have got down to nothing. . . . All the boys may have been like my boy in the Boy's Town, in having each an inward being that was not the least like their outward being, but that somehow seemed to be their real self, whether it truly was so or not. (171)

The constitutive multiplicity of boyhood character and the contingency of the boy's accession to adulthood are quite startling in this passage. A boy, for Howells, is not a singular and distinct individual; he is an agglomeration of "many characters," of "twenty or thirty" other boys. "To be a man" consists in the ability to condense this multiplicity into "one life and one character." The attainment of such coherence and singularity is "a good thing," but the nostalgic tone of every bad-boy book, including *The Adventures of Tom Sawyer*,

---

6. The Composite Order is an architectural term designating a Roman capital formed by superimposing an Ionic volute on a Corinthian capital.

along with the image of some men as hollow sets of "hulls," makes the path to adult masculinity seem a complex, risky, and possibly fraudulent process, implying that manhood is an only partly desirable state. Even the assertion that a boy's veiled "inward being" is his "real self" is qualified by the phrase "somehow seemed," and this qualification is underscored when the final phrase questions the 'truth' of this "real self." Distinctions between singularity and multiplicity, particularity and generality, interiority and exterior appearance, are apparently foreign to "the nature of boys," even though nineteenth-century advice for young men usually assumed that these same distinctions are essential for the bourgeois individual's participation in contractual exchange and the masculine public sphere.

This image of manhood as plural and radically contingent is evidence of conflicting tendencies in the male subjectivity imagined and addressed by *The Adventures of Tom Sawyer* and the bad-boy book in general. On the one hand the reader is encouraged to desire the self-mastery and theatricality figured in Tom's most dramatic scenes, when he is able to manipulate the entire town of St. Petersburg into enthusiastic participation in his own spectacles. And at the same time the reader is expected to take vicarious pleasure in the boy's freedom from the ego constraints of masculine individuality. The boy's contradictory appeal to a reader thus becomes a source of anxiety. The risk and pleasure of identifying with such a multiple and fragmented figure are that the (male) reader may give up his own sense of singularity, coherence, and self-possession. Howells's figure of failed adult masculinity, the set of "hulls" with nothing at the center, sets out concisely the poles between which the bad-boy book's reader is meant to situate himself: Masculine character may be an irreducible multiplicity or it may be no character at all. Howells acknowledges that the transcendence of this opposition may never occur, that the ideals of unity and coherent self-possession are always in tension with the fantasies of multiplicity and fluid subjectivity associated with boyhood.

Even Tom Sawyer's most attractive and seemingly masterful characteristic—his theatricality—has as its most common subtext a radical threat to his individuality. Tom repeatedly imagines how theatrically effective his own death would be as a way of attracting attention to himself. Each time he stages or fantasizes a death or disappearance he transforms the arousal of sympathy into a form of mastery and even violent revenge. After Aunt Polly has punished him unjustly, "He pictured himself lying sick unto death and his aunt bending over him beseeching one little forgiving word, but he would turn his face to the wall, and die with that word unsaid. Ah, how would she feel then?" (III:22). He wants to display his mastery over an audience by evoking its sympathy: "she would be sorry some day—

maybe when it was too late," he thinks when Becky rejects him (VIII: 64). However, like Eva in *Uncle Tom's Cabin* or any other dying sentimental heroine, he exerts his power most effectively through a theatricalization of his own self-negation. Twain most succinctly expresses the paradox of Tom's position by writing, "Ah, if he could only die *temporarily*" (VIII:64).

Although Tom's death fantasies are usually planned as manipulative and masterful hoaxes, they have a peculiar tendency to turn back on themselves, to transform him into the tearful, sentimental spectator he means to produce. Tom's theatricalized subjectivity is especially narcissistic because it is based in a sympathetic identification in which he occupies both roles, switching from suffering hero(ine) to sympathetic spectator at a moment's notice, oscillating between affectively absorbed audience and masterful male performer (Peck 233). In fact, he is often the most sympathetic spectator of his own performances. Fantasizing his own death, "[h]e so worked upon his feelings with the pathos of these dreams that he had to keep swallowing, he was so like to choke; and his eyes swam in a blur of water . . ." (III:22–23). And the image of Becky discovering his death "brought such an agony of pleasurable suffering that he worked it over and over again in his mind and set it up in new and varied lights till he worked it threadbare" (III:24). Hidden under Aunt Polly's bed, watching the scene of mourning he has created by running away to Jackson's Island, Tom's emotions reach a climax: "Tom was snuffling, now, himself—and more in pity of himself than anybody else" (XV:116). Although he is tempted to relieve his aunt's agony by coming out from under the bed—"and the theatrical gorgeousness of the thing appealed strongly to his nature"—he prefers the form of theatricality he has planned, the dramatic appearance at his own funeral service, so he "resisted and lay still" (XV:117).

Whereas at some moments it is clear that Tom wishes to "die temporarily" as the ultimate expression of his power over his audience, at others his death drive appears as a result of having no audience to perform for. He expresses this wish in the few scenes in which he is entirely solitary, cut off from his domestic life by his aunt's punishment, from his romantic life by Becky's whims, and from his male friends by his own melancholy. "He wandered far from the accustomed haunts of boys, and sought desolate places that were in harmony with his spirit" (III:23). For Tom, whose very identity depends on his being the center of attention, solitude brings out a potentially fatal form of his constitutive theatricality. He sits by the river, "wishing, the while, that he could only be drowned, all at once and unconsciously, without undergoing the uncomfortable routine devised by nature. . . . He wondered if *she* [Becky] would pity him if she knew? Would she cry, and wish that she had a right to put her arms around his neck and comfort him? Or would she turn coldly away like all the hollow world? . . . At last he rose up sighing, and departed in the darkness" (III:23–24).

Both the sentimental death scene and Tom's fantasy reworkings of it rely on the assumption that a female "audience"—in this case, both Becky and Aunt Polly—responds sympathetically. Tom is even able to confirm this when he sneaks back to his aunt's house to observe the women family members grieving and his cousin Sid's envy. But Tom's audience is never only female, for one aim of his fantasy is to separate him from the feminized private sphere epitomized by the deathbed scene. While he hides under Polly's bed to observe her mourning, the theatricality of his own position is evident only to himself and the novel's readers; the women in the scene are excluded from the audience. This passage does more than mock sentimental death scenes; it rewrites their conventions by excluding women—and the "good boy" figure, Sid—from such scenes' web of identifications. Whereas the sentimental reader is positioned as a sympathetic spectator to the angelic character's death, identified as much with the sinners gathered around her bed as with the dying girl herself, Twain's reader is positioned under the bed with Tom, sharing his cognitive and affective ascendance over his female audience and even the almost supernatural ability to enjoy his own mourning and funeral.

In identifying with Tom's desire to die "temporarily," with a consciously theatricalized sympathy, Twain's audience is again differentiated from a sympathetic, feminine readership. Instead of disavowing the theatricality of Tom's position, Twain underscores it, figuring the character's position—and, by extension, the identifying reader's—as an active, masterful performer rather than a passive, affective spectator. Tom's masterful theatricality always seems to entail his own absorption in the scenario he has constructed. Indeed, the oscillation between theatricality and absorption, "agony" and "pleasurable suffering," sympathy and distance, performer and spectator is Tom's defining characteristic; such oscillations motivate his actions and drive the novel's plot. The anxiety at the center of the genre is, then, the possibility that an identification with a protagonist whose masculinity and individuality are always destabilized by self-absorption might destabilize the masculinity and individuality of the reader as well.

I have argued elsewhere that women's sentimental fiction juxtaposes its scenes of sympathy with images of death and self-effacement, thereby registering nineteenth-century limits of female individuality (Hendler 113–46). *Tom Sawyer* and other bad-boy books similarly juxtapose their characters' theatricalized masculine individuality with emphatic gestures toward self-negation. Even as the boy's theatrical self-mastery is asserted, he repeatedly fantasizes his own non-existence, wallowing in perversely pleasurable fantasies of death and disappearance that are apparently designed to place him back at the center of attention. In his death fantasies, Tom's desire is to enact the same kind of sympathetic identification that sentimental death scenes evoke in women's fiction. Tom's performances of sympathy are strikingly effective; they produce tears and forgiveness from his Aunt Polly, and often a wider adulation from the rest of St. Petersburg. But the fluidity and reversibility of roles in a scene like this one—the way death turns into life, performer into spectator, activity into immobility, sadism into masochism— entail the possibility that his fake death will become a real loss of individuality, that Tom will become the sentimental heroine and/or reader whose role is so often parodied in Twain's fiction. In the process of mastering his audience, he risks losing himself in his own performance.

What does it mean to identify with such a boy, with someone whose masculinity and individuality seem always to be in crisis? Variants of this question helped motivate the explosion in the 1870s of articles and conferences on the reading of boys and young men, a discourse that almost replaced the worries over women's reading which had pervaded literary criticism in the first half of the century (Horlick; Macleod; Mailloux, *Rhetorical Power*; Ross).[7] Bad-boy books were not just examples used in these newer debates; they implicitly participated in the arguments themselves by raising questions about readerly identification. After all, literary bad boys are themselves constituted by what they read. As Lionel Trilling has observed, Tom Sawyer's mind has "literary furnishings"; he is constructed out of the texts he encounters:[8] the *Arabian Nights*, *Don Quixote*, sensational boys' adventure stories by popular authors like Ned Buntline, and other sources (Trilling 110).[9] In his *Atlantic*

7. For some examples of this debate, see the various contributions to *Library Journal* 4.9–10 (September–October 1879).
8. The same is true of other Twain stories involving Tom. For instance, in the unfinished tale "Huck Finn and Tom Sawyer Among the Indians," Tom blames his mishaps on the misconceptions about Indians he got from reading "Cooper's novels" (50). James Fenimore Cooper was one of Twain's favorite targets for ridicule ("Fenimore Cooper's Literary Offenses" 169–81). Here, as elsewhere in his writings on boys, Twain joins the critics of bad-boy books in claiming that fantastic and unrealistic tales like those of Cooper are capable of taking hold of a boy's mind and influencing his actions.
9. Each of the "lines of action" Walter Blair identifies in *The Adventures of Tom Sawyer*— "the story of Tom and Becky, the story of Tom and Muff Potter, the Jackson's Island episode, and the series of happenings (which might be called the Injun Joe story) leading to the discovery of the treasure"—is more or less directly inspired by Tom's attempt to act out his own version of a narrative he has read, to identify with its hero (Blair 84). All but the first are clearly variations on or parodies of sensational adventure stories and include typical elements such as grave robbing, piracy, running away from home, and the deciphering of a cryptic message. The "love story" is a bit more ambiguous in its literary

review of *Tom Sawyer* William Dean Howells remarks approvingly that "though every boy has wild and fantastic dreams, this boy cannot rest till he has somehow realized them" (621). He argues that this relation to fiction or fantasy, though somewhat extreme in Tom's case, is typical of "the boy-mind." As if to prove his own point, fourteen years later Howells again used the word "realize" to describe his own bad-boy, who "was not different from other boys in his desire to localize, to realize, what he read" (*Boy's Town* 176–77). The "composite architecture" of boyhood is apparently built of books.

Boys in these texts clearly invest themselves quite intensely in the fiction they consume. Howells describes his boy's affective investment in his reading as constituting the little interiority his character possesses—"the world within him"—as well as his "outward" behavior. Referring to the exotic stories of which his protagonist is fond, Howells says: "He was always contriving in fancy scenes and encounters of the greatest splendor, in which he bore a chief part. Inwardly he was all thrones, principalities, and powers, the foe of tyrants, the friend of good emperors . . . [O]utwardly he was an incorrigible little sloven, who suffered in all social exigencies from the direst bashfulness, and wished nothing so much as to shrink out of the sight of men if they spoke to him" (*Boy's Town* 177). It is a boy's nature, Howells asserts, to assimilate what he reads into his subjectivity, "inwardly" to become the protagonist of a book, a play, a story. Howells, like other writers of the time, represented boys' reading as a form of incorporation, an almost literal absorption into and of the book and its protagonist.[1]

The effects of such reading are, for these fictional boys, unstable. A boy's character is constituted by his incorporations, by the "thrones, principalities, and powers" that make up his "inward" self. It is at the same time the multiplicity of these identifications which makes it difficult and perhaps even undesirable to consolidate the "many lives" and "many characters" of boyhood into the "one life and one character" of manhood. The bad boy thus exhibits a paradoxically public form of interiority. His incorporative nature inverts the normative masculine relation to the public realm; his virtuousness, heroic nature, and publicness are entirely "inward" characteristics, while "outwardly" he wishes to "shrink out of the sight of men." And

sources, but Tom's attempt to win Becky's favor by fraudulently claiming a reading prize in Sunday School (IV:34–36) can easily be seen as an attempt to take on the role of the hero of a "good boy" Sunday School story.

1. For discussions of the way this metaphorics was often literalized, see Mailloux, "Rhetorical Use," and Ross. Though Twain wrote before the development of psychoanalysis, nineteenth-century theories of reading often resonate with Freudian theories of identification. Freud sometimes describes identification as incorporation, though the latter term more often designates the infantile, physical model for the later development of the process of identification. See Laplanche and Pontalis 211–12; Freud, *Interpretation* 183. The connection between identification and incorporation is developed more fully in Klein 55–98.

without his compulsion to identify, the boy ceases to exist. As Howells writes, "I dare say this was not quite a wholesome frame of mind for a boy of ten years; but I do not defend it; I only portray it. . . . At any rate, it was a phase of being that could not have been prevented without literally destroying him" (*Boy's Town* 181–82). Even though the boy's drive to identify disrupts the putative singularity of male subjectivity, its absence is equated with the effacement of the self.

The precariousness and ambiguous moral valence of this figuration of reading and subjectivity are nowhere more evident than in the writings of another adult reader of bad-boy books, the moral crusader and professional censor Anthony Comstock.[2] Comstock's 1883 book *Traps for the Young* is a compendium of evils threatening to seduce nineteenth-century youth from the path of virtue, evils that include bad-boy books and adventure fiction for boys.[3] From its first paragraph, *Traps for the Young* conceives of readerly subjectivity through a confused but relentless metaphorics of assimilation and absorption. "Each birth begins a history," he announces in the book's first sentence, and makes clear that this history is a written one. "The pages are filled out, one by one, by the records of daily life. The mind is the source of action. Thoughts are the aliment upon which it feeds. We assimilate what we read. The pages of printed matter become our companions. Memory unites them indissolubly, so that, unlike an enemy, we cannot get away from them" (ix).[4]

For Comstock, you are what you read. A boy *is* a book, and his and his "companions" are so fully incorporated into himself that they can be described as the "pages" of his own book. The language of the passage—"the aliment upon which it feeds," "we assimilate what we read"—metaphorizes both reading and intersubjective relations in general as forms of incorporation. This was not an uncommon way to represent the reader's relation to a text; he could have drawn it from the novels themselves as easily as from the Lockean *tabula rasa* rhetoric he is obviously deploying. But Comstock's equation of book and reader makes this textual absorption curiously reciprocal, as if there were no difference between the "pages" of the individual's "daily life," the "pages" that represent other people, and the "pages

2. The best work on Comstock's long and complex career is Beisel's.
3. Of course, Comstock's rage is generally directed against the more sensational forms of boys' literature, for which Howells as well had little affection. But Comstock is quite explicit that no matter how mild or extreme, the depiction of immoral acts leads to immoral responses from readers. Thus the pranks, disrespect for authority, petty theft, and lying in *A Boy's Town*, like the arson, theft, bribery, and escape from jail in Aldrich's *Story of a Bad Boy* (much of which, in both books, remains undiscovered and unpunished) would qualify each for Comstock's condemnation.
4. This opening paragraph's account of the formation of subjectivity through incorporative identification is meant as a description of the lures of all the "traps" the book denounces. However, its metaphorics is most fully developed in Comstock's chapter on bad-boy books, and its consistency with the rhetoric of other denunciations of the genre justifies its use as an example in this context.

of printed matter" which he or she reads. Inherent in the process of reading is the possibility that the distinctions between self and other, text and reader, experiential history and fictional story, will be ambiguated. This blurring of boundaries, Comstock makes clear, is what makes it essential to control what children read, and what makes the unconstrained drive to identify figured in bad-boy books so dangerous.

In Comstock's theory of reading, these incorporative identifications absorb readers into a fictional "world," thus threatening to lure a boy from his direct path to an ideally singular, coherent, and morally upright manhood. This absorption and consequent de-individuation is figured in Comstock's writing as the transformation of bonds between boys and books into bonds between boys and other boys. In short, absorbed boy-readers are incorporated into gangs. *Traps for the Young* is thus filled with stories of and interviews with young criminals who cite bad-boy books and sensational story-papers as the inspiration for their formation of "gangs of boy bandits." "[C]lassical literature," explains one boy, "didn't seem to belong to my real life, but these stories did." This boy—the son of a judge, and therefore presumed to be well-read—attributes his life of crime to his identification with the heroes of these stories: "They were boys like myself who did these wonderful things . . . and they lived in a world like ours" (31).

These boys' minds, like Tom Sawyer's, have "literary furnishings." In fact, Twain and other writers of bad-boy books seem to share Comstock's assumption that boys' absorption in their reading leads to the formation of gangs. Strangely, the narrative structure of the main anecdotes in *The Adventures of Tom Sawyer* is virtually identical to that of Comstock's cautionary anecdotes, and their accounts of the consequences of reading are strikingly similar as well. Whatever Tom reads—boys' adventure stories, *Don Quixote*, or history books—he interprets as a model for action, and his first step in "realizing" what he reads is always to reconstitute "Tom Sawyer's Gang." "[O]f course there's got to be a Gang," he exclaims, "or else there wouldn't be any style about it" (XXXIII:243). In the course of Tom's adventures, his gang becomes pirates, holy crusaders, treasure hunters, conspirators, abolitionists, and other unsavory imaginary groups. The identities of bad-boy books' protagonists are always inextricably tied to their membership in groups like the gang in Aldrich's novel, the "Rivermouth Centipedes," as if a boy's central fantasy were to see himself as one of the legs of a single organism.[5]

Of course, Comstock condemns the gangs he depicts, while bad-

5. For a somewhat different interpretation of the figure of the gang in the bad-boy book, see Habegger 206–19.

boy books revel in them. But both discourses represent the seduc-
tiveness of gang-formation as essential to the popular pleasures of
reading. For Comstock, the gang draws a boy away from honesty and
public virtue. This is precisely the appeal of the gang for the bad-
boy hero and his reader; it initiates him into an all-male world in
which boys can constitute their own identities, write their own
"pages," without the constraints of adult, properly public masculinity.[6] The pleasures of being a part of Tom's gang of robbers are even
enough to motivate Huck Finn to submit to the Widow Douglas's
confining care at the end of *Tom Sawyer*. "Well," he says, "I'll go
back to the widder for a month and tackle it and see if I can come
to stand it, if you'll let me b'long to the gang, Tom" (XXXV:259).

The idea that boyhood mischief could be linked to respectable
public manhood was by no means a new one in the late nineteenth
century. Early in Benjamin Franklin's *Autobiography* he describes an
incident that "shows an early projecting public Spirit, tho' not then
justly conducted" (7), in which he and some other boys steal some
stones from a building site to make into a wharf in a nearby salt
marsh. What seems to me to be different in the bad-boy book is the
way it offers the male homosocial identification of the gang as an
end in itself, without the external "projecting public spirit" materi-
alized and metaphorized by Franklin's wharf. In this genre, the boy's
identity is presented as most complete when he has become part of
a gang. The book's reader is invited to join as well, to participate in
a homosocial identification. Howells explicitly interpellates[7] his
reader with this offer: "the reader can be a boy with him there on
the intimate terms which are the only terms of true friendship" (*Boy's
Town* 10). In both the bad-boy book and the discourses condemning
it, the pleasure and danger of identifying with a boy are the multiplicity and unfixity of the unstable object of that identification. A
reader who is not necessarily a boy can "be a boy with" the protagonist, who is himself made up of "twenty or thirty" boys. The figure
of the gang, then, can represent both the source and the result of
that multiplicity. The pleasure of "being a boy" is to negate, or at
least defer, the reduction to "one life and one character." And the
pleasures of reading the bad-boy book lie in the fantasy of accompanying the boy in this simultaneous self-negation and self-
constitution.

I use the word "pleasure" here with every intention of evoking its
erotic connotations, for the bad-boy book represents identification

---

6. Adult men in the late nineteenth century were also searching for escape from the constraints of public masculinity in the rituals of organizations like the Freemasons and the
Odd Fellows. For a discussion of the importance of secret societies in the construction of
nineteenth-century masculinity, see Carnes.
7. Interpellation is Louis Althusser's term for the way ideology addresses and constitutes the
subject, constituting identity through the very act of "hailing" the individual (127–93).

as significantly sexualized. The genre represents masculine identification as a pleasurable form of self-possession, defined in opposition to the self-negation of feminine sympathy. The logic of sympathy in the bad-boy book is just as powerfully gendered as it is in women's fiction, but in the former reading is linked to sexuality. I am not claiming that bad-boy books represent and provoke sexual *desires*, as Leslie Fiedler contends in his influential analysis of *Adventures of Huckleberry Finn* ("Come Back"). Rather, I am arguing that the novels work to address a masculine readership by figuring and inspiring sexualized *identifications*. One scene in *The Adventures of Tom Sawyer* may illustrate this point. At the beginning of Chapter XX, Tom Sawyer attempts to apologize to Becky Thatcher for an early hostile act, but is haughtily spurned. Tom's wish for reconciliation is quickly transformed into a desire that combines and equates violence and a gender reversal: he "moped into the school-yard wishing she were a boy, and imagining how he would trounce her if she were." A few minutes later, he returns to the classroom, surprising Becky in the act of stealing a peek at the book which the schoolmaster pores over every day. This book, for the children, contains an inaccessible but fascinating secret: "Every boy and girl had a theory about the nature of that book; but no two theories were alike, and there was no way of getting at the facts in the case." Twain's phrasing here recalls Freud's account of children's attempts to discern the secrets of sexual difference and reproduction ("Sexual Theories"), and this is exactly what the book contains: it is a book of anatomy, featuring "a handsomely engraved and colored frontispiece—a human figure, stark naked" (XX:148).

Becky, for whom "the title-page—Professor somebody's 'Anatomy' " means nothing, opens to the image of the naked body just as Tom looks over her shoulder. For a brief, disruptive moment, an act of reading is shared by both genders on equal terms—something that rarely happens in nineteenth-century American fiction. And what they read together is an image that could only have been perceived by Twain's readers as sexual; indeed, Howells and Twain's wife Olivia Clemens convinced Twain to censor this scene because of its sexual connotations (DeVoto 12–14). Tom "caught a glimpse of the picture," and in her attempt to conceal it from him Becky "had the hard luck to tear the pictured page half down the middle" (XX:148).

What follows is a drama simultaneously sexual, visual, epistemological, and interpretive. In tears, Becky scolds Tom for "sneak[ing] up on a person and look[ing] at what they're looking at," while Tom retorts, "How could *I* know you was looking at anything?" (XX:148). Becky tries to assert her superior knowledge—she has seen another boy spill ink on Tom's spelling book, which is sure to get Tom punished—by responding, "*I* know something that's going to happen.

You just wait and you'll see!" Each child then goes on to fantasize
about the punishment the other will receive, a "licking" from the
schoolmaster. Tom goes on to imagine the scene of Becky's discovery
and punishment in some detail, but his initial sadistic pleasure in
the idea of Becky being whipped is contaminated by an involuntary
sympathetic identification: "Considering all things, he did not want
to pity her, and yet it was all he could do to help it. He could get up
no exultation that was really worthy the name" (XX:149). Then, after
the teacher's discovery of the torn illustration, Tom falsely but heroically claims responsibility, drawing upon himself his second whipping that day in order to prevent Becky from having to endure the
first "licking" of her life. Identification has turned a desire into its
opposite, transforming a sadistic fantasy into a masochistic reality,
in which Tom undergoes what Twain refers to as "pleasurable suffering." The most immediate consequence of Tom's selfless act is the
revival of Becky's affections for him; in fact, she doesn't spurn him
again for the rest of the book. But the price of this affection is a
temporary and painful loss of self. Tom's substitution of his own body
for that of a girl leads to both a literal and a figurative violation of
his bodily integrity, as he "gather[s] his dismembered faculties" and
receives "the most merciless flaying that even Mr. Dobbins had ever
administered" (XX:152). The sexual ambiguity of the act of reading
and the moral ambiguity of Tom's "heroic lie" lead to an act of
extreme violence, as if the teacher's role were to enforce the gender
difference pictured in the anatomy book.

What is most interesting about this scene is the way it constructs
connections linking sexuality, reading, and a fluidity of gender roles,
all resulting from an act of male sympathy. An act of reading shared
by both sexes—looking at an image of a naked body whose gender
is never specified—leads to an act of male homosocial violence that
itself borders on the erotic; the master "seemed to take a vindictive
pleasure" in whipping the boy, and Tom is "dismembered" by the
punishment. Like so much else in the novel, however, this scene
serves to constitute Tom's masculinity. The effects of the schoolmaster's acts are precisely the opposite of their intentions; the adult
man's "vindictive pleasure" transforms Tom's transgressions into virtues, and the boy's "dismemberment" leads to his heroization. At the
end of the book, Becky's father compares Tom's "noble lie" to George
Washington and the cherry tree, and offers to send Tom to West
Point and law school, thus doubly prefiguring the boy's potential
positioning in some of the most masculine sectors of the public
sphere.[8] The scene also solidifies the relationship between Tom and

8. Tom's position in a conventional domestic space is anticipated in an earlier scene, in which

Becky; the chapter concludes when Tom falls asleep "with Becky's latest words lingering dreamily in his ear—'Tom, how *could* you be so noble!' " (XX:152).

The contradiction between the homosocial violence of the scene and its heterosexual outcome is only apparent, of course. As Eve Kosofsky Sedgwick and others have argued, homosocial bonds—economic, political, and personal ties between men—are often essential underpinnings for both compulsory heterosexuality and the exclusion of women from power, even when this homosociality is itself an eroticized, violent, or asymmetrical relation of power. Here Sedgwick's point is demonstrated by Tom's almost magical transformation of the power relations in the situation. The master's exertion of power and Tom's violent emasculation ultimately serve to confirm the boy's masculine virtue and to solidify his position in a relationship that it is only slightly anachronistic to call heterosexual. One of the rare moments when the novel represents a normative, moral, discrete masculinity occurs as a direct result of the eroticized disintegration of the boy's body.

Thus *Tom Sawyer*'s pleasures rely on an uneasy proximity between masculine individuality and its dissolution, on the almost explicit claim that radical self-loss is the prerequisite for the attainment of normative masculinity. The bad-boy book offers several ways of containing the risk that an identification with such an unstable position may lead to a loss of self, of affirming the reader's difference from the character undergoing these experiences while evoking the reader's identification with him, an identification that implies that the two are similar and in some sense equivalent. C. B. Macpherson has aptly described the Lockean model of subjectivity as "possessive individualism," and the novels draw on a rhetoric of possession and self-possession in their characterization of their protagonists. However, it is rarely the boy's own self-possession which is asserted. Howells, for instance, insulates adult male readers from his boy's constitutive instability by figuring the relation between boy and reader as one of ownership. In order to emphasize that the hero of *A Boy's Town* is "merely and exactly an ordinary boy," Howells says early in the book, "[f]or convenience, I shall call this boy, my boy; but I hope he might have been almost anybody's boy" (2). In fact,

---

he mentions that if he ever finds a treasure he will "buy a new drum, and a sure-'nough sword, and a red neck-tie and a bull pup, and get married." This depresses Huck, for "if you get married I'll be more lonesomer than ever." But Tom states authoritatively: "No you won't. You'll come and live with me" (XXV:178–79). Like Alger, who refigures the domestic realm as a homosocial space, Twain places a homosocial bond at the center of his utopian image of domesticity. Alger's brief visions of homosocial domesticity seem to exclude marriage, whereas Twain's even briefer vision of married domesticity includes homosociality. On homosociality in Alger, see Moon.

the character remains nameless throughout the novel; he is never referred to as anything but "my boy."

The epithet posits ownership as the man's relation to his former self, possession as a way of asserting the continuity of manhood with boyhood. But the singularity and self-possession of both men and boys are again problematized by this sentence's qualifications: "I hope he might have been almost anybody's boy" and the assertion of ownership between two subjects who are both the same as and different from one another. This dynamic of equivalence and difference is central to the way the genre constitutes and addresses its audience by inducing an identification with a boy. The bad-boy book images a form of masculine identity constituted out of the tension between norms of masculine individuality and boyhood's alleged dissolution of identity. But while this instability and its reiteration produce the pleasures of the genre, the novels' narrative trajectories imply that the tension is unsustainable. In the end, the destabilizing characteristics of boyhood subjectivity are projected onto others. Through this process of projection, bad-boy books transform the multiplicity, contingency, and instability of their male protagonists into a version of the singularity, autonomy, and self-possession which, they assume, their readers have always already possessed.

Becky Thatcher is the screen for such a projection toward the end of *The Adventures of Tom Sawyer*. The chapters in which Becky and Tom are lost in McDougal's cave—the only episode in which adventure plot and romantic plot come together—have as their subtext the projection of all Tom's fantasies of self-negation onto Becky. While just beforehand the girl has been as active as the boys, playing " 'hi-spy' and 'gully-keeper' " with Tom and the others, when they get lost in the darkness Becky suddenly seems to become the dying heroine of a sentimental novel. In what could almost be a direct reference to Eva's death in *Uncle Tom's Cabin*, Becky falls into a peaceful sleep. Tom "sat looking into her drawn face and saw it grow smooth and natural under the influence of pleasant dreams; and by and by a smile dawned and rested there." Tom is inspired by this sight much as Eva's observers are moved by the sight of the "bright, the glorious smile [that] passed over her face" in her last moments, and when Becky awakens she utters a sentence that could have come from Eva: "I've seen such a beautiful country in my dream. I reckon we are going there" (Stowe 428; *Tom Sawyer* XXXI:227).

If this projection of Tom's death fantasies were a mere passing incident it might not be very significant. However, it marks the novel's emphatic exclusion of Becky and enables a crucial transformation in Tom. The girl is permanently reduced to a powerless, tearful figure and thoroughly marginalized for the rest of the narrative. Even when Tom tells Becky he has found the way out of the cave, she continues in her role of dying little girl, absorbing both Tom's fears and his death fantasies: "she told him not to fret her with such stuff, for she was tired, and knew she was going to die, and wanted to" (XXXII:235). The last time we see Becky we are told that she "did not leave her room until Sunday, and then she looked as if she had passed through a wasting illness" (XXXII:236). The expulsion of Becky from the plot coincides with Tom's acquisition of traits which, though somewhat ironized, still amount to an image of stability, autonomy, and self-possession. At the same moment when Tom finds the exit to the cave he deduces where the treasure is hidden. *Tom Sawyer* is not usually read as a "rags to riches" story, but Tom here does become quite wealthy, more so than most Horatio Alger heroes. And his trajectory toward public masculinity similarly parallels that of the Alger protagonist, whose ascension to respectability is often signaled by the appearance of his name in print. Earlier, when Tom was "a glittering hero" for discovering the murderer of Dr. Robinson, "[h]is name even went into immortal print, for the village paper magnified him. There were some that believed he could be President, yet, if he escaped hanging" (XXIV:173). Here he again appears in print, as "the village paper published biographical sketches" of Tom and Huck. Judge Thatcher praises Tom both for his rescue of his daughter and his earlier lie to the teacher which prevented Becky from getting a whipping. The judge even associates him with republican virtue by comparing this lie with "George Washington's lauded Truth about the hatchet!" (XXXV:255). Tom never again expresses a desire to die or experience any other feeling of self-loss. Although *The Adventures of Tom Sawyer*, unlike *Adventures of Huckleberry Finn*, is usually interpreted as lacking an emphasis on a boy's emotional or moral growth, Tom does develop a degree of virtuous publicity and financial and affective autonomy that he lacked earlier in the book. He has become an exemplar of nineteenth-century ideals of middle-class public masculinity and audience-oriented subjectivity.

By projecting Tom's self-negating traits onto Becky and then expunging her from his world, Twain formulates a relatively stable representation of masculine individuality and reasserts dichotomizing representations of gender roles with a vengeance. The boy acquires his individuality and autonomy only when he has definitively rejected the girl. And Twain does more than marginalize Becky from the plot; he incorporates that act of containment and exclusion into the renewed fantasy of "Tom Sawyer's Gang" which serves as the novel's conclusion. Toward the end of the book, standing at the spot where he and Becky had escaped from the cave, Tom describes the glories of life in a gang of robbers, reveling in the prospect of kidnapping, extortion, and murder. "Only you don't kill the women," he tells Huck: "You shut up the women, but you don't kill them. . . . Well the women get to loving you, and after they've been in the cave a week or two weeks they stop crying and after that you couldn't get them to leave. If you drove them out they'd turn right around and come back. It's so in all the books" (XXXIII:244). "It's so" in *The Adventures of Tom Sawyer* as well. Tom has once again merged his reading with his life, referring here both to boys' adventure stories and his own experience with Becky in the cave, where she cried for days, became meek and dependent, and refused to leave.

This dynamic is exemplified in condensed form in Twain's unpublished "Boy's Manuscript" of 1868. The story is written as if it were the diary of a young boy by the name of William T. Rogers, and it is clearly the antecedent to the Becky Thatcher plot in *The Adventures of Tom Sawyer*, following the same pattern of heterosexual attraction and violent rejection. It outlines the vicissitudes of Billy's affections for a girl named Amy. Billy's attempts to get Amy's attention run the same gamut as Tom's theatrical gestures, including the staging of a torchlight procession by her house and the sentence, written in a letter: "I love you to destruction Amy and I can't live if you don't come back" (17). Such statements of self-negation characterize Billy's courtship methods, and are backed up by a failed suicide attempt.

Billy's actions, like Tom's, have ambiguous effects and connotations; although his aborted poisoning attracts Amy's sympathy, it also makes him quite ill and leads him to be portrayed as the bedridden, usually female invalid in a sentimental novel. As Billy writes: "I had lost all interest in things, and didn't care whether I lived or died" (11). But almost immediately the emotionality of the scene is projected onto Amy, who rushes to his bedside and sheds enough tears for the both of them.

Toward the end of "Boy's Manuscript," Billy announces that he definitively rejects not only Amy but girls in general. If heterosexual marriage turns out to be compulsory, he says, he will "hunt up a wife" in a manner that projects his own anxieties about individuality, anonymity, and even his desire for death onto his object of choice: "I would just go in amongst a crowd of girls and say / 'Eggs, cheese, butter, bread / Stick, stock, stone—DEAD!' and take the one it lit on just the same as if I was choosing up for fox or baste or three-cornered cat or hide'n'whoop or anything like that." He describes this decision as his first assertion of individuality and autonomy. "I'm thankful that I'm free," Billy proclaims. "I've come to myself. I'll never love another girl again. There's no dependence [sic] in them" (17).

The violent expulsion and containment of the girl—anticipated and condensed in Billy's shout of "DEAD!" at the end of his rhyme—

provide both closure for the boys' stories and suture for their potentially fragmented subjectivity. This closure comes at the expense of
both the girl and, more surprisingly, everything that makes the boy
an attractive site of identification, the distance from normative masculine individuality which makes him appealing. It thus raises the
same question raised by the conclusion of *Tom Sawyer* and other
bad-boy books: Why would a story whose pleasures and cultural work
depend on an identification with a boy conclude by negating everything appealing about its protagonist?[9]

The answer to this question brings us back to the issue I raised
early in this essay, the problem of creating, in a sentimental world,
a protagonist who is both masculine and "sympathetic." The *telos* of
the bad-boy book is this protagonist's existence, which entails an
affirmation of boyhood's difference from adult manhood. But it can
not, of course, construct boy-nature as entirely antithetical to or
distant from manhood. While the stories never narrate their heroes'
maturation to adulthood, they refer humorously though sincerely to
the idea that bad boys often grow up to be good men. Warner
describes one boy who compulsively stole pies from his mother's
pantry, "who afterwards grew up to be a selectman, and brushed his
hair straight up like General Jackson, and went to the legislature"
(69). Aldrich notes in passing that one of his more mischievous
friends has grown up to be "a judge, sedate and wise," and that the
others "are rather elderly boys by this time—lawyers, merchants, sea-
captains, soldiers, authors, what not" (4–5).

Twain's "Conclusion" to *The Adventures of Tom Sawyer* demon-
strates a remarkable self-consciousness about the contradictions in
this dynamic: "So endeth this chronicle," Twain writes. "It being

9. One possible answer to this question is that this shift in Tom is the novel's weakness.
Some of Twain's critics have claimed that, as readers, they lose interest in Tom at the end,
even charging that Tom betrays Huck by convincing him to resubmit to the Widow Douglas's care. Others, agreeing with the premise that Tom becomes less attractive at the end
of the novel, argue that Twain deliberately ironizes Tom's character, especially his tendency to subordinate reality to what he has read in books. This interpretation makes the
end of *Tom Sawyer* consistent with a similarly ironic reading of *Huckleberry Finn*, in which
Tom's insistence that Jim's escape from slavery be "by the book" results in Jim's humiliation
and pain.

To sustain either of these interpretations, however, it would be necessary to reconceive
the entirety of *The Adventures of Tom Sawyer* as ironic, for all the traits satirized at the
end of *Huckleberry Finn* exist in Tom from the beginning of the earlier book. From the
start, the "literary furnishings" of Tom's mind determine his actions, and he is willing to
cause pain to others in order to make things come out "by the book," as for instance when
despite his awareness of Aunt Polly's sorrow and Joe Harper's homesickness he delays the
boys' return from Jackson's Island. And the same letter to Howells in which Twain insists
that the book "is *not* a boy's book, at all" records his decision to refuse to narrate Tom's
ascension to manhood as based precisely in a desire to avoid arousing this distaste in the
reader. "If I went on, now, & took him into manhood, he would just be like all the one-
horse men in literature & the reader would conceive a hearty contempt for him" (*Twain–
Howells Letters* 91).

strictly a history of a *boy*, it must stop here; the story could not go much further without becoming the history of a *man*. When one writes a novel about grown people, he knows exactly where to stop—that is, with a marriage; but when he writes of juveniles, he must stop where he best can" (260). Twain seems here to be placing boys and men in contradistinction to one another, but the paragraph's underlying opposition is between a *history* of a boy and a *history* of a man. The distinction asserted here is not primarily one of generation, but one of genre and ultimately gender. For it was not merely novels "about grown people" which conventionally ended in marriage; it was primarily novels about women. At least since Leslie Fiedler's 1948 essay on *Huckleberry Finn* and his expansion of his thesis in *Love and Death in the American Novel*, it has been clear that one element distinguishing the boys' books which he claims make up the mainstream of the American canon from Cooper to Hemingway from the sentimental tradition is the boy's aversion to sexual and romantic desires for girls, or at least to marriage. But it is misleading to call this phenomenon, with Fiedler, an evasion of heterosexuality. Indeed, it is more plausible to conceive of bad-boy books as participating in the construction or reconstruction of sexualities, both hetero- and homo-, as aspects of character—as *identities*. What is new here is that such identities get constituted, embodied, and enforced through individual emotional and psychological processes such as identification and projection, rather than through institutions like marriage. Boy-books construct identificatory identities, structuring gender and sexuality through the identifications figured in their plots. They represent the practices and pleasures of reading as constitutive of gendered sexual identities.

Despite Twain's claim in *Tom Sawyer*'s preface that the book addresses all ages and genders, the bad-boy book's disavowal of a target audience is in fact the genre's way of interpellating a specific audience. The genre's distinction between "boy-nature" and self-identical, self-possessed individuality moves the reader toward a masculinity which it assumes the reader already possesses, and yet represents as being constitutively in crisis. In its images of homosocial violence, its fantasies of de-individuation, and the unstable, multiple identifications figured in the male gang, the genre bears the traces of the work—the repression as well as the production of fantasies—necessary for the construction of a heterosexualized male identity based on the violent exclusion of women. Paradoxically but powerfully, the novels imagine a masculine individuality that is not rooted in a singular and stable male identity, and a heterosexuality that does not require women.

The bad-boy book thus deploys and contains the risky pleasures of identifying with a boy. Although it appears to open up a playful, less stringently gendered position for its audience, the genre models and produces identifications that interpellate readers as masculine, heterosexualized subjects. *The Adventures of Tom Sawyer* itself can be read as a series of such interpellations. Its opening words are in fact a failed hailing, as aunt Polly cries out "TOM!" and "You TOM!" but receives "no answer" to this attempt to address Tom as the self-identical subject of her disciplinary gaze (I:1). Similarly, in the scene where he is unable to recite the requested Bible verses in front of Judge Thatcher, the teacher has to coax him to refer to himself by his full name, Thomas Sawyer. And when he first meets Becky Thatcher, she says that she knows his name, "Thomas Sawyer," but he replies, "That's the name they lick me by. I'm Tom, when I'm good. You call me Tom, will you?" (VI:55). Just as the Horatio Alger hero changes his name to fit his station in life—Ragged Dick becomes Dick and then Richard Hunter—Tom Sawyer changes his name depending on his relation to the public sphere. I think it is safe to assume that when his "biographical sketch" is published, he appears as "Thomas Sawyer," and that the bank account in which he places his share of the treasure is also under his full, adult, public name, "the name they lick [him] by."

Even though the narrative of *The Adventures of Tom Sawyer* ends with its female character relegated to silence and its male protagonist wealthy and publicly virtuous, it does not fully resolve all the contradictions inherent in the attempt to interpellate an audience though its identification with a boy. The provisional nature of Huck's assimilation into society—marked most prominently by the cache of guns and ammunition he and Tom have hidden in the cave—signals the possibility that both the narrative and the reader's identification with the boys' instability may pick up again. On the one hand this openness is a canny marketing move on Twain's part, for it remobilizes the reader's pleasure in one of the more unstable aspects of boy-nature, the identification with the gang, and allies that attachment with the desire for a sequel. At the same time, the promise of more plot is inseparable from those aspects of boy-nature which both constitute and destabilize masculine individuality. The pleasures and dangers of identifying with a boy are thus infinitely repeatable, as are their contributions to masculine self-fashioning.

Works Cited

Aldrich, Thomas Bailey. *The Story of a Bad Boy.* 1869. Vol. VII of *The Writings of Thomas Bailey Aldrich.* Boston: Houghton Mifflin, 1897.

Althusser, Louis. *Lenin and Philosophy.* Trans. Ben Brewster. New York: Monthly Review, 1971.

Beisel, Nicola. *Imperiled Innocents: Anthony Comstock and Family Repro-*

duction in Victorian America. Princeton: Princeton University Press, 1997.

Blair, Walter. "On the Structure of *Tom Sawyer*." *Modern Philology* 37 (August 1939): 75–88.

Camfield, Gregg. *Sentimental Twain: Samuel Clemens in the Maze of Moral Philosophy*. Philadelphia: University of Pennsylvania Press, 1994.

Carnes, Mark C. *Secret Ritual and Manhood in Victorian America*. New Haven: Yale University Press, 1989.

Chapman, Mary, and Glenn Hendler, ed. *Sentimental Men: Masculinity and the Politics of Affect in American Culture*. Berkeley: University of California Press, 1999.

Comstock, Anthony. *Traps for the Young*. 1883. New York: Funk and Wagnalls, 1884.

DeVoto, Bernard. *Mark Twain at Work*. 1942. Bound with *Mark Twain's America*. Boston: Houghton Mifflin, 1967.

Fiedler, Leslie. "Come Back to the Raft Ag'in, Huck Honey!" 1948. *A Fiedler Reader*. New York: Stein and Day, 1977. 3–12.

———. *Love and Death in the American Novel*. 1960. Rev. ed. New York: Anchor, 1992.

Franklin, Benjamin. *Benjamin Franklin's Autobiography*. 1791. Ed. J. A. Leo Lemay and P. M. Zall. New York: Norton, 1986.

Freud, Sigmund. *The Interpretation of Dreams*. 1900. Trans. James Strachey. New York: Avon, 1965.

———. "On the Sexual Theories of Children." 1908. *The Sexual Enlightenment of Children*. Ed. Philip Rieff. New York: Collier Books, 1963. 25–40.

Habegger, Alfred. *Gender, Fantasy, and Realism in American Literature*. New York: Columbia University Press, 1982.

Hendler, Glenn. *Public Sentiments: Structures of Feeling in Nineteenth-Century American Literature*. Chapel Hill: University of North Carolina Press, 2001.

Horlick, Allan Stanley. *Country Boys and Merchant Princes: The Social Control of Young Men in New York*. Lewisburg, PA: Bucknell University Press, 1975.

Howells, William Dean. *A Boy's Town, Described for* Harper's Young People. 1890. New York: Harper, 1904.

———. Review of *The Adventures of Tom Sawyer*, by Mark Twain. *Atlantic Monthly*, May 1876, 621–22.

Klein, Melanie. "On Identification." In *Our Adult World and Other Essays*. New York: Basic, 1963. 55–98.

Laplanche, J., and J.-B. Pontalis. *The Language of Psychoanalysis*. Trans. Donald Nicholson-Smith. New York: Norton, 1973.

Macleod, David I. *Building Character in the American Boy: The Boy Scouts, YMCA, and Their Forerunners, 1870–1920*. Madison: University of Wisconsin Press, 1983.

Macpherson, C. B. *The Political Theory of Possessive Individualism: Hobbes to Locke*. New York: Oxford University Press, 1964.

Mailloux, Steven. *Rhetorical Power*. Ithaca: Cornell University Press, 1989.

———. "The Rhetorical Use and Abuse of Fiction: Eating Books in Late

Nineteenth-Century America," *Boundary 2* 17.1 (Spring 1990): 133–57.

Moon, Michael. " 'The Gentle Boy from the Dangerous Classes': Pederasty, Domesticity, and Capitalism in Horatio Alger." *Representations* 19 (Summer 1987): 87–110.

Peck, Elizabeth P. "Tom Sawyer: Character in Search of an Audience." *American Transcendental Quarterly* n.s. 2 (September 1988): 223–36.

Ross, Catherine Sheldrick. "Metaphors of Reading." *Journal of Library History* 22 (Spring 1987): 147–63.

Sedgwick, Eve Kosofsky. *Between Men: English Literature and Male Homosocial Desire*. New York: Columbia University Press, 1985.

Stowe, Harriet Beecher. *Uncle Tom's Cabin*. 1852. New York: Norton, 1994.

Trensky, Anne. "The Bad Boy in Nineteenth-Century American Fiction." *Georgia Review* 27 (Winter 1973): 503–17.

Trilling, Lionel. *The Liberal Imagination: Essays on Literature and Society*. 1948. New York: Harcourt, 1979.

Twain, Mark. *The Adventures of Tom Sawyer*. 1876. Berkeley: University of California Press, 1982.

———. "Boy's Manuscript." 1868. *Huck Finn and Tom Sawyer Among the Indians and Other Unfinished Stories*. Berkeley: University of California Press, 1989. 1–19.

———. "Fenimore Cooper's Literary Offenses." In *Great Short Works of Mark Twain*. Ed. Justin Kaplan. New York: Harper and Row, 1967. 169–81.

———. "Huck Finn and Tom Sawyer Among the Indians." 1884. *Huck Finn and Tom Sawyer Among the Indians and Other Unfinished Stories*. Berkeley: University of California Press, 1989. 33–81.

———. "Story of the Bad Little Boy." *Sketches New and Old*. Vol. 19 of *The Writings of Mark Twain*. New York: Harper and Brothers, 1904. 54–59.

———. "The Story of the Good Little Boy." *Sketches New and Old*. Vol. 19 of *The Writings of Mark Twain*. New York: Harper and Brothers, 1904. 60–67.

Twain, Mark, and William Dean Howells. *Mark Twain–Howells Letters: The Correspondence of Samuel L. Clemens and William D. Howells, 1872–1910*. Ed. Henry Nash Smith and William M. Gibson. 2 vols. Cambridge: Belknap–Harvard University Press, 1960.

Warner, Charles Dudley. *Being a Boy*. 1877. Boston: Houghton, Mifflin, 1897.

CARTER REVARD

Why Mark Twain Murdered Injun Joe—and Will Never Be Indicted†

Mark Twain is an author whose work can be read with delight and wonder, a writer as deep and humane as Henry James or Joseph Conrad. Yet Twain hated Indians, expressed this hatred quite viciously in books that remain very popular—and no one in the American literary and cultural establishment has looked closely at this hatred and its violently racist expression. I want therefore to ask two questions: first, why Twain hated Indians so fiercely;[1] second, why this silence about his hatred?

An individual psychological explanation for Twain's hatred, I will suggest, would involve what the pre-adolescent Sam Clemens saw, and who showed it to him, in McDowell's Cave near Hannibal, Missouri—the site, in *Tom Sawyer*, where Mark Twain says he killed Injun Joe.[2] Behind the critical silence, however, is the fact that a

---

† From *Massachusetts Review* 40.4 (Winter 1999–2000): 643–70. Reprinted by permission of Carter Revard. All notes are Revard's.

1. I am fully aware that Indian-hating was usual in the Missouri of 1835–1875 (before publication of *The Adventures of Tom Sawyer*), but it seems to me Twain's is a particularly intense and illuminating case. The hatred was not merely endemic among the less formally educated, such as Twain. Consider, for instance, the account by Laban Miles—later appointed agent for the Osage Indians in Oklahoma—of a moment during his freshman year at the University of Iowa in the 1860s. When Miles arrived, new student accommodations were not yet ready, and he joined seven other young men assigned to sleep on pallets in a basement:

   > There had recently been some trouble in the northwest between the whites and the Indian, and there was considerable disturbance in the community in reference to the matter. That night the question came up and was discussed among us young men together in the room, and finally near bed time one of the young men made a little speech, setting out his views and what he would like to do. He said, "I would like to be a Cavalryman of a thousand men armed with nothing but swords. I would like to have all the Indians of the United States rounded up into one corral; then I would like to ride in and cut and slash, and cut and slash until there was not a red man, woman or child living." And when he had finished he remarked, "I think it is time to retire. I've always been used to having services before retiring. Let us have a little season of prayer." I have never forgotten that night, and have always felt that I was on the opposite side of the Indian question from that young man.

   For more on Miles as Osage agent in Oklahoma, see John Joseph Mathews, *Wah'kon-tah, The Osage and the White Man's Road* (Norman: University of Oklahoma Press, 1932), from which the above excerpt is quoted (p. 14).

2. In his *Autobiography* Twain says: "In the book called *Tom Sawyer* I starved him entirely to death in the cave but that was in the interest of art; it never happened." The "real-life" Injun Joe, Twain says, did get lost in that cave, but survived by eating bats. What was in that cave, and what Sam Clemens and "Injun Joe" may have had to do with it, are considered later in the present essay. For the present discussion I have used Charles Neider, ed., *The Autobiography of Mark Twain* (New York: Harper, 1959), where the real-life "Injun Joe of Hannibal MO" appears on pp. 8–9, 43, 68. Recent editions of pieces of Twain's autobiography include Michael J. Kiskis, *Mark Twain's Own Autobiography: The Chapters from the* North American Review (Madison: University of Wisconsin Press, 1990); see also *Chapters from My Autobiography*, foreword by Shelley Fisher Fishkin,

good many scholars cannot accept that there have been Holocausts on this continent, evidently believing that such things could only be done overseas and by un-American monsters.[3] A pattern for such denial is clear in Twain's work: we can see how the "screen memories" of *Tom Sawyer* cover the events of Twain's lifetime—both of his individual and of American communal history. Moreover, if we went on from viewing *Tom Sawyer* to see how Twain, a man of great and generous soul, in his later years worked free of these psychic knots, this fury of Indian-hating, and turned his rage against the real American monsters, we could see more clearly the dimensions of his later work, which critics and biographers have tended to devalue in favor of his work up to *Huckleberry Finn* in 1886—but that may wait for another occasion.

1. *Injun Joe,* Tom Sawyer, *and the Critics*

Two things about *Tom Sawyer* astonish me. The first is that at every reading its racism seems more obvious; the second, that every time I ask people whether it is a racist book they look amazed and say it is not.[4] Moreover, some of these readers tell me that *Huckle-*

---

introduction by Arthur Miller, afterword by Michael J. Kiskis (New York: Oxford University Press, 1996).

3. There have certainly been general discussions—for instance, Richard Slotkin's *Regeneration through Violence: The Mythology of the American Frontier* (Middletown: Wesleyan University Press, 1973), and *The Fatal Environment: The Myth of the Frontier in the Age of Industrialization, 1800–1890* (New York: Atheneum, 1985); in the latter, Slotkin brilliantly describes "the myth/ideological system that took shape around the Indian wars and labor struggles of the [Custer's] Last Stand period," and discusses "literary" works as they interact with "history" in nineteenth-century America—but his discussion of *Tom Sawyer* (519–22) does not even mention Injun Joe. Valuable further discussion is found in Richard Drinnon, *Facing West: The Metaphysics of Indian-Hating and Empire-Building* (Minneapolis: University of Minnesota Press, 1980); and Kirkpatrick Sale, *The Conquest of Paradise: Christopher Columbus and the Columbian Legacy* (New York: Knopf, 1990). Leslie Fiedler, cited below, speaks pungently of Twain's Indian-hating. For the perspective of one American Indian historian, see Ward Churchill, *Fantasies of the Master Race: Literature, Cinema, and the Colonization of American Indians* (San Francisco: City Lights Books, 1998) and *A Little Matter of Genocide: Holocaust and Denial in the Americas, 1492 to the Present* (San Francisco: City Lights Books, 1997).

4. An exception—at first sight—would seem to be Shelley Fisher Fishkin's *Lighting Out for the Territory* (New York: Oxford University Press, 1997); but her account of *The Adventures of Tom Sawyer* (42–48) turns out to be primarily a demonstration that the people of Hannibal, Missouri, have used that book to hide their own tacit racism while erasing the Black history which, Fishkin believes, is integral to the book's artistic achievement. Not Twain, but Hannibal—then and now—is racist, according to Fishkin. However, Fishkin takes a very Black and White view of racism. The minute she looks at a newspaper photograph of Joe Douglas, the man whom Hannibal townspeople persistently (against his protests) identified as the "real-life model" for Injun Joe, Fishkin says: "Joe Douglas was black." She never talks about Twain's *Injun* Joe, she asks only why the townspeople chose to "identify" the "historical Injun Joe" as Joe Douglas—dismissing the newspaper's report that Joe Douglas was part Osage Indian by saying (43): "The 'one-drop rule' that pervaded legal racial categories in the United States would have defined him as black despite the fact that he was also part Osage Indian." In other words, while proclaiming that Americans erase Black history, Fishkin proceeds to erase Indian history. It does not matter whether he was Indian, what matters is only that he was (also) Black. So when Fishkin asks (43–

berry Finn is racist—taking, it seems, the view that heroicizing the
slave Jim is at best plantation-owner paternalism—while sniffing at
Tom Sawyer as "just a boy's book," with hardly any slaves in it: no
slaves, therefore no racism.[5] Here for instance are the editors of the
Norton Anthology of American Literature:

> For all its charm and lasting appeal, *The Adventures of Tom
> Sawyer* (1876) is in certain respects a backward step. There is
> no mistaking its failure to integrate its self-consciously fine writ-
> ing, addressed to adults, with its account in plain diction of
> thrilling adventures designed to appeal to young people. Twain
> had returned imaginatively to the Hannibal of his youth; before
> he could realize the deepest potential of his material he would

---

44) the obvious question—"How did Joe Douglas become the model for a base and murderous figure like Injun Joe?"—she says that is the "wrong question," because

> the real question was why the good people of Hannibal had *decided* he was the model.
> Mark Twain never said Joe Douglas was Injun Joe. No, it was the citizens of Hannibal,
> giddy with the challenge of pairing each fictional creation of Twain's with a real-life
> counterpart, who had made the match. (44)

In Fishkin's account, Twain's "Injun" has disappeared because Hannibal's "Nigger" is
being mistreated. She simply ignores Dixon Wecter's alternative "identification" of the
"historical" Injun Joe as an Osage boy scalped and left for dead by Pawnees and later
brought by cattlemen to Hannibal, where he lived in a hollow sycamore tree, wore a red
wig to hide the scar from his scalping, and did odd jobs around Hannibal including carrying
baggage from the wharf to "Injun Joe's Cave": for these details see Wecter, *Sam Clemens
of Hannibal* (Boston: Houghton Mifflin, 1952), 151.
5. Lee Clark Mitchell, in a long and perceptive introduction to the World's Classics edition
of *The Adventures of Tom Sawyer* (Oxford: Oxford University Press, 1993), vii–xxxiv, quotes
a sentence from William Dean Howells's review of the novel that brings out with stunning
clarity the paternal tolerance of Howells's view of Indians, in contrast to the nasty racism
of Twain's: Tom Sawyer's courage, says Howells, "is the Indian sort, full of prudence and
mindful of retreat as one of the conditions of prolonged hostilities. In a word, he is a boy,
and merely and exactly an ordinary boy on the moral side" (quoted by Mitchell, xvi). For
Howells, Tom Sawyer as an apparently Bad but really good Boy is like an Indian in that
he is mischievous, adventurous, unorthodoxly religious, deceptive but not a liar, cruel out
of ignorance, generous within strict limits—and courageous in never giving up his "prolonged hostilities" but having the prudence and self-control to run away but come back
and fight another day. What to Howells is admirable likeness between Tom and Indians
(after all, both are just children), is to Twain based on Tom's naive faith in the Fenimore
Cooper Indian, totally belied by the treachery, sadism, and vengefulness of the "real"
halfbreed Injun Joe.
      Mitchell pays no attention, however, to the Indianness of Injun Joe. He points out that
this is the most popular novel ever written by an American, and (xxii–xxiii) compares and
contrasts Tom and Injun Joe, agreeing with Cynthia Griffin Wolff's remark that "Injun
Joe is Tom's shadow self," but insisting that the portrait of Injun Joe is "extremely thin"
in physical details, and that he is "never described"—then citing Twain's descriptions of
him as a "stolid face . . . iron faced," finally asserting that "the remarkable feature of Injun
Joe's appearance lies less in the vagueness of his physical characteristics than in the fre-
quency with which he is signalled in the novel by sound alone"—that is, his voice is
unmistakable. This insight at once is used, however, to assert that "many of the novel's
characters are denoted by their distinctive voices," implying that Injun Joe is just like all
of them, with personality conveyed most "fully in a characteristic manner of speech." Injun
Joe has been "disappeared" by Mitchell almost as effectively as the Argentine and Chilean
generals "disappeared" their victims. And Mitchell's is a standard way of dissolving Joe's
being "Injun" into Greek mythology or Freudian psychology: see, below, discussion of how
Forrest Robinson and contributors to his *Cambridge Companion to Mark Twain* "handle"
Injun Joe (and the notes for references).

have to put aside the psychological impediments of his civilized adulthood. *Tom Sawyer* creates a compelling myth of the endless summer of childhood pleasures mixed with terror, but as Twain hints in the opening sentence of *Huck Finn*, the earlier novel is important primarily as the place of origin of *Huckleberry Finn*. . . . [6]

There are three clever critical moves here. The first judges *Tom Sawyer* purely on style and rhetoric, dismissing it for "failure to integrate" upscale filigree with cheap pewter, while cocking a snook at *both* pewter and filigree. A second critical move is the Freud-and-Darwin gambit—seeing *Tom Sawyer* as the work of a psyche not yet free to recognize and re-present its Id-forces, still too immature (Freud) or primitive (Darwin) to write *Huckleberry Finn*. But the third and slickest critical move is to seal off all the race-haunted houses in Tom Sawyer's Hannibal, leaving open for business only the "childhood nostalgia" souvenir-shop. In plain terms, this critic allows only the general term "terror" to represent the book's central plot—which in fact turns on the murder of the doctor by Injun Joe, the witnessing of it and later testifying to it by Tom and Huck, and the desperate struggle against Injun Joe from that moment to the end of the book, in which Huck and Tom get rich from the gold stolen by Injun Joe and released by his death in the cave, where Tom found it. "A boy's book," the critics say—winking away its gaudy staging of Manifest Destiny and California Dreaming.

For what these readers have turned their eyes from is that the great antagonist in *Tom Sawyer*—the sadistic murderer defeated by Tom and Huck—is *"Injun"* Joe, a *"half-breed,"* whose Indian blood is said by the most trustworthy adults in the book to be the true cause of his sociopathic sadism and vengefulness.[7] The book, how-

---

6. *The Norton Anthology of American Literature*, vol. 2, 3rd ed. (New York: Norton, 1989), 11.

7. For instance, the "Welshman" who, after hearing Huck's revelation that it was Injun Joe who was planning to rob and mutilate the Widow Douglas, says: "When you talked about notching ears and slitting noses I judged that was your own embellishment, because white men don't take that sort of revenge. But an Injun! That's a different matter, altogether." The most "damning" view of Joe's evil as due to his Indian blood is, of course, put into Joe's own mouth. Preparing to murder Dr. Robinson in the graveyard, Injun Joe says he now wants revenge for something Dr. Robinson did to Joe five years before, when he drove Joe from his door, where he had begged for food, and had him jailed as a vagrant. "Did you think I'd forget?" Joe says. "The Injun blood ain't in me for nothing. And now I've got you and you got to *settle*, you know!" Later, when Joe's partner wants to leave town with their stolen gold and forget about attacking the Widow Douglas, Joe refuses because it was her husband who had had Joe publicly horsewhipped and, as Justice of the Peace, had jailed him as a vagrant. Joe says grimly of Justice Douglas: "He took advantage of me and died. But I'll take it out of *her*." When his shocked partner says, "Oh, don't kill her!" Joe responds: "Kill? Who said anything about killing? I would kill *him* if he was here: but not her. When you want to get revenge on a woman you don't kill her—bosh! You go for her looks. You slit her nostrils—you notch her ears, like a sow's!" and adds, when the partner starts to say something, "Keep your opinion to yourself! It will be safest for you. I'll tie her to the bed. If she bleeds to death, is that my fault?"

The picture could not be clearer: vengefulness, sadism, delight in torturing and demean-

ever brilliantly done, was written by an Indian-hating and Indian-fearing author who brought to life in its pages two of the major heroes of American literature, characters on whose creation Twain's great and enduring popularity mostly depends, and as their major heroic action presented the defeat of a wily, savage and treacherous Indian.[8] The critics who are alive to every nuance of how Twain, in *Huckleberry Finn*, kid-gloves the Black and White issues, blatantly ignore his mauling of Red and White questions in *Tom Sawyer*.

To illustrate, we can turn from the *Norton Anthology* to a recent scholarly guide, *The Cambridge Companion to Mark Twain*.[9] The most substantial of its few and perfunctory mentions of *The Adventures of Tom Sawyer* is a brief discussion in Stanley Brodwin's essay, "Mark Twain's Theology: The Gods of a Brevet Presbyterian." In considering Twain's account of humankind's "natural" and "hellish" instincts, Brodwin says:

> To watch these instincts at play we must go back to 1876, the year both "The Carnival of Crime in Connecticut" and *The Adventures of Tom Sawyer* were published. The former story offers us a Poesque demonstration of how to kill our conscience. . . . On the other hand, we have the Edenic, hymnal fairy tale of *Tom Sawyer*, another version of the natural in the world of youth clinging to and playing out its instincts and need for adventure in a society . . . asserting its authority over that play. . . . Tom, the rebel-conformist . . . manages to play out his instincts without subverting the world that allows him to do so—within limits. The satanic in its midst, Injun Joe, is destroyed by Tom's heroic actions. . . . If Tom and Becky confront the horrors of the underworld in the cave, they also achieve "salvation" and triumph. . . . The essence of *Tom Sawyer*, therefore, remains profoundly Adamic despite some of its darker subterranean flashes. (224–26)

Brodwin's critical orientation is "psychological" (literature is to be read as Freudian "screen memory" of the author's, and then related to "culture-myths" such as that of Oedipus or Adam and Eve which are also literary projections of "screen memories"), so he presents *Tom Sawyer* as Twain's take on the culture-myth of Eden—tweaked by Twain so that Satan, who somehow gets called Injun Joe, is "destroyed by Tom's heroic actions." It does not matter, to this psychoanalytical account, that Twain's Satan is a half-breed Indian.

ing (especially of women), are precisely due to Joe's being an Indian, as attested both by the wise old Welshman and by Joe himself.

8. For the depth and extent of that popularity, see Louis J. Budd, "Mark Twain as an American Icon," in Forrest G. Robinson, ed., *The Cambridge Companion to Mark Twain* (Cambridge: Cambridge University Press, 1995), 1–26.

9. Robinson, *ibid.*

Nor is Brodwin's contribution in any way untypical of the other ten essays by Twain specialists in the *Cambridge Companion*. These include an essay on "Mark Twain and Women," one on "Black Critics and Mark Twain," a third on "Mr. Clemens and Jim Crow: Twain, Race, and Blackface," a fourth on "Mark Twain's Travels in the Racial Occult: *Following the Equator* and the Dream Tales": that is, the critics are alert to Twain's management of the hot issues of race and gender, but the issues are seen to touch only Blacks, Jews, and Women. In the volume's Index, the word "Indians" does not occur, while under "Twain, Mark," we are pointed to pages on the following topics: *Americanism, fraud, free trade, humor, imperialism and colonialism, individualism, the "Jewish Question"* (seven pages), *lies, Orientalism, pessimism, politics, the psychological, publicity and advertising, race and slavery, religion, spiritualism,* and *women*. It is indeed a useful and wide-ranging handbook—but so far as this *Cambridge Companion to Mark Twain* is concerned, there are no Indians in Twain's work or in Twain's America.

The omission in this handbook is the more startling because its editor, Forrest Robinson, in an earlier book had given *The Adventures of Tom Sawyer* both extensive and sophisticated critical attention.[1] Yet even there, Robinson shoves the Indian question first behind the Psychological Reading and then behind the Black Problem, as handy ways to dismiss "Indian matters" so he can get on to what really interests him—race as defined by slavery and black/white questions. Here is what he says:

> Most readers of *Tom Sawyer* are prepared to recognize that Injun Joe is a victim of racial prejudices; the text makes this clear enough. It is equally notable that for most readers the novel seems to invite the absorption of racial considerations into much larger, "universal" anthropological or psychological frames of reference. Thus we are inclined to lose sight of the half-breed in the scapegoat, or in the dark bearer of society's repressed sexual energy. But the racism that figures in the abuse of Jim is not so easily dealt with. Indeed, where we witness the fear and hatred and mistreatment and death of Injun Joe with relative equanimity, we bring anxious, lingering uncertainty to a story that features long intervals of relative racial amity and that culminates in the liberation of a slave. (*Bad Faith*, 131)

It is a very smooth presentation. Robinson acknowledges that Injun Joe is a "victim" of racism, that the book's text makes this clear, and that "most readers are prepared to recognize" this. ("Oh yeah, *very*

---

1. Forrest Robinson, *In Bad Faith* (Cambridge: Harvard University Press, 1986), hereafter cited as *Bad Faith*; references to Injun Joe occur on pages 20, 35, 50–51, 52–54, 169, 97–98, 102–3, and 131.

racist stuff—*we* know that.") He then says "most readers"—at the invitation of "the novel" itself, of course—re-categorize Injun Joe not as historical Indian, but as mythic or psychic scapegoat.[2] So far, it seems he is merely reporting some survey of American readers—but then he uses the royal *we* to speak for all of us: "we are inclined to lose sight of the half-breed in the scapegoat."

That phrasing implies, with just a hint of apology, that since Robinson is not himself Indian, he and "most readers" (how many Injuns can read?) don't really give a damn about Injun Joe or Indians in general, and anyhow the novel itself "invites" readers to convert the overtly anti-Indian text into mythic or psychodramatic hypertext. In contrast, he insists, "most readers" cannot dismiss what happens to Nigger Jim the way they can dismiss what happens to Injun Joe; as he goes on to say (*Bad Faith*, 132), "we grow uncomfortable with images of racism . . . when they are drawn into direct association with the familiar circumstances of slavery in America." *We know what was done to Blacks, so we care about Jim; we don't know what was done to Indians, so we care nothing for Joe.*

I'll grant that Robinson is a more intelligent and sensitive reader than the above account allows. He says, for instance (*Bad Faith*, 73), that *Tom Sawyer's* readers have connived at its "illusion of calm by preferring not to pursue vigorously or systematically the clues that the novel provides to its troubled undercurrents." And he suggests (*Bad Faith*, 35) that when the village learns of Injun Joe's death in the cave, and the village women then get up a petition for a post-humous pardon for Joe, this petition is "the manifestation of an unconscious admission that the half-breed terror of the village is in fact the victim of a cruel racial lie, and is hounded to his misdeeds, and ultimately to his death, by heartless prejudice." Further, Robinson claims, Twain's own feelings about Joe are hardly as severe as we might suppose from Twain's sarcasm at the sentimentality of the women's petition: "Subsequent references to Joe as 'prisoner,' 'captive,' 'the poor unfortunate' and 'the hapless half-breed' . . . contrast dramatically with the diatribe against 'sappy women' that immediately follows" (*Bad Faith*, 53). And later, Robinson says, Twain "slipped into an identification with" Tom Sawyer's feelings of pity for the miserable cave-death of Injun Joe (*Bad Faith*, 54, 220). Most tellingly, Robinson tries to clarify just how the novel's racism works, by applying to Injun Joe precisely the terms usually applied to Blacks:

> Sexuality in general, sexual aggressiveness in particular, deceit, greed, varieties of perversity and violence and the resistance to social restraint—these are the kinds of energies and impulses

2. Scapegoating seems more what Hawthorne does in "Young Goodman Brown" or "The Maypole of Merry Mount" or *The Scarlet Letter*, than what Twain does in *Tom Sawyer*.

which the town fears, and which it attempts to cast away from itself and to control by heaping them on Injun Joe.[3] The clearly applied social construction has it that all irremediable social forces are traceable to the darkness in the half-breed. . . . The community's cultural blindness, its inability to see clearly and consciously that Joe is a kindred spirit, is at once a leading symptom and a primary cause of its bad faith. So long as the townspeople fail to recognize Joe as their fellow equal, the alien halfbreed will continue to flourish in their midst. . . . (*Bad Faith*, 102–3)

It is a very accurate and perceptive account, but notice that it is "the *darkness* in the half-breed," and not "the *Indian*" in him, which Robinson identifies as source of the town's racist fear and hatred. Notice that Robinson never points to the book's careful and explicit identification of Joe *not* as particularly "dark" but as predominantly "Injun" or "Indian"; notice that Robinson never mentions that in *Tom Sawyer* the slaves who do appear (including the precursor of Jim) are not in the least sexually aggressive or greedy, but merely buffoonish, so it is not those with darkest skins who behave worst in this book. No doubt "color" was terribly important in 1876, but in *Tom Sawyer* it is not so dreadful as "Injun," and the weakness of Robinson's account is in his refusing to see Injun Joe as an Indian, and—so far as he sees Joe as racist victim—describing him in terms that effectively make him a Black manqué.[4]

There is, moreover, a whole historical dimension missing from Robinson's *Tom Sawyer*: the dimension that would connect the theft of a continent with the theft of the gold which ultimately is "inherited" by Tom and Huck from their "father" Injun Joe.[5] Robinson can

3. Robinson's Injun Joe sounds awfully like Faulkner's Joe Christmas (*Light in August*).
4. Twain presents Injun Joe as insisting on *not* being black—as, indeed, most rabidly revengeful over having been treated as if he *were* black. When the Widow Douglas's husband had jailed Joe as vagrant, the worst part (says Joe) was not the jailing: "He had me horsewhipped!—horsewhipped in front of the jail *like a nigger*! Horsewhipped!—do you understand?" When Injun Joe speaks of his being Indian, it is with injured pride in how fearsome he is, and he regards Blacks and the way they are treated as far beneath what *he* deserves. It is clear that Twain regards such an "Injun half-breed" as much worse than the Blacks Joe despises. He is nearer the white trash stratum than the Black slave stratum of society, but his companion in the graverobbing scene, Muff Potter, who is also "white trash," is only bad when drunk, and when sober is a sweet, unselfish, humbly gullible and pitiable man, whereas Injun Joe drunk or sober is a wily, Satanic, sadistic, treacherous, utterly heartless and proud monster. Injun Joe is actually *proud* of being Indian—and that, perhaps, is the deepest insult to the people of Hannibal, something they pretend the Blacks would never dare assert—pride in *not* being white! As mentioned, in *Tom Sawyer* the Blacks are happy-go-lucky and friendly, unthreatening figures, but when Twain refers to the threats of a slave revolt it is in his contrasting the lesser outlaw Jesse James with the greater outlaw Murrell, one of whose most nightmarish and powerful threats was that he might lead a slave-insurrection.
5. John Seelye, in his introduction to *The Adventures of Tom Sawyer* (New York: Penguin, 1986), xix, likens the way Tom and Huck get rich to the way the Forty-Niners got rich in California:

speak tellingly of sexual and psychological dimensions, and when he turns to *Huckleberry Finn* he puts the history of slavery on this continent powerfully into play—yet he says nothing whatever of Injun Joe in relation to the Conquest of the West, Manifest Destiny, or ethnic cleansing, surely aspects of American history as crucial to Twain's time as were slavery and the Civil War and Reconstruction. Nor does he consider what Twain had absorbed from the popular media of his day, the newspaper reports of Indian massacres, the accounts of heroic cavalry protecting innocent travelers of the Oregon Trail or Forty-Niners headed for California, or what Twain scavenged from popular "science" with its racial classifications and horror of "miscegenation" (a new word just then).

But let's turn from such deplorable omissions to the questions with which we began. *First*, why did Twain *hate* Indians so fiercely, and is the hatred important only in *Tom Sawyer*? I have already suggested that a partial answer will be found in certain parts of Twain's *Autobiography* involving Sam Clemens's experiences in McDowell's Cave; and as we will see, the Indian-hating crops up in Twain's work before *Tom Sawyer*. *Second*, why has so little notice of the evidence for this been taken by readers and critics? *Third*, and finally, what do Twain's bigotry, and (more important) its invisibility to readers both academic and popular, imply about American literature, Amer-

---

Tom Sawyer . . . realizes the American Dream at the threshold of adolescence . . . by striking it rich California-style, imitating in miniature the Gold Rush that Mark Twain so persistently lamented as the national event that signaled an end to the old American dream of pastoral, rural contentment, even while, as Sam Clemens, he did everything he could to increase his personal fortune, whether prospecting for silver in Nevada or plowing the profits from his books into ill-fated investments . . .

In "What's in a Name: Sounding the Depths of *Tom Sawyer*" (*Sewanee Review* 90 [1982], 408–29), Seelye offers considerable discussion of Injun Joe (416 ff.), essentially dismissing him as on the one hand an Indian villain out of Fenimore Cooper (Magua in *Last of the Mohicans*), and on the other "the conventional villain of melodrama, his evilness enhanced by his mixed blood, the half-breed being a miscegenetic type depicted in much nineteenth-century American literature as being inherently vicious" (426–27). As for why Twain himself presented "the American aborigine . . . as a subspecies of Yahoo," Seelye calmly says this is "largely because Sam Clemens's own experience with Indians was limited to *degenerate tribes in Nevada and California*" (my emphasis). I wonder whether such present-day poets and novelists as Adrian Louis and Nila Northsun would agree that their Nevada tribes were, or are, quite so "degenerate" as Seelye must think; and I suppose the Tule River or Round Valley Reservation "yahoos" might object to the ignorant racism shown by Seelye in that astonishing aside. Even after thus dismissing the "aborigine" model for Injun Joe, Seelye still has to deal with Twain's *Injun* Joe—and does so by refashioning him into a Greek myth. In the McDougal's Cave episode, Seelye considers that Injun Joe becomes the "resident Minotaur," one of "the cannibalist ogres who populate folk and fairy tales"— everything but an Indian half-breed meant by Twain to be a "real" Indian, not a Fenimore Cooper fiction.

I admire Seelye for connecting the Hannibal and the California gold-strikes, but must point out that in neither case does he connect Indians with that gold. For slaughter of Indians by California miners, see *General George Crook, His Autobiography* (Norman: University of Oklahoma Press, 1946). Crook, later a Union general in the Civil War, went on to fight the Sioux and Cheyenne at the Battle of the Rosebud in 1876, and was later the nemesis of Geronimo.

ican history, and the education of American citizens? Lest this inquiry be taken as rack-and-thumbscrew Inquisition, I hope to show that there are ways of making the answers to these questions part of a positive education in what Twain and we can see, in place of the "real" Indians he so brilliantly fantasized.

2. *Before Injun Joe:* Innocents Abroad *and* Roughing It

Not everybody has ignored Twain's view of Indians. Leslie Fiedler says, in *The Return of the Vanishing American*, "Twain is . . . an absolute Indian hater, consumed by the desire to destroy not merely real Indians, but any image of Indian life which stands between White America and a total commitment to genocide."[6] As evidence, Fiedler cites Twain's nasty aside in *The Innocents Abroad* about the Digger Indians of Nevada and California,[7] which shows us it was not just in *Tom Sawyer* that Twain went after Indians. *Innocents Abroad* of course was a very early book (1869)—but Twain repeated the diatribe, then foamed more rabidly still, in *Roughing It* (1872),[8] published between *Innocents Abroad* and *Tom Sawyer* (1876).

Roughing It narrates Twain's journey in 1861 from St. Louis to Carson City, Nevada, and points west, and tells of his experiences as miner and journalist in the Western territories for the next several years. It has marvelously funny stories and is full of information, which as Twain modestly remarks in his Preface "appears to stew out of me naturally, like the precious otter of roses out of the otter." One such drop stews out in Chapter 5:

> It is considered that the cayote, and the obscene bird, and the Indian of the desert, testify their blood kinship with each other in that they live together in the waste places of the earth on

6. Leslie Fiedler, *The Return of the Vanishing American* (1968; reprint, New York: Stein and Day, 1969), 122–23.
7. Twain was comparing the beauties of the Italian Lake Como, where his traveling party was staying, to those of Lake Tahoe, mention of which led him to complain that "Tahoe" was such a wretched name for a beautiful place:

> Tahoe means grasshoppers. It means grasshopper soup. It is Indian and suggestive of Indians. They say it is Piute—possibly it is Digger. I am satisfied it was named by the Diggers—those degraded savages who roast their dead relatives, then mix the human grease and ashes of bones with tar, and "gaum" it thick all over their heads and foreheads and ears, and go caterwauling about the hills and call it *mourning. These* are the gentry that named the Lake. . . . It isn't worth while, in these practical times, to talk about Indian poetry—there never was any in them—except in the Fenimore Cooper Indians. But *they* are an extinct tribe that never existed. I know the Noble Red Man. I have camped with the Indians; I have been on the warpath with them, taken part in the chase with them—for grasshoppers; helped them steal cattle; I have roamed with them, scalped them, had them for breakfast. I would gladly eat the whole race if I had a chance. But I am growing unreliable. I will return to my comparison of the Lakes.

(Quoted here from p. 205 of a facsimile of the 1869 edition of *The Innocents Abroad* by Hippocrene Books, New York).

8. *Roughing It*, ed. Franklin R. Rogers and Paul Baender (Berkeley: University of California Press, 1972), cited hereafter as *RI* with page numbers in parentheses.

terms of perfect confidence and friendship, while hating all
other creatures and yearning to assist at their funerals. (*RI*, 69)

This might seem incidental comment, dropped as occasion allowed,
but Twain returns to the attack in Chapter 19, alleging the utter
bestiality of "Goshoot" Indians.[9] He had tried, he tells us, to find
other examples of human beings as degraded as they are, but only
after poring through all the bulky volumes of Wood's *Uncivilized
Races of Men* could he find their match, and then only one tribe—
these being the Bushmen of South Africa—on whom such a "shameful verdict" must be pronounced:

> The Bushmen and our Goshoots are manifestly descended from
> the self-same gorilla, or kangaroo, or Norway rat, whichever ani-
> mal-Adam the Darwinians trace them to. (*RI*, 144–45)

Twain then tells a nasty story of how these gorilla-descendants
attacked a stage and killed its heroic driver[1]—after which he claims
to have once been an Indian worshiper, a disciple of James Fenimore
Cooper, but these Goshoots so nauseated him as to set him

> examining authorities, to see if perchance I had been over-
> estimating the Red Man. . . . It was curious to see how quickly
> the paint and tinsel fell away from him and left him treacherous,
> filthy and repulsive—and how quickly the evidence accumu-
> lated that wherever one finds an Indian tribe he has only found
> Goshoots more or less modified by circumstances and surround-
> ings—but Goshoots, after all. They deserve pity, poor creatures;
> and they can have mine—at this distance. Nearer by, they never
> get anybody's. (*RI*, 146)

Twain is joking about having been a disciple of Cooper—but he is
unmistakably serious about slurring Indians: not just the Goshoots,
but *all* Indians.

3. *Any White Bad Guys?*

In 1872, then, Twain laced his writing with contemptuous bigotry
and corrosive hatred of Indians generally. Might we, however, in

9. Rogers (*RI*, 566–67) identifies Twain's "Goshoot" Indians as "properly Gosiute Indians,
which is a contraction of Go-ship or Gossip, the name of a former chief combined with
the tribal name *Ute*. They were a small tribe (460 members in 1873) of the Shoshonean
family, affiliated with such other tribes as the Paiutes and the Utes. . . . Although they
were one of the least culturally advanced of the Shoshonean tribes, they were not so
degraded as Mark Twain makes them. He exaggerates here to emphasize the disillusion-
ment of one who expected to see 'Noble Savages.' "

1. *RI*, 145–46. Twain's version, as Franklin Rogers nicely notes (567), "differs somewhat
from the facts." The incident, as Rogers says, "began the so-called Goshute War of 1863."
It might be worth asking why the Goshutes would do such an "Indian" thing as rob a
stagecoach and kill its passengers, or for that matter asking how the resulting "war" was
fought, and whether the Goshutes behaved as bestially as the whites before, during, and
after it. Or whether the Goshute War had anything to do with the small size of the Goshute
tribe in the 1873 census, cited by Rogers (preceding note).

charity suppose that he would have hated *any*one, white or black or red, who lived by squalid begging or by murderous robbery—the way he describes Goshoots as living, by begging in the passage just quoted, or (just before that, *RI*, 145–46) by treacherously attacking a stagecoach? We might believe that his outburst against Indians showed moral rather than racist hatred, had not Twain spent much of the previous eighteen chapters of *Roughing It* in heroicizing the exploits of murderous white gunslingers and robbers, observed or heard about, during his stagecoach journey from Missouri to Nevada. For some reason, he never (in *Roughing It*) draws the implication that such treachery and violence are typical of the white race in general, nor searches through anthropological tomes to see if their squalid treachery has any match among uncivilized savages.

In Chapter 9, for instance, *Roughing It*'s Table of Contents had promised us that the journey would be "Among the Indians," and early on we are told that the travelers "had now reached a hostile Indian country" and were "aware that many of the trees we dashed by at arm's length concealed a lurking Indian or two"—one of whom, Twain says, the night before had shot at a passing Pony Express rider, so the travelers doze uneasily as their stage moves by night through such dangers. But when the passengers are actually wakened by a shot, then a "long, wild, agonizing shriek," followed by the cries of a man begging for his life or for a pistol to defend himself, and then the sounds of his being clubbed and shot to death even as he whines ("Don't, gentlemen, please don't—I'm a dead man!"), all the terrible words *are in English*. Silence falls, a whip cracks, and the stage speeds away from the station where it has just changed drivers—but not till the next morning do the passengers learn that the murdered man was the driver who had just finished his stint. He had "been talking roughly about some of the outlaws that infested the region"; the outlaws had heard of it, waited for him, and murdered him when he drove in.

Having earwitnessed this brutal murder, Twain and his fellow passengers—so he reports (*RI*, 88)—"fed on that mystery the rest of the night," and not being able to get it explained until morning, they "lay there in the dark, listening to each other's story of how he first felt and how many thousand Indians he first thought had hurled themselves upon us"—and yet, as he says, "there was never a theory that would account for . . . Indian murderers talking such good English, if they were Indians." The next day, having learned what actually occurred, he notices that neither the new driver nor the conductor

> were much concerned about the matter. They plainly had little respect for a man who would deliver offensive opinions of peo-
> ple and then be so simple as to come into their presence unpre-

pared to "back his judgment," as they pleasantly phrased the killing of any fellow-being who did not like said opinions. (*RI*, 89)

Twain's attitudes here grow quite complex: he is condemning what he also admires. His ambivalence grows when the conductor remarks that speaking roughly of outlaws like those was "as much as Slade himself wants to do." As Twain tells us,

> This remark created an entire revolution in my curiosity. I cared nothing now about the Indians, and even lost interest in the murdered driver. There was such magic in that name, SLADE! . . . Slade was a man whose heart and hands and soul were steeped in the blood of offenders against his dignity; a man who awfully avenged all injuries, affronts, insults or slights, of whatever kind—on the spot if he could, years afterward if lack of earlier opportunity compelled it; a man whose hate tortured him day and night till vengeance appeased it—and not an ordinary vengeance either, but his enemy's absolute death—nothing less; a man whose face would light up with a terrible joy when he surprised a foe and had him at a disadvantage. A high and efficient servant of the Overland, an outlaw among outlaws and yet their relentless scourge, Slade was at once the most bloody, the most dangerous and the most valuable citizen that inhabited the savage fastnesses of the mountains. (*RI*, 89–90)

Slade, then, is described almost exactly as Twain has described the Goshutes, and as he will presently describe Injun Joe in *Tom Sawyer*: violent, treacherous, insatiably and sadistically vengeful. Yet Slade is also a man of very high status in the white society he dominates: he gets to murder, loot, revenge himself by torture and mutilation against every real or perceived insult, act in every way like a totally uncivilized human being, and yet is regarded as a bulwark of civilization. In short, Slade is exactly what Twain wants to be and knows he must not be. He is also exactly what Tom Sawyer, and Huck Finn the Red-handed, and their companions, play at being—the pirates, and the Indians, whom they practice being, not only in *Tom Sawyer* but in *Huckleberry Finn*—the Indians whom Huck and Tom were to go out among in the unfinished novel which Twain began in those years. Had Twain, to learn about Indians before writing about them, consulted his contemporary Thomas Tibbles, who in the late 1850s, aged sixteen, actually went out and lived among Plains Indians for more than a year (eventually, in fact, marrying one of them)—then not only Twain's view of Indians, but of the United States, might have been very different indeed.[2]

2. For the novel-fragment, see *Huck Finn and Tom Sawyer among the Indians*, ed. Dahlia Armon, Walter Blair, William Gibson, and Franklin Rogers (Berkeley: University of Cal-

4. Twain as Slade as Injun-Fighter

Consider, now, a moment in *Roughing It* (chapter 17) when Twain describes himself as insulted, and as taking a Slade-like revenge—a moment when the insult comes from an Indian man. Twain introduces this by explaining that everything in Salt Lake City cost at least a quarter, whereas the travelers were used to paying only five or ten cents at most for "a cigar, . . . a peach, or a candle, or a newspaper, or a shave." The first time Twain was in Salt Lake City, in his ignorance of this he was (or so he tells us) deeply embarrassed. It would be just another funny story, except that Twain carefully identifies the person who embarrassed him as a *half-breed*:

> A young half-breed with a complexion like a yellow-jacket asked me if I would have my boots blacked. . . . I said yes, and he blacked them. Then I handed him a silver five-cent piece, with the benevolent air of a person who is conferring wealth and blessedness upon poverty and suffering. The yellow-jacket took it with what I judged to be suppressed emotion, and laid it reverently down in the middle of his broad hand. Then he began to contemplate it, much as a philosopher contemplates a gnat's ear in the ample field of his microscope. Several mountaineers, teamsters, stage-drivers, etc., drew near and dropped into the tableau and fell to surveying the money with that attractive indifference to formality which is noticeable in the hardy pioneer. Presently the yellow-jacket handed the half dime back to me and told me I ought to keep my money in my pocket-book instead of in my soul, and then I wouldn't get it cramped and shriveled up so!
>
> What a roar of vulgar laughter there was! I destroyed the mongrel reptile on the spot, but I smiled and smiled all the time I was detaching his scalp, for the remark he made *was* good for an "Injun." (*RI*, 138)

The satire in this little story seems aimed at Twain himself as innocent tenderfoot, more than at the "half-breed" who embarrasses him,

ifornia Press, 1989). Tibbles narrates his 1856–57 adventures among Indians, and later marriage to Susette La Flesche (Omaha), in *Buckskin and Blanket Days* (Lincoln: University of Nebraska Press, 1969). Fishkin, in *Lighting Out for the Territory* (73–125), notes that in 1871–89 Twain summered and wrote in Elmira, New York, where his wife's Langdon family were strong Abolitionists (her father worked with the Underground Railroad); and that Twain through the Langdons met and heard Frederick Douglass. She suggests that this "educated" Twain and (73–74) helps explain his shift from hostility toward "uppity" blacks in earlier letters to his mother, to the sympathetic views found in *Huckleberry Finn* and later works. I know of no such contact between Twain and "Friends of the Indians," and wonder what he made of Helen Hunt Jackson's 1881 *A Century of Dishonor* and 1884 *Ramona*, both published not long before Twain wrote *Huck and Tom among the Indians* and completed *Huckleberry Finn*. It would be particularly interesting to know whether Twain read, in *A Century of Dishonor*, Jackson's account (chapter nine) of three massacres of Indians by whites.

and the "revenge" Twain takes is of course fantasy. Yet the story's humor would not be the same were the boot-black white instead of "half-breed" or "Injun" or "yellowjacket." And when Twain calls him a "mongrel reptile" the slur is not so merely humorous as we might think—not if we recall what both "mongrel" and "half-breed" implied in Twain's day. A *mongrel* dog was one of *mixed* breed, and to call someone a mongrel, at a time when the term *miscegenation* was being put into the vocabulary as a way of denigrating the mixture of "white" with "Negro" people, was not a merely humorous turn.[3] Had Twain just called the boot-black a "reptile," the case would have been very different.

We may also recall, here, what "half-breed" would have implied, in that time and place: not only the bastard son of white father and Indian woman, but likely of an Indian woman used as prostitute. "Half-breed" carried not only racist but legal, moral, social, and religious sting; half-breeds were not only "naturally" apt to be of poor character by being products of miscegenation, but apt to be really bad people because they were children of society's "dregs"—not merely, like Shakespeare's Edmund in *King Lear*, the children of a nobleman's adulterous passion, but children of criminal sex between drunks and whores.[4]

Roughing It, then, shows us that not long before he wrote *Tom Sawyer*, Twain considered Indians generally to be low and degraded, hardly human creatures; that when he observed a white man (Slade) acting as brutally as such Indians, he nevertheless both feared and admired even while deploring that white man's actions; and that when he told of being embarrassed by a boot-black in Salt Lake City he first went out of his way to emphasize that the man who insulted him was a half-breed Indian, and then described his own "revenge" on this half-breed in terms very like those used for Slade's revenges. Now let us look again at *Tom Sawyer*'s "compelling myth of the endless summer of childhood pleasures mixed with terrors," as the editors of the *Norton Anthology* describe it.

3. The *OED* entries for *mongrel* and *miscegenation* are highly relevant here. Even more relevant is Twain's own usage of the word *mongrel*—in, for instance, *Following the Equator*'s listing of the different population groups on Mauritius: "The majority . . . is East Indian; then mongrels; then negroes . . . ; then French; then English. . . . The mongrels are the result of all kinds of mixtures; black and white, mulatto and white, octoroon and white. And so there is every shade of complexion" (quoted here from p. 206 of Susan Gillman's "Mark Twain's Travels in the Racial Occult: *Following the Equator* and the Dream Tales," 193–219, of Robinson, *Cambridge Companion to Twain*).

4. That is one reason why it is often difficult for Americans who in the late 20th century want to document their "Indian blood": their grandparents or great-great-grandparents may either have wanted, or felt forced, to hide any such connections.

5. Tom Sawyer *as a Stephen King Novel*

Among the early reviewers of *Tom Sawyer*, the critic for the *New York Times* in 1877 was more discerning than most twentieth-century critics have been, commenting: "With less, then, of Injun Joe and 'revenge' and 'slitting women's ears' and the shadow of the gallows, which throws an unnecessary sinister tinge over the story (and the story is really intended for boys and girls), we should have liked Tom Sawyer better."[5] The one critic who has recently viewed *Tom Sawyer* as a terrifying book is Cynthia Griffin Wolff, whose account deserves notice here. She points out that "violence is everywhere in Tom's world," and suggests that Tom's own fantasy-games are "carefully constructed rituals of devastation" in which he can express the "rebellion and rage that never fully surface in his dealings with Aunt Polly."[6] The major figures in his rituals, she remarks, are "pirates and robbers and Indians," and when we notice how precarious is the balance between violence and control in these fantasies, "we can easily comprehend his terrified fascination with Injun Joe's incursions into the 'safety' of St. Petersburg." Injun Joe can be seen, says Wolff, as "one element in Tom's fantasy world . . . torn loose and broken away from him, roaming restlessly—a ruthless predator—genuinely and mortally dangerous." She notes that Injun Joe has murdered a man but does not flee; instead, he hides and waits his chance to take revenge on the Widow Douglas for what the Widow's husband had once done to Joe. In this, Wolff suggests, Joe is like Tom Sawyer—having "a grievance against the absence of the man who would be his natural antagonist, and . . . the woman who has inherited the man's property and authority . . . *Injun Joe is Tom's shadow self, a potential for retrogression and destructiveness that cannot be permitted abroad*" (emphasis mine).

Wolff argues that to control a threat not only so powerful but living within Tom's psyche, only death is strong enough: Tom must himself suffer a kind of death and rebirth in the cave ("a dark and savage place, both fascinating and deadly"). The fact that Injun Joe's death in the cave is quite accidental is (Wolff says) mere repression, "an ending with no resolution at all," a device to "lock away the small boy's anger; lock away his anti-social impulses; shut up his resentments at this totally feminine world; stifle rebellion; ignore adult male hostility; they are all too dangerous to traffic with." With such an irresolute ending, she concludes, Twain's creative vision has fal-

---

5. Quoted from John C. Gerber, Paul Baender, and Terry Firkins, *The Works of Mark Twain, Vol. 4, The Adventures of Tom Sawyer, Tom Sawyer Abroad, Tom Sawyer, Detective* (Berkeley: University of California Press, 1980), 28.

6. Cynthia Griffin Wolff, "*Tom Sawyer*: A Nightmare Vision of American Boyhood," *The Massachusetts Review* (Winter 1980), quoted from reprinted version in Harold Bloom's collection of critical essays, *Mark Twain* (New York: Chelsea House, 1986), 93–105.

tered: "Twain averts his attention from the struggle that should be central and shrinks from uncivilized inclinations."

Wolff's essay brilliantly lights up the haunted houses and piratical presences of Twain's novel. What it does not address, what it never even mentions, is the fact that *Twain makes his shadow self an Indian.* Why has Wolff herself suppressed *this* fact? But even before we listen for what her silence can tell us, how might we account for the fact itself—that the "shadow self" *is* an Indian? Why, in short, did Twain make the villain of *Tom Sawyer* a half-breed Indian?

I have already suggested that part of the answer lies in the contents of McDowell's Cave—the "real-life" version of "Injun Joe's Cave" not far south of Hannibal, Missouri, in which Twain and his boyhood friends actually did their "adventuring." In Twain's *Autobiography* he tells us there was also a "real-life" Injun Joe in Hannibal, but that he was a harmless town drunk. He says the "real" Injun Joe did get lost in the cave once,

> and would have starved to death if the bats had run short. But there was no chance of that; there were myriads of them. He told me all his story. In the book called *Tom Sawyer* I starved him entirely to death in the cave but that was in the interest of art; it never happened.[7]

Twain here carefully distinguishes between "real" and "literary" Injun Joes. Then he goes on, apparently casually, to mention something else about that cave:

> . . . it contained a corpse—the corpse of a young girl of fourteen. It was in a glass cylinder inclosed in a copper one . . . The body was preserved in alcohol and it was said that loafers and rowdies used to drag it up by the hair and look at the dead face. The girl was the daughter of a St. Louis surgeon of extraordinary ability and wide celebrity. He was an eccentric man and did many strange things. (*Autobiography*, 8–9)

Who were those "loafers and rowdies" that dragged up this presumably naked and nubile girl's corpse to be looked at? Without a doubt, some of them would have been the town drunks of the time, whom Twain has named elsewhere in his *Autobiography*. One, "General" Gaines, is explicitly linked to the cave by Twain, who says that Gaines

> was lost in [the cave] for the space of a week and finally pushed his handkerchief out of a hole in a hilltop . . . , and somebody saw it and dug him out. There is nothing the matter with his statistics except the handkerchief. I knew him for years and he

7. Neider, *Autobiography of Mark Twain*, 8–9; hereafter cited in text as *Autobiography*.

hadn't any. But it could have been his nose. That would have attracted attention. (*Autobiography*, 8–9)

The second town drunk was Jimmy Finn (the "literary" father of Huck Finn), and the third was "Injun Joe." Twain's father, Judge Clemens, tried to "reform" both these men:

> My father tried to reform [Jimmy Finn] once but did not suc-
> ceed. . . . Once he tried to reform Injun Joe. That also was a
> failure . . . and we boys were glad. For Injun Joe, drunk, was
> interesting and a benefaction to us, but Injun Joe sober was a
> dreary spectacle. We watched my father's experiments upon him
> with a good deal of anxiety but it came out all right and we were
> satisfied. Injun Joe got drunk oftener than before and became
> intolerably interesting. (*Autobiography*, 68)

That Injun Joe also got lost in the cave had been mentioned by Twain in a previous bit of the *Autobiography* (8–9); now, after telling us that Joe fell off the wagon, Twain describes both the literary doom he meted out to Joe, and Joe's actual death:

> I think that in *Tom Sawyer* I starved Injun Joe to death in the
> cave. But that may have been to meet the exigencies of romantic
> literature. I can't remember now whether the real Injun Joe died
> in the cave or out of it but I do remember that the news of his
> death came to me at a most unhappy time . . . just at bedtime
> on a summer night, when a prodigious storm of thunder and
> lightning caused me to repent and resolve to lead a better life.
> . . . I perfectly well knew what all that wild rumpus was for—
> Satan had come to get Injun Joe. . . . With every glare of light-
> ning I shriveled and shrank together in mortal terror, . . . poured
> out my lamentings over my lost condition, and my supplications
> for just one more chance. . . . But in the morning I saw that it
> was a false alarm and concluded to resume business at the old
> stand and wait for another reminder. (*Autobiography*, 68).[8]

6. Injun Joe and Hannibal, MO

Twain, then, "found" in his memories of Hannibal a set of town drunks, including the original of Injun Joe, with whom he and his

8. Forrest Robinson (*Bad Faith*, 76) perceptively links the measles infection of Tom Sawyer both to Tom's guilt-pangs at leaving the jailed Muff Potter to face hanging for the death of the doctor, and to the measles suffered by the young Sam Clemens. Robinson also mentions the "dreadful storm" which seems to the guilty Tom to "threaten imminent retribution"—but Robinson does *not* link this storm, as Twain in his *Autobiography* (quoted here) links it, to the death of Injun Joe. Surely we can concatenate the guilt of Tom Sawyer, which the thunderstorm makes him think is tied to the death-throes of Muff Potter, and the guilt of Sam Clemens, which the Satanic storm makes him think tied to the death of Injun Joe—whom he "starved to death in a cave."

boyhood friends had spent a good deal of time, and his language shows that he felt intensely guilty for whatever he and the boys had done to Injun Joe, and probably intensely ashamed of what they had done with him. *At this point I hope the reader will think briefly about what sorts of things those boys probably did to Injun Joe, and with Injun Joe.* To the boys, Twain tells us, Joe was of no interest reformed and sober, but of great interest sinful and drunk. What *would* boys have done to a town drunk—or, in academic language, to an alcoholic? Would not such doings, at the moment and in a small mob, have been greatly entertaining, but afterwards be painful to remember—much like what we see the mob doing with the town drunk Boggs who, in a famous chapter of *Huckleberry Finn*, is eventually shot dead?

More interesting, however, is the question of what sort of things this drunken "Injun Joe" would have been doing that so entertained the boys. One thing Twain does tell us was done by the town's loafers and rowdies was to go down to McDowell's Cave where the fourteen-year-old girl was preserved in alcohol, and to drag her up by the hair to be stared at. Did Twain and his friends get part of their sexual education in that way? And even if they did, is such an education really relatable to such a "children's book" as *Tom Sawyer*?

One way to answer that question is to consider an apparently unrelated moment in *Tom Sawyer*—the occasion when Tom's light of love, Becky Thatcher, is caught by Tom in the schoolroom staring at an illustration of a naked man: in her haste to get rid of the evidence she tears the page—which is in a book belonging to the schoolteacher. Tom and Becky know the teacher will return and, since the teacher habitually enjoys this book's pictures (as a pornographic relief, Twain seems to imply, from his pedantic duties), they know the teacher will discover the torn illustration and realize that one of the children has seen the book and has been looking at that picture. Becky thinks this means she will surely be found out, and that this will disgrace her for life—as it would have done. But Tom at once sees this will allow him to do a Noble Thing, and he does it: when the teacher's inquisition has all but turned the spotlight on Becky as culprit, Tom steps up and shouts "I done it!" This naturally gets him a terrible whipping from the teacher, but also—as he expected—gets him the undying gratitude and love of Becky Thatcher. So Tom and Becky have looked at full frontal nudity together, Tom has been punished for it, Becky's initiation has been kept secret, and they are practically married, though no one knows it.

The critical trail from this point is so obvious it need not be traced in detail. One thicket it would lead readers through is Twain's effort to make a stageable drama of *Tom Sawyer*, which presents Tom—

once he has heroically outwitted Injun Joe in the cave, and got Becky and himself out of it—as telling his Aunt Polly that he and Becky were "married" in the cave. For this "nonsense" he is suitably chastised when Aunt Polly cracks his head with a thimble.[9] But I need not speculate further about the psychological reasons why Twain's hatred of Indians is so virulent in *Tom Sawyer*; it may safely be left to the great army of expert Freudian critics, now that I have provided the evidence, to interpret this at leisure.[1] I want, instead, to conclude by hinting at how Twain, twenty years after publishing *Tom Sawyer*, discovered America—and realized what it was he so hated about Indians—by sailing eastward around the world: like a new Columbus, but this time through the Looking Glass.

7. By Sailing East, Mark Twain Discovers America

Twain, like America, went bankrupt in the 1890s when the Frontier closed,[2] and like America, had to recoup his fortune by assuming (as a writer) international-imperial rather than regional-national dimensions.[3] In America's case, two "new" sources of income were

9. The play is printed in *Mark Twain's Hannibal, Huck & Tom*, ed. Walter Blair (Berkeley: University of California Press, 1969), 243–324.
1. I have above suggested mainly two points: the sexual initiation in McDowell's Cave, and the kind of public humiliation by a "mongrel half-breed" recorded, if not invented, in *Roughing It*. Another suggestion may be worth considering: perhaps Twain had more to do with the Indians of Nevada and California, and in less morally upright ways, than his descriptions in *The Innocents Abroad* and *Roughing It* were meant to show. His phrasing in *Innocents Abroad*, for instance, is meant to establish that he (unlike the Cooper romanticizers) has actually spent time and "lived with" real Indians: "I have camped with the Indians; I have been on the warpath with them, taken part in the chase with them—for grasshoppers; helped them steal cattle; I have roamed with them, scalped them, had them for breakfast. I would gladly eat the whole race if I had a chance" (205). The last part of the passage ascends, like a balloon that has finally filled with hot air, into sheer fantasy— but may that not be a quick defensive move to cover whatever Twain actually did? When he says he "camped with them" and "helped them steal cattle," does that not seem perfectly plausible for Samuel Clemens to have done when he was out camping in Nevada and California? Is it also possible that he had sexual dealings with Indian women, and that he was afterward horribly angry and ashamed about it? Or is it more likely that Twain simply observed Indian women who for money, food, or whisky provided sex for the white saloon-goers and bully-boys, or Twain's miner-companions, and that Twain judged these women as depraved and immoral for it, perhaps hating them the more because he too would have liked to lay them?
2. For light on Twain's financial history see Justin Kaplan's biography, *Mr. Clemens and Mark Twain* (New York: Simon and Schuster, 1966); and interesting details in Samuel C. Webster, ed., *Mark Twain, Business Man* (Boston: Little, Brown, 1946).
3. By 1897, when Twain had completed his round-the-world trip and arrived in Vienna, he was an international celebrity who would go on to be given an honorary degree from Oxford University (which must have graveled Henry James). Twain's arrival in Vienna was noted in the newspapers of the time, which remarked that he was expected to write much of interest while there, as he had an excellent command of the German language both in speaking and in writing it (*International Herald Tribune*, reprinting in October 1997 a notice from October 1897 papers). See Carl Dolmetsch, *"Our Famous Guest": Mark Twain in Vienna* (Athens: University of Georgia Press, 1992), for an excellent account of Twain's Vienna years from September 1897, when he wrote much of his finest late work in one of the most cultivated European cities while participating in its social and intellectual life. For his work after the Vienna years, see Jim Zwick, ed., *Mark Twain's Weapons of Satire: Anti-Imperialist Writings on the Philippine-American War* (Syracuse: Syracuse University

developed between 1890 and 1910: the first was the "Indian Territory" that had carelessly been "given" to Indians forever:[4] and the
second was the remnants of European empires, especially of the
Spanish, which could be "liberated" to become part of the new American Empire. Only when Twain left America for a trip round the
world by which he hoped to pay off the creditors he owed, did he
make his great discovery that the American takeovers of Indian Territory and of the Spanish Empire were closely related, which led him
to realize that what he had thought he hated about Indians was what
he actually hated about Americans, and still more what he hated
about "the damned human race." He had prepared for the trip by
time-travel with the grown-up Tom Sawyer as the *Connecticut Yankee*, by race-travel in *Pudd'nhead Wilson*—but once he had reversed
Columbus, Tom Sawyer would become his angelic Satan as Mysterious Stranger, Injun Joe the Person Sitting In Darkness. Twain had
more than earned the doctorate from Oxford that was given him not
long before he died.[5]

Press, 1992); and William Macnaughton, *Mark Twain's Last Years as a Writer* (Columbia:
University of Missouri Press, 1979). An excellent discussion of Twain's later work is Max-
well Geismar's *Mark Twain: An American Prophet* (Boston: Houghton Mifflin, 1970).

4. The period between 1876, when Custer was killed and *Tom Sawyer* was published, and
1890, when Frederick Turner declared that the American frontier was closed, was the
time when the last free American Indian nations were defeated and forced onto reservation—and the time when Congress, which in 1871 had unilaterally reduced all those
nations (formerly dealt with by treaties, as befitting nations dealing with nations) to mere
"wards" of the U.S. Government, was working out legal ways to take away those same
"reservations." The largest block of land that had been assigned to them was what is now
called the state of Oklahoma, which from the early nineteenth century had been desig-
nated as the dumping-ground for the "Five Civilized Tribes" (Cherokees, Chickasaws,
Choctaws, Creeks and Seminoles), and from the mid-nineteenth century was the place to
which dozens of other nations, fragments from the Eastern United States and larger groups
from west of the Mississippi, had been "moved." See, for some history of this, Vine Deloria
Jr. and Clifford Lytle, *The Nations Within: The Past and Future of American Indian Sovereignty* (New York: Pantheon, 1984); and Richard Drinnon, *Facing West: The Metaphysics
of Indian-Hating and Empire-Building* (Minneapolis: University of Minnesota Press,
1980). For the Indian resistance to the "allotment" of tribal lands to individuals, meant
by Congress to "break up the tribal mass" and make the Indians "melt into the pot," see
Blue Clark, *Lone Wolf vs. Hitchcock: Treaty Rights and Indian Law at the End of the
Nineteenth Century* (Lincoln: University of Nebraska Press, 1994), which details the suit
brought by Lone Wolf (also named Mammedaty, the Kiowa grandfather of the poet and
novelist N. Scott Momaday) to force the U.S. to keep its treaties with the Kiowa and
Comanche people, by whose terms no such allotment was ever to be forced upon them
unless agreed to by a full vote of all tribal members. The Supreme Court's decision against
the Indians (on the grounds that the U.S. could do as it pleased with Indians) justified
the "runs" of white people across the "borders" to stake their claims to the "Indian Territory," once given "so long as the grass grows and water flows" to Indian nations. A good
account of what happened to Indians and the land allotted to them in the new state of
Oklahoma, between 1904 and 1940, is given by Angie Debo, *And Still the Waters Run*
(Princeton: Princeton University Press, 1941).

5. A useful recent biography is Andrew Jay Hoffman, *Inventing Mark Twain: The Lives of
Samuel Langhorne Clemens* (New York: William Morrow, 1997).

SUSAN R. GANNON

"200 Rattling Pictures": True Williams and the Imagetext of the First American Edition of *The Adventures of Tom Sawyer*†

Mark Twain's *The Adventures of Tom Sawyer*[1] has been illustrated, adapted, and dramatized so often that even people who have never actually *read* the book feel they know it. The text of his novel may be permanently fixed in Twain's words, but the story, as re-created in its many retellings, has changed as often as "the reasons for its retelling" have changed (Davis 4). Over the years, visual interpretations and dramatizations of *Tom Sawyer* have come to focus on its affectionate presentation of an irresistibly appealing iconic image of American boyhood. So today a mention of the book tends to evoke a few familiar images of Tom—flourishing his brush before a yet-to-be-whitewashed fence; dodging out of reach as Aunt Polly tries to deliver retribution; flirting with Becky Thatcher. The power and the ambivalence of Twain's narrative performance, the darker, more unsettling elements of the novel, and its immediate satiric take on popular culture have long been downplayed in retellings sweetened to suit the tastes of a sentimental public, nostalgic for the supposed simplicities of an earlier time.

Among those invited to illustrate Twain's novel over the years have been many artists with distinctive personal styles and a keen sense of what their immediate public wanted to make of it. For the 1903 Uniform Author's Edition J. G. Brown created an album of pictures featuring the kind of ragged, cherubic boys with artfully tousled hair and bare feet who figured in his commercially successful genre paintings. When Norman Rockwell was commissioned by the Heritage Press in 1935 to do eight color paintings and a number of small black-and-white sketches for a deluxe edition, he produced a sentimental tribute to small-town boy's life, featuring his trademark ordinary American boys, caught in mid-action, and posed in impossibly strenuous cute situations. A detail from Rockwell's depiction of the whitewashing scene was reproduced on a postage stamp in 1972, indicating, perhaps, how much his pictures had contributed to making Tom Sawyer synonymous with American boyhood. On

† This essay appears for the first time in this Norton Critical Edition. Copyright © 2006 by Susan R. Gannon.

1. Unless otherwise specified, the text of *The Adventures of Tom Sawyer* to which I refer is the facsimile of the first American edition published in 1876 by the American Publishing Company of Hartford, Connecticut, and reprinted in the Oxford Mark Twain. I provide both chapter and page numbers.

Barry Moser's cover for his 1989 HarperCollins Books of Wonder edition, Tom has made one dramatic sweep of whitewash on the fence and turns around, with brush in hand, as if tempting the viewer to have a go. Moser's other pictures for this edition are his usual accomplished portraits of carefully chosen models who stand in for the characters in the novel, including a plump and sun-dazzled Becky Thatcher, a fiery preacher resembling actor Hal Holbrook, and a Widow Douglas who looks hauntingly like Emily Dickinson. The appealing, technically skillful pictures provided by these very different artists have much to tell us about fashions in illustration and the history of the novel's reception, but for a reading of *The Adventures of Tom Sawyer* that does more justice both to its edgy complexity and its embeddedness in its own cultural moment we must turn to Twain's own choice as an illustrator, Truman W. Williams, whose drawings and decorations helped shape the reading experience offered the audience of the first American edition of the novel—and pleased the author mightily. Twain called them "200 rattling pictures"[2] and marveled at Williams's ability to rise to the challenge of his text, saying, "He takes a book of mine, & without suggestion from anybody builds no end of pictures just from his reading of it" (Clemens to William Dean Howells, 26 April 1876, quoted in David 1:236).

I. *True Williams and the Challenge of Illustrating* Tom Sawyer

By 1875, when Twain and Elisha Bliss of the American Publishing Company were contemplating publishing *The Adventures of Tom Sawyer*, True Williams had already worked on illustrations for Twain's *Innocents Abroad*, *Roughing It*, *The Gilded Age*, and *Sketches, New and Old*.[3] He understood the way Twain's performance-oriented style of narration worked, relished his sense of humor, and enjoyed trying to match Twain's verbal playfulness with appropriately "over-the-top" visual imagery. Twain, for his part, appreciated Williams's talent and originality, as well as his "good heart and good intentions" (1905 speech to Society of Illustrators, quoted in Schmidt), though he regretted the fondness for rum that threatened to "murder" his "genius" and make him an unreliable collaborator (Clemens to Howells, 26 April 1876, quoted in David 1:236). In 1875 Twain and Bliss agreed that Williams would illus-

2. The phrase "200 rattling pictures" *is* the way Twain put it. The word *rattling* is more commonly used as an intensifier with a word like *good*, as in the familiar phrase, *a rattling good yarn*. But used all by itself, as Twain has used it here, it means "remarkably good" according to the OED (*The Compact Edition of the Oxford English Dictionary*, vol. 2 [Oxford: Oxford University Press, 1971]).
3. Their work together is described in detail in David's invaluable *Mark Twain and His Illustrators*. David, in turn, has drawn on the research of Hamilton as well as the remarkable literary detective work of Schmidt.

trate *The Adventures of Tom Sawyer* using the same format he had used in *Sketches*. At Twain's request, a copy of the complete manuscript was sent to Williams before he began work so that he could "make the pictures more understandingly" (Clemens to Bliss, 5 November [1875], quoted in David 1:219). The somewhat down-market audience for the American Publishing Company's subscription books preferred large, elaborately illustrated volumes with impressive covers. For this public, *Tom Sawyer* would be a very skimpy offering unless profusely illustrated and decorated to make up the desired bulk. But the novel would also be a bid for fame and status, meant to establish Twain's place in the literary world and to appeal to a more demanding audience, for whom some toning down of the broad humor and high-flying absurdities of earlier collaborative efforts between Twain and Williams would be necessary. Since it was a "crossover" item, aimed at a dual audience of children and adults, the illustrations would have to be suitable for the young, yet satisfying to their elders. The many comic scenes and sardonic asides in the novel would be right up Williams's alley, but there would be occasional moments of pathos and a few passages of "fine writing" that would also need to be illustrated sympathetically. The novel's episodic, rambling nature would be problematic, its chameleon protagonist impossible to pin down in a convincingly consistent image. And how could even the most skilled artist do complete justice to the variety and suppleness of Twain's narrative style, his sly humor, his oddly ambivalent attitude toward his material?

Tom Sawyer is both a nostalgic portrait of Twain's long-lost Missouri boyhood and an unsparing assessment of the manners, morals, cultural values, and aspirations of the residents of Hannibal, his "St. Petersburg." The book's tone is mixed, its sympathies divided. The narrator may offer prose poems about the river at night or the place of a drop of water in the great flow of history, but such rhapsodies never last long. Tender moments and rhetorical flights are deliberately intermingled with passages of merciless satire, deadpan humor, mischievous exaggeration. The story begins as domestic comedy but gradually becomes something of a fairy tale. The romance formula in which a boy hero tries one way after another to escape the restrictions of the adult world; does battle with the powers of darkness; and goes on to win treasure, glory, and the gratitude of all is a familiar and satisfying one, especially appealing to younger readers. (It worked for Twain's contemporary, R. L. Stevenson, and seems to be doing pretty well for J. K. Rowling, today.) More experienced readers may be moved by the book's affectionate re-creation of an archetypal American boyhood, but Williams and Twain won't let them miss the narrator's pungent asides, the deliberately deflationary quality of the ending, or the unforgiving shrewdness with which Twain has captured the follies, hypocrisies, and cruelties of the citizens of St. Petersburg—young and old.

Twain's evident pleasure in the "200 rattling pictures" (actually 163) Williams supplied, then, may have been mixed with a certain relief. Williams, "without suggestion from anybody," had built his pictorial contribution to their joint venture into a model reading of the text that responded to its contradictions and ambiguities, and invited readers to enter into the pleasurable process of making sense of a book full of boldly mixed signals. Together, they managed to create an intriguing "imagetext,"[4] a composite, synthetic work combining Twain's masterful narrative, his ingenious typographical variations, playful page headings, and documentary pastiche, with Williams's sympathetic, conceptually interesting illustrations and decorative format.

II. Reading the Format of the Imagetext

For Twain, organizing the first half of *Tom Sawyer* was like preparing one of his famous lectures. The challenge was to arrange a set of good "bits" to best advantage, fitting them into an overall framework in just the right places and moving from one to another in such a graceful way that his audience would not notice any awkward discontinuities. On the lecture stage Twain could rely on the smoothness and conversational ease of his delivery to manage sudden shifts from pathos to humor, from "the devious pokerface to apparently guileless transparency" (Knoper 58). As a novelist he was able to project a narrative persona whose artful performance would lend continuity to the telling of a very episodic tale. And the format proposed for the new book offered Williams a chance to help Twain emphasize thematic repetitions; foreshadow events to come; clarify relations of cause and effect; and handle adjustments in tone, lapses of time, and shifts of scene through deft chaptering.

As in his work for *Sketches*, here Williams was required to provide elaborate chapter headings, with headpieces that took up the left half of the first page, numerous smaller illustrations set into the text adjacent to the passages to which they referred, and—often enough—small tailpieces at the end of a chapter. The latter might be original drawings of his own, or some stock image. Among the pictures supplied in the opening cuts would be portraits of most of the major characters, and there would be a frontispiece with a portrait of Tom Sawyer himself. Critics have justly complained that Williams's depictions of Tom and other characters are inconsistent.

---

4. With Mitchell, I am using the term *imagetext* as a convenient way to designate "composite, synthetic works . . . that combine image and text" (89 n.9).

Sometimes the easiest way to identify Tom in a picture is by the checked trousers Williams gives him to wear. As Tom steals sugar from Aunt Polly's table in Chapter I he seems a well-built teenager (19); in his Sunday school appearances a few chapters later (IV:45, 51), he looks no more than seven or eight. But of course, the age of Twain's Tom is similarly hard to pin down. More puzzling are some of Williams's other choices. His Muff Potter is in one scene a silver-haired gentleman (IX:91), in another a debauched-looking wretch (XI:101); Injun Joe's accomplice, known only in the text as "the ragged man," is well-dressed in a suit, tie, and hat (XXVI:205); and Injun Joe is never shown with his trademark eye patch.

The stilted and sentimental portrait of Tom in the frontispiece has been worked over perhaps too carefully, and darkened with cross-hatching to provide more realistic solidity than the other sketches (Figure 1). Tom sits (somewhat unconvincingly) on the riverbank, with a fishing rod loosely held in his left hand. Unlike the lively young boy with childish features in many of the later sketches, the subject of this portrait, with his decided profile, dreamy eyes, and rosebud mouth, is a romantically idealized adolescent. This stiff but ambitious frontispiece may have been an effort at accommodating Twain's desire to have the novel received as a serious literary effort, for at this time, Twain was still thought of primarily as a humorist, and "drawings were thought to be appropriate mainly for reinforcing the texts of 'comic' writings" while the works of " 'serious' authors appeared in printed forms devoid of illustrations" (Gribben vii–viii). The mood and atmosphere of the picture do suit Twain's description of the book as a hymn celebrating boyhood. And the portrait introduces the important theme of Tom as a daydreamer whose imaginings often presage events to come. Its imagery reappears later in an illustration in which "Tom Meditates" on heroic outlaw roles he might play in life (pirate, soldier, Indian warrior), while lounging "on a mossy spot under a spreading oak" in Chapter VIII (81), and in the headpiece to Chapter XIV where, as "the marvel of Nature shaking off sleep and going to work unfolded itself to the musing boy," he leans back on yet another convenient grassy bank (121–22).

The static frontispiece does not prepare the reader for the energy with which the characters of the story swarm through the pictures in the following pages. The tiny figure of Tom seems in perpetual motion as he scrambles over fences and in and out of windows, flirts with Becky Thatcher, cringes from his schoolmaster's blows, emerges wide-eyed from McDougal's cave. The images Williams created provide a movie-like continuity of action that exists parallel to the written text and might complement the table of contents as a "preview of coming attractions" for the casual browser. But Tom's adventures begin properly with the first page of the first chapter,

Figure 1. Frontispiece.

with its elaborate heading in which the letters of the book's title and the chapter heading together with the first word of the chapter, "TOM!" are drawn to resemble three-dimensional carved capitals entwined with ivy-like vines. The heading takes up the upper third of the page, and a long cut depicting "Tom at Home" covers what remains of the lower left half of the page (Figure 2). Each chapter has a distinctive introductory apparatus, with chapter heading/first word decoratively presented in hand lettering and a long vertical cut or vignette stretching down the left side of the page. In most of these cuts, the visual dynamics of the picture or the header propel the reader's attention forward, into the text itself. Even when characters face left in a headpiece, other elements in the design often focus reader attention to the right. Becky demurely turns a bit to the left in the header for Chapter III (33), but her position only emphasizes the coy glance directed over her shoulder, up and rightward at the first word of the text, which is, once more, "TOM" (Figure 3). The knowing, deliberate flirtatiousness of Becky's expression hints at her future role in Tom's story and prepares the reader for her prompt acknowledgment of Tom's interest a few pages later, when she tosses him, from the bouquet she has been shown gathering in the head-piece, a pansy, representative in the nineteenth-century "language of flowers" of her thoughts for him (Pickston n.p.)

The cuts that introduce chapters can quickly establish time, place, and atmosphere, as in the scary nighttime sequences introduced by pictures of a dog howling at the moon (X:93), an ominous owl (IX: 85), a flock of bats in McDougal's cave (XXXI:236). They can accent the thematic importance of a seemingly casual item, as in the case of the lush and romantic gravesite of a little Jimmy Hodges, thought of briefly in one of Tom's self-pitying reveries (VIII:79). The opening cuts often offer portraits of characters who will have important roles in the chapter to follow, like the genial Uncle Jake who has fed and befriended Huck (XXVIII:212) or the sinister, disguised Injun Joe in green spectacles and serape who broods over Chapter XXVI (199). Sometimes they lure the young reader to read on through material that might be more appealing to adults, as in the picture labeled "Tom Declaims" showing the usually nonchalant Tom with his hands pressed to his sides, his eyes starting from his head, as he freezes with stage-fright during his very momentary appearance in the exam-ination day program so extensively described in Chapter XXI (167).

Even the design of the words hand-lettered by Williams in the chapter headers and the sketches or decorations surrounding them can manage to suggest the subject or tone of the chapter to come. In Chapter XVI, where the boys learn to smoke, the opening cut shows Tom facing left, his back to the text, but the upward curve of the smoke rising from his corncob pipe forms itself into the words of the heading (134). In Chapter XXIII, in which Tom testifies on behalf of Muff Potter, the letters of the title are entangled with "scales of justice" that appear to have been upset (181). When "a raging desire to go somewhere and dig for hidden treasure" over-comes Tom in Chapter XXV, the chapter heading is draped with chains and lockets (191), and in Chapter XXVII when the boys make

Figure 2. Tom at Home.

plans to find and open the locked room where the treasure may be stashed, the words of the heading are cleverly constructed of a lock and keys (208).

In the table of contents for the first American edition, each chapter number is followed by a few cryptic, often humorous, phrases identifying significant incidents from that chapter. These same phrases are printed at the top of the right-hand pages throughout the book. These page-headings—unfortunately not always reproduced in modern editions of the novel—seem carefully planned to manipulate the reader's experience of the text, foreshadowing what

Figure 3. Becky Thatcher.

will happen, making jokes, suggesting the implications of various turns of event. As Mark West has pointed out, many of them "only make sense after one has read the chapter." Sometimes, like the header "A Sensation" (XIV:125), they arouse curiosity; sometimes, like the alarming "Found But Not Saved" (XXXI:245), when Tom and Becky are lost, they deliberately mislead in order to create tension. They can be used ironically: "Youthful Eloquence" heads the page (XXI:169) on which Tom is overcome by stage-fright as he recites Patrick Henry's "Give me liberty or give me death" speech.

Or they can offer a needed "distancing" from some unpleasant subject matter, like the punning "Grave Subjects Introduced" (IX:89) as Injun Joe prepares to murder Dr. Robinson.

These page-headers have their counterparts in the briefer but equally sly captions for many of the Williams illustrations. Sometimes the reader is invited to check out the picture with its caption and then to re-evaluate the label after reading further. "Tom's Effort at Prayer" (IX:88) shows Tom and Huck devoutly on their knees in the dark graveyard, staring at a mysterious, spooky light in the distance, but the reader soon discovers that in this crisis Tom's "effort" only extends to the opening line of "Now I lay me down to sleep." Similarly, the true merits of the "Prize Authors" (XXI:173) on examination day can be gauged only after the reader has been able to sample their eloquence. The caption "Injun Joe's Two Victims" might seem at first to refer to the body of Doctor Robinson and the hapless Muff Potter, who stands by the graveside about to confess to a murder he didn't commit. But the mischievous illustrator has insinuated a tombstone bearing the words "Sacred to the Memory of T. W. Williams" into the scene, making the precise identity of the second of Joe's victims a trifle uncertain (XI:103).

One of the devices Williams used to comment on Twain's text was the tailpiece, a small image either created by Williams or drawn from stock and used to fill space left on the last page of a chapter, as well as to make a general comment, reflect on some turn of events, or set a mood. The chapter in which Tom and Huck begin to feel shocked and conscience-stricken over their role in Muff Potter's plight concludes with a stock image titled "In the Coils," showing a serpent savagely crushing a bird (XI:106). "Fate of the Ragged Man" who "had been drowned while trying to escape, perhaps" (XXXII:250), shows his body floating in the moonlit river, as predatory birds circle round (251). And for Chapter IV, in which Twain had swept his deeply embarrassed hero offstage with the pious suggestion "Let us draw the curtain of charity over the rest of the scene," the mischievous tailpiece depicts the glittering prize the young trader in Sunday school tickets had pursued with such ruthless effectiveness: a Bible, nestled in a mound of artistically arranged flowers (52). The conventional spiritual associations of this image perhaps invite second thoughts about the dubious game that Tom—and the teachers who knew quite well he hadn't come by those tickets honestly—have been playing for the benefit of visiting dignitaries.

III. The Intertextuality of the Imagetext

It has been said that the original illustrations for Twain's works are important because they are "a documentary source in their own

right, a window into Twain's world and our own" (David and Sapirstein 22). Yet in the case of True Williams's pictures and decorations
for Tom Sawyer, what you more often see is the world as it was
conventionally presented in the popular graphic traditions in which
Williams was working. Just as Twain's novel is a collage of polished
anecdotes told many times before, memories carefully re-cast in
terms of a tradition of domestic comedy full of formulaic conventions, Williams's images bear the traces of previous use. Illustrated
magazines and humorous fiction of the time often used cartoon-like
sketches that provided readers with a system of notation, a visual
vocabulary for picturing and thinking about their world. This tradition was often painfully limited in its sensitivities. Its expressive dis-
tortion and exaggeration conveyed action and feeling with great
economy, but tended to reduce human beings to social types cate-
gorized by distinctive costuming, theatrical gesture, and facial caricature. Though such work abounded in trite, sentimental images, it
could also be brutally racist, sexist, ageist.

The grotesque depiction of young Jim, the slave Tom tries to persuade to do his whitewashing, is a case in point. Williams has made
no effort to show the happy little boy who skips out of the gate, on
a Saturday morning, singing. His Jim is not only a racist stereotype
with exaggerated features and rolling eyes, but is quite inappropri-
ately adult in appearance (II:26, 28). The images of Aunt Polly seem
to be patterned on the fussy old ladies who gave grief to the young
in the world of humorous journalism, and who were often carica-
tured as stiff, angular creatures with grim expressions and unbecom-
ing bonnets. In fact, most of the pictures of Aunt Polly provided by
Williams resemble his own drawings of just such a woman: the
grandmother who lays down the law in Twain's sketch "History
Repeats Itself," which Williams had just finished illustrating for
Sketches, New and Old. At least two other images Williams had
devised for Sketches also were adapted for Tom Sawyer, which is to
an extent a parody of the sort of boys' book that had been popular
earlier in the century, where the good prosper and the bad come,
inevitably, to grief. Williams had done the illustrations for two of
Twain's earlier pieces, reprinted in Sketches as "Story of the Bad
Little Boy" for whom everything comes up roses (Figure 4), and "The
Story of the Good Little Boy" whose virtue is not rewarded. Williams
adapted the introductory cut for the bad boy story to introduce the
chapter in which Tom's traffic in Sunday School tickets wins him an
undeserved Bible (IV:42) (Figure 5), while the image of a miserable
"Huck Transformed" (Figure 6) when dressed up by the well-
meaning Widow Douglas (XXXV:268) appears to be an adaptation
of a picture of little Jacob Blevins (Figure 7), Twain's very unfortunate good boy (David 1:216–17).

IV. Imaging the Storyteller's Performance:
From Ironic Comedy to Romance

Richard Adams has observed that what unity and coherence *Tom Sawyer* has "are thematic and symbolic . . . fused in an organization of imagery that transcends any concept of plot or story line as a series of causally related events" (385). Williams's visual narrative doesn't

STORY OF THE BAD LITTLE BOY.

ONCE there was a bad little boy whose name was Jim—though, if you will notice, you will find that bad little boys are nearly always called James in your Sunday-school books It was strange, but still it was true that this one was called Jim.

He didn't have any sick mother either—a sick mother who was pious and had the consumption, and would be glad to lie down in the grave and be at rest but for the strong love she bore her boy, and the anxiety she felt that the world might be harsh and cold towards him when she was gone. Most bad boys in the Sunday-books are named James, and have sick mothers,

Figure 4. "Story of the Bad Little Boy."

Figure 5. Boyhood.

just parallel Twain's verbal performance. It supplements it, interacts with it, emphasizes certain effects, foreshadows events to come, sets incidents in new contexts. So the copious illustrations for the novel help bind the elements of the text together thematically. Even a casual glance at a list of Williams's illustrations shows that he has repeatedly chosen to illustrate scenes with similar subject matter. In the first half of the book we see Tom's comical transgressions and the retribution meted out to him; his efforts to escape, and his returns home; his daydreams of outlawry, of "temporary" death; his unsuccessful courtship of Becky Thatcher. Later, we see his encounters with real death and danger, real outlaws; his escape to Jackson's

Figure 6. Huck Transformed.

Island and "return from the dead"; his descent into the underworld and triumphant return with untold wealth; his winning of the affections of Becky, her family, and everyone else in sight. In the early part of the book, the reader is invited to look at Tom's behavior in an indulgent but detached way. The narrator is clearly having fun, and a surprising number of Williams's pictures relate not so much to details of the story but to the skillful performance of the story-teller. When "Twain" pauses to philosophize on Tom's success in conning his friends, he concludes that "Work consists of whatever a body is *obliged* to do, and that Play consists of whatever a body is not obliged to do," adding that this is why "climbing Mont Blanc is only amusement." Williams provides a cut beside these reflections

Figure 7. "The Story of the Good Little Boy."

of a little figure painfully laboring up a snowy mountainside, and labels it "Amusement" (II:32). The labels on Williams's sketches are usually part of the game, because they suggest ways to think about the pictures, but sometimes there is no need for one. When Tom cons the local boys into giving him their possessions in exchange for a chance to whitewash the fence, we learn that in addition to Ben's apple, Billy Fisher's kite, and Johnny Miller's dead rat on a string, Tom's new wealth included forty-five other items. These are presented in an artfully arranged E. B. White-like list that Williams obviously admired, because right beneath it in the text he placed a lovingly exact picture of all the loot, as though inviting the reader to pause and check out the accuracy with which he has catalogued it (II:31). Other passages to which Williams gives special treatment are the marvelous description of Huck Finn's costume and way of life (VI:64), and the dramatic set piece describing the storm on Jackson's Island, illustrated by a vertical cut showing a lightning bolt streaking down the page as the tiny figures of the boys crouch and cover their eyes, preferring not to see the scene so extravagantly described by the narrator (XVI:141). Williams provided appropriately "dainty" imagery of the starry night on the river when the boys look

at the town from their stolen raft, as "two or three glimmering lights
showed where it lay, peacefully sleeping beyond the vague vast sweep
of star-gemmed water, unconscious of the tremendous event that
was happening" (XIII:117). But his equally pretty later cut illustrating "Twain's" effusions over the water dripping from the stalactite
into "Injun Joe's cup" features a male tourist gesturing theatrically
as he carries on about the matter to a lady-friend, and helps to set
the reader up for the narrator's later mocking subversion of the emotion projected in this passage (XXXIII:254).

Sometimes Williams amplifies the text by showing in specific
detail something the narrator has just hinted at. When Tom gets a
"sure-enough" Barlow knife from Mary (IV:43), and goes on to carve
up the household furniture, Williams shows us Tom's crude artwork,
too, in the style of the one illustration Twain himself is said to have
supplied, the house Tom draws for Becky in class (VI:70). Twain
mentions a church choir's tittering and whispering all through the
service, but Williams's picture tells us *why*: the young fellows and
girls are far too busy flirting with each other to pay attention to
anything else (V:55). Occasionally, Williams adds amusing comments of his own to the scene he is describing. The examination
room in which a series of relentlessly pious and inane compositions
are declaimed by their young authors is just described in the text as
"brilliantly lighted, and adorned with festoons of foliage and flowers."
Williams has added a set of mottoes on the walls, informing those
trapped in the audience that "Time Flies," "Knowledge is Power,"
"The Pen is Mightier Than the Sword," and "Industry Must Thrive"
(XXI:168).

Williams's treatment of the illustrated page from the anatomy
book torn by Becky Thatcher is discreet, though like Twain's text,
teasingly so. His picture of Mr. Dobbins discovering that his book
has been vandalized lets us see only the vague outline of the human
figure depicted in the frontispiece (XX:161) (Figure 8). When William Dean Howells read the draft manuscript, he had cautioned
Twain, "I should be afraid of this picture incident" (quoted in Baender 457) and Twain's subsequent revisions "deemphasized the picture and Becky's interest in it" (Baender 457). The likely model for
the anatomy book in question included as frontispiece only a modest,
stylized diagram of the human form (see p. 208 herein), but by leaving the precise details of the illustration on that torn page uncertain,
Twain and Williams slyly allowed young and old to find in it whatever
they were prepared to imagine.

The first part of the novel is full of the kind of deflationary visual
jokes Williams loved, like having a picture of Tom on one page day-
dreaming about how sorry Becky would be if he drowned, followed
on the overleaf by a long vertical cut in which the boy, playing dead

Figure 8. The Discovery.

outside Becky's house, is jolted to his senses by a basin of water dumped on him from above (III:39, 40). But this sort of fun would only be a distraction from the intensity of the dark and compelling adventure sequences in which Tom becomes Injun Joe's nemesis—and his heir. As Tom is drawn into the drama surrounding the murder of Dr. Robinson, the illustrations provided by Williams become melodramatic enough to have attracted negative comment in the press. An anonymous reviewer for *The New York Times* objected to "an ugly murder in the book, over-minutely described and too fully illustrated" (Scharnhorst 56). Though Williams's two pictures of the crime scene are more restrained than Twain's descriptions, they do bring to life Twain's striking theatrical tableaus in romantic terms a contemporary audience would have relished. Both feature stage-blocking in which the main figures face each other as they might in a theater, their body language sending stylized but nonetheless powerful messages. In the first one, Joe, who has persuaded the muddled and half-drunk Muff Potter that *he* is the killer, sits thoughtfully, hand under his chin, coolly considering what Potter is saying (Figure 9). Potter bends on one knee, in the traditional posture of a suppliant, his hands dramatically clasped before him, pleading with Joe not to tell anyone what he has done (IX:91). In the second scene, Williams artfully presents three consecutive actions in a single pictured moment (Figure 10). In the text, as Tom worms his way through the crowd of onlookers at the graveside, Huck pinches his arm, and their eyes meet. In the picture they are shown crouching in the background as they glance at each other. A minute later in the story, the sheriff comes through the crowd, leading Potter by the arm. We see him in the picture with one arm around Potter, the other gesturing toward the body, but we also see Potter's response to the sight, as he puts his face in his hands and bursts into tears (XI:103).

Injun Joe, in this graveyard confrontation scene, is for once shown as a stereotypical stage "Indian": stern, impenetrable of expression, arms folded across his chest. But when Williams dramatizes his lightning-like escape from the courtroom, Joe becomes a tall, commanding figure, who, as he leaps for the window, looks back with a contemptuous smile on the fools who have let him get away (XXIII:

Figure 9. Muff Potter Outwitted.

Figure 10. Injun Joe's Two Victims.

188). In later pictures, as Tom's fear of him increases, he seems to take on a demonic power. The following chapter details Tom's enjoyment by day of the new celebrity he has won by testifying at the trial, and his torment by night as "Injun Joe infested all his dreams. And always with doom in his eye" (XXIV:189). Williams conveys Tom's misery by showing him in bed, menaced by a huge dream-like emanation of Injun Joe with staring eyes, glittering teeth and a long knife (XXIV:190) (Figure 11). The monstrous apparition looms over a Tom whose sleeping body lies draped across the bed, head thrown back, one arm hanging limply to the floor, in the style of Henry Fuseli's well-known painting *The Nightmare* (Figure 12). As this picture suggests, the figure of Injun Joe may represent "Tom's shadow self, a potential for retrogression and destructiveness that cannot be permitted abroad" (Wolff 156). Some pages later, Williams will picture a furtive Tom standing—in his turn—over the sleeping Joe, and carrying an improvised "dark lantern" (a burglar's tool) (XXVIII:214). Later still, Williams will provide a dramatic picture of the terrifying moment of revelation when Joe appears to Tom—in the utterly black depths of McDougal's cave—bearing a candle like the one he had used to mark the location of the ill-gotten treasure, so soon to be Tom's and Huck's (XXXI:245).

Many of the pictures in the latter part of the book are effectively drawn, atmospheric night pieces, and their recapitulation of the mat-

Figure 11. Tom Dreams.

Figure 12. Henry Fuseli, *The Nightmare*.

ter of previously depicted scenes underlines the way so much in the latter part of the novel repeats—in the romantic mode and for higher stakes—material that appeared earlier in terms of play and day-dream. But the kind of commitment to the text invited by ironic comedy and that demanded by romance are quite different. The detached reader of the early part of the book may have time to enjoy Williams's visual take on Twain's droll asides, but the latter part of the novel is a page-turner, relatively uninterrupted by such digressions until, in the very last chapters, Tom's adventures come to their somewhat awkward conclusion.[5] Then the time has come for author and illustrator to remind their readers that life is more complicated, less consoling, than romance.

And what do readers find when they are nudged awake by mocking jokes and satiric pictures like the one of the weepy committee determined to persuade the governor to pardon Injun Joe? Tom's being lionized by the leading citizens of St. Petersburg might, as some critics have suggested, indicate that we are meant to think of him as having grown up a bit by the end of the novel, and to find a certain satisfaction in that line of development. But Judith Fetterley has rightly observed that these particular adults have been shown to be hypocrites and worse, and "it hardly makes sense to assume that they provide the yardstick which charts a growth from something negative to something positive" (127; see p. 287 herein). Moreover, as Williams's pictures have hinted, Tom himself is bound to the demonic Injun Joe in a new way by the end of the book. He might not have been responsible for Joe's escape, but despite overhearing Joe's talk of a revenge job yet to come, Tom deliberately let the murderer remain at large so that he and Huck might stalk him and find the treasure. When Tom claims Joe's hoard, he also inherits the far more valuable (and even more tainted) treasure Joe had found in the haunted house. This had been hidden by "Murrel's gang." As Twain himself tells it in Chapter XXIX of Life on the Mississippi, Murrel (a.k.a. John A. Murrell) was a master criminal with a vast network of associates reputed to come from every rank in society, a golden-

5. Twain observes in the "Conclusion" to *Tom Sawyer* that when an author "writes of juveniles, he must stop where he best can" (275). But, abrupt as the inconclusive ending of this novel may seem, it is not ineffective, for it leaves readers slightly unsettled, perhaps anxious to read more. And Twain admits in the "Conclusion" to a practical motive for ending just this way: his desire to leave open the option of revisiting the same characters and material in future. In fact, when, in 1892, he wrote *Tom Sawyer Abroad*, Twain proposed to his publisher, Fred J. Hall, that he hoped to expand it into a lucrative series, detailing Tom's adventures in various foreign locales (Hill 313–15). When he submitted the manuscript of *Tom Sawyer Abroad* to Mary Mapes Dodge for publication in *St. Nicholas Magazine*, in 1892, she was appalled at "its ending, or rather its no ending," and begged him to "round off the story" in such a way as to "lure the fascinated reader into the belief that he had it all." In response to her insistence on the "clamorous" demand of young readers for definite endings, Twain reluctantly supplied an only slightly more conclusive ending that still left open the possibility of sequels to come (quoted in Wright 183).

tongued con-man who could pose as a traveling preacher and melt the hearts of a congregation while his confederates stole their horses. But his real fortune was based on the stealing and reselling of slaves whom he routinely murdered when they were of no more use to him. Murrel was as well known as Jesse James in his day, and readers who recognized the allusion would know that the capital to finance Tom and Huck in their proposed careers as "respectable robbers" was blood money—money that like Murrel's would circulate in the respectable world, put out at interest for the boys by the irreproachable Widow Douglas and Judge Thatcher.

Williams's tailpieces usually provide a visual approximation of one of Twain's favorite effects, the artful, unexpected observation that sheds a whole new light on the passage preceding it. So it is well to consider the implications of the tailpiece that closes the entire book (Figure 13). The portrait of a smiling old lady dressed in the Aunt

Figure 13. Contentment.

Polly mode and titled "Contentment" might at first glance seem simply to signify Aunt Polly's pleasure that everything has turned out well (XXXV:274). However, the sketch actually represents a well-known character named Mrs. Partington, created by Twain's friend, the humorist Benjamin P. Shillaber.[6] The picture is based on an image originally drawn "by Josiah Wolcott for the *Boston Pathfinder*," and later copied for Shillaber's magazine *The Carpet-Bag* by artist Frederick M. Coffin (David 1:224). Twain acknowledged that his own depiction of the Aunt Polly–Tom relationship owes a debt to Shillaber's work, and since Twain and his mother "were said to have joked about their own parallels with Mrs. Partington and her nephew Ike" (David and Sapirstein 26), the picture would have worked as a genial private joke for Twain and his circle. But a closer look at what a reference to "Mrs. Partington" would have meant to the readers of Shillaber's popular sketches is in order. Shillaber used Mrs. Partington to deliver gently humorous satiric messages on American manners and morals. Her most striking comic foible was to be so utterly without guile or malice as to be incapable of discerning it in others, especially her devious nephew. (In the well-known original version of this image, Ike was shown surreptitiously stealing sugar from his ever-smiling aunt.) Any "contentment" the innocent old lady might feel about Ike was likely to be ill-founded, and in choosing as tailpiece to their entire imagetext the smiling likeness of a simple soul to whom the more unsettling implications of Tom's story would never occur, Twain and Williams may well have given the narrative one last satiric tweak aimed at readers too easily "contented" with an unexamined happy ending.

Williams's pictures differ from Twain's text in certain ways, but as W. J. T. Mitchell has said, "The real question to ask when confronted with these kinds of image/text relations is not 'what is the difference (or similarity) between the words and the images?' but what difference do the differences (and similarities) make?" (91). At various moments Williams's pictures support Twain's text, extend it, limit it, contradict it. They make amusing passages funnier, suggest unsuspected ironies, introduce alternative ways of looking at a situation. Often they point up some intertextual relationship, whether by direct allusion or by drawing on reader familiarity with particular conventions of representation. The net effect is to open up a multiplicity of meanings in Twain's text, built out of Williams's own sympathetic reading of it. Twain said some years after Williams's death that he was "a very good artist . . . who had never taken a lesson in drawing. Everything he did was original" (1905 speech to Society of Illustrators, quoted in Schmidt). Twain valued the way Williams read—at

6. For a careful bibliographical account of the origins of this sketch, see David 1:224–30.

once "understandingly," and imaginatively. And the unsentimental, conceptually rich imagetext of *The Adventures of Tom Sawyer* they created together still invites a reading of the novel unusually open to its complexities, sensitive to its cultural context, and appreciative of its playful performativity.

Works Cited

Adams, Richard P. "The Unity and Coherence of *Huckleberry Finn*." *Tulane Studies in English* 6 (1956): 86–103. Rpt. in. *Huck Finn and His Critics*. Ed. Richard Lettis, Robert F. McDonnell, and William E. Morris. Toronto: Collier–Macmillan, 1972. 384–401.

Baender, Paul. "W. D. Howells' Comments in the Secretarial Copy." Supplement B. *The Adventures of Tom Sawyer; Tom Sawyer Abroad; and Tom Sawyer, Detective*. By Mark Twain. Ed. John C. Gerber et al. 457.

David, Beverly R. *Mark Twain and His Illustrators*. 2 vols. to date. Troy, NY: Whitston, 1986–.

David, Beverly R., and Ray Sapirstein. "Reading the Illustrations in *Tom Sawyer*." *The Adventures of Tom Sawyer*. By Mark Twain. The Oxford Mark Twain. New York: Oxford University Press, 1996. 24–31. (Editorial matter separately paged following p. 280 of the facsimile of the 1876 edition.)

Davis, Paul. *The Lives and Times of Ebenezer Scrooge*. New Haven, CT: Yale University Press, 1990.

Fetterley, Judith. "The Sanctioned Rebel." *Studies in the Novel* 3 (Fall 1971): 293–304. Rpt. in Scharnhorst 119–29.

Gribben, Alan. Foreword. David. 1:vii–viii.

Hamilton, Sinclair. *Nineteenth Century American Book Illustration*. Princeton, NJ: Princeton University Press, 1958.

Hill, Hamlin, ed. *Mark Twain's Letters to His Publishers, 1867–1894*. Berkeley: University of California Press, 1967.

Knoper, Randall. *Acting Naturally: Mark Twain in the Culture of Performance*. Berkeley: University of California Press, 1995.

Mitchell, W.J.T. *Picture Theory*. Chicago: University of Chicago Press, 1994.

Pickston, Margaret, copyright holder. *The Language of Flowers*. Facsimile of handmade album [1913]. London: Michael Joseph, 1968.

Review of *The Adventures of Tom Sawyer*. *New York Times*, 13 January 1877, 3:2–3. Rpt. in Scharnhorst 54–57.

Scharnhorst, Gary, ed. *Critical Essays on* The Adventures of Tom Sawyer. New York: G. K. Hall, 1993.

Schmidt, Barbara. "A Closer Look at the Lives of True Williams and Alexander Belford." Paper presented at the Fourth Annual International Conference on the State of Mark Twain Studies, Elmira, NY, August 18, 2001. Available at www.twainquotes.com/TWW/TWW.html; accessed 17 February 2005.

Shillaber, Benjamin Penhallow. *Life and Sayings of Mrs. Partington and Others of the Family*. New York: J. C. Derby, 1854.

Twain, Mark. *The Adventures of Tom Sawyer*. Facsimile of the First American Edition. Hartford: American Publishing Company, 1876. The Oxford Mark Twain. New York: Oxford University Press, 1996.

————. *The Adventures of Tom Sawyer*. The Uniform Author's Edition. Illustrated by J. G. Brown. New York: Harper & Brothers, 1903.

————. *The Adventures of Tom Sawyer*. Illustrated by Barry Moser. New York: Books of Wonder–HarperCollins, 1989.

————. *The Adventures of Tom Sawyer*. Illustrated by Norman Rockwell. Norwalk, CT: Heritage, 2000.

————. *The Adventures of Tom Sawyer; Tom Sawyer Abroad; and Tom Sawyer Detective*. Ed. John C. Gerber, Paul Baender, and Terry Firkins. The Works of Mark Twain. Berkeley: Published for the Iowa Center for Textual Studies by University of California Press, 1980.

————. *Life on the Mississippi*. New York: Harper & Brothers, 1906.

West. Mark. "The Strange Case of *Tom Sawyer* and the Disappearing Chapter Headings." Available at faculty.citadel.edu/leonard/od00c.htm; accessed 24 May 2005.

Wolff, Cynthia Griffin. "*The Adventures of Tom Sawyer*: A Nightmare Vision of American Boyhood." *Massachusetts Review* 21 (Winter 1980): 637–52. Rpt. in Scharnhorst 148–59.

Wright, Catharine Morris. *Lady of the Silver Skates: The Life and Correspondence of Mary Mapes Dodge*. Jamestown, RI: Clingstone, 1979.

Figure Credits

Figures 1, 2, 3, 5, 6, 8, 9, 10, 11, 13 are from pp. [iii], [17], 33, 42, 268, 161, 91, 103, 190, and 274 of the 1996 Oxford facsimile of the first U.S. edition of *The Adventures of Tom Sawyer* (1876).

Figures 4 and 7 are from Twain's *Sketches, New and Old* (Hartford: American Publishing Company, 1875), pp. 51, 60, reproduced from a copy held by the Beinecke Rare Book and Manuscript Library, Yale University.

Figure 12: *The Nightmare*, 1781
  Henry Fuseli
  Founders Society Purchase with funds from Mr. and Mrs. Bert L. Smokler and Mr. and Mrs. Lawrence A. Fleischman
Photograph © 1997 The Detroit Institute of Arts.

Mark Twain: A Chronology

1835   Samuel Clemens born to Jane Lampton Clemens and John Marshall Clemens in Florida, Missouri.

1839   Family moves to Hannibal, Missouri.

1847   Father dies.

1848   Clemens apprenticed to a newspaper.

1857   Begins lessons as cub pilot.

1859   Obtains river pilot license.

1861   Briefly serves in the Missouri State Guard; moves to Nevada.

1863   First publishes as Mark Twain.

1864   Moves to California.

1865   Publishes "Jim Smiley and His Jumping Frog," which leads to national fame.

1869   *The Innocents Abroad*.

1870   Marries Olivia Langdon and settles in Buffalo, New York; son Langdon born.

1871   Moves to Hartford, Connecticut.

1872   Daughter Susy born; Langdon dies; *Roughing It*.

1873   *The Gilded Age*, co-authored with Charles Dudley Warner.

1874   Daughter Clara born.

1876   *The Adventures of Tom Sawyer*.

1880   *A Tramp Abroad*; daughter Jean born.

1881   *The Prince and the Pauper*.

1883   *Life on the Mississippi*.

1885   *Adventures of Huckleberry Finn*.

1889   *A Connecticut Yankee in King Arthur's Court*.

1890   Mother dies.

1891   Leaves Hartford for Europe because of financial difficulties.

1894   *The Tragedy of Pudd'nhead Wilson*.

1895   Begins world lecture tour to pay off debts.

1896   *Personal Recollections of Joan of Arc*; Susy dies.

1901   Honorary doctorate from Yale.

1904   Wife dies.

1906   Starts wearing trademark white suits.

1907   Honorary doctorate from Oxford.

1908   Moves to Redding, Connecticut.
1909   Jean dies.
1910   Samuel Clemens dies.
1916   *The Mysterious Stranger*, compiled by Albert Bigelow Paine.

Selected Bibliography

Good sources of biographical information include Justin Kaplan's *Mr. Clemens and Mark Twain* (Simon, 1966), Everett Emerson's *Mark Twain: A Literary Life* (University of Pennsylvania Press, 2000), and Ron Powers' *Mark Twain: A Life* (Free Press, 2005). The University of California Press is publishing authoritative editions of Twain's letters; the first six volumes include letters through 1875. A good Web site, with links to other Twain sites, is Jim Zwick's at www.boondocksnet.com/twainwww/index.html. Of the many book-length studies that address Twain, in whole or in part, I have listed a few with particularly interesting discussions of *The Adventures of Tom Sawyer*.

● indicates a work included or excerpted in this Norton Critical Edition.

Criticism

Aspiz, Harold. "Tom Sawyer's Games of Death." *Studies in the Novel* 27.2 (Summer 1995): 141–53.

Baender, Paul. Introduction. *The Adventures of Tom Sawyer: A Facsimile of the Author's Holograph Manuscript.* Frederick, MD: University Publications of America, 1982. 1:ix–xxxvi.

Blair, Walter, ed. *Mark Twain's Hannibal, Huck and Tom.* Berkeley: University of California Press, 1969.

———. "On the Structure of *Tom Sawyer*." *Modern Philology* 37 (August 1939): 75–88.

Blues, Thomas. "The Strategy of Compromise in Mark Twain's 'Boy Books.' " *Modern Fiction Studies* 14.1 (Spring 1968): 21–31.

Brown, Gillian. "Child's Play." *differences* 11.3 (1999): 76–106.

Budd, Louis J., ed. *Mark Twain: The Contemporary Reviews.* Cambridge: Cambridge University Press, 1999.

Byers, John R., Jr. "A Hannibal Summer: The Framework of *The Adventures of Tom Sawyer*." *Studies in American Fiction* 8 (Spring 1980): 81–88.

Campbell, Neil. "The 'Seductive Outside' and the 'Sacred Precincts': Boundaries and Transgressions in *The Adventures of Tom Sawyer*." *Children's Literature in Education* 25.2 (June 1994): 125–38.

Clark, Beverly Lyon. *Kiddie Lit: The Cultural Construction of Children's Literature in America.* Baltimore: Johns Hopkins University Press, 2003.

Cox, James M. *Mark Twain: The Fate of Humor.* Princeton, NJ: Princeton University Press, 1966.

de Koster, Katie, ed. *Readings on* The Adventures of Tom Sawyer. San Diego: Greenhaven, 1999.

● DeVoto, Bernard. *Mark Twain at Work.* Cambridge: Harvard University Press, 1942.

Dillingham, William B. "Setting and Theme in *Tom Sawyer*." *Mark Twain Journal* 12.2 (Spring 1964):6–8.

Ensor, Allison R. " 'Norman Rockwell Sentimentality': The Rockwell Illustrations for *Tom*

Sawyer and *Huckleberry Finn.*" In *The Mythologizing of Mark Twain*. Ed. Sara deSaussure Davis and Philip D. Beidler. N.p.: University of Alabama Press, 1984. 15–36.

Evans, John D. *A Tom Sawyer Companion: An Autobiographical Guided Tour with Mark Twain*. Lanham, MD: University Press of America, 1993.

● Fetterley, Judith. "The Sanctioned Rebel." *Studies in the Novel* 3.3 (Fall 1971): 293–304.

Fields, Wayne. "When the Fences Are Down: Language and Order in *The Adventures of Tom Sawyer* and *Huckleberry Finn.*" *Journal of American Studies* 24.3 (1990): 369–86.

Fishkin, Shelley Fisher, ed. *A Historical Guide to Mark Twain*. New York: Oxford University Press, 2002.

Geller, Evelyn. "Tom Sawyer, Tom Bailey, and the Bad-Boy Genre." *Wilson Library Bulletin* 51.3 (November 1976): 245–50.

Gerber, John. Introduction. *The Adventures of Tom Sawyer; Tom Sawyer Abroad; Tom Sawyer, Detective*. Ed. John Gerber et al. Vol. 4 of *The Works of Mark Twain*. Iowa Center for Textual Studies. Berkeley: University of California Press, 1980. 3–30.

Gerber, John C. *Mark Twain*. Boston: Twayne, 1988.

Gribben, Alan. "How Tom Sawyer Played Robin Hood 'by the Book.'" *English Language Notes* 13.3 (March 1976): 201–4.

● ———. "'I Did Wish Tom Sawyer Was There': Boy-Book Elements in *Tom Sawyer* and *Huckleberry Finn.*" *One Hundred Years of* Huckleberry Finn: *The Boy, His Book, and American Culture*. Ed. Robert Sattelmeyer and J. Donald Crowley. Columbia: University of Missouri Press, 1985. 149–70.

● ———. "Manipulating a Genre: *Huckleberry Finn* as Boy Book." *South Central Review* 5 (Winter 1988): 15–21.

Griswold, Jerry. *Audacious Kids: Coming of Age in America's Classic Children's Books*. New York: Oxford University Press, 1992.

Harris, Susan K. *Mark Twain's Escape from Time: A Study of Patterns and Images*. Columbia: University of Missouri Press, 1982.

● Hendler, Glenn. "Tom Sawyer's Masculinity." *Arizona Quarterly* 49.4 (Winter 1993): 33–59.

● Hill, Hamlin L. "The Composition and the Structure of *Tom Sawyer.*" *American Literature* 32.4 (January 1961): 379–92.

——— . "Mark Twain: Audience and Artistry." *American Quarterly* 15.1 (Spring 1963): 25–40.

Hirsch, Tim. "Banned by Neglect: *Tom Sawyer*, Teaching the Conflicts." In *Censored Books II: Critical Viewpoints, 1985–2000*. Ed. Nicholas J. Karolides. Lanham, MD: Scarecrow, 2002. 1–9.

● [Howells, William Dean]. Review of *The Adventures of Tom Sawyer*. *Atlantic Monthly*, May 1876, 621–22.

Hutchinson, Stuart, ed. *Mark Twain*: Tom Sawyer *and* Huckleberry Finn. Columbia Critical Guides. New York: Columbia University Press, 1998.

Jacobson, Marcia. *Being a Boy Again: Autobiography and the American Boy Book*. Tuscaloosa: University of Alabama Press, 1994.

● Jackson, Robert. "The Emergence of Mark Twain's Missouri: Regional Theory and *Adventures of Huckleberry Finn.*" *Southern Literary Journal* 35.1 (2002): 47–69.

Johnson, James L. *Mark Twain and the Limits of Power: Emerson's God in Ruins*. Knoxville: University of Tennessee Press, 1982.

Krauth, Leland. *Proper Mark Twain*. Athens: University of Georgia Press, 1999.

LeMaster, J. R., and James D. Wilson, ed. *Mark Twain Encyclopedia*. New York: Garland, 1993.

Lowry, Richard S. *"Littery Man": Mark Twain and Modern Authorship*. New York: Oxford University Press, 1996.

Maik, Thomas A. "The Village in *Tom Sawyer*: Myth and Reality." *Arizona Quarterly* 42.2 (Summer 1986): 157–64.

Mailloux, Steven. *Rhetorical Power*. Ithaca, NY: Cornell University Press, 1989.

Messent, Peter. "Discipline and Punishment in *The Adventures of Tom Sawyer.*" *Journal of American Studies* 32.2 (1998): 219–35.

Michaelsen, Scott. "Tom Sawyer's Capitalisms and the Destructuring of Huck Finn." *Prospects* 22 (1997): 133–51.

Million, Elmer M. "Sawyer et al. v. Administrator of Injun Joe." *Missouri Law Review* 16 (1951): 27–38.

Mitchell, Lee Clark. Introduction. *The Adventures of Tom Sawyer*. By Mark Twain. Oxford: Oxford University Press, 1993. vii–xxxvi.

Norton, Charles A. *Writing* Tom Sawyer: *The Adventures of a Classic*. Jefferson, NC: McFarland, 1983.

Peck, Elizabeth G. "Tom Sawyer: Character in Search of an Audience." *ATQ* n.s. 2.3 (September 1988): 223–36.

Pinsker, Sanford. "*The Adventures of Tom Sawyer*, Play Theory, and the Critic's Job of Work." *Midwest Quarterly* 29.3 (Spring 1988): 357–65.

Powers, Ron. *Dangerous Water: A Biography of the Boy Who Became Mark Twain*. New York: Basic, 1999.

Railton, Stephen. *Mark Twain: A Short Introduction*. Malden, MA: Blackwell, 2004.

• Revard, Carter. "Why Mark Twain Murdered Injun Joe—and Will Never Be Indicted." *Massachusetts Review* 40.4 (Winter 1999–2000): 643–70.

Robinson, Forrest G. "Social Play and Bad Faith in *The Adventures of Tom Sawyer*." *Nineteenth Century Fiction* 39.1 (June 1984): 1–24.

Rubin, Louis D., Jr. "Mark Twain: *The Adventures of Tom Sawyer*." In *Landmarks of American Writing*. Ed. Hennig Cohen. New York: Basic, 1969. 157–71.

Scharnhorst, Gary, ed. *Critical Essays on* The Adventures of Tom Sawyer. New York: Hall, 1993.

See, Fred. G. "Tom Sawyer and Children's Literature." *Essays in Literature* 12.2 (Fall 1985): 251–71.

Seelye, John. "What's in a Name: Sounding the Depths of *Tom Sawyer*." *Sewanee Review* 90.3 (Summer 1982): 408–29.

Smith, Henry Nash. *Mark Twain: The Development of a Writer*. Cambridge: Belknap–Harvard University Press, 1962.

Spengemann, William C. *Mark Twain and the Backwoods Angel: The Matter of Innocence in the Works of Samuel L. Clemens*. [Kent, OH]: Kent State University Press, 1966.

Steinbrink, Jeffrey. "Who Shot Tom Sawyer?" *American Literary Realism* 35.1 (Fall 2002): 29–38.

Stone, Albert E., Jr. *The Innocent Eye: Childhood in Mark Twain's Imagination*. New Haven, CT: Yale University Press, 1961.

Towers, Tom H. " 'I Never Thought We Might Want to Come Back': Strategies of Transcendence in *Tom Sawyer*." *Modern Fiction Studies* 21.4 (Winter 1975–1976): 509–20.

Tracy, Robert. "Myth and Reality in *The Adventures of Tom Sawyer*." *Southern Review* n.s. 4.2 (April 1968): 530–41.

Trensky, Anne. "The Bad Boy in Nineteenth-Century American Fiction." *Georgia Review* 27 (1973): 503–17.

Wexman, Virginia. "The Role of Structure in *Tom Sawyer* and *Huckleberry Finn*." *American Literary Realism* 6.1 (Winter 1973): 1–11.

Wolff, Cynthia Griffin. "*The Adventures of Tom Sawyer*: A Nightmare Vision of American Boyhood." *Massachusetts Review* 21 (Winter 1980): 637–52.

Wonham, Henry B. *Mark Twain and the Art of the Tall Tale*. New York: Oxford University Press, 1993.

Contexts

Brown, Harry J. *Injun Joe's Ghost: The Indian Mixed-Blood in American Writing*. Columbia: University of Missouri Press, 2004.

Dempsey, Terrell. *Searching for Jim: Slavery in Sam Clemens's World*. Columbia: University of Missouri Press, 2003.

Finkelstein, Barbara, ed. *Governing the Young: Teacher Behavior in Popular Primary Schools in Nineteenth-Century United States*. New York: Falmer, 1989.

Jaffa, Henry V. *The Conditions of Freedom: Essays in Political Philosophy*. Baltimore: Johns Hopkins University Press, 1975.

Kidd, Kenneth B. *Making American Boys: Boyology and the Feral Tale*. Minneapolis: University of Minnesota Press, 2004.

• Ober, K. Patrick. *Mark Twain and Medicine: "Any Mummery Will Cure."* Columbia: University of Missouri Press, 2003.

• Rotundo, E. Anthony. *American Manhood: Transformations in Masculinity from the Revolution to the Modern Era*. New York: Basic, 1993.

Sappol, Michael. *A Traffic of Dead Bodies: Anatomy and Embodied Social Identity in Nineteenth-Century America*. Princeton, NJ: Princeton University Press, 2002.